True to the Law

Berkley Sensation titles by Jo Goodman

KISSING COMFORT
THE LAST RENEGADE
TRUE TO THE LAW

True to
the Law

JO GOODMAN

BERKLEY SENSATION, NEW YORK

THE BERKLEY PUBLISHING GROUP
Published by the Penguin Group
Penguin Group (USA) Inc.
375 Hudson Street, New York, New York 10014, USA

USA | Canada | UK | Ireland | Australia | New Zealand | India | South Africa | China

Penguin Books Ltd., Registered Offices: 80 Strand, London WC2R 0RL, England

TRUE TO THE LAW

A Berkley Sensation Book / published by arrangement with the author

Berkley Sensation Books are published by The Berkley Publishing Group.
BERKLEY SENSATION® is a registered trademark of Penguin Group (USA) Inc.
The "B" design is a trademark of Penguin Group (USA) Inc.

ISBN: 978-162490-498-1

PRINTED IN THE UNITED STATES OF AMERICA

Cover photo by Claudio Marinesco.
Cover design by Rita Frangie.

This is a work of fiction. Names, characters, places, and incidents either are the product
of the author's imagination or are used fictitiously, and any resemblance to actual persons,
living or dead, business establishments, events, or locales is entirely coincidental.
The publisher does not have any control over and does not assume any responsibility for
author or third-party websites or their content.

In memory of my mother,
whose gift was believing in her children,
and in honor of my sister, a teacher,
who believes in every one of hers.

Prologue

August 1889
Chicago

"Find her."

Cobb Bridger gave no indication that he was inclined to accept or dismiss the job. Most men in his position would have taken this opportunity to ask a question, perhaps several questions. Cobb remained silent. In his experience, silence was a powerful motivator, and he judged that it would be a useful tool now.

It was.

Andrew Charles Mackey III stopped turning over the envelope in his hand and set it on the desk blotter. He laid his palm over it. "Is it the money? I was given to understand that what I'm offering is well in excess of your usual retainer. I'm aware there will be other expenses. We will settle those when you find her."

Cobb said nothing. He tilted his head slightly to one side. His eyes narrowed a fraction. The look was a calculating one, thoughtful in the way one was when taking the full measure of a man. In Cobb's case, it was also a sham. He was bone weary. Worse, he was bored. No amount of money was an incentive when he was bored. Besides that, he had taken Mackey's measure at their introduction and distilled all the details to a single salient point: Here was a man with no expectation that he would be, or should be, challenged.

"I was told you would not ask questions," said Mackey.

"I don't believe I have."

The hand over the envelope curled slightly. Mackey began to drum it lightly with his fingertips. "Then you'll do it."

"I don't believe I've said I will." Cobb's eyes never left Mackey's face. He heard rather than saw the drumming fingers miss several beats. After a brief pause, they resumed their tattoo. That's when Cobb knew Andrew Mackey had made his decision.

"Miss Morrow has something that belongs to me. I want it back."

Cobb detected a hesitation; something in Mackey's speech suggested he was choosing his words carefully. Although he did not rouse himself to attention, Cobb Bridger was marginally less bored than he had been moments earlier.

"It is not just for me," Mackey said after another hesitation. "The family also has an interest in recovering what she has stolen."

Not *my* family, Cobb noted. *The* family. Cobb wondered if Mackey were aware that a distinction had been made. Probably not. One of the reasons Cobb had a reputation for asking so few questions was that he knew the answers to many of them before he scheduled the first meeting.

Andrew Charles Mackey III was still a bachelor at thirty. As Cobb himself was only one year younger and also unmarried, Mackey's single state was not by itself very interesting. The fact that Mackey had been engaged three times and all of them ended abruptly, was. As far as Cobb was able to determine, Mackey had no bastards. An only child, his parents had died within months of each other when he was still at Princeton. More recently, in fact just two months ago, his only remaining grandparent, his paternal grandmother, passed away. The death of Charlotte Mackey left a not insignificant hole for the society pages to fill; yet that hole was nothing compared with the one left in the business pages.

The Mackey empire was in want of an . . . emperor? Empress?

Andrew Mackey's failure to marry and produce any offspring, and the death of his parents and now the Mackey matriarch, did not, however, mean that he was without family. Cobb counted one uncle on the Mackey side and half a dozen Mackey cousins. Charlotte Mackey's death meant there was a vacancy at the head of the family and an opportunity for someone to fill it.

It seemed that Andrew Mackey was speaking for the family. Cobb was uncertain if he had appointed himself to this front-and-center position or if he had been thrust there by the Mackey collective, and neither was he sure that it mattered. What piqued his curiosity was the missing item. What had Gertrude Morrow taken with her when she disappeared? What was important enough to Andrew Mackey, and ostensibly to the rest of the family, that hiring a private detective was a reasonable solution?

Cobb asked, "Is it bigger than, say, my fist?"

Mackey blinked. "What?"

"This *something* that you allege Miss Morrow stole . . . is it bigger than my fist?"

Now Andrew Mackey frowned. "Miss Morrow took it. That is what is important. The size is of no consequence."

Cobb wondered how that was possible. Mackey had given him a useful description of Miss Morrow, discussed at length her former position in the house and the access she had to every part of it, but especially the access she had to his grandmother, and finally, albeit without fanfare, shared the classified section of the newspaper he recently discovered in Miss Morrow's former room—with seven advertisements for employment neatly removed from the pages. The newspaper, which he described as having been secreted away by Miss Morrow, had been found in a stack of similar papers bundled for removal. In Mackey's mind this was further proof of Miss Morrow's clever and concealing nature.

Cobb did not point out that a more clever and concealing woman would have burnt the paper, not left its discovery to chance. Mackey had a great deal to say about Miss Gertrude Morrow and nothing at all to say about what she took.

"The size," said Cobb, "has some bearing on finding what's been taken . . . and returning it to you."

Andrew Mackey picked up the envelope and tapped one corner of it against the blotter. Before he spoke, his mouth thinned briefly. "You mistake the assignment, Mr. Bridger. I am not hiring you to find and return what's been stolen. I don't believe I ever said as much. For the matter of the theft to be resolved, you only have to find Miss Morrow. She is, you will note from my description, bigger than your fist."

Cobb thought he probably deserved Mackey's condescension. It did not make it more palatable, but it did stay the aforementioned fist from mashing Mackey's patrician nose. "And when I find her?"

"You will inform me. I expect you will observe her until I can arrange a meeting. It is a precaution, nothing more, in the event she decides to disappear again. At all costs, you should prevent that."

"At all costs," Cobb repeated, shrugging. "It's your money, Mr. Mackey."

"Yes, it is."

On the face of it, the job was straightforward. Cobb doubted that was the case. The point of hiring someone with his particular skills generally meant that the face of it was a façade.

All the better, else where was the challenge?

"Very well," said Cobb, rising to his feet and extending his hand across the desk.

Mackey also stood. He offered Cobb the envelope, not his hand.

Cobb thought he correctly read the intent of the exchange in Mackey's taut expression. No gentleman's agreement here. This was business.

Cobb Bridger was fine with that.

Chapter One

October 1889
Bitter Springs, Wyoming

Finn Collins decided he would stare at Priscilla Taylor's braid
until his eyes crossed. The braid, perfectly plaited with every
hair still in place at the end of the day, rested along the line
of Priscilla's ramrod straight backbone. Priscilla never
slumped on her bench. She never fidgeted. The braid never
moved except when Priscilla raised her hand to answer a
question, then it slid ever so slightly to one side and the tip
curled like an apostrophe. Or maybe a comma. Those punc-
tuation marks were suspiciously similar, except one was high
and one was low. It was no wonder he got them confused.

"Finn?"

Finn did not stir. In point of fact, he did not hear his name
being called. He sat with his elbows on the desk, his head
cupped in his hands. His chin and cheeks rested warmly
between his palms. His eyes had begun to relax. Priscilla had
two braids now. Two ramrods. And when she raised her hand
to show everyone that she knew the answer to something no

one cared about—like the name of the fifth president—the tail of one braid curled in a comma, the other in an apostrophe.

"Carpenter Addison Collins."

Finn came to attention with the jerkiness of someone suddenly roused from a deep sleep. His elbows slid off the edge of the desk, his head snapped up, and his feet, which had been swinging in a lazy rhythm under the bench, kicked spasmodically before slamming hard to the floor. He blinked widely. There was only one person who called him by all three of his proper names.

"Gran?"

Thirteen of Finn's classmates were moved to laughter. Finn's brother, Rabbit, was an exception. He glanced over his shoulder at Finn and rolled his eyes. Somehow he managed to convey disapproval *and* embarrassment. Just like Granny.

Finn felt color rush into his face and knew his cheeks were glowing like hot coals. If someone poked at him, he would burst into flames. For himself, he didn't mind so much. In some ways it would be a relief. More concerning was that no one would be safe from the conflagration. Priscilla's braid would take to the fire like a candlewick. She'd whip her head around then, he was certain of it, and shoot tongues of fire at anyone who tried to save her. Stupid girl. She would burn down the school. Probably the town. It would be his fault because no one ever blamed girls. To save the school, the town, to save everyone, really, he had to act. The solution was clear.

He yanked hard on Priscilla's offending braid.

She squealed. It was a sound no one had ever heard her make before, but everyone knew how a piglet sounded when it was in want of its mother's teat. Priscilla squealed like that, and all eyes shifted to her. A moment later, so did the laughter.

Priscilla swiveled on her bench seat, slate in hand, and swung it at Finn's head. Finn ducked instinctively, but he was never in any danger. Miss Morrow stepped in and stayed Priscilla's arm. Out of the corner of his eye, Finn saw her calmly remove the slate from Priscilla's hand and set it gently on the desk. She had a small, quiet smile for Priscilla, one that was more understanding than quelling. For the class, she effectively used a single raised eyebrow to stopper the laughter. It was Finn for whom she had words. He held his breath, waiting for the pronouncement.

"Finn, you will stay after the others leave today."

Finn kept his head down, his eyes averted. He knew better than to look pleased. He kept his voice small, penitent. "Yes, ma'am."

"Is there something you want to say to Priscilla?"

Now Finn looked up and stared squarely at Priscilla's back. "Sure is. Prissy, that pigtail is nuthin' but a temptation. And now that I heard you squeal, well, giving it a yank now and again is a thing that can't be resisted." He risked a glance at Miss Morrow. For reasons he did not entirely understand, she looked as if she was going to choke on her spit. "That's all I got to say, ma'am."

Tru Morrow covered her mouth with the back of her hand and politely cleared her throat. "We will speak later, and you can write your apology."

Finn's narrow shoulders slumped. Staying after school with Miss Morrow was nothing but a pleasure. Writing, whether it was an apology to Priscilla or "I will raise my hand before I speak" twenty times, well, that cast a long shadow on the pleasure of Miss Morrow's company. His pap would tell him that a man has to pay for his pleasure, and it seemed to Finn that his pap was proved right again. He tucked that thought away so he could use it when Pap asked him to account for his behavior today. There was nothing like flattering a man with the rightness of his thinking to stay another lecture on the same subject. Granny would be a little trickier. She wasn't impressed by flattery, and it seemed that a man paying for his pleasure had a different meaning to her because when Pap said it she snorted and set his plate down hard. If she didn't have a plate in her hand, she just cuffed him.

Finn sighed. He would consider the problem of his granny later. Miss Morrow was walking to the front of the classroom. His eyes followed her. The carefully tied bow at the small of her back perched as daintily above her bustle as a bird hovering on the edge of its nest. It was as severe a temptation as Priscilla Taylor's braid. Even if he could keep himself from tugging on it, he still might blurt out the question he was asking himself: How did she tie it?

Finn sat on his hands. For the moment, it was the best way to stay out of trouble.

Tru Morrow stood to one side of the door as she ushered her students out. She made certain they left with their coats, hats, and scarves. Most of the girls wore mittens or carried a muff. The boys, if they had gloves, wore them. Those with mittens simply jammed their hands into their pockets. Mittens were for girls and babies, she'd learned. Finn had explained it to her.

She closed the door as soon as the last student filed out. The "bitter" in "Bitter Springs" didn't refer to the quality of the water, but the quality of the wind. Born and raised in Chicago, she had been confident that she understood cold. She was familiar with the wind blowing over the water of Lake Michigan, funneling ice into the collective breath of the city. That was frigid. It was only October, and she was coming to learn that there was a qualitative difference between frigid and bitter. Here in the high plains country, wind seared her lungs. It was so cold, it was hot, and even when she sipped it carefully, she seemed to taste it at the very back of her tongue. Bitter.

Tru lifted her poppy red shawl and drew it more closely around her shoulders. The wool felt substantial and warm and smelled faintly of smoke from the stove.

"Finn, would you add some coals to the stove? Half a scoop. That will keep us warm long enough for you to write your apology."

Finn stood. Tru sensed his uncertainty as she passed him.

"What is it?" she asked without pausing.

"Well, it's just that you're awful confident that I know what I'm apologizin' for."

Careful not to smile, Tru took her seat behind her desk.

She folded her hands and placed them in front of her where Finn could see them. Her posture was correct, her spine perfectly aligned, shoulders back, chin lifted. She envisioned herself as a model of rectitude, and she was impressed with herself even if she could see that Finn wasn't. It was probably her eyes that gave her away, she thought. She had been told they were a merry shade of green, a color, according to her father, that could not be easily captured by an artist's palette because the substance of it was a quality of character as much as a quality of light. It was a fanciful notion, but one she brought to mind when she was in danger of taking herself too seriously.

Now was such a time. She relaxed her spine and leaned forward, unclasping her hands as Finn moved to the stove to add coals. She smoothed back a wayward coil of hair that had been pushed out of place by her brief encounter with the wind. She could not help but notice that Finn's eyes followed this small movement, and when her hand fell away from her hair, he remained exactly as he was a moment longer, transfixed. She could only guess at what he was thinking.

"Are you tempted to give my hair a tug?" she asked.

Finn blinked. "How's that again, ma'am?"

"I wondered if you were tempted to yank on my hair."

He ducked his head, cheeks flushing, and hurried to the stove. "Uh, no. No, ma'am." Finn used the sleeve of his shirt like a mitt to open the stove door and tossed half a scoop of coals inside. "Wasn't tempted at all."

Tru watched Finn poke at the fire and warm himself in front of the stove long enough to provide an explanation for his rosy cheeks. "I just wondered," she said. "After all, my hair is the same color as Priscilla's."

Finn turned his backside to the stove and stared at her. "I sure hope you'll pardon me for setting you straight, Miss Morrow, but you ever hear tell of a man named Rumple Sticks?"

"Rumpelstiltskin?"

"That's the fellow. You know of him?"

"I believe I've heard of him."

"That's good because I couldn't explain it all. Rabbit's better with stories than I am. Well, anyway, I can see you want me to get on with it. It's like this: Priscilla's got hair that puts me in mind of the straw that Mr. Stiltskin wanted for his spinning wheel, and your hair is what Mr. Stiltskin spun it into. So you see, one color's not at all like the other. Yellow. Gold. I got some idea there's a big difference." Finn rocked back on his heels. "Besides, you got your hair lassoed so tight to your head that it would be hard to know what thread to pull."

Now it was Tru who blinked and blushed. "How old are you again, Finn?"

"Ten. Or I will be soon enough."

"So you're nine. Maybe you shouldn't be in such a hurry to grow up."

Finn moved away from the stove and shut the door. "That's what everyone says. Even Rabbit. He's eleven and thinks he can say things like that now. Sort of like he's wise. He's not."

Tru knew better than to make any judgment on Rabbit's wisdom. Finn was certain to carry the tale, and it did not take much provocation to start a war of words between the brothers. She'd seen them use elbows and fists like periods and exclamation points to punctuate their threats.

"Sit down, Finn, and clean your slate. I trust that given sufficient contemplation you'll arrive at what you need to write."

His shoulders slumped, and he jammed his hands in his pockets. "Suppose I will."

"You'll read it to the class tomorrow morning, first thing after prayers."

He grimaced but slid into his seat without a word.

"And perhaps at the end of the day, you will be so kind as to help me clean all the slates." She reasoned that if she found small tasks for him to do, he might not choose getting into trouble in order to remain in her company. He would probably tire of that soon enough. This was her first encounter with a boy's infatuation, and she had been slow to recognize it for what it was. Her sense was that it would pass quickly. She thought she might be a little sorry when it did.

Tru left the schoolhouse ten minutes after Finn shuffled out. He had done everything he could think of to draw out his time. She admired his creativity, was even a tad flattered by his motives, but was careful not to encourage either. She listened with half an ear when he prattled on about the most recent visitor to Bitter Springs and nodded at what she hoped were the proper intervals when he gave a full account of the birth of a foal in Mr. Ransom's livery just that morning. He also added a rapid, if somewhat incoherent, story about the milliner's daughter accepting Mr. Irvin's proposal of marriage. Finn wasn't clear if it was Millicent Garvin who was marrying the undertaker, or her younger sister Marianna, but there was definitely a wedding being planned because Mrs. Garvin was ordering catalogs and silk from Paris.

Tru thought that even if she hadn't been apprised of some of the town's more interesting citizens when she interviewed for the teaching position, it would not have taken her long to identify Heather Collins, grandmother of Rabbit and Finn, as the one who invariably had her ear to the ground and her tongue positioned for wagging. While her husband was the station agent for Bitter Springs, and privy to all the comings and goings of the trains and travelers, he was still merely the human hub. Mrs. Collins, on the other hand, was the human hubbub.

Tru had a suspicion that Finn's ear was similarly pressed and his mouth similarly positioned.

Pulling her scarf up so that it covered her mouth and the bottom half of her nose, Tru stepped out of the schoolhouse. Wind whipped at her skirts. She ignored the flare of her petticoats but surrendered to the shiver that rattled her teeth. She tucked her chin against her chest and watched her step on the uneven sidewalk as she bucked the wind.

She would have been knocked to the ground if the same

force that stopped her forward progress had not also stopped her downward plunge. In that first moment, she lost her breath. In the next, she recovered it.

And promptly lost a little of it again when she met the direct, crystalline blue gaze of the man who was at once an obstruction and her protection.

"I beg your pardon," he said.

Feeling rather foolish, Tru sought purchase on the ground with the toes of her boots. He immediately set her down.

"Better?"

"Yes." Tru could feel her bonnet slipping backward. She made a grab for it, exposing her tightly coiled hair to the wind's icy teeth, and set it properly on her head before it could blow away.

Still watching her, he frowned. "Are you all right?"

Tru realized that her scarf had muffled her answer. Rather than expose her face to the cold, she nodded.

"I'm afraid I wasn't watching where I was going," he said.

She nodded again and pointed to herself, hoping he understood she was offering the same explanation.

"Are you certain you can walk? You didn't twist an ankle?"

The answer to the first required another nod. The answer to the second required a shake. It would be too confusing if she did both. Tru pulled the scarf just below her bottom lip. "Really, I'm fine." Her moist breath was made visible by the cold air. She burrowed her mouth and nose into the warm wool again. When he continued to stare at her as though gauging the truth of her words, Tru took a step sideways. The wind slipped under her petticoats and her skirt fluttered wildly against his legs as she made to pass.

"You're Miss Morrow. The schoolteacher."

Tru stopped. She supposed that if he had any doubt about her identity, the simple act of pausing was sufficient to confirm it.

"My name's Bridger," he said, touching the brim of his pearl gray Stetson with a gloved hand. "Cobb Bridger."

She sighed and tugged on her scarf again. "I know who you are, Mr. Bridger."

"You do?"

She felt strangely pleased that she had surprised him. "I eliminated all the faces I know. Since I don't know yours, that makes you new to town and therefore the gambler who has taken up lodgings at the Pennyroyal."

"I'm staying at the Pennyroyal."

"I don't pass any judgment about gambling, Mr. Bridger. Or drinking for that matter." The Pennyroyal was a hotel *and* saloon. "Your affairs are your own." She thought she sounded a bit priggish for someone who professed to pass no judgment, but it was too late to make amends for it. "Excuse me, please."

He retreated a step and let her move out of his reach before he said, "I thought you'd be more curious."

If he'd put out a hand to block her path, he could not have stopped her with more ease. Tru turned her head and arched a single spun-gold eyebrow.

"Don't you wonder how I recognized you, Miss Morrow?"

Tru yanked on her scarf. "I imagine you learned something about everyone in Bitter Springs in the same manner I did. You cannot get from the train station to the hotel without the assistance of Rabbit and Finn Collins, and no personal detail is too small for them to miss about you or relate about others. As the young masters are both my pupils, I can suppose one or both pointed me out to you as you rode by or told you all of the six ways I've made their lives miserable by accepting the position to teach in Bitter Springs. You probably noticed my horns and cloven feet."

Almost immediately, Tru regretted calling attention to herself in that manner. Cobb Bridger's scrutiny was thorough, though not particularly personal. He regarded her with a certain remoteness that was almost clinical, more akin to the dispassionate observation of a scientist. She was most definitely not flattered, but then neither, she realized, was she embarrassed.

"What I noticed," he said, returning his eyes to hers, "is that the color of your hair is as fine as Rumpelstiltskin could spin it."

Tru felt her jaw go slack. Gaping like a fish was unattractive, and she recovered quickly. Quite against her will, though, the dimple on the left side of her mouth appeared as a short laugh changed the shape of her lips. "Pardon me, Mr. Bridger, but this is the second time today that someone has made that rather odd comparison. I do have to ask myself whether you heard it first from Finn or whether he came by it from you."

"No doubt about it, Miss Morrow. That's a puzzler."

Tru smiled again, this time appreciatively. Mr. Bridger had obviously decided to give nothing away. "So you and Finn have become fast friends."

"I don't remember that he gave me a choice."

"No, I don't suppose he did." Her smile faltered, became earnest. "You'll have a care with him, won't you? He doesn't know a stranger, and I understand from his grandmother that he's drawn most particularly to gamblers."

"He asked me right off if I knew his father."

She nodded. "He believes his father is riding the rails playing high-stakes poker from one end of the country to the other. He might be. No one knows, but no one but Finn holds out any hope that one day he'll turn up in Bitter Springs with his winnings in a wheelbarrow."

"I see."

Tru wasn't sure what he saw. When he tilted his head, the brim of his hat cast a shadow over his eyes. She couldn't tell whether he was being reflective or dismissive. "So you'll have a care," she repeated. "It would be a kindness if you did."

"You are certain of that?"

His question seemed to suggest that she could be wrong. She felt herself bristling and responded with rather more sharpness than she intended. "It's no burden to show kindness."

"What if kindness is merely a deceit? There's a burden there, I think, and usually unfortunate consequences."

Tru shivered inside her coat. She tried to form a response, but her teeth chattered so violently that she would have bitten her tongue.

"Perhaps we should agree to disagree," he said. "Before you are chilled to the bone."

"T-too l-l-late."

"May I escort you home?"

She shook her head.

"As you wish." He tapped his brim again. "Good day, Miss Morrow."

Tru thought she might have seen something like humor play about his mouth, but she couldn't be sure. He did not strike her as a man who smiled as a matter of course but as one who offered it more judiciously and to far more devastating effect.

Tru covered the lower half of her face again and turned away. She fought the temptation to glance over her shoulder to see if he was watching her. She had the sensation that he was. The most disturbing thing about that particular fancy was that she was warmed by it.

Like many Western towns built around driving cattle to market, Bitter Springs had a wide thoroughfare through the center of town. Businesses, often with living space above them for the owners, lined both sides of the street. What had once been a tent city for the worst vices of transient rail workers, barkeeps, gamblers, and whores had become a town of more or less permanent citizens with some notion of respectability and pride.

The railroad gave Bitter Springs a link east and west and south. North was still the territory of outlaw hideouts, ranches so large they were measured in square miles, not acres, and all of the Montana Territory. To hear the citizens of Bitter Springs tell it, there was no good reason to go north.

Cobb Bridger watched the schoolteacher until she turned the corner. He knew from Finn that Miss Morrow lived in a home built expressly for the purpose of attracting a qualified teacher to Bitter Springs. According to the boy, the previous teacher had been murdered, and someone—he called her the widder Berry—was to blame. With some help from Finn's older brother, Cobb came to understand that the widder Berry was to blame for wanting the town to have a new teacher, not the murder of the former one. Rabbit also clarified that the widder Berry was now Mrs. Kellen Coltrane, but Cobb had worked that out for himself by then.

It was Mrs. Coltrane who placed the advertisement for a teacher in the Chicago paper, one of the seven positions that Gertrude Morrow had cut out, and one of five for which she was invited to interview. He had no difficulty in locating and speaking to the other potential employers, but it was experience and persistence in equal measure that led him to finding Mrs. Coltrane. As it happened, she was not a resident of Chicago but a visitor to the city, and the information she left with the paper gave her address as the Palmer House.

Andrew Mackey III had discovered the newspaper lead so late that Cobb had no expectation that Mrs. Coltrane would still be a guest at the Palmer months after placing her advertisement. At the time, he had no way of knowing if Gertrude Morrow had responded to this particular notice, but as he eliminated the other leads he was given he had to follow the one that remained. If Miss Morrow had never met with Mrs. Coltrane, then Cobb had nothing.

It hadn't come to that. He'd verified that she was in Bitter Springs and now all that remained was to make certain she stayed and inform Andrew Mackey of her whereabouts. Keeping her close was no hardship, but he had spent his first few days in town learning about her, and what he knew about the schoolteacher made him question the wisdom of informing on her too quickly.

"Nothing adds up."

"Pardon?" Walter Mangold cut his lumbering stride short and drew up beside Cobb. "D'you say something to me, Mr. Bridger?"

The deep voice intruded on Cobb's reverie. He glanced sideways and then up. Walt Mangold stood half a head taller than Cobb's six feet and had shoulders broad enough to clear the sidewalks of passersby if he didn't tread carefully. Cobb had observed that Walt *did* tread carefully. He was not merely conscious of those around him; he was conscientious. It did not escape Cobb's notice that Walt needed more time to think about things than most people, but Cobb thought that might be a point in his favor. It would be a mistake to suppose that pondering made him slow-witted.

"Sorry, Walt. I was just thinking out loud."

"I do that myself from time to time. Mrs. Sterling doesn't much like it. She thinks she's supposed to answer me, and she's got no time for it. That's what she tells me."

"You stay busy at the hotel."

"Sure do. And if I don't, she has something to say about that."

One corner of Cobb's mouth turned up. Ida Mae Sterling managed the hotel and saloon in the absence of the owner, another fact he'd learned from Finn and Rabbit before they set his bags on the front porch. That's where Walt scooped them up in his hamlike fists. Mrs. Sterling introduced herself at the registration desk and gave him a key to his room, but not before she looked him over and asked what brought him to town. It said something about Mrs. Sterling's suffer-no-fools manner that Cobb almost told her the truth. Instead he told her that he had no particular reason for stopping in Bitter Springs. It was just a place on the way to somewhere else.

He didn't know if she believed him, but she accepted it, and Cobb supposed it was right about then that they all con- ceived the idea that he was a gambling man. Finn and Rabbit had certainly been hanging on his every word.

Cobb began walking again and Walt fell in step. "Is Mrs. Sterling serving up apple pie tonight?" he asked. "I don't know when I've tasted better."

"She sure is. Funny you should ask about it. I'm on my way to pick up a couple of pies right now."

"Pick them up? What do you mean?"

"Oh, Mrs. Sterling don't make her own pies. When she took over managing the place from Mrs. Coltrane, well, she had to give something up, and baking pies was it. Mrs. Phillips, that's who makes them now." Walt raised his arm to point across the street. "That's her place over there."

Cobb ducked under Walt's extended arm in time to avoid a crushed windpipe and glanced in the direction of Walt's fingerpost. Large, neatly painted letters above the window proclaimed the shop to be exactly what it was: BAKERY. "So it is."

Walt pulled up short. "You want to come with me, Mr. Bridger? Jenny usually gives me something for my trouble. Could be she'd have something for you, or I can share."

"That's a tempting offer, but I'm on my way to the station."

"The station? You're leaving?" Deep furrows appeared in Walt's broad brow. "No, of course you're not. You don't have your bags. Then again, you don't need them if you're running out. Is that what you're doing, running out? Mrs. Sterling will hunt you down herself if you didn't pay your bill. We've seen that happen before, and it doesn't set right with her. Can't say I like it too much myself, especially since you won better than fifty dollars last night from Charlie Patterson and the Davis boys."

Cobb held up a hand. "Walt." When he had the other man's attention, he went on. "I'm looking for Mr. Collins, Walt. That's why I'm going to the station."

"Oh."

"And ease your mind on the matter of me leaving and not settling up. I can promise you that won't happen. I keep my promises and pay my debts."

Walt shifted his weight uncomfortably. "I shouldn't have said all that. Sometimes my mouth runs ahead of my wits. You been real good for us, so I hope you know I was just blatherin'."

Cobb regarded Walt's ruddy cheeks and wondered how much color was embarrassment and how much was the result of the beating wind. "What do you mean that I've been good for you?"

"You bring in business. Folks like to take a hand with a card sharp now and again. Makes them feel real skilled if they beat you and just unlucky if they don't. Wouldn't do for a permanent gaming man to set up at the Pennyroyal, but a now-and-again fellow suits everyone."

"I see."

"It'd be real good if you stayed about a month or so."

"I'll be careful not to wear out my welcome."

Walt shifted again, and his eyes darted sideways. "I didn't mean that. I figured you wouldn't want to get caught here when winter sets in."

"You mean this isn't it?"

Walt's laughter boomed. "This? A day like this is just a hint. Just a little ol' hint."

"Then I'll consider myself warned." He touched his hat. "I'll see you this evening, Walt."

"You will, Mr. Bridger. I'll be bringing you your pie."

Jefferson Collins found his spectacles on his forehead after looking for them on the counter, under the counter, and in all twelve of the cubbyholes on the wall behind the counter. He slid them down to his nose and regarded his grandsons over the wire rims.

"You knew I was looking for them, didn't you?"

"I had a suspicion," said Finn. As soon as he spoke, he lost his rhythm with the three leather beanbags he was trying to juggle. "Shucks."

"My turn," said Rabbit.

"That's not fair. Pap made me miss."

"It's fair. He asked a question and you answered and that's what made you miss. It's my turn."

"Boys." The station agent's voice was infused with equal parts impatience and affection. He told anyone who asked after his grandsons that they were the light of his life and the bane of his existence. It was not so long ago that they could be mistaken for twins, but Rabbit shot up around the time of his eleventh birthday and it seemed that now he towered over his younger brother. They were both still tow-headed, but Collins could see that Rabbit's hair was darkening ever so slightly at the roots. Neither of the boys weighed much soaking wet, but there was a contrast between Finn's sharp angles and Rabbit's sturdier frame. There was no denying that Rabbit was filling out and growing up.

The station agent was making peace with it. It was the way

of things. Finn, though, did not like being left behind. Collins watched his younger grandson make as if he was going to throw the beanbags hard at his brother's head, but Rabbit flinched, and that apparently was all Finn had been looking for. He tossed them underhand one at a time.

Jeff Collins returned to his perch on the stool behind the station counter and checked his pocket watch. He had receipts to prepare for the crates and packages due to leave Bitter Springs on the next westbound train. He pushed aside the receipt book and set his forearms on the counter, clasping his hands together.

"I haven't heard yet why you were kept after school, Finn."

Finn did not look in his grandfather's direction. He watched Rabbit carefully, willing his brother to miss just one toss. "Didn't Rabbit tell you?"

"I didn't ask him. I thought it was your story to tell."

"Thought he might have told you anyway."

Not missing a beat, Rabbit said, "I'm not a tattletale."

"Only since you got to be eleven." He stole a look at his grandfather. "You want a story or you want the truth?"

"Sometimes they're the same, but if there is a distinction in your mind, I'd like the truth."

"Well, the truth is I like talking to Miss Morrow."

"You do?"

"Uh-huh. She's nice, and she talks to me like I'm eleven."

"She does."

"Yep. Even though she says I shouldn't be in a hurry to grow up."

"She's got that right."

"Oh, she knows a whole lot of things. I suspect she's right about most of them. Same as you."

"I'm right about all of them."

"Yes, sir. That's what I meant to say."

Collins's mouth twitched. "So I can tell your granny that you were late for afternoon chores because you preferred your teacher's company."

Finn frowned deeply. "That'd be the truth," he said slowly,

"but I think Granny would take to a story better. Maybe you could tell her that I had chores to do at school. I will tomorrow. Miss Morrow asked me to help her clean slates, so I'll be staying after again."

A beanbag thumped to the floor. "You just made that up," said Rabbit.

"Did not." Finn scooped the fallen beanbag off the floor and held out one hand for the other two.

Disgusted, Rabbit dropped them on the floor for Finn to pick up. "Robby Fox and I asked her this morning if there was anything we could do for her after school and she said no."

"She needs my help tomorrow," Finn said. "You and Robby just asked too early. She didn't give me anything special to do today."

Rabbit put the toe of his shoe on one of the beanbags when Finn stooped to pick it up. "Maybe because you were too busy writing 'I am surely sorry for making Prissy Taylor squeal like a piglet.' I bet you misspelled most of the words just so you could keep Miss Morrow busy correcting you."

Finn tugged on the beanbag and pulled it free. Rabbit promptly stepped on the other one. "So what if I did? She was real kind about it. You just wish you'd thought of giving Prissy's hair a good yank. Robby Fox probably wishes he did too. You both looked real jealous when Miss Morrow told me to stay. I would have wrote my apology on every slate if she'd asked." He glanced sideways at his grandfather. "A man's gotta pay for his pleasure."

Rabbit set his fists on his hips. "You didn't even like her when she came to town. You musta told everyone she came here to bedevil you."

Finn didn't deny it. "Well, you said it, too, and besides, I changed my mind since then." He grabbed one corner of the beanbag still held captive beneath Rabbit's shoe and yanked hard. The stitching gave way as he freed it and dozens of small white beans spilled out. They bounced and rolled across the floor.

Jeff Collins shook his head. "Now, didn't I just see that

coming? Get a broom, boys. And a dustpan. I'm not asking your granny to fix that bag either. About time you two learned your way around a needle and thread."

Rabbit and Finn glared at each other but neither pointed a finger. Finn placed the two good beanbags on the counter for safekeeping and slunk off behind his brother to get the broom and dustpan in the back room.

The station agent was still shaking his head when the door leading to the train platform opened. He extended his arm, palm out, warning Cobb Bridger when he stepped past the threshold. "Have a care you don't get beans underfoot. I don't reckon there's anything more graceless than a grown man going down on his backside."

"And few things more amusing."

"That's what I was thinking."

Cobb examined the floor for evidence of what caused the mishap. His glance fell on the split leather beanbag and then the two bags on the counter. "Rabbit and Finn are around, I gather."

"In the back, getting the proper implements for cleaning up." He sat up and adjusted his spectacles. "What brings you here, Mr. Bridger?"

Cobb carefully picked his way to the counter. He hefted one of the beanbags. "Always surprises me how many beans one of these can hold. Your grandsons are learning to juggle?"

"Rabbit's got the knack of it. Finn's learning."

Nodding, Cobb set the bag down and leaned an elbow on the countertop. The caped shoulder of his duster brushed against the receipt book that Collins had pushed to the side. "I want to send a letter to someone in Chicago. About how long will it take to get there?"

"Well, if it's speed you're after, I can send it over the wire. It'd have to be short, though. You pay by the word and every word is dear."

"No, I prefer a letter for this."

"Then it would take about three days express train, weather permitting, and upward of six days regular mail coach."

"That's faster than I thought."

"Yes, sir. The country's shrinking. I hear Montana Territory will be a state soon. Maybe next month. Wyoming can't be far behind. Seems like the railroad is swallowing us up. Hard to know what speed will bring next. I'm taking deliveries all the time from Chicago and St. Louis. Folks see something in a magazine and they think they got to have it. Even Mrs. Garvin's ordering from Paris, France."

Cobb's eyes narrowed as he tried to place the name. He couldn't draw it out, but before he asked, Mr. Collins offered the information.

"That'd be the milliner. It's her older daughter, Millicent, who's getting hitched. She's marrying Mr. Irvin. He's the undertaker. My wife says I shouldn't be so surprised that Mrs. Garvin is ordering from Paris, France, but then she doesn't have much of a head for geography and the notion of distance."

Cobb angled his ear toward the back room when the sounds of a scuffle erupted. "The boys?"

Collins remained unperturbed. "Better be, else the station's infested with the biggest rats this side of the Continental Divide. You have that letter, Mr. Bridger?"

"No. I haven't written it yet."

"Three days express. Six days regular."

"I remember." He paused. "What's the slowest way to get a letter to Chicago."

"Slower than six days, you mean?"

"That's right."

"Well, I suppose putting off writing it would take care of that."

One corner of Cobb's mouth edged upward. "I'd prefer to write it this evening, post it tomorrow, and have it take a month to arrive."

"A month? The pony express was three weeks faster than that. I suppose I could get Finn or Rabbit to walk it there."

"Something more practical," Cobb said dryly.

"It's an interesting idea, sending something by way of a slow boat to China. That's just an expression, you understand.

No telling what would become of your letter if it went by way of China. You *do* want it to reach Chicago, don't you?"

"I do."

"You expecting a reply to your correspondence?"

"I am."

"Then I guess it's your intention to stay put for a while."

"For a while."

"I pegged you for a gambling man right off."

"I remember."

"My wife will tell you that I've made that judgment before and been wrong about it."

"She already has."

"Sure. I should have known." The station agent looked Cobb Bridger in the eye. "Am I wrong?"

"No one seems to think so, not even your wife."

"I'm asking you."

"I've been playing poker at the Pennyroyal every night since I arrived. That's four evenings running. Tonight will make my fifth, and I'm winning more than I'm losing. Just this afternoon, Walt Mangold told me I'm good for business."

"I reckon he's right. He might have mentioned I don't hold much with gamblers."

"Walt never said a word. Mrs. Collins warned me."

"That so? Well, I reckon she was right to, but maybe she also told you it's not personal."

"She said your son left Bitter Springs to take up the sporting life. I'd say that was very personal."

Jefferson Collins snorted softly. His Adam's apple bobbed above his stiff collar when he swallowed. "More like he was run out of town. Couldn't pay his debts, and the Burdicks would have taken it out of his hide. I paid up, but he still had to leave. The Burdicks are gone now, but I don't suppose he knows that, and I don't suppose it would matter if he did."

The station agent's mouth curled to one side, regret stamped on his narrow face. He knuckled his bearded chin. "I can't think why I'm telling you this."

Cobb said nothing. He didn't have to. The reasons for the station agent's confession chose that moment to charge out of the back room. Rabbit wielded the broom with the flair and deadly purpose of St. George wielding Ascalon, and Finn used the dustpan like a shield to protect his flank. To their credit, they made an attempt to put on the brakes when they spied him. The beans made that impossible. Both boys lost their footing at the same time, and all their flailing was in aid of nothing except comic effect. They landed on their backsides hard enough to jar the floor. Rabbit managed to hold on to the broom. Finn's dustpan flew out of his hand and would have conked him on the head if Cobb hadn't caught it.

"Yep," said their grandfather, leaning over the counter for a good look. "Nothing as graceless."

"Or as amusing." Cobb handed the dustpan back to Finn.

"Hey, Mr. Bridger."

"Hey, Finn." His eyes darted to Rabbit. "Hey, Rabbit."

"Hello." He turned on one hip and rubbed his backside. Beans were stuck to his denim overalls. Grimacing, he swept them aside.

"Better than picking out buckshot," Cobb said.

"I was thinking the same thing," said Rabbit's grandfather.

Cobb extended a hand to help Rabbit up. When the boy had sure footing, he extended the same courtesy to Finn. Rabbit started sweeping, but Finn just set the dustpan on the floor and sidled up to the counter. He was too short to prop his elbow on it, but that didn't stop him from trying to mimic Cobb's casual pose.

"What'd you come for, Mr. Bridger?" asked Finn. "You have an errand for me? I do errands for people, you know." He shrugged his thin shoulders. "But I probably told you that already."

"You did. I haven't forgotten. There might be something you can do for me later."

"Sure. As long as it's not after I'm supposed to be in bed. Granny wouldn't like that."

Collins tapped the counter. "I wouldn't like it either."

"Oh, I know that, but you'd understand."

"Maybe. Maybe not. Better you don't test the waters."

Cobb nudged the toe of Finn's shoe with his. "Tomorrow.

I'm still trying to work out a few things with your grand-father."

"He's real good at working things out."

Collins reached over the counter and flicked Finn's temple. "And you're real good at not working at things. Help your brother."

Finn made a show of rubbing his head, but he returned to the dustpan and held it in place while Rabbit swept.

The station agent winked at Cobb. "Now about that letter. I'm thinking that if it went west first, by mistake of course, well, that'd add some days to its journey. Upwards of two weeks, I should think. Mistakes like that take some time to sort out. You have to allow that you're making an unusual request."

"I know that."

"I suppose you have your reasons."

"I suppose I do."

Collins waited a full ten seconds before he shrugged. "You're not going to tell me. I guess playing cards close to your vest is second nature."

"It probably seems that way.

"All right. Let's see. There's one more thing you can do that might work. How's your handwriting?"

"My handwriting? It's not copperplate, but it's legible."

"I'm thinking you don't want it to be. Legible, that is. Now, you can't write so bad that no one can read it, but you might make some of your letters look like other letters. Confuse things some. Or change the address just a bit. Send it to the west part of the street instead of the east, for example. After that, I'm plum out of ideas. You sure you just don't want to wait to send your letter off?"

"I'm sure. You'll have it tomorrow."

Collins nodded. "All right, then."

Cobb turned and regarded the boys. "I met your teacher today." Their heads came up simultaneously. Bird dogs could hardly have been more alert. "We collided on the sidewalk."

A crease appeared between Rabbit's eyebrows. "You didn't

knock her down, did you? I have some experience landing on my backside. It's not for ladies."

"I didn't knock her down."

"She's not hurt?" asked Finn. "I'm supposed to help her after school. Maybe she won't care about that if you smashed her foot."

"I managed to avoid every one of her toes."

Finn's cheeks puffed out like a chipmunk's as he blew out a breath. "That's good news. Did you say you were sorry? That'd be the mannerly thing to do. She talks about manners. A lot."

"She sure does," said Rabbit. "Talks about them all the time. We even read stories about manners. I don't care for them much, but the girls act as if they like them."

"I was sincerely contrite."

"Yeah," Finn said, "but did you say you were sorry?"

Cobb heard Finn's grandfather chuckle. "I did say I was sorry. I also introduced myself, but she already knew who I was."

"She did?" asked Rabbit.

Finn told his brother, "I might have said something or other about Mr. Bridger being new to town. Just by way of makin' conversation." He returned his attention to Cobb. "You knew it was her right off, didn't you?"

"I did."

"Now how did you know that?" asked Collins.

"Finn here told me there was no mistaking the color of her hair."

"And I was right. Remember, Pap? Mr. Stiltskin? You said he spun gold from straw? He's the one, isn't he?"

"Rumpelstiltskin," said Rabbit.

"Sure. That's him."

"I remember, but I'm not following what one has to do with the other."

Rabbit leaned against his broom. "Finn thinks Miss Morrow's hair was spun by Rumpelstiltskin."

Finn glared at his brother, his eyes accusing. "You agreed with me."

"What if I did?"

"Well, I told her what I thought. Told her straight out that Prissy's hair was yellow like straw and her hair was like gold. And *I'm* the one she invited to stay after school."

There didn't seem to be anything to say after that.

Chapter Two

"Will you have a table by the window tonight?"

Tru glanced quickly around the dining room. She had at least a passing acquaintance with all of the diners at the tables this evening, and Mr. Cobb Bridger was not among them. She felt a small measure of relief followed by a wash of disappointment and chided herself for feeling either. He was no one to her. And she was less than no one to him.

"I don't mind sharing a table if you'd like to save the window seat for someone else," she said.

Cecilia Ross brought up her hand in a dismissive gesture. "It's yours if you want it. I know you're partial to sitting by the window so I sorta saved it for you, this being Monday and all, and you being a regular Monday through Thursday."

"Well then, yes. I'd be pleased to sit there."

Cecilia nodded, satisfied. The fulsome smile that she used to greet guests turned mischievous. Under her breath, for Tru's ears alone, she said, "And wouldn't I just like to join you, but Mrs. Sterling has me running around tonight like there's two of me." Cil drew back and spoke up in her normal tone. "I'll bring you tea, unless you'd rather have beer or a sarsa-parilla."

"Tea is exactly what I want."

"It's chicken and dumplings tonight. Lots of Mrs. Sterling's good gravy besides."

"I see." Tru's nostrils pinched slightly as she sniffed the air. "Better than that, I smell it." She parted company with Cil and wended her way among the diners, pausing at each table she passed to respond to a greeting. She was invited twice to take a chair with others, but she politely declined both times. While she had told Cil honestly that she had no objections to sharing a table, she would not have chosen to share one with the family or extended family of her students. She had learned that she must consider the perception of favoritism. There were only thirteen regular pupils at the school and six others who came when they could, but it seemed all of them were related in one way or another to every adult in Bitter Springs. To avoid problems, her dinner companions were almost exclusively the overnight guests at the Pennyroyal.

The cup of tea that Cil placed before her was too hot to drink immediately. Tru set the cup back in its saucer and stared out the window while she waited for it to cool. It was already too dark outside to make out much beyond the glass, but the warm lamplight inside the dining room gave the window the reflective quality of a mirror. Tru watched Howard Wheeler make broad gestures with his hands as he conversed with his longtime friend. Jack Clifton's lean, weathered features were indistinct in the glass, but Tru imagined his expression was impassively fixed as he waited his turn for rebuttal.

Tru wondered what argument was entertaining them now and if Ida Mae Sterling figured into it. She had it from Heather Collins, then from Cil Ross, and later from Mrs. Sterling herself, that Howard and Jack were sweet on the widow Sterling, even sweeter on her cooking, but that they couldn't settle on who should make the first proposal. Tru smiled as Jack took over the conversation, using his hands as expansively as Howard.

"May I join you?"

Startled, Tru's head snapped up. The back of her hand brushed her teacup. The cup bobbled in the saucer, splashing her with hot tea. "Oh!" She pressed the back of her hand to her lips before she thought to reach for the napkin in her lap.

"I beg your pardon," Cobb Bridger said. "Again."

Tru waved aside his concern with her free hand and indicated he could sit.

"Are you certain? I seem to be well on my way to causing you serious injury."

She regarded him over her hand and saw that a hint of a smile played about his mouth. In spite of his words, she thought he was not at all concerned about the possibility that she would turn him away. It made her wonder what he knew about her that she did not know about herself. Drawing back her hand and placing it in her lap, she said, "I think we might manage to negotiate chicken and dumplings, Mr. Bridger."

Cobb pulled out the chair opposite Tru and sat. He carefully maneuvered his long legs under the table so that neither his knees nor his feet bumped it.

"Well done, Mr. Bridger, but I think you exaggerate the threat you present to me. You could not have known that I would startle so easily."

"I should have recognized the signs of someone whose mind was otherwise occupied."

"Oh? Why is that?"

"Some familiarity with that state myself, I'm afraid."

Cecilia Ross arrived with a beer for Cobb and a plate of rolls. When she set it down in front of him, Tru picked up her teacup and watched with a measure of detachment as Cil flirted quite shamelessly with the Pennyroyal's most recent guest. The part of her that was not as detached as she might have wished still could find no fault with Cecilia, and she suspected that Cobb Bridger was used to the kind of attention he was receiving.

It did not seem likely that he was unaware of his good looks. His blue eyes—and it was not an exaggeration to call them bright to the point of brilliance—were his most compelling feature, but an argument could be made for the sensual mouth with the full lower lip and the smile that hovered there like a promise. His narrow, clean-shaven face clearly defined his jaw and chin. Even the line of his nose did not shift from its vertical plane to break the perfect symmetry of his features. He was saved the awkwardness of being pretty because every aspect of his face had been sculpted by a deft hand but not a fine one. There was a boldness to his features that made them seem of this earth rather than the heavens. His thatch of finger-combed hair might be shot through with threads of radiant sunlight, but there was no mistaking it for a halo.

In Tru's mind, angels would not claim Cobb Bridger as one of their own.

It was apparent to Tru that Cil thought otherwise. She hovered at Cobb's side until a request from another diner required her attention, and even then her departure was noticeably reluctant.

Tru's gaze followed Cecilia, but she spoke to Cobb. "I believe you have made a conquest." She heard him make a sound at the back of his throat that might have meant anything. She turned back to him, smiling knowingly. "It's probably better that you don't comment."

Cobb lifted his beer and took a full swallow. "She has a cousin, I believe."

"Renee? Miss Harrison's not working tonight." She studied his face, wondering why he brought up Cil's cousin. "You prefer her to Cecilia?"

"I prefer present company, Miss Morrow."

"A pretty compliment, but I must point out that you don't know me."

"I thought it was obvious that I mean to rectify that." He returned her study, his gaze direct but vaguely remote, seeing more than he gave away. "It can be . . . wearing . . . when the cousins work together. That's why I inquired after Miss Harrison."

"I've observed that men are generally flattered by their attentions."

"I didn't say I wasn't flattered."

Tru laughed. "No, you didn't, did you?" She helped herself to a crusty roll from the plate Cil left and broke it in two. She set one half down and drizzled honey on the other. When she looked up, he was still watching her. "You're staring, Mr. Bridger. You've seen someone put honey on bread before, haven't you?"

"No one with your concentration for the task. Your tongue was peeping out." He touched the right corner of his own mouth with a fingertip. "Right here."

She nodded and wondered if she should be embarrassed. She didn't feel embarrassed. It was odd that he didn't make her feel that way. "I've been told it also happens when I write or do particularly difficult sums." She took a delicate bite of her roll.

"Who told you that?"

Tru savored the roll as it melted on her tongue. She tasted honey on her lips. "My father thought it was a habit I should be able to manage better. Applications of pepper sauce proved unsuccessful."

Cobb's eyebrows lifted.

"It wasn't as awful as it sounds."

"I don't know. It sounds painful."

She shrugged. "I do try to be mindful around my students. I've caught some of the girls aping me. Well, mimicking me. Aping makes it sound as if they mean to be cruel, and I don't think that is their intention."

"I'm sure it's not."

Tru stayed her hand on the way to her mouth and regarded Cobb Bridger with new interest. "How can you be sure? To my knowledge, you've only met two of my students, neither of whom are young ladies."

"No, they're young men, and I don't think I'm wrong that they find the gesture as fascinating as I do. Your girls, at least the older ones, come by that knowledge through some instinct as old as Eve, and they act on it without scruple. We, and by 'we' I mean all men, will never be able to resist the apple."

Tru blinked. She required a moment to recover. "You present a rather disturbing image. I believe I will try the pepper sauce again."

"Do not do it on my account."

"There is no reason to flatter yourself. I'm doing it for my young ladies, the ones who think that a female is of no account unless she has an apple to offer." It was wholly satisfying that it was Cobb Bridger who blinked this time. She claimed that as a victory of sorts because he did not strike her as a man who was easily taken aback. "I may be almost as new to Wyoming as you, Mr. Bridger, but I fully embrace the notion that women here are of equal standing, at least in the eyes of territory law."

Tru thought it was a proper construction of her position, clear and concise, and conveyed that she was a serious person and one who should be taken seriously, then the corners of his mouth curved upward and the promise of his smile was fully realized. She could not make out condescension in his features. All evidence pointed to genuine enjoyment. He set down his beer and gave sound to a full-throated laugh. Tru finished off her roll in the time it took him to rein in his amusement. When he was quiet, she raised a single eyebrow and simply waited him out.

Cobb cleared his throat and took another swallow of beer. "I stand corrected," he said. "And in awe."

It was not disapproval that made Tru press her lips together. She needed to suppress the urge to laugh. She waited until it passed and then asked, "Why are you really here, Mr. Bridger?"

He shrugged. "Just passing through."

"So Finn told me, but I meant why are you sitting with me now? I did not see you Thursday night, and I believe you had already arrived."

"Fishing for compliments?"

"Not at all," she said, and meant it. "I know my value as a comfortable companion, and I am not unfamiliar with the attentions of men, but a sporting man such as yourself always keeps his distance out of respect for my position. You recognized me as the schoolteacher this afternoon and still put yourself at my table this evening."

"You did not object."

"I was curious."

"Are we attracting notice?"

Her smile was edged with disappointment. "Please, Mr. Bridger, do not pretend that you don't know. When you're not looking at me, your attention is drawn to the window. I know very well what you can see in that black mirror. You may not be able to identify each surreptitious stare, but you can certainly count the number of heads turning in our direction."

Tru watched Cobb sit back. She could almost feel him regard her with new appreciation. "The only reason I'm rising in your estimation is that you underestimated me in the first place. Did I seem as though I might be an easy mark? The unattached schoolmarm, lonely, perhaps a little sad, virtually an old maid at twenty-six. It is unpalatable to even say it, more so because it is the stuff of dime novels and badly written melodramas, but it is difficult to refute an archetype that exists in the minds of so many as a truth."

Frowning, a crease appeared between his eyebrows. Cobb angled his head and worried one earlobe with his thumb and forefinger. "Is it your opinion that I have certain—shall I call them designs—on your person?"

"I don't know. Do you?"

"Are you always this straightforward?"

"I believe I am, yes. And you have not answered the question."

"I cannot decide if you think so much of yourself or so little, but the answer is no. I thought you might provide more in the way of lively conversation than any of my dinner companions of the last few days, and I wasn't wrong about that. Do you mind that my attentions have attracted notice?"

"No. But do not ask to escort me home. That would give rise to more speculation than is good for a town this size. I won't permit it."

He smiled then. "And you shouldn't expect that you'll always have your way. You won't." His eyes darted to the window. The door from the kitchen swept open. "Here comes Miss Ross with our dinner."

Tru waited until Cil moved away from their table before she picked up her fork. "How does one become a gambler, Mr. Bridger? Did you eliminate other professions first to arrive at this one, or is it a consequence of winning a single game and not being able to turn back?"

"I can't speak for all gamblers, but I came to it as a diversion."

"A diversion. That's a rather more intriguing answer than I expected."

Cobb speared a slice of chicken and added half a dumpling. "I've earned a living in more traditional ways, Miss Morrow. I've worked inside banks, stockyards, rail coaches, hospitals, and on two separate occasions, city hall. I was also the marshal of Hempstead, Indiana, for six weeks. I left after hunting down and bringing in a father and son who were using their traveling tent church to prey on young women." He paused, sighed. Regret touched his eyes. "That was an unfortunate choice of words."

He paused again, then took a mouthful of food and washed it down with a sip of beer. "After Hempstead, I set a different course."

Tru considered that. "So you might not always play at the tables for your livelihood."

"I might. I might not. I'm making no plans." He jabbed at another dumpling. "Is it important? I recall you saying that you do not pass judgment on gaming." He pointed to his beer. "Or drinking."

"I haven't forgotten what I said. I meant it."

Cobb's eyes narrowed slightly. "You've got something in mind, though. I can see it."

She touched the corner of her mouth self-consciously. No, she hadn't pushed out her tongue. "What gave me away?"

"You don't really expect me to tell you."

She shrugged and took a bite of food. "Bitter Springs has no marshal. Did you know that?"

"No. No one's mentioned it."

"I didn't hear about it until weeks after I arrived. Most folks think it should be kept quiet around strangers, at least until they're fairly confident the strangers aren't bank robbers or cattle thieves."

"Or card cheats."

"Especially not card cheats."

"You don't think it should be kept secret?"

"I think the town should have a lawman. There used to be a deputy. If I recall correctly, his name was Dan Sugar. But he's gone now, and no one has a good word to say about him anyway. Mrs. Sterling's husband was marshal years ago, and he was well liked. He was killed in an ambush outside of town."

"I was aware of what happened to Marshal Sterling. Finn told me. He left out the part about the position still being vacant."

"It's hard to imagine, but I suppose even Finn can mind his tongue from time to time."

Cobb jabbed a dumpling. "Why do you believe Bitter Springs needs a marshal? Is there some problem Finn hasn't shared with me?"

"I don't think so. There are disputes, of course, but Terry McCormick settles those. He's the mayor. If it's a property dispute, Harry Sample or his cousin Charles from the land office gets involved. Sometimes it's a matter for a judge to decide and one comes in from Rawlins. That's only happened once since I arrived."

"And when did you arrive?"

"The first week of June."

"So you've been here a little more than four months. Do you think you know enough to say whether or not Bitter Springs needs another marshal?"

"I'm allowed to have an opinion."

"Of course. It's generally better if it's an informed one.

There's probably a good reason why no one is clamoring to fill the vacancy."

"But I think I—"

Cobb interrupted her. "It doesn't matter, Miss Morrow. Even if I could get elected to the position, I'm not interested in wearing a badge again or staying in Bitter Springs that long."

Tru felt as if she had been pushed back in her chair. Cobb Bridger had not raised his voice in the least, rather it had become softer at the same time it was gathering intensity. There was a real force to it. She did not think she had imagined that. Her father had spoken similarly when he felt passionate about his subject, which he frequently did standing at the pulpit above the congregation at Olde St. John's Episcopal Church. Tru also had occasion to hear her father practice his sermons and knew that the modulation of his voice was often carefully calculated to underscore a point.

Tru folded her hands around her teacup, warming them. "I don't know if you could be clearer, Mr. Bridger, but I am compelled to correct an assumption you made. There is no election. The mayor and council can appoint you. They have that federal authority by virtue of their offices."

"Miss Morrow."

She recognized the feigned patience in his tone. "Yes?"

"I am not interested."

"Now," she said. "You are not interested now. You might find yourself in need of another diversion. It's hard to say how a losing streak at the card table might influence your thinking."

Cobb shook his head, but it was more in admiration than negation. "And I thought you could be dissuaded." He lifted his beer before he inched forward in his chair just enough so he could recline. Beneath the table he crossed his legs at the ankles. "Very well. But why me, Miss Morrow? Why now? You've had months to apply yourself to the problem of law and order in Bitter Springs. Given what I have observed of your tenacity, it is astonishing that you haven't already sworn in a new marshal. All by yourself."

"I have heard it said that sarcasm is the language of the devil."

"Then you know who you're dealing with."

The line of Tru's full lips thinned as she suppressed another smile. His sardonic wit brought Charlotte Mackey to mind, although Mrs. Mackey's pronouncements veered toward acerbic, while Cobb Bridger's remarks were wry and dry.

"In spite of what you think, Mr. Bridger, the idea that you might make a reasonably competent marshal only occurred to me when you mentioned your experience. There have been discussions at public council meetings so it is not as if I am the only one who has been entertaining the notion. Not of you specifically, I mean. How could any of us have anticipated that someone with your experience would arrive in Bitter Springs? I'm talking about the *idea* that the town could benefit from a man like you. Since no one's come forward to apply for the position, there's been a proposal that the town should make the vacancy public."

"Like they did with you."

"As a matter of fact, yes. But how did you know?" She shook her head, blowing out an audible breath. "Finn."

"And his grandmother. And Walt. Miss Ross said something about it as well. Or it could have been Miss Harrison. People seem to be delighted that the new teacher hails from Chicago and has an education to match her position. It's a point of pride and the reason they talk about it so easily. Even Finn has come around, but then you know that."

"It's disquieting what a complete stranger can learn in a matter of days."

"Most of it in the matter of a single day. Although it seems when the town agrees that some things are better not shared with strangers, like the absence of a marshal, for instance, there is almost universal silence."

Tru flushed at what she felt was a rebuke. The fact that it was delivered by a virtual stranger made it all the more galling.

"When there is no such restriction," he said, "I've learned that people in Bitter Springs have more to say than the *New York World*."

"There is a lot of talk here," she said. "And no town newspaper."

"You don't need one. Just like you probably don't need a marshal."

"I beg to differ on both counts."

"Yet you did not ask me to be a publisher."

"Do you have experience operating a newspaper?"

"No."

"Experience is the salient point here. You carry a gun, don't you?"

"Not to dinner."

"But you know how to use one."

"Yes. And so do the men robbing banks, stealing cattle, and challenging card cheats. One of the reasons people aren't clamoring to be marshal is because it's dangerous. Mrs. Sterling knows that all too well."

Tru fell silent. Cecilia appeared again, this time to take their plates away and replace them with warm slices of apple pie. Tru thanked her and hoped she would recognize it for the dismissal it was. Cecilia lingered long enough to watch Cobb savor his first bite and agree to carry his compliments back to the cook.

"Mrs. Sterling doesn't make the pies," Tru said.

"I know. Mrs. Phillips does. But Mrs. Sterling deserves praise for purchasing them from someone so profoundly competent."

"I will tell Jenny. She is a friend."

"Then you should definitely tell her."

"She thinks we need a marshal."

He shrugged and took another bite of pie.

"The time to look for a marshal is when we don't need one. If we are faced with the decision at the point of some calamity, it will be more difficult to be thoughtful."

"Miss Morrow, there is more to being marshal than knowing how to shoot, although as a predictor of success in the job, it's a reasonably good beginning." He relished his last bite of pie but declined Tru's serving when she pushed it toward him.

"What other qualities are important?" she asked.

"Very well. I suggest evenhandedness. Objectivity. A better than average knowledge of the law, particularly the ones that govern the town. The man you're looking for won't take the job if there are laws that are inherently flawed."

"For example?"

"Laws that favor one group over another without regard to merit."

"Like supporting the rights of men over women. Husbands over wives."

Cobb's mouth twisted in a wry smile. "I opened that door wide, didn't I?"

"You did. What else?"

"Skill at tracking, investigation. Someone who can lead."

"Someone who commands respect."

"Precisely. A point not in my favor, by the way."

"You should not be so quick to judge the citizens of Bitter Springs. People respect a gambler who runs a fair game."

"I swear, Miss Morrow, you are sorely tempting me to reveal the ace I keep up my sleeve."

Tru's mouth twisted to one side as she studied him. Her lips settled into their normal line once she arrived at her conclusion. "You don't have an ace anywhere on your person. You don't play with marked cards. And you don't deal from the bottom of the deck."

"You are more trusting than is good for you."

"You are not the first person to say so."

"Your father again?"

She shook her head. "My former employer. Mrs. Mackey chided me regularly, but then she was suspicious of everyone. I asked her once if she was born cynical, and she assured me that she wasn't. Family, she said, had made her that way. I told it her that it was the same for mc."

"How do you mean?"

"Trusting others to be at least as good as they can be. Trusting that some will be better. That thinking is compliments of my father. He was a minister and great believer in the good."

Both of Cobb's eyebrows lifted. "So you're a schoolteacher *and* a minister's daughter. You really aren't going to allow me to escort you home."

She laughed. "I told you."

Cecilia Ross visited each table one more time, collecting plates and refilling coffee cups. She arrived at Cobb and Tru's table last. "I let Mrs. Sterling know you liked the pie." She glanced at the slice Tru had barely touched. "Something wrong with yours, Miss Morrow?"

"Not at all. I was chattering."

"I noticed. I surely did."

Tru was careful to temper her response. "I'm sure you weren't alone. May I have my pie wrapped? I'd like to take it home." She thought Cecilia looked as if she wanted to say no, but in the end she acquiesced.

"Of course." She stopped short of saying she would be happy to do it.

"Thank you, Cil."

Cecilia was already turning toward Cobb. "Is there anything else you'd like, Mr. Bridger?"

"Nothing for me."

"Will you be going to the saloon before long? Folks have been asking."

"Within the hour. There's something I need to do first."

"You don't mind if I let people know? Jem and Jessop Davis are looking to win back what they lost last night. Jake says they're fools, but he'd like to watch his brothers lose their shirts. I think he means to collect them for you."

"I doubt it will come to that. Thank you, Miss Ross. Certainly you can let people know I intend to play this evening."

"Oh, you're welcome, Mr. Bridger. It'll be my pleasure."

When she walked away Tru checked to see if Cil's feet were touching the ground. They were, but only just. She glanced at Cobb. "I hope you do not mean to break that girl's heart, though I imagine she would bear as much responsibility for the breakage as you."

Cobb said, "You're making too much of her attention."

Tru shrugged lightly.

Cobb's eyes fell to the plate in front of Tru. "She forgot to take your pie."

"I rest my case."

Cobb sat at the small oak writing desk beside his bed, his feet propped sideways on a three-legged stool he had carried out of the bathing room. Walter delivered the paper, pen, and ink to him mere minutes after he made his request, and Cobb had given him a gold piece for his trouble. It was an extravagant gesture, one that Cobb could not afford to regularly repeat, but he had been feeling generous. It was a mood that lingered.

She had something to do with it. Gertrude Morrow. He reached into the inside pocket of his vest and gingerly extracted the sketch he had made of her in Andrew Mackey's study. The lawyer's description had been correct on general points, but he had not been able to convey the finer ones.

Miss Morrow did indeed have an oval face, but there had been no mention of the faint indentation at the base of her chin or that in spite of features that were perfectly proportioned, there was an intriguing asymmetry that was visible when she smiled. The shallow dimple on the left side of her mouth had no twin on the right. Cobb wondered if Mackey hadn't noticed or didn't think it was important enough to bring up. For Cobb it was precisely that kind of detail that raised a sketch to the level of a portrait. Cobb had spent a considerable portion of the evening committing certain aspects of Gertrude Morrow's face to his memory and wondering if Andrew Mackey had ever noticed her except in passing.

Her eyes were a shade of green that he did not believe existed in any other form in nature and therefore defied his ability to describe them. Warmer and a shade lighter than emerald, brighter than the green underside of an orchid leaf, they absorbed and reflected light in a way that softened the color in one moment and then brought it brilliantly into sharp relief in the next.

Cobb reined in that thought, his mouth twisting with wry humor. He had been interviewing witnesses and suspects for years and never once gave this much consideration to identifying the color of a pair of eyes. Neither, he reflected, had he surrendered so much control of an interview, and when he had asked Miss Morrow if he might join her for dinner, interviewing her had been the purpose of his request.

Or he had fooled himself into believing that was his motive. He could admit that he had not put up much of a fight. The only details on a personal note that she shared with him were her former connection to Charlotte Mackey and the fact that her father was a minister, both pieces of information that Cobb already knew. She, on the other hand, learned one fact—that he was not a dedicated gambler—and chased it with the single-mindedness of a greyhound after a rabbit.

Cobb still wondered why he told her about Hempstead, Indiana. He had had sense enough to keep his answers close to the truth so he would not trip over himself, but his intention had been to offer only broad strokes. He *had* worked in banks, stockyards, and hospitals, also for the railroad and twice for city hall. In every instance he had been employed as an investigator, first with the powerful Pinkerton Detective Agency behind him, and later on his own. He had never been marshal for one day in Hempstead, let alone six weeks, but it had taken him that long to establish the connection between the molestation, rape, and on two occasions, murder, of seven young women in rural Indiana towns and run the itinerant preacher and his son responsible for the acts to ground.

What happened after that turned out to be a lesson to him, not his finest hour.

He studied his sketch again. Owing to his critical judgment, he decided that he had placed her eyes rather more closely together than they actually were. Neither was her nose as pinched as he'd been led to believe. Mackey had nothing at all to say about her neck, and Cobb's sketch only suggested the line so that her head would not appear to float on the paper. He picked up the pen and extended that line so the long stem of her neck became the graceful curve of her shoulder. He made small changes to her eyes and nose, put in shading to hint at the luster of her hair, and added the faint indentation to her chin. He widened her mouth, lifted the corners slightly to intimate a smile, and then considered the problem of that maddening dimple. Without it, the sketch looked incomplete, but if he rendered it wrong, the sketch would never satisfy him.

He flicked the nib of the pen over the paper, making a comma just to the left of her lips. The effect was to immediately deepen her smile.

Cobb returned her greeting with an ironic half smile of his own. "There's still the matter of you being a thief, Miss Morrow. I haven't forgotten that."

The problem was that he didn't believe it with the same conviction his employer seemed to.

Sliding the sketch out of his way, Cobb slanted the writing paper on the desk and dipped his pen in the inkwell. He planned to keep his correspondence brief.

He had considered telling Mackey that he had discovered Miss Morrow's whereabouts before he left for Bitter Springs but decided in the end to exercise more caution. Clients did not always act in their own best interests, and Mackey might have done something to send Miss Morrow packing. At the very least, Mackey would press for details, and Cobb was not prepared to give him Miss Morrow's connection to Mrs. Kellen Coltrane.

It turned out that Mrs. Coltrane, once he was finally able to speak with her and present himself as a candidate for the teaching position, had been both apologetic and helpful. She informed him that she had hired someone months earlier and regretted that Bitter Springs was too small to support or have need of a second teacher, especially since his letter of interest was as impressive as the woman who accepted the position.

"Miss Morrow does not have your experience minding a school," Mrs. Coltrane had informed him, "but I have assured myself her education and temperament make her admirably suited."

She had questioned Cobb as to why he had not made his application earlier, and he told her the truth: He had not seen the advertisement when it first appeared and learned about it from an acquaintance. She was impressed that he continued to pursue the opportunity even after he discovered that she was gone from the Palmer House. Without prompting, she offered the information that her husband's work required extensive travel, although she never mentioned what manner of business occupied him. Cobb had to learn that for himself.

By the time Cobb left the interview at the Peabody Hotel in Memphis, he possessed enough information about Mrs. Coltrane, Bitter Springs, and the teacher who had taken the position to whet his appetite, not satisfy it. Rather than telling Mackey anything definitive, he only revealed that he had several promising leads. The lawyer was not impressed, but he still advanced Cobb money for his expenses. Watching Mackey write the draft, Cobb could not help but think there was something desperate in the act. There was no shaking the notion that Andrew Mackey had something to fear from Gertrude Morrow. Spending time with her this evening had not made Cobb change his mind.

Cobb's hand moved swiftly across the page, leaving a scrawl of letters behind that bore only a passing resemblance to the careful script he had practiced as a youth. In two sentences, he explained the situation to his employer. He added a third, this time to say that he would remain in Bitter Springs and wait for further instructions. Cobb could envision Mackey changing his mind when he learned how far he would have to travel to meet Miss Morrow. It was possible he would want Cobb to escort her back to Chicago. That would effectively end his assignment, because regardless of the payment due him, he already determined he wouldn't perform that task.

Cobb waited for the ink to dry before he folded the letter. His employer would be unhappy that Cobb had not sent word by telegram, but if Mackey thought about it, he would realize that any message, even a cryptic one, could not be kept confidential from the person who operated the telegraph, and if the lawyer had any appreciation for the breadth of gossip that passed for conversation in Bitter Springs, he would be downright grateful for Cobb's discretion, even if that message came by way of the most circuitous route possible.

Cobb slipped the letter under his vest. It was still a question in his mind if he would allow Finn to send the letter for him. The boy wanted to run an errand in the worst way, but Cobb wondered if he shouldn't think of something with a less problematic outcome if Finn should fail.

Cobb stepped away from the desk. Out of the corner of his eye, he caught a glimpse of the sketch he had pushed aside. There was no need to carry the sketch when he had Miss Morrow in his sights, but he found himself picking it up and slipping it back into the inside pocket of his vest anyway.

When Tru led her students in prayer the following morning, she heard Finn Collins's voice rise above the others. It seemed he also put considerably more feeling into the effort than was his usual recitation; however, neither his volume nor his vehemence saved him from being summoned to her desk to read his apology to Priscilla Taylor and the class. She kept one eye on Rabbit and his friends to make sure they didn't snigger and with the other took note of Priscilla to be certain she didn't gloat. Her watchfulness was rewarded because neither of those things occurred.

Properly chastened, if not sincerely sorry, Finn returned to his seat and folded his hands on his desk. He also put his feet flat on the floor. Tru was trying to guess how long he could possibly maintain that pose when she noticed he was eyeing the smudged slates around him as if anticipating the end of the day when he would be cleaning them. She wondered if perhaps she shouldn't read the class something from *Tom Sawyer* very soon; the chapter where Tom slyly engages Ben in whitewashing the fence seemed particularly apropos of Finn's situation. Even if Finn did not grasp the implication, it would be a balm on her conscience.

Tru raised the map at the front of the classroom to reveal the multiplication and division problems she had put on the blackboard before the students arrived. The older children groaned, recognizing it as work for them. Her younger pupils dutifully took out their *McGuffey's First Eclectic Reader* when she asked and turned to Lesson Thirty, in which Kate and Nell fashioned a boat for their dolls out of a tub and set it loose on the pond. There was slate work that followed, and while they were engaged in that, Tru checked the work of the older students.

"You have a head for numbers, Mr. Fox," she said, lightly laying her hand on Robby's shoulder. "Better than I recollect from yesterday." She felt his uneasy shrug. "But I wonder if it's not your neighbor's work I should be praising."

Rabbit's head swiveled around and up. "It's not his fault, Miss Morrow. I told him he could copy from my slate. I don't mind."

"I mind, Cabot."

"It's Rabbit, Miss Morrow. Really. I hardly recognize the other."

"You mean your Christian name."

"The way I figure it, the Christian thing to do would have been for my parents to name me William or Robert or even Jefferson, like my pap. Cabot Theodore just about guarantees a boy's going to have his head pushed in a trough at least once before he turns seven."

"I hadn't considered that. How many times has it happened to you?"

"Never. I'm called Rabbit on account of I'm fast as one, not because it rhymes with 'Cabot.'"

"Or 'Blabbit,'" Finn said. "But you do that, too." His comment, made in an aside to his neighbor loudly enough to be heard by the class, earned him some titters from his friends and a silent rebuke from his teacher. He ducked his head and reapplied himself to his slate.

"Very well," Tru said, "but Cabot is a name rich with history."

Rabbit looked doubtful.

"It's all right, Rabbit. Some other time. For now, I want you and Robby to work independently." She addressed her other students. "That's intended for all of you unless I indicate otherwise." She lightly squeezed Robby Fox's shoulder. "Try the first problem again, Robby. I want to watch."

And so it went. Tru nudged and encouraged, scolded and praised. She taught each subject using methods she had studied at Chicago's Normal School in Junction Grove, but the manner she adopted with her students was not always embraced by her own teachers. It was not that she did not appreciate the need for order, obedience, and discipline in her classroom, but that she had an equal appreciation for the need for free thinking, for learning through one's own experience, and for feeding the mind, body, and soul of a child.

It was just that sort of free thinking that kept her from getting a position after graduation. In interview after interview, she was turned away for being, well, not quite right. She considered being less than frank when asked about her views, but she was never quite able to articulate what every superintendent and principal wanted to hear.

She never doubted that her father understood her disappointment, but as much as he professed to want her to succeed, she also knew he was content with the situation as it was. Keeping her close was reason enough to pray for her failure.

Tru tried not to judge him harshly for that, and she did not regret a single day that she spent caring for him before he died. Looking back, she was not even sure that she had been prepared to forgo her responsibilities with his ministry to take a position that would demand equal time. When he fell ill, it seemed that all the right choices had been made, and now that she had the position in Bitter Springs, it was easier to make peace with them.

She still missed him though. At times, desperately.

"Miss Morrow?"

Tru brought herself to the present. She blinked in quick succession to stay the wash of tears before turning away from the map. She rested the tip of her pointer on the edge of her desk. "Yes, Priscilla? What is it?"

"My mother said I should ask to be excused early today."

"How early?"

"One hour before the usual."

Tru checked the watch she wore on a black grosgrain fob above her heart. The watch was hers, but the ribbon fob had belonged to her father. She would have to replace it someday— it was fraying at the edges—but not just yet.

"You are already twenty minutes late."

Priscilla sighed and closed her book. "I hoped it was more."

Tru could sympathize with the girl's reluctance. It was true that Priscilla sometimes tripped over her own feet because she had her nose so high in the air, but she was an earnest student and genuinely enjoyed attending school. The Taylors took in laundry and operated a bathhouse, and for whatever reason, Tuesdays were busier than other days of the week. If Priscilla was going to ask to be excused before the rest of the class, it was going to happen on a Tuesday.

"Would you like to take a book with you, Priscilla?" she asked.

Priscilla's eyes widened. "Could I? I'd be ever so careful with it."

"I wouldn't have offered if I thought otherwise." Tru went to the bookcase and ran her finger along the middle shelf. She passed over the moralizing works of Edward Lear's *A Book of Nonsense* and John Ruskin's *The King of the Golden River* and chose instead *Alice's Adventures in Wonderland*.

She carried it to Priscilla and placed it firmly in the girl's hands. "You will find this challenging and much too long to read in one evening. Bring it back tomorrow, and we'll talk about what you've read. Once you've read it all, I will expect you to write a letter to Mrs. Coltrane thanking her for providing our school with such fine books."

Priscilla nodded eagerly and tucked the book under her coat before she bolted for the door. She flung it open, prepared to charge out into the cold, and squealed like a piglet when she plowed into Cobb Bridger.

Chapter Three

Cobb steadied the girl so she didn't fall. Before he could apologize she eluded his hold and squeezed past him, as quick and unpredictable as a bead of mercury. He teetered on the threshold, caught himself, and then entered.

"Please close the door," Tru said. "Class. Our guest is Mr. Bridger. Say hello."

Cobb was aware that every student was already turned in his direction and that they probably had not caught the inflection in their teacher's voice that made the word "guest" a rather stiff but polite substitute for the word "intruder." He closed the door.

"Hell-o, Mr. Bridger!"

The wall of sound that was their enthusiastic greeting rolled over Cobb. He nearly reared back. "Hello."

With all the children turned in their seats to face Cobb, Tru was free to express her disapproval. She did not go as far as setting her hands on her hips and tapping her foot. Her narrow-eyed stare was sufficient.

Cobb favored her with an apologetic smile while he reached under one arm to reveal he had come bearing a gift.

He dangled the sack from his fingertips and gave it a little shake. "From Mrs. Phillips," he said. "Sand tarts."

The children clapped, delighted. More important from his perspective, their teacher stopped glaring at him.

Tru examined her watch. "I dismiss the class at three o'clock, Mr. Bridger. You may leave the sack on my desk if you like, or stay and pass out the cookies as the children are leaving."

"They cannot have them now?"

Tru was aware of every child's head swiveling in her direction. "No," she said firmly. She did not explain herself. The disappointment that was leveled at her was palpable, but she remained resolute.

"Then if it's all the same to you, I'd like to stay."

Tru pointed to the seat left vacant by Priscilla. "You may sit there. Your bench neighbor is Mary Ransom. Mary, please make room for Mr. Bridger."

Cobb looked doubtfully at the bench as Mary scooted to the edge and pulled in her skirts. His knees would not fit under the desk. He would have to make room for them under his chin. "Perhaps I should stand."

"No, really," said Tru. "You should sit."

Cobb was familiar with standoffs, and this had all the makings of one. He saw Miss Morrow come to the same realization a moment after he did. The flash of panic in her eyes was revealing, and he let her wrestle with the implications of starting a skirmish that might have no clear winner. Her students were watching him, but it was their respect for her that was in jeopardy.

Cobb's decision to comply was a strategic one. There was the battle, and then there was the war.

"Yes, ma'am," he said. Cobb observed relief on Finn's face as he began his march down the center aisle. He held the sack of sand tarts in front of him like the offering of a penitent and gingerly took his place beside the diminutive Mary Ransom. He did not have to tuck his knees under his chin as he feared, but there was no doubt in his mind that he cut a comical figure. He removed his Stetson and set it and the sack of cookies to one side. He wanted the slate uncovered in the event she required him to use it.

"Thank you, Mr. Bridger. Class, eyes here." She motioned to herself. "Who remembers where we left off?" Three hands shot up. Tru called on Charity Burnside.

"The capital of Pennsylvania," she said. "The Keystone State."

"Thank you, Charity." Tru picked up her pointer and indicated Pennsylvania on the map. She did not assume that Charity knew the capital so she put the question to the class. She was prepared to ignore Cobb if he raised his hand, but apparently he had decided not to be more disruptive than he already had been. That, or he didn't know the capital.

"Harrisburg," Tom Sedgwick said when she acknowledged him.

"Very good. Would you share an interesting fact about the state?"

"The name means 'Penn's woods.'"

"It certainly does. Now Maryland."

The lesson continued in this fashion until they had covered all the states east of the Mississippi. Finn was the last to volunteer an answer. He offered to name the capital of Delaware but struggled when he had to come up with an interesting fact. She let it pass when Cobb scribbled something on his slate and held it over his shoulder for Finn to read. Finn announced to the class that it was the first state to sign the constipation.

When the class erupted with laughter, Tru set down her pointer and called it a day. Without meeting Cobb's eyes squarely, she indicated that he should go to the door. The children were still giggling and ribbing each other as they filed out, but they all managed to mind their manners long enough to thank him when he placed a sand tart in their hand.

Finn remained at his seat, his head lowered so far that his small, pointed chin rested on his chest. Tru picked up the slate that Cobb used and examined it before she set it down on top of Finn's.

"It looks like 'constipation' to me," she said. "I would have to say that Mr. Bridger did not practice his script as he ought to have done when he was your age. That accounts for these badly formed letters. And truly, Finn, when it is written out, there is little to distinguish 'constitution' from 'constipation.'" Because she could not help herself, she flicked his cowlick. It immediately sprang back up. "You made everyone laugh. Usually you don't mind that." When he said nothing, she added, "I suppose it makes a difference when you didn't mean to do it."

He shrugged.

"Maybe you could pretend that you did mean to make them laugh."

Finn lifted his head and regarded her suspiciously. "Lie?"

Cobb had been trying to listen to what she was saying to Finn as the children shuffled out. He caught a few words here and there, but when the last pupil filed past him, he was able to shut the door and clearly hear her comment. Curious, he leaned back against the door and folded his arms across his chest. The sack, with four cookies left in it, dangled from his fingertips.

"Certainly not," she said. "The best course is not to comment on it. When Rabbit teases you about it, and you know he will, say nothing."

"Nothing?"

"That's right. Nothing at all. Just smile."

"I'll want to punch him."

"I'm sure you will, but if you smile as if you know something he doesn't, he will always wonder."

"I know lots of things he doesn't, and he's eleven."

Tru patted him on the shoulder. "You think about it while you start on the slates. There's a rag and bucket in the broom closet, but you'll have to pump water."

"Sure thing." He jumped to his feet when Tru stepped aside and went to get his coat. He put on gloves and jammed his hat on his head before he retrieved the bucket. At the door he accepted a cookie from Cobb, but he put it in his pocket for later. "You should have practiced making your letters, Mr. Bridger. Things can get all twisted up on account of poor penmanship."

Cobb thought about the letter he was carrying inside his jacket. "You make an excellent point, Finn." He let the boy out and then extended the hand that held the sand tarts toward Miss Morrow. The sack swung like a pendulum from the end of his fingertips. "There is one in here for you. Mrs. Phillips took pains to make sure of it. Also one for the little girl who nearly flattened me. Priscilla Taylor, was it?"

"Yes." Tru closed the distance between them and reached out to take the sack. At the last moment, he withdrew his hand. Her arm remained suspended as he opened the sack and took out a sand tart for himself. He put a third of the rectangular cookie between his lips while he rewound the string around the sack's neck. Only then did he place it in Tru's open palm.

Her fingers closed around it while the line of her mouth settled somewhere between disapproval and amusement. One of her eyebrows lifted. "How *old* are you, Mr. Bridger?"

Before he answered, Cobb bit off the portion of the cookie between his lips and pushed it into his cheek. "Twenty nine, ma'am."

"There's a wonder," she said, turning away. "Have a mind you step back from the door before Finn knocks you over."

Her warning came just in time. Cobb had just sidled sideways when Finn barreled through.

Finn spared a glance for Cobb as he passed. "You're still here, Mr. Bridger. You in some kind of trouble?"

Cobb answered the boy, but his eyes were fixed on Miss Morrow's slender back as she walked away. He swallowed. "Sure feels like some kind of trouble, Finn."

Finn hefted the bucket onto his bench. "She makin' you write something? She likes doing that."

Tru looked over her shoulder as she set the sack on her desk. She also spoke to Finn while her eyes remained steady on Cobb. "Mr. Bridger is leaving."

"I'm being banished, Finn." He took another bite of his sand tart. "Like Napoleon to Elba."

Finn's attention was all for making sure he didn't slop water onto the floor. The looks exchanged between the adults in the room went literally and figuratively over his head. He pulled the cleaning rag from his pocket with the flourish of a magician. "Never heard of Napoleon," he said. "Elba neither, but if you mean you're goin' back to the Pennyroyal, I guess I'll see you later."

"I hope so. There's that errand we talked about."

Finn stopped twisting the cleaning rag over the bucket and looked at Cobb. "Really? You got something for me to do?"

"I do."

"What is it?"

"Later."

"I'll come directly after I'm done here."

Tru had started toward the broom closet, but now she paused. "You better go home first, Finn."

The boy sighed feelingly. "Miss Morrow's right, Mr. Bridger. There'll be hell to pay if I don't, and you and me ain't come to money terms yet."

"It doesn't matter how much I pay you," said Cobb. "The devil always charges a nickel more than a man's got. Go see your granny before you come by the hotel."

Nodding, Finn turned back to his task.

Over her shoulder, Tru mouthed a thank-you to Cobb.

He shrugged. "I guess I'll be going, then." No one said he shouldn't. Cobb saw that Finn's concentration was all for the slate he was cleaning. When the boy was done there would be no evidence of what Delaware signed, and very likely no black left on the slate. He also noticed that Finn's tongue was peeping out of the corner of his mouth. He looked back at Miss Morrow. Andrew Mackey's alleged thief had a broom in her hand and was using the butt of it to push the closet door closed. When she turned around, he glimpsed surprise in her eyes.

"Oh, Mr. Bridger. You're still here."

"I thought I would finish my cookie first." Although he

only had a third of it left, he bit that part in two. Crumbs fell on the floor. He brushed more off the front of his duster. When he looked up and saw Miss Morrow was watching him, he stamped his slim smile with equal parts guilt and remorse.

Tru saw right through to the guile. It was all she could do not to roll her eyes. She held out the broom. "You can sweep the floor," she said. "Mind you get the mud under Sam Burnside's desk." She cast her eyes in the direction of Sam's seat. "Every day he carries in clods of earth in his shoes. I believe he is moving a mountain." She thrust the broom in Cobb's hand when he came forward to collect it. "I'm going to pick up the slates for Finn."

Cobb put what remained of the sand tart in his mouth. He passed the broom from hand to hand while he shrugged out of his duster. He hung it on a hook next to Finn's coat and then started sweeping.

Tru began gathering slates at the front and wound between the rows until she had them all. She stacked them on Finn's bench beside the water bucket and went to get a cloth to wipe away the excess water. She engaged him in conversation while they worked, although it hardly required effort. Finn had something to say about everything and even more to say when he didn't know his subject.

Although Finn had her attention, Tru was not unaware of Cobb Bridger moving around the schoolroom. She had had no particular expectations when she handed him the broom. For practical reasons she would have been pleased if he just swept away his own crumbs and Sam Burnside's muddy footprints, but he was doing much more than that. She heard him moving desks, lifting benches, and digging the broom straws deep into the four corners of the room. He didn't interrupt her to ask for a dustpan but found it in the closet on his own. She also noticed that he took particular care around the stove not to scatter ashes into the air.

When he was done, he put the broom and dustpan away but made no move to leave. Instead, he sat on the other side of the classroom and thumbed through one of the readers lying on a desk.

Tru returned the last clean slate to its proper place and briskly brushed off her hands. "We're done here, Finn. Thank you."

"Will you have something for me to do tomorrow?"

"Let me think about that this evening."

He nodded. "All right. I need to empty the bucket before I go."

"Very well. Don't play in the water."

As soon as Finn was gone, Cobb stood. "Not to worry, Miss Morrow. I'm leaving now. I have a letter to post at the station. I don't suppose that Finn will have any objection if I walk him home."

Tru got to her feet; her eyes followed him as he went to get his coat. "Why did you come here, Mr. Bridger?"

He turned to face her as he slipped into his duster. "The cookies, remember?"

"Yes, well, that's what you said. You do recall that Jennifer Phillips is my friend."

"I certainly do, but I suppose you're bringing it up because you want me to know that you can verify my story."

She shrugged. "In the event that you'd like to change it."

"Just because it's a story, Miss Morrow, doesn't mean it's not true. They're not mutually exclusive."

Tru remained suspicious. "Why were you visiting the bakery?"

"I had some thought that I might buy you a slice of apple pie since yours remained on your plate last night, but Mrs. Phillips was taking sand tarts out of the oven when I got there and that was that."

"You bought them, didn't you?"

"It would have been wrong to steal them." He retrieved his hat from where he left it on Priscilla's desk but did not put it on. "There are still two cookies left. One is yours and the other is for Priscilla."

Tru picked up the sack, unwound the string, and took out one sand tart. "Thank you, Mr. Bridger." She held out the sack. "I would be pleased if you and Finn would take this to her. Finn knows where she lives." She dropped it in his open palm. "Perhaps you'd tell me how you know it was Priscilla who left. I wondered about it earlier but let it pass. I find that I'm still curious."

Cobb tapped the top of Priscilla's desk. "Finn's grandfather explained what Finn did yesterday to get himself in trouble. When you told me to take a seat here, and the seat put me directly in front of Finn, it seemed likely that the little girl had occupied it. Finn would have found the proximity of her braid too tempting to ignore."

Tru nodded slowly, thoughtful. "You seem to have a particular talent for making a picture with only a few pieces of the puzzle. I begin to understand how you brought that father and son to justice in Hempstead."

"I brought the pair in, Miss Morrow."

It was what he did not say that intrigued Tru. She sensed that he chose to answer carefully, and it was the absence of "justice" that made her wonder what it was she didn't know. His response begged for a question, but she saw immediately that he would not entertain one. His expression, while not cold, had become remote and was fixed in a manner that did not invite further inquiry.

Cobb put on his hat and gave her a short nod as he tapped the brim. "I'll see that the last sand tart is delivered." He turned to go.

Tru said, "Perhaps I'll see you this evening." She did not intend her statement to be anything but matter of fact, and it spoke to her lingering discomfort that she heard these words delivered in a tone that might politely be called hopeful and more harshly described as desperate. "At the hotel," she added quickly. As a clarification, she thought it was less than perfect. It sounded vaguely as if she were planning a tryst. "In the dining room."

Heat warmed her cheeks when he turned around to face her again, and she saw that humor had lifted one corner of his mouth the narrowest of fractions. Even under the shading brim of his hat, she could see that his gaze was no longer distant, but intimate and amused.

"I look forward to seeing you there, Miss Morrow."

This time when he headed back to the door, Tru let him go.

The dining room had several empty tables, including the one closest to the window. When neither Cecilia nor her cousin greeted her, Tru took her usual place. Once again, other diners invited her to sit with them, including the older couple from Denver. They had been staying at the Pennyroyal so the husband could recuperate from injuries he sustained during a mishap on the station platform. Tru found them lively conversationalists up to the point that they began repeating themselves. When they emphasized all the same points and laughed in precisely the same places, it was difficult not to allow her mind to wander.

As it was wandering now. Tru fiddled with her fork, turning it over and over on the tablecloth while she entertained all her earlier doubts about coming to the hotel this evening. The fact that the hotel staff expected her was a deciding factor in favor of returning. Her teaching contract specified that she could take meals as often as she liked at the Pennyroyal. It was a generous allowance, but Tru also liked to cook, and she usually managed for herself on Friday and Saturday. On Sundays she frequently invited Andrew Robbins, the pastor of Grace Church, and his wife to join her for dinner, or she took her meal after services with Jennifer Phillips and her husband.

Her routine varied little from day to day. Her absence at the Pennyroyal on a Tuesday would have been noted and discussed. Most likely someone from the hotel, probably Walt, would have been sent to make sure she was all right. It was a fine thing the way they cared for her, and it had everything to do with Mrs. Coltrane's influence, but sometimes Tru felt that by observing a routine she had become predictable to the point of boring herself.

Cobb Bridger was proving to be an excellent diversion. She was pleased to see that he had sense enough not to arrive before she did. It would have been awkward to refuse the invitation of other diners in favor of his, especially as this would be the second time they shared a table in as many days. The problem with diversion was that it would inevitably lead to speculation, and while Tru could accept that as a consequence, she was not of a mind to provoke it unnecessarily.

Tru did not have to look up to know when Cobb reached the threshold. She supposed that it was because she was anticipating his arrival that she sensed a stirring among the other diners. Within moments of him stepping into the room, people were greeting him. She noticed that he was invariably polite but also that he did not encourage conversation. He managed to disengage himself at each table with the skill of a seasoned politician.

There was no doubt in her mind that if it ever came to him running for a town office, he could get himself elected.

"Miss Morrow."

She lifted her head and offered him a modest smile. "Mr. Bridger."

"It's hard to believe you are dining alone again. May I join you?"

"If you like."

"I believe I do." With the public niceties out of the way, he sat. "Where is Miss Ross?"

Tru shrugged. "No one from the kitchen has come out since I arrived. I imagine they've been waiting for you."

He chuckled. "I doubt that."

As if recognizing a cue, Cecilia Ross and her cousin entered the dining room, stage left. Tru conveyed her satisfaction upon being proved right by regarding him from under raised eyebrows.

Renee Harrison and Cecilia took different routes to reach the table, but high road or low road, they came to a stop beside Cobb at the same time. After they informed him that stew was being served this evening, they inquired about his preference in drink. When he asked for coffee, Cecilia hurried away to fetch it, leaving Renee to attend to Tru.

"It's amusing," Tru said once Renee was out of hearing.

Cobb merely grunted softly.

Tru chuckled. "This kind of attention cannot be a novelty to you, and if it is, you should enjoy it more."

"Do you speak from experience?"

"A very modest experience. When I came to Bitter Springs, the welcome I received was overwhelming, all out of proportion to what I was hired to do. Or at least that's what I thought. I've since come to understand that the people here see me as some sort of ambassador for Mrs. Coltrane, the woman who hired me. She corresponds regularly with me and with Mrs. Sterling, but I am the last person in town to have spoken with her."

Cobb did not say otherwise. He let her go on.

"The town sets great store by her—and her husband, I should add. It has to do with some trouble a while back. You won't find anyone here with a criticism for either of them."

Cobb asked, "What interested you in the position?"

"I've always wanted to teach, but even with the very generous arrangement I was offered, I thought a long time about traveling so far. It was Mrs. Mackey who convinced me to go. She was adamant, in fact."

He drew his eyebrows together as though struggling to place the name and cleared his brow as he feigned coming upon it. "Your former employer, is that right?"

"Yes. I was her companion for about two years. She was a member of Olde St. John's, the parish where my father was rector. She was quite influential in the Episcopal community."

"She sounds formidable."

"Oh, yes. She certainly was that." Quite unexpectedly, Tru felt an ache behind her eyes that meant tears were threatening. She blinked several times and managed a watery smile. "I didn't know that was going to happen. I thought . . . well, it doesn't matter what I thought. Not enough time has passed, I suppose."

"You miss her."

She nodded and didn't speak until she had collected herself and her thoughts. "I do. She was a grand lady, worthy of admiration and respect, but I also miss her for selfish reasons.

She was a connection to my father, his works, his life. When I learned she passed, it felt as if I'd lost him again." Tears welled, and this time she blew out a long breath, seeking composure before she was forced to dab at her eyes with a handkerchief and draw every diner's attention to her. She pressed a hand to her temple, blocking her profile. "This is not how I imagined our conversation. You must wish yourself anywhere but here."

"Must I?"

Tru slowly lowered her hand. "Don't you?"

"No, not when you've made me curious about what you imagined our conversation would be."

"I didn't mean—"

Cobb shook his head slowly, his blue eyes leveled knowingly on hers. "Yes, you did. You've thought about meeting me here, probably thought about *not* meeting me. You were telling the truth when you said you imagined what we might talk about . . . and how it would go."

"You are too confident by half."

"You think so? If I am, it's because I had imaginings of my own."

Tru felt her cheeks coloring. She resisted the urge to shield her face again and fiddled with her fork to distract herself. "I went to the bakery after you left."

"All right," he said easily. "We can talk about that."

"You made an impression on Jenny. I believe the word is 'charmed.' I barely set foot inside the door when she began to regale me with your visit to her shop, and she was delighted when you wanted to buy sand tarts for my class." She frowned slightly and regarded him frankly. "It is not at all usual for a guest in town to involve himself in such a way. Why did you do it, Mr. Bridger?"

"Cobb, please. My grandfather was Jacob, my father, Jake. I'm Cobb so the family can keep it straight."

"Very well. Why did you do it . . . Cobb? I find myself wondering how you might be something other than you appear."

He angled his head slightly. "Suspicious?"

"I prefer cautious."

"Because I bought and delivered sand tarts to the school? From now on, I will more carefully consider acts of kindness."

"Jenny thinks you would make a fine marshal." Tru's lips curled when Cobb groaned softly. "So does our mayor. I spoke to Terry McCormick after I left the bakery."

"So *this* is how you imagined our conversation would go. I am disappointed, Miss Morrow. I expected something more inspired."

Her dimple appeared when her smile deepened. "Well, I did think we would have it over a meal."

"Ah." He glanced toward the door to the kitchen. "I wonder what's keeping them."

"Probably the fact that they're arguing over who is going to bring your food and drink."

Cobb's lips quirked. "You are overstating their interest."

At that moment, the kitchen door opened and Mrs. Sterling stepped through to the dining room. She wore her spectacles above her salt-and-pepper widow's peak and a militant expression on her open face. She looked as if she wanted to throw the heavy tray she was carrying rather than deliver it.

Tru and Cobb exchanged glances as Mrs. Sterling advanced on their table. "Don't shrink," she said under her breath. "Stay strong."

Cobb jumped to his feet before the cook reached the table and swept the tray out of her hand. "Allow me," he said and gave her no choice but that she should. "It smells delicious, Mrs. Sterling."

"Of course it does," she said flatly. "I used a good cut of roast for that stew." Now that her hands were empty, she was able to set them on her hips. Her apron stretched taut across her middle. "I'm not fooled by your nonsense, Mr. Bridger. I like you just fine, and you haven't caused me a lick of trouble in the saloon like some folks I could mention." Here, her head snapped to the left, and she shot a narrow-eyed glance at Howard Wheeler and Jack Clifton. They immediately averted their eyes from the spectacle and applied themselves to their food. Her head came around again and settled the same accusing look on Cobb.

"My dining room's another matter. You've got my two girls spitting and snarling at each other like alley cats. And bein' cousins only makes it worse. Now, I don't know what you're doing that's giving them the conniptions, but it has to stop. I lost my best girl a while back to a cowpoke who had nothing to recommend him but an agreeable smile and an ornery horse. When Sue Hage married Charlie Patterson I wondered how I was going to manage without her. Together, Cecilia and Renee hardly make one of my Sue, but mostly they do for me what I ask, and when they don't, I let them know it."

She looked past Cobb to Tru. "I'm not sure this should be a regular occurrence, you sitting with him at dinner. Maybe you should think about joining other folks now and again. I'm saying it plainly, Miss Morrow. It would cause less stir with the girls."

Tru blinked. It required considerable mettle not to flinch. "You've given me something to consider."

Mrs. Sterling harrumphed, but in moments the lines around her eyes and mouth softened. "I'd appreciate it, Miss Morrow. You know the girls don't have the sense of a bag of hair between them, and this one"—she jerked her sharp chin at Cobb—"and this one's kind don't come around that often. I hope you aren't moved to fluttering when he looks at you sideways."

"No," said Tru. "I'm not."

She nodded. "Well, that's all I'm saying." Mrs. Sterling put one hand to her heart as she gave Cobb a thorough look. "It's a fact, Mr. Bridger, that if I weren't a woman of advanced years, I'd probably be in the kitchen scrappin' with Cil and Renee myself. Now let me set those plates on your table and get back to my kitchen."

Cobb stood at attention while Mrs. Sterling made short work of putting their meal in order. He remained standing until the kitchen door closed behind her, and then he slowly sat. "I clearly underestimated her as a force of nature."

"Wyoming women are fierce."

"So I'm learning." He picked up his coffee cup. "I thought she made a good point, though."

"Yes, and I believe I made it earlier. Cil and Renee are both taken with you."

He took a drink, swallowed, and dismissed her comment with a wave of his hand. "I was thinking that perhaps we could eat separately and meet privately."

She sighed. "Sometimes you are predictable to the point of being tedious, Mr. Bridger."

"Cobb."

"Cobb," she repeated. "You're not offended?"

He pretended to think about it. "No."

Tru abandoned her fork in favor of a spoon and dipped it into her stew. Steam rose from the meat and potatoes as she lifted it to her mouth. She blew on it lightly.

Cobb tore his eyes away from her puckered lips and tucked into his own meal. What was it that Andrew Mackey was so sure she had taken from his family? It no longer mattered to Cobb that he had not been hired to find what was stolen. There was no possibility that he would let it rest after meeting Gertrude Morrow. Either she was the best at the con he had ever encountered, or she was innocent. It was difficult to imagine what there might be in between.

He wanted to see the inside of her house. It would be better if he were invited, although it was not necessary. From the chatty Jennifer Phillips, he learned most of what he needed to know about her routine; the rest he had gleaned from a variety of sources, not the least of which was Heather Collins.

"Were you able to post your letter this afternoon?" asked Tru.

Her question made him wonder if she was prescient since he had just been thinking about Mrs. Collins. "I was. Finn's grandmother took it off my hands. And you should know that we delivered the last cookie."

"And the errand? You said you had something for Finn to do for you."

"He took one of my bags to the leather goods store and

waited for the handle to be stitched and remounted." Cobb had had to cut the stitching and break the handle first, but Finn would never know that. He took on the task with the solemnity of one asked to carry stone tablets down from the mount, and Cobb made it worth his while to go carefully.

"That was good of him." She paused. "And you."

He shrugged.

Tru chuckled at his discomfort. "You are impervious to insults, but it seems as if a kind word might be your Achilles' heel. Very well. I won't keep poking at it. Allow me to tell you what Mr. McCormick had to say when I spoke to him."

"Could I stop you?"

"No."

Cobb turned over his palm, indicating she could proceed. He did not waste the gesture on merely giving her permission; he also snagged a biscuit.

"I told him that we might already have a candidate for marshal in Bitter Springs. He warmed to the idea after I mentioned your name. He said you are acquainted."

"I think he had ten dollars in the pot when I took it from the table the other night. Did you tell him that I'm not interested?"

"I did not."

"I'll tell him myself."

"I don't think it will matter. He can be very persuasive."

"Besides being the mayor, what is it that Mr. McCormick does?"

"He owns the eatery that serves the railway. He owns another one in Easterville."

Cobb was familiar enough with the railway restaurants to know they were a lucrative operation for their owners. And Terrence McCormick owned two. He probably thought he was a man in a position to bring pressure to bear. Cobb wished now that he had relieved the mayor of more than ten dollars.

He expected her to press her case again, but she didn't. Unlike him, on certain matters, she was not predictable.

They finished their meal in companionable silence. Their

plates were swept away by Cecilia, and Renee replaced them with bowls of hot apple pudding. The girls did not linger this time. They barely looked up.

"Was that a scratch on Renee's face?" asked Tru when they were gone.

"I don't know. I had my eyes front and center."

"Because Mrs. Sterling put the fear of God in you?"

He shook his head. "Because I'd rather look at you, Miss Morrow." His mouth curved briefly and his voice was huskier than it had been a moment before. "Because I'd rather look at you."

Jennifer Phillips set her knitting needles down hard in her lap and regarded Tru with patent disbelief. "You should have let him walk you home. I don't see how there can be harm in that." She looked askance at her husband who was sitting on the other side of the lamp, reading. "Jim?" When he offered no response, she rolled her eyes. "He's only pretending not to pay us any mind. He heard every word. He just does not want to involve himself."

"I don't think I blame him." Tru glanced at the knitting needles. "You have weapons."

Shrugging as if it were not important, Jennifer picked up the needles, confirmed that she had not dropped a stitch, and began working them furiously. She was a slight woman with hands made strong by pounding and kneading dough. The faint blue network of veins on the back of her hands stood out as she plied her needles. "I don't know why you're bein' so cautious. The man's not a hardship to look at, he showed a real particular kindness buying my sand tarts for your school, and word is, he runs an honest game. He's not going to be around forever, Tru. As long as you have a care not to get your heart broken, I don't see that you can't allow yourself to enjoy his company."

"Mrs. Sterling thinks otherwise. She was thinking of his effect on Cil and Renee."

Jennifer lifted one dark eyebrow in a dramatic arch.

"Inviting him to sit with you is not the same as inviting him to bed. Ask Jim."

"Don't ask me," Jim said. He kept his head down and his eyes on the page.

Jennifer's needles continued clicking. "Why are you hesitating? Is it your contract? I don't remember ever hearing there was some morals clause in it. I have nothing but respect for Mrs. Coltrane, but she'd be a pot calling the kettle black if she attached a morals clause to your position."

"Jenny! I don't have any intention of doing something immoral."

"No one ever does," Jennifer intoned gravely. "And then . . ." She paused, counting stitches. "And then intentions go to hell in a handcart."

Tru threw up her hands. "Do you trust me or not?"

"Seems to me the question is whether you trust yourself. I'm not hearing much confidence in that regard. That piece you said about your intentions sounded to me like you were trying to convince yourself."

Exasperated, Tru let her hands fall back in her lap. "Why did I even come here?"

Jennifer opened her mouth to answer, but out of the corner of her eye she saw her husband shaking his head. "Well?" she asked him.

"That was what you call a rhetorical question," he said. "The answer to one is usually self-evident." With that, he returned to his reading.

Jennifer smiled proudly at Tru. "He's a bright one, my Jim."

Tru nodded. "You don't see how he looks at me," she said. "Jim?"

"No, Cobb."

"So it's Cobb now."

"He asked me to call him Cobb. I haven't given him permission to call me Tru."

"Well, you better. Otherwise he might take to thinking of you as Gertie, Gert, or Trudy."

"My mother's mother was Gertie."

"And I'm sure she was a fine woman, but do you want to

be your grandmother? That's a rhetorical question. Tell me how he looks at you."

"It's hard to explain. He says all the right things, kind things, flattering things, but sometimes I feel as if he's studying me."

"That doesn't sound awful."

Tru shook her head. "You know how boys study something they stumble over by the creek or in the grass or in the middle of the road?"

"I know what you mean. Usually it's something dead." Her needles clicked for another couple of beats then stopped completely. "You better say more about that. Jim will want to hear it. I know I do."

"Well, he easily carries on a conversation, but I have the impression that he's not really engaged, that he's watching me at least as much as he's listening, trying to decide which wing he wants to pluck, or what will happen if he pokes me with a stick."

Jennifer pulled her mouth to one side as she considered what Tru was saying. "I don't know, Tru. Could be he's just got that way about him and doesn't mean anything by it."

"Did you notice it when he was in your shop?"

"I honestly can't say that I did. Oh, he looked around some, but then you have to allow for that, as it was his first time in. I thought it was all kinds of thoughtful that he wanted to buy you a slice of apple pie."

"So you've said. Several times."

Shrugging, Jenny returned to her knitting. "You're right about him being easy with conversation. Not like Jim here. I think I would have told him my life story if he'd asked. He and I talked up a storm anyway."

"I didn't realize," Tru said. "What did you talk about?"

"This and that. The school. How you've taken to the town like a duck to water. I think I mentioned that folks are tickled to have a teacher again."

"But you talked about things that weren't related to me, didn't you?"

Jennifer angled her head, thinking. "I'm sure we did,

though nothing comes to mind. Wait, I did tell him how you and I became friends on account of you helping me in the shop when that storm blew through and my roof leaked like a sieve."

"That has something to do with me as well," Tru pointed out.

"You are determined to pick all the enjoyment out of this. If you ask me, you're the one pokin' and studying this thing from all sides. The man barrels into you in the street, apologizes, sits with you at dinner, shows a kindness to your students, takes his meal with you a second time, and you are ten ways suspicious that he's up to no good."

"I never said that."

"Well, what other reason do you have to be so guarded?"

Tru recalled that Cobb had also said the same about her. "I think I'm being prudent."

"Prudish is not the same as prudent. You don't want to mistake the two."

Agitated, Tru stood. She ran her palms over her midriff, smoothing the fabric of her lettuce green gown. Her hands came to rest at her sides, but the tight-fitting skirt made no allowance for hiding them. It was a struggle not to curl them into fists.

"You're leaving?" Jennifer began to put her knitting aside, but Tru stopped her.

"Don't trouble yourself to see me out. I have a lesson to prepare, and I want to look over something I'm considering reading to the students."

"You're out of sorts with me. Don't deny it. I can read the signs same as I can with Jim."

"I'm not out of sorts with you, Jenny. I'm out of sorts with myself."

Jennifer gave her a thorough look, measuring Tru's words against what she saw in her face. "All right. I believe you. You follow your conscience where Mr. Bridger is concerned and don't pay me any mind. Jim never does and we bump along all right. It's six years that we've been married."

"Seven," Jim said.

Jennifer shook her head and mouthed the word "six" to

Tru. "Maybe you'll stop by after dinner tomorrow?" she asked. "You'll take your meal at the hotel, won't you?"

"I haven't decided."

"I'll look for you anyway. If it makes a difference to you, Walt's dropping by in the afternoon to pick up a couple of molasses pound cakes that Mrs. Sterling ordered for dessert."

"I'll keep that in mind." Tru pulled her mittens and scarf from the sleeve of her coat before she put it on. Once she was properly bundled, she bid them good evening.

Jim finally looked up from his book. "Always nice chatting with you, Tru."

Cobb folded his cards, laid them on the table, and waved the pot in the direction of Ted Rush. The hardware store owner cackled gleefully as he raked in his winnings. It was all Cobb could do not to wince at the sound. The other men at the table showed their annoyance outright. Jake Davis stuck his index finger in his ear and wiggled it. Richard Allen screwed his face so hard to the left it looked as if he'd erased all the features on the right. Harry Sample from the land office had a few choice words for Ted, none of which Ted took offense to.

Cobb pushed his chair back. "I'm stepping out for a spell," he said, getting to his feet. "Losing three hands in a row makes me think I need some fresh air."

"Another whiskey would do you good," Ted Rush said. "'Course, it would do us better." This time when he cackled at his own humor, Richard Allen cuffed him on the back of the head.

Cobb abandoned the table before he cuffed Rush himself. He glanced back at the bar and gave Walt a finger salute as he stepped outside.

The saloon had an outside entrance separate from the hotel. An archway on the inside connected the establishments, but overnight guests could come and go without stepping into the saloon if they wished to avoid it. Rocking chairs lined the long porch that fronted the hotel. The saloon did not invite lingering on the wrong side of its doors.

Cobb glanced in the direction of the rocking chairs, but it was too chilly to make a seat there tempting. He elected to shake off his unrest by walking toward the center of town. He estimated he'd gone about twenty yards before a figure turned the corner from the drugstore and stepped directly into his path.

Terrence McCormick was brought up short as well. He clapped his hands together, beaming as he recognized Cobb. "How about this?" he said. "And wasn't I just on my way to the Pennyroyal to see you. It's providence, that's what it is. Could be that folks are right about you. C'mon. I'll walk with you. We can talk about this marshal business as we go."

Chapter Four

It was not the molasses pound cake that decided Tru in favor of dining in the hotel on Wednesday evening. Plain and simple, it was Cobb Bridger. In spite of the way he regarded her as though she were a puzzle with too many missing pieces, she favored his company. It was not as if anything would—or could—come of it. She reminded herself of all the ways that spending time with Cobb was different from spending time with the last man who had wanted her to be his dinner companion. For all his scrutiny, she could allow that at least Cobb Bridger wanted to know her. Andrew Mackey III, on the other hand, thought he already did.

It was a fine distinction, but in Tru's mind, an important one, and Mrs. Sterling would just have to accept her decision.

She waited patiently at her table for Cobb to make an appearance. She had a pot of tea to keep her company and the mirrored window to keep her amused.

Mrs. Sterling made it her mission to intercept Cobb before he reached the dining room. With Walt's help, she was able to leave the kitchen in time to catch him coming down the stairs. She waited until he reached the landing before she returned his greeting. She knew a thing or two about giving up the high ground, and Cobb's height already gave him a distinct advantage.

Cobb straightened the sleeves of his black wool jacket and ran his hands over the buttons of his vest. The cook made him want to present himself like a soldier for inspection. "Mrs. Sterling."

"Mr. Bridger." She wiped her damp hands on her apron front. "I know it's none of my business, but that's never stopped me from telling folks what I think. I don't know what you have in mind for that gal in there, but she's a good soul, and I think I'd have to cut you off at the knees if your aim is to enjoy yourself with no heed as to how she might be left the worse for it. I got the sense that when she came here she was startin' over, leavin' something behind that near to broke her heart. Now, that could be a fancy on my part. Her father passed on, and then that woman she worked for died, and that is surely enough to make any good heart heavy, but I'm holding on to a suspicion that there was more. Usually that means a man, and another man is never the cure for what grieves a woman in times like that."

"What are you proposing I do, Mrs. Sterling?"

She took off her spectacles and cleaned them with one corner of her apron. "I'm not proposing you do or you don't. I'm just sayin', Mr. Bridger. I'm just sayin'." She returned her gold-wired rimmed glasses to her nose and regarded Cobb over the top. "Looks to me like she's ignoring my advice and waiting for you, but you think about whether it's a good idea to sit with her this evening. There's a place at the table with Mr. and Mrs. Washington."

"The couple in the room next to mine from Denver?"

"Yes."

Cobb regarded her with a flat expression. "Did I offend you in some way? Surely what you are suggesting is a punishment."

"You take it as you like," she said tartly. "I'm doing my

duty." With that, Mrs. Sterling turned on her heel with the precision of a praetorian and left the lobby for the kitchen.

Cobb's eyes followed her. He wasn't sure what he was going to do until he walked into the dining room and saw Gertrude Morrow sitting at her usual table, her face visible only in three-quarter view as she looked at the dining room reflected in the window. He thought she might have seen him. The slight lift in her chin made him think she had. Smiling with more grit than pleasure, he walked straight to the table— of Mr. and Mrs. Washington.

The main thoroughfare was largely deserted when Tru left the hotel. Lamplight illuminated windows above the store-fronts where some of the owners lived with their families. Most of the businesses were dark, having closed for the evening. Light and music streamed from the town's only other saloon. Tru gave it a wide berth because it tended to draw a rowdier crowd of young, restless cowhands than the Penny-royal. Hurrying along, she glanced at Dr. Kent's lighted window as she passed and saw him sitting at his desk hovering over a microscope. She thought it must be fascinating, the things that he saw.

Tru did not pause as she walked by Jennifer's bakery. She had nothing to say to her friend that would not sound pitiful. Perhaps tomorrow, when she was in a better frame of mind, she would be able to share how Cobb Bridger had come to the dining room and acted as if he didn't know she were there.

The few people she met on her way nodded a greeting or stopped to inquire about her health and report on their own. She spent several minutes with Mrs. Garvin hearing about the plans for Millicent's wedding. It was no hardship to listen to the milliner's chatter, but her enthusiasm for her subject was not contagious.

By the time Tru opened the front door to her dark home, she had given some thought as to what would occupy her after she readied for bed, and the idea of pouring a couple of fingers of whiskey and reading *Oliver Twist* was rather more inviting than not.

She set down the wrapped pound cake on the table just inside the front door and lighted an oil lamp. The small entry-way was bathed in a warm, welcoming glow. Tru took off her coat, hung it up with her mittens and scarf, and carried the cake and the lamp to the kitchen where she set both on the table.

Her home was modest, much smaller than the rectory where she had lived with her father, and not much larger than a child's playhouse when compared with Charlotte Mackey's granite mansion on Michigan Avenue. None of that mattered. Tru felt as if she belonged here the moment she crossed the threshold.

The house was built to accommodate a family in the event that the teacher who was hired was married. Tru knew that the prevailing thought was that the teacher would be a man. Most female teachers who married ceased to work, either by their own volition or because it was a requirement of their situation that they remain single. Tru's contract had no such requirement, but she didn't think it mattered. She had no intention of marrying.

The certainty with which the thought came to her gave her pause. What was it that Jennifer told her yesterday? Some-thing about intentions going to hell in a handcart. It was prob-ably worth keeping in mind.

Tru glanced up as the floorboards creaked above her head. The house was still settling and every pop and groan of the wood drew her notice. The colder the evening, the worse it was. She left the cake behind and carried the lamp into the parlor where she set a fire in the stove. She stayed nearby long enough for the heat to penetrate her marrow and then she hur-ried upstairs to her bedroom to change into her nightclothes.

There were three bedrooms on the second floor but only two doors leading off the hallway from the landing. An inte-rior door connected the smaller bedrooms, so that reaching the bedroom at the rear of the house was only possible by going through the forward room. The back bedroom had noth-ing in it, and the front one was furnished with a few pieces

donated by Mrs. Coltrane that came from the hotel. There
were no personal items. She had no use for the rooms and
kept the door closed so they didn't draw heat away from the
rest of the house.

The first thing Tru did when she reached her bedroom was
close the curtains. One window faced the street; the other had
a bird's-eye view of her neighbor's roof and chimney. When
there was benefit of a clear sky and moonlight, she could
make out the school, Grace Church, and through an opening
between the mercantile and the bank, she could see the
entrance to the Pennyroyal. She was always conscious that
someone could be looking back.

Tru undressed, carefully smoothing the material of her
gown and checking it for stains before she hung it in the
wardrobe. Her bustle was next; she fussed with its shape
before putting it away. She loosened the laces on her black
kid boots and pulled them off, dropping them to the floor one
by one and pushing them under the bed with her foot. She sat
at the vanity to remove her stockings, corset, and take down
her hair, barely glancing at her reflection in the mirror as she
removed the pins. She brushed her hair until it crackled,
plaited it, and finally tied it off with a green grosgrain ribbon.
Afterward, she exchanged her chemise and knickers for a
cotton nightgown and soft flannel robe. She stepped into a
pair of slippers while she belted the robe. Once she was suf-
ficiently warm again, she poured fresh water into the bowl on
the commode and washed her face and cleaned her teeth.

Feeling less like a stranger in her own skin, Tru picked up
Oliver Twist from the nightstand and the lamp from the vanity
and made her way back to the parlor. The warmth from the
stove invited her in. This was her favorite room. The appointments were serviceable, not fancy. All of the pieces came
from townsfolk, but there was not a castoff among them.
Richard Allen, owner of the lumberyard, made the lamp
tables that stood on either end of the sofa. They were matched
in size and design, but each was unique because of the scrap
wood he salvaged to complete them. He used walnut and
cherry and oak in different ways on each, making them more

like fraternal twins rather than identical ones. The overstuffed armchair and sofa came from Mr. and Mrs. George Johnson, owners of the mercantile. They swore the pieces were meant for their own apartments above the store, but when they were delivered, no amount of twisting and turning would get them up the stairs. Tru was not sure she believed them, but whether by mistake or on purpose, the furniture was a generous gift.

The parlor was spacious enough to accommodate a table suitable for card playing and four chairs. The set was compliments of the mayor who took them from his station restaurant before they were scarred or damaged by passenger traffic. Besides the lamp that she always returned to the table by the door, the parlor could be warmly lighted by a lamp with a frosted red globe, another with a gold one, and a third that had purple and yellow pansies painted on the glass. Jennifer offered several times to find her lamps that matched, but Tru liked these, liked the reminder that with very little provocation, people were moved to act kindly.

The gold-and-navy area rug came from Ted Rush of the hardware store. He had no children or grandchildren in the school, but he wanted to contribute. The rug had once been in his dining room, a pure waste, he said, since he ate his meals in the kitchen or dined at the Pennyroyal.

Pastor Robbins had painted a landscape for the parlor's one windowless wall. The rolling fields were saturated with sunlight and bright waves of Wyoming wildflowers. The hues in the columbine, Indian paintbrush, and lupine were so brilliant that they might have been the banded arcs of a rainbow. Tru had seen similar, though more modest, works hanging in the parsonage, but this piece was arguably his finest painting to date and she was delighted to have it displayed in her home for as long as he was willing to part with it.

Walter Mangold donated the drinks cabinet. He'd found it in a storage room at the back of the saloon and buffed the wood until it shone in the lamplight. He also stocked the cabinet for Tru with whiskey, ginger beer, red wine, and sherry when he could get it.

Tru opened the cabinet, removed the bottle of whiskey,

and measured out two fingers thicker than her own for her glass. She waited until she was curled in her reading chair by the stove before she sipped. The whiskey was smooth on her tongue and warm all the way down. The heat in her belly was satisfying. She had another sip before she exchanged the tumbler for *Oliver Twist*. Tilting the book in the direction of the lamplight, she began to read.

She had no recollection of falling asleep, only of being jarred awake. In those first disorienting moments, Tru thought she must have dropped the book. That would explain the thump. She even started to reach for Dickens only to realize that the book still lay open in her lap.

Thump.

Tru blinked and angled her head toward the door. The *back* door. It made no sense that the sound would be coming from that direction. An animal? she wondered.

She set the book aside, uncurled her legs, and rose. When the thump came again and was closely followed by another, she recognized the rhythm. Someone was knocking. Grabbing the lamp, she hurried to the kitchen. Evelyn Stillwell from next door regularly came to this entrance, but she was usually carrying a quart of bean or vegetable soup, and she had never visited at night. Tru could only imagine that some calamity had brought Evelyn out.

Tru's senses were sharper now than when she had awakened. She resisted throwing the door wide in the event that Evelyn was standing directly in front of it. She held up the lamp as she carefully pushed the door open.

"Evelyn? What—"

But it wasn't her neighbor, or even her neighbor's husband.

Cobb Bridger touched one hand to his hat and filled the silence that followed her aborted greeting with his smooth baritone and a mildly apologetic grin. "Evening, Miss Morrow."

Tru lowered the lamp and started to pull the door closed. There was immediate resistance. Looking down, she saw the toe of Cobb's boot was acting as a doorstop. "Remove your foot, Mr. Bridger."

"Mr. Bridger?" When she said nothing, he shrugged. He did not remove his boot. "Don't you want to know what I'm doing here?"

"I don't believe I do, no. Please step back."

He didn't move. "I wanted to explain about earlier at the hotel."

"You're letting the cold in."

"The cold will stay out here if you invite me in."

Tru set her mouth stubbornly.

"Very well," Cobb said. "I thought you would want to know that Mrs. Sterling cornered me before I got to the dining room."

Tru watched shadow chasing light across Cobb's face as the oil lamp's flame flickered. She was aware her hand was trembling and only a small part of that was accounted for by the weight of the lamp. A shiver shook her spine. She was mere seconds away from chattering teeth.

There was no real welcome in her voice when she said, "Come in." She backed up. "Close the door."

Cobb stepped over the threshold and pulled the door shut behind him. He whipped off his hat and held it in front of him with one hand while the other made a quick pass through his hair. He glanced around before his eyes settled on her face. He raised his eyebrows. "Is this where you want to talk?"

"I don't want to talk at all. You woke me."

"You were sleeping in a chair. It looked as if you nodded off while you were reading. Some people would appreciate being woken before their neck had a permanent crick."

Now Tru's eyebrows lifted, and their arc was more dramatic than Cobb's mildly expectant expression. "You were spying on me?"

"Spying puts it in a harsh light. I saw you from the street. You should close your parlor curtains at night. Anyone passing can see in."

Tru recalled that on her way home she had seen Dr. Kent through his window. "What were you doing on my street?"

"Coming to see you."

Tru's nostrils flared as she took in a sharp breath. Frustrated, she could not count as high as ten before she was done exhaling. She set the lamp on the kitchen table and folded her arms in front of her. "Whatever you came here to say, please say it and say it quickly. It's late."

His eyes dropped to her chest momentarily. "You're not wearing your watch and fob."

"On my robe? You're being ridiculous."

He shrugged. "It looked to me as though it might be part of your uniform. When I saw it this afternoon, it put me in mind of a general sporting his medal."

Since Tru had had the same thought at times, it felt wrong to take issue with his remark. Still, she was wearing a *robe*. "Do you mean to be annoying as a strategy or is it a character flaw?"

Cobb grinned. "If those are my choices, I'd better not answer." He angled his chin toward the table. "Do you mind if we sit?"

"I don't suppose that it matters if I do." She pointed to the chair closest to the sink. "Sit there." Tru pulled out the chair at a right angle to his but waited for him to be seated before she decided to follow suit. It occurred to her that standing over him might present some sort of advantage, then she considered the manner in which he watched her and thought she was probably only fooling herself.

Cobb set his hat beside the wrapped parcel lying on the table. "Molasses pound cake?" he asked.

"It is. And it's mine."

"I wouldn't think of asking you to share. I already ate my fill." He held up two fingers. "A little whiskey, though . . . I wouldn't turn that down."

"Mr. Bridger," she said in a tone that every one of her students would recognize as the precursor to the last straw. "I have no intention of playing hostess. I am suffering your presence, not enjoying it."

"No one saw me."

Tru could not follow the change of subject. "Pardon?"

"No one saw me come here. You can rest easy."

"I was resting easy before you began pounding on my door. Tell me what you meant about Mrs. Sterling cornering you."

"You know she frightens me," he said, straight-faced.

"I know you'd like me to believe that. You probably want Mrs. Sterling to believe it as well. I can't speak for her, but I don't think there's much that frightens you."

"You'd be wrong."

She shrugged.

"Why would I say it if it weren't true?" he asked.

Tru gave him a considering look. "I suspect it's to make you appear less dangerous."

One corner of his mouth kicked up. "Dangerous? What have you been reading this evening that has your imagination wound tight as a top?"

"Of course it must be my imagination that is at fault. And how did you know I was reading?"

"I told you I saw you through the window. The book was in your lap."

"And you don't know the name of it? That surprises."

"I left my spyglass in my room. So, what were you reading?"

Tru sighed. What was it he had said to her that first night? *And you shouldn't expect that you'll always have your way. You won't.* Here was the proof of that. She didn't think she could hurry him along if she set his hair on fire. "*Oliver Twist.*"

"Of course," he said after a moment's thought.

"You do not put me in mind of Fagin," she said flatly. "In spite of your way with the children."

"No, not Fagin. Bill Sikes. He cuts the most romantic figure."

Tru's eyes widened. "He murdered the woman who loved him."

"My point. You've been acting as if you think I mean to do the same to you."

She closed her eyes briefly while she raised one hand to her temple and massaged the area with her fingertips. There was no doubt that he was responsible for the fog rolling over her judgment. She gave voice to the first clear thought that emerged.

"I don't love you." Hearing the words, belatedly realizing that she had spoken them, Tru winced. She gave Cobb credit for not doing the same. His reaction was to have none at all. He simply continued to study her as though she were an insect pinned to a felt board. "I mean I'm not Nancy to your Bill. My imagination is not wound that tightly."

"So you say."

Tru watched his eyes lower to her mouth. She felt his gaze as a physical touch, his pale blue eyes grazing her lips as his fingers might. She kept her hands on the table, unwilling to reveal by raising one to her mouth that she was affected in any way. It was only when she made to speak that she realized she had pressed her lips together.

"I *do* say, Mr. Bridger."

His faint smile communicated what he thought of her formality. "Mrs. Sterling warned me to stay away from you."

"You mean to explain that, don't you?"

"I'm a little parched." He touched his throat.

She stared at him, shaking her head. "You are extraordinary."

"I'm not sensing that you mean that as a compliment."

"Oh, good for you, Mr. Bridger." She stood and put out her hand to indicate he was to stay precisely where he was. "I'll be right back with your whiskey." It was tempting to glance over her shoulder as she walked away. She was certain he had a sly smile on his face, and equally certain that confronting it would turn her to stone or a pillar of salt depending if she referenced the Greeks or the Hebrews. Tru had no real hope that he would remain at the table.

She wasn't wrong. When she returned with a tumbler of whiskey for him and what remained of the drink she had poured for herself earlier, he was standing with his back to the sink, his feet slightly parted, hands at his back, surveying her kitchen as if he were a ship's captain and this area was his deck and domain. Her eyes went to the table to confirm that she still had a slice of pound cake sitting there.

Cobb followed her glance. "As tempting as it was, I left it for you."

Tru set his whiskey on the table and pointed to the chair. Again, she waited for him to sit before she did. "About Ida Mae Sterling."

Cobb sipped, lifted his eyebrows. "This is excellent."

"My father taught me to appreciate fine spirits."

He raised his glass, studied the amber liquid against the golden glow of the lamp. "To your father, then. Even if he could claim no other accomplishments, it would be enough that he educated his daughter to know an excellent whiskey."

"He would be glad to hear it," she said dryly and continued to regard him expectantly over the rim of her glass.

"Yes. Your good friend Mrs. Sterling. She cautioned me against enjoying myself with no heed as to how I left you. She didn't tell me what to do one way or the other, but she did indicate that there was an empty seat at Mr. and Mrs. Washington's table."

"This really happened?" asked Tru. "You're not making this up?"

He raised his right hand. "Swear."

Tru sighed. "It's not very flattering, is it?"

"No, I was almost offended."

"I wasn't talking about you. What she did is not very flattering to me. I think I'm the one she doesn't trust. She truly must believe that I am a single dinner away from having my head turned and my heart turned over."

"Are you?"

"No. And don't pretend that you were hopeful."

"I was a little hopeful."

Tru snorted. "Admit it, Mr. Bridger, you wouldn't know what to do with my heart if you had it." She anticipated a quick reply, something flippant and of no worth, but Cobb fell unexpectedly silent and his level gaze held hers. His eyes darkened and she couldn't look away.

"Don't be so sure, Miss Morrow. I'd know."

Tru felt her breath hitch. She quickly lifted her glass and

took a sip. "It won't come to that. My heart—and my head—will remain my own."

Cobb did not challenge her assertion on the surface. Instead, he said, "Perhaps you'll want to assure Mrs. Sterling. She's the one who seems to think you might be vulnerable."

"I don't know why she has that impression."

"I suspect you gave it to her."

"Me?"

He nodded, watching her carefully. "You'll have to think back to when you arrived in Bitter Springs. Mrs. Sterling said she had the sense that you were leaving something behind. Running away was how she described it. She acknowledged that she might have it wrong, but—"

"She has it all wrong," Tru said.

Cobb ignored her. "But she thinks that if she peels the layers away from this onion, she'll find there's a man."

"There's no man."

Again, Cobb went on as if Tru hadn't. "Mrs. Sterling knows about the deaths of your father and your employer, but she is still betting that it's a man."

"It's a bad wager. There is no man."

This time Cobb allowed her words to lie there.

"No man," she repeated, this time quietly and more to herself than to Cobb.

"You might want to tell Mrs. Sterling," he said after a while. "She has some notion that it's her duty to protect you."

Tru finished off her drink. "I have no idea what she means by that."

Cobb had nothing to offer.

"I will speak to her," said Tru. "Of course I will. I'm sure she has my best interests in mind, but I am not her responsibility."

"If I may make a suggestion, it would be not to tell her that."

"What? That I am not her responsibility?"

He nodded. "At least not say it in your usual straightforward manner. She strikes me as someone who lives to take care of others. She wouldn't know how to stop if you asked. It comes as naturally as breathing."

"I know she means well, but I am not a child. I am not even one of her girls."

Cobb slowly turned his tumbler in his hands. "I saw you as you were leaving the dining room. You looked . . . unhappy."

"And you naturally thought it must have something to do with you."

"I *hoped* it had something to do with me. Was I wrong?"

"My, but it's a wonder you found a hat big enough for your head."

"You didn't answer my question. Were you unhappy because I didn't join you this evening?"

"I was disappointed that you did not bother to acknowledge my presence, but that was short-lived, and I was not unhappy when I left the hotel. I had excellent company at dinner."

"Jack and Howard."

"Yes."

"Then I suppose I mistook what I saw. Was Mrs. Sterling right to warn me off?"

"No. That's for me to do."

"Then if I ask to join you tomorrow evening, I'll be welcome?"

Tru lifted her chin a notch. "Ask me tomorrow evening."

He nodded slowly. "I will, Miss Morrow." He finished his drink and set down the glass. "And about Mrs. Sterling?"

"I'll find a way to tell her that I did not arrive in Bitter Springs with a broken heart. As for the rest, I'll let it lie."

Cobb pushed his chair back and stood. "All right. I'm going."

Tru got to her feet and skirted the corner of the table. He stepped in front of her so smoothly that she didn't have time to react. She walked into him, and when his arms came around her waist to steady her, she was struck by the thought that she hadn't been off balance until she was in his embrace.

She didn't struggle. She raised her face and met his eyes.

"Warn me off," he said.

Almost infinitesimally, Tru shook her head. The agitation she felt moments earlier fled, and now she understood that the source of it wasn't anything Cobb Bridger had done, but what he hadn't done. She had wanted this. Wanted it still. How had he known?

His head came down slowly; slow enough to allow her another opportunity to say no or turn away. She did neither. Just before his mouth touched hers, her lips parted. She took a breath; cool at first and then warmed by him.

He touched her mouth lightly, and she thought this kiss was like his smile, not fully realized, but a promise of what might be. She held herself very still, waiting.

Cobb kept one hand at the small of her back just below her belted robe while the other slid upward along her spine. The small space that separated them ceased to exist. Her body arched, curving into his until her breasts and belly were snug against him. She wished she had asked him to take off his coat. Why hadn't she invited him to do that?

His hand fisted around her braid at the base of her neck. He tugged, not hard, but insistently, and changed the tilt of her head so that when his mouth left hers, he had access to the hollow just below her ear.

Tru sought purchase by clutching the front of Cobb's duster. Her knuckles whitened when she felt the damp edge of his tongue against her skin. Her breath hitched and lodged at the back of her throat. Light-headed, she felt all of her senses stirring. It took a gasp to move air into her lungs, but it was the suck of his mouth on her neck that forced the gasp.

His lips returned to hers but not before he cupped her face and touched his thumb to the faint indentation at the base of her chin. His kiss was different this time, no longer a hint of what might be, but everything his first touch had promised.

This kiss was a claim.

He took her mouth at his leisure, nudging her lips open so that he could have the fullness of her offering. His tongue traced the underside of her upper lip before it dipped inside to meet hers. She was reminded that they both had had the whiskey. The taste of it lingered on his tongue, smooth and velvety and warm. Tru was glad she had learned to appreciate fine spirits.

The kiss deepened. In subtle measures, the tenor of it

changed. His lips firmed, pressed, and what had been explora-
tion became something more than that. It felt like a *need*. It
felt like hunger.

Tru wanted it too, wanted it from this man, wanted to feel
it with him. In that most secret part of her heart, the truth was
there. She couldn't say as much, but there wasn't any part of
her that wasn't responding as if she were shouting it.

Her fingers slowly uncurled from his coat and slid up his
chest. She raised her hands. They hovered just above his
shoulders for a moment before clasping behind his neck.
He wore his sun-beaten hair slightly longer than what passed
for fashion in Bitter Springs. Tru smoothed his nape with her
fingertips, dragging her nails against his skin. She felt his
shoulders roll. She ruffled his hair and heard him growl low in
his throat. The sound of it raised a shiver in her.

Tru felt the edge of the table pressing just below her bottom. She had no idea when he'd turned her, no recollection
of resisting him. With very little effort, he lifted her onto the
table. Her robe parted below the belt. She was aware of the
warm imprint of one of his hands at the center of her back
and the even warmer impression of his other hand in the act
of raising her nightgown. His palm lightly cupped her calf,
lifting the hem with his thumb as it traveled upward toward
her knee.

Tru felt cool air against her skin from ankle to thigh before
it ever occurred to her that she could stop him. Not that she
should. Only that she *could*. She had stopped thinking altogether by the time he parted her knees and stepped between
them. He pulled her toward him.

She could not distinguish between one kiss and the next.
The pauses that had punctuated his first forays were gone. He
made each transition smoothly, angling her head and then his,
tasting the corner of her mouth, teasing her bottom lip with
the tip of his tongue. He never directed her, never told her
what to do, but she found her way in spite of that and sensed
he was not entirely in command of his every action. It was
a heady notion that she was giving as good as she got, not

with her wits this time, but with her hands and mouth and clever fingers.

Tru wedged her hands between their bodies and slipped them inside his duster. She lifted the caped shoulders to ease him out of it. He was impatient with the act, as though loath to release her long enough to shrug it off. This time she was insistent, pulling the duster down his arms until it fell to the floor.

He took her back then, holding her close enough to flatten her to his chest. The pressure felt good against her swelling breasts, and when he made to put some space between them, she arched her spine and rubbed.

"Your belt," he whispered against her mouth.

It seemed forever since she had heard his voice, and this voice was not quite as she remembered it. She was reminded of whiskey again, smooth and velvety and warm, and perhaps even better aged than she was used to.

Without looking away, Tru found his hands and laid hers over them. She felt his fingers still. He was waiting for her, she realized, searching her face with eyes that were darker now with wanting. He tugged at the knot she'd made in her belt and opened her robe.

Then she waited.

His hands moved to her waist. He held her like that for a long time, his palms filling the curves, the pads of his thumbs making a pass across the smooth fabric of her nightgown. Tru wanted to raise his hands to her breasts but anticipation was too rich an experience to be hurried. When he finally cupped their undersides, she gave no thought to coming out of her nightgown. She thought she might come out of her skin.

Tru lifted her face and found Cobb's mouth. She closed her eyes and moved her lips over his. Her breasts felt heavy in his hands. Her nipples were taut and tender. She wanted his thumbs to make another pass, this time across the budding flesh. When he did, she could barely draw a breath for the sensation of skittering sparks.

A current of electricity went through her, not so charged

that it was painful, but with enough energy to make her aware that her toes were curling. It was so wholly unexpected that it made her smile, and she surrendered that smile in her kiss.

Cobb broke the kiss and looked at her again but with something different in his eyes.

A question.

She did not let him ask it, and she did not suppose that she knew him well enough to guess at what it might be. She simply nodded and invited him back to her mouth with lips that parted around her smile.

Groaning softly, Cobb bent his head. His fingers scrabbled at the ribbon closure on her nightgown. He did not ask for Tru's help this time, and she did not offer it. Their kiss was long and slow and deep. He drew open the neckline of her gown and slipped one hand inside.

At the first touch of his fingers against her skin, Tru released what was left of the breath she had been holding. Her sigh was lost in the kiss.

Tru released Cobb and sought to steady herself by placing her hands slightly behind her and flat on the table. One of her palms found the purchase she was seeking. The other landed squarely on the wrapped slice of molasses pound cake.

Jenny came to mind immediately. Jenny who had made the pound cake and said to her on the subject of morals and intentions, *"And then intentions go to hell in a handcart."*

On the heels of that thought came Mrs. Sterling. Ida Mae who had served the cake in her dining room and said to her on the subject of Cobb Bridger, *"I hope you aren't moved to fluttering when he looks at you sideways."*

Tru realized she was proving her friend right and her self-appointed guardian angel wrong. Neither set well with her. Before she said a word, Cobb was straightening and closing the gap in her neckline. His fingers tugged gently on the ribbons. His hands were not entirely steady as he tied them. She let him smooth the robe over her shoulders without shrugging him off, but she stiffened when his hands began to run down the length of her arms. He let her go and stepped back. She closed her legs and pushed her nightgown over her knees.

"What happened?" he asked. His voice was still like whiskey, but with some grit in it now, as if it had been poured over sand.

Tru stared at her hands in her lap long enough to recognize her avoidance for cowardice. She lifted her eyes to his. "I'm sorry."

"So am I. But I wasn't asking for an apology. I asked what happened."

Tru reached behind her and found the molasses pound cake. She showed him the parcel.

"It looks as if you flattened it."

"I did."

"Did I sit you on it?"

Tru shook her head and held up the offending hand. "This." She hesitated, uncertain that she could explain. In the end, she didn't have to.

"A slice of reality, I imagine." Cobb relieved her of the cake and examined it from all sides. "Even so, it's probably still tasty."

She couldn't help herself. She laughed, and it felt better than good. It felt right. "Would you like to share it, Mr. Bridger?"

He cocked an eyebrow at her.

"Would you like to share it, Cobb?"

"That's better. Yes, I'd like that."

She didn't say anything about the two slices he claimed to have eaten earlier in the evening. Even if it were true, he probably had an appetite that matched hers now. She took the cake back when he stooped to pick up his coat.

"You can hang that by the back door. Your hat also."

Cobb took both away while Tru got out plates. She set them on the table, belted her robe, and then found a knife and two forks. She carefully unwrapped the misshapen cake and sliced it in two. "You choose," she told him when he returned to the table. "I did the cutting."

He smiled. "That's a mother's trick."

"And a teacher's."

Cobb eyed both slices and made his selection. "If there's a difference in their size, I can't tell."

"Good. That's the way it's supposed to work." She sat down and pulled her plate toward her. "You said it was a mother's trick. Is that where you learned it? Your mother?"

"I did."

"Then you must have had at least one sibling."

Cobb put down his fork and held up eight fingers. He nodded when her eyes widened. "Farm family."

Tru couldn't keep her eyes from widening further. "Farmers? Tilling-the-soil and reaping-the-harvest farmers?"

"I'm not sure I understand your surprise, but yes, tilling and reaping. You neglected to mention planting. That's at least as important as the others. My father did it all. His father before him. My brother Adam is taking over. Farming's always been in his blood."

"Not yours?"

"Never."

"And the rest of your family? Are they still connected to the farm?"

"Some more than others. Saul is a minister. Edie's married to a druggist. They own a shop not far from the farm in Lima."

"You're from Ohio?"

"Born and raised."

"I took you for city bred."

"Oh? On what evidence?"

"None at all, I'm realizing. Merely a wrong-headed assumption." She took a bite of cake. "What about your other siblings? You've named three."

"Teddy died of scarlet fever when he was eight. He was two years older. Michael didn't live to see his first birthday. He was six years younger. Amy came after me, and Jeremiah after her. Amy married a farmer. Jeremiah joined the Army. He's stationed at the military prison at Alcatraz. Seth is the youngest. He's still on the farm and probably will stay there until he marries."

"Your mother and father?"

"Both well and working as hard as they did when they were my age."

"You're in the middle."

"Four ahead. Four behind. A brother dead on either side, so I'm still in the middle."

Tru tried to imagine what it would be like to be part of a family that large. It was one of the few times her imagination failed her. "I had two younger sisters. Amity and Clara. They died in '71. October. The Chicago Fire. My mother also."

Cobb said nothing for a time, taking it in. "How is it that you and your father were spared?"

"We were at the church. It was Sunday evening. I was helping my father look for a piece of jewelry one of the parishioners lost. Mrs. Mackey sent—"

Cobb interrupted. "The same Mrs. Mackey that would later employ you?"

"Yes," she said, surprised that he remembered. "The same. She lost a brooch in church that morning, or at least she thought she had. Father and I were alone at the rectory when her message arrived so we went to the church together. Mother had taken my sisters with her when she went to visit her parents and hadn't returned. My grandparents lived only a few blocks northeast of DeKoven Street." She waited to see if he reacted to that. Sometimes people did. When he remained silent, she went on. "You probably heard that the O'Learys' cow started the fire. I don't concern myself with whether that's true or not. It's the least important thing. What is true is that the fire began on DeKoven Street and spread northeast.

"It was a conflagration. I thought hell had come to earth. It very nearly did. No one who wasn't there can properly imagine how fast the flames spread. They leaped from roof to roof, spire to spire. The heat was so terrible that wooden houses burst into flame in advance of the fire. Father and I escaped, but my mother and sisters did not."

"Your grandparents?"

She shook her head. "The fire burned for days, and it was days after that before we could return. I wasn't allowed to help my father search. He made me stay with parishioners whose homes were spared while he went back again and again to look for their bodies."

"Did he find them?"

"He said he did. I think it might be the only time my father lied to me. We had a service, a burial. We mourned. Two weeks later, he sent me to Mrs. Henry Winston's Academy for the Advancement of Education and Refinement of Young Ladies. I was eight." She stopped abruptly and looked down at her hands.

Cobb recognized the signs of someone who was done talking, of someone who was perhaps regretting having said so much. He did not press, and after a long silence that neither of them was inclined to fill, he rose and let himself out, touching her ever so lightly on the shoulder as he passed.

Chapter Five

Cobb sat alone at dinner. No one asked to join him, and he did not offer an invitation. He had waited as long as he could, watching for her from his hotel window, but restlessness and a dislike for his own company finally drove him downstairs. Hunger was never a factor.

He did justice to his meal because to do otherwise would have caused comment in the kitchen. Renee came by his table several times, ostensibly to bring more coffee and inquire after the tenderness of the mutton chops, but each time she gave him a thorough eye, measuring his mood as much as what was left of his meal.

He wondered why he had expected to see Gertrude Morrow this evening. It probably no longer mattered that they had parted on easy terms last night. She had had considerable time since then to reflect on his behavior—and her own. He could not imagine anything good coming of that.

If he presented himself at her back door tonight, it was quite possible she would greet him from behind a shotgun, and it was no flight of fancy that his thoughts went in that direction. She owned a shotgun. He saw it when she directed him to hang his coat and hat by the door. It was mounted on a rack above the hooks, and it looked as if it had been cared for properly, moving parts oiled and the maple stock polished. He had no desire to discover at the point of the barrel whether she knew how to use the gun. Here, he leaned on the side of caution. If she had it, she probably had a reason for it, and any reason at all dictated that she learn how to use it.

That she had not come to the hotel tonight meant that he had to revise his thinking. He had hoped he might use this evening to secure an invitation from her for dinner in her home. After last night, he wryly acknowledged to himself that it was perhaps too optimistic, even if he was far and away more interested in proving her innocence than her guilt. Mackey's allegation hung overhead regardless of whether he believed it and having access to her home was the surest way he would find something . . . or not.

"Will you have dessert?" asked Renee.

Cobb's head came up slowly, and he stared at Renee blankly, unsure why she was standing at his table. Had she spoken to him? Or had he just been listening to his own thoughts?

"Bread pudding." When he didn't say anything, she added. "That's the dessert tonight. Bread pudding."

"Oh." He shook his head. "None for me. Thank you."

Renee picked up his plate. "More coffee? A beer?"

"Coffee."

"You goin' to be in the saloon later?"

"I haven't decided."

"Word is that you lost your shirt last night."

"*Almost*," he corrected. "Almost lost my shirt." At a kitchen table, he reminded himself. Not a poker table. "If that's the word, then I suspect it's Ted Rush who's saying it."

"Sure. I don't figure it takes long for visitors to learn that Ted's got more stories than the Good Book's got chapters."

"I've already heard a fair sampling."

"Don't fool yourself, Mr. Bridger. There's no such thing as a fair sampling where Ted is concerned."

Cobb's smile was polite, but cool. He held up his empty cup. "I'd be pleased to get that coffee."

Renee's eyes swiveled from Cobb's face to his cup. Flustered, her apple cheeks turned a deeper shade of rose. "Sure. Right away." She started to go, hesitated, and after a moment's indecision, squared her shoulders.

Cobb's brows lifted. Unable to imagine what she wanted to say to him, he waited.

"I couldn't help but notice that you're at sixes and sevens tonight, Mr. Bridger, and I thought you might be grieving your losses or maybe pining after Miss Morrow since she ain't come by, but if it's neither one of those, or even if it is, there's nothing like a walk to clear your head and put your mind at ease. If you need another reason, you could walk me home. I'd be obliged."

Renee's little speech, for all that it came at him like a shotgun blast, was surprisingly coherent. She wasn't wrong about the walk, and if he was with her, he couldn't very well end up somewhere he shouldn't. Like Gertrude Morrow's.

Cobb consulted his pocket watch. "When will you be done?"

"I have a couple of hours of chores left. Mrs. Sterling wants me to sweep up real good and give the chairs a shine, but I don't work in the saloon tonight."

"All right. I'll walk you home."

"I'll find you when I'm done."

"That's fine." He pointed to his cup again. "Coffee?"

"Oh, yes. Of course." Remembering herself, her smile faltered. "I'm going now." The wash of color left in her cheeks was already brightening as she hurried away.

It did not take long for fresh coffee to arrive at his table, but it was Mrs. Sterling who brought it.

"Renee says you're walking her home," she said while she poured. "Is there a misunderstanding?"

Cobb waited until Mrs. Sterling withdrew the pot before he answered. He didn't think she would pour hot coffee in his lap, but again, caution was the wiser course. "No misunderstanding. I want to go for a walk, and she said she'd be obliged for the escort home."

"Won't be much of a walk, Mr. Bridger. Unless you have it

in your mind to take your constitutional by way of the cemetery or the creek, the Harrisons don't live but a stone's throw from here."

"I had a different impression. I don't know what Miss Harrison has in mind."

Mrs. Sterling snorted. "Then you're the only one who doesn't. You better mind yourself, Mr. Bridger. Folks will start thinking you aren't fit to be our marshal if a little gal like Renee can lead you around by the nose."

Cobb came very close to spilling his coffee. He set the cup down. "Mrs. Sterling," he said carefully. "I will cheerfully allow Miss Harrison to lead me anywhere she likes if it will end this talk about me being marshal."

"What's wrong with being marshal?"

Whatever he expected, it was not that Mrs. Sterling would take offense. Cobb could hardly make the point to her that her husband had been murdered doing his job. "Nothing," he said. "I respect the position, but that doesn't mean I want it. I don't."

"That's neither here nor there. Do you respect duty, Mr. Bridger? Because I'm thinking you have one."

"A duty? To whom? I'm just passing through, Mrs. Sterling."

"Dallying, some folks would say."

"I thought you agreed with Walt that I'm good for the saloon."

"Well, I'm having second thoughts about that." She bent her head and looked at him over the rim of her spectacles. "Now, if you weren't just passing through, maybe I could take a different view. Not with Renee, mind you, but I could be persuaded that your intentions regarding Miss Tru Morrow might just be honorable."

Mrs. Sterling smiled sweetly, if not sincerely. "Just something to think about, Mr. Bridger, when you're taking your walk."

Cobb watched her go. He did not trust her to not turn and take another snipe at him. The last time he was the target of so much advice and moral instruction he had been in the farmhouse in Lima, surrounded by his family and enough pumpkin pie to make the comments almost palatable. Cobb thought he should have had dessert.

Renee buttoned her coat as she approached the table where Cobb was playing poker. No one but Jem Davis looked at her as she sidled up to Cobb. Jem had already folded. Everyone else was studying their cards or studying Cobb Bridger.

She cleared her throat. "I'm finished now."

Cobb nodded but didn't glance up. "Jem's going to walk you home, Miss Harrison. My luck is building up a head of steam. I'm not putting that engine on a sidetrack."

Jem started to rise, but Renee said, "I can wait," and he sat down again.

Cobb folded his cards, placed them face down on the table, and tossed three bills in the pot. "See and raise," he said. His face was virtually without expression when he finally looked at Renee. "I don't think that's a good idea," he told her. "It could be a while, and you don't want to be the cause of my luck turning."

Renee protested. "It wouldn't be my fault."

"Maybe not, but I'd hold you responsible just the same. Gambling invites superstition."

Jem nodded. He had a broad, open face and a crooked smile that made him seem even younger than his twenty-four years. "You know that's true, Renee. Remember when Mr. Burdick used to come in here? He always sat in the same chair. Not at the same table. In the same *chair*. See?" He stood again and pointed to the deep gouge in the seat of the chair he'd just vacated. "This one. Uriah swore by it, but it's never done any good by me." He pushed it in under the table and grinned at Renee. "C'mon, gal. You let me see you home, and maybe I'll think my luck's improving."

Renee's tightly clamped jaw loosened a bit. "Get your coat." Chin up, she turned sharply and marched out.

Jem yanked his coat off the back of his chair, jammed on his hat, and loped after her.

Terry McCormick was chuckling when he looked up from his cards. "That was a fine thing you did there, Cobb, providing for Jem to walk her home. The boy can hardly look anywhere else when she's around, and she looks every place he isn't. They're a pair."

"Sure enough," Ted Rush said. "They're sweet on each other but only one of them knows it. Reminds me of the time I almost asked Marjorie Stockinglass to marry me. Came about as close as a man can to putting the question to her, but I held back on account of Mrs. Rush."

"Your mother?" asked Cobb.

"My wife."

Shaking his head, Cobb let Ted's gleeful cackling roll off him. The lesson here was not to comment on one of Ted's stories. Ever. Judging by the grins that met him as he looked around the table, it was a lesson everyone else had learned.

It was almost midnight when the game broke up. Cobb walked out of the saloon with the mayor. It was no pretext that he wanted to stretch his legs. The confinement of the hotel and saloon was wearing. Tomorrow, he decided, he would rent a horse from Ransom's Livery and go riding. In the meantime, he asked Terry to point him in the direction of the cemetery.

A three-quarter moon on the wane helped Cobb find his way in the dark. He walked among the grave markers, unable to read any of them, but finding that he needed the peace of the place to order his thoughts.

Miss Morrow was lying. He'd had trouble understanding that last night, but he was clearer about it now. What made detection more difficult was that she was also lying to herself. It was perhaps a harsher judgment than she deserved. The lie was in the form of denial, and Cobb didn't know what would bring her around to the truth of it. He didn't even know if it was necessary for her to admit the truth, but there *was* a man. More important, in his view, was the possibility that she was lying to herself about the theft. It could be that if she had taken something from the Mackeys, she believed she had every right to it. She would not consider that theft. Few people in that same circumstance would.

That led Cobb back to the conversation in her kitchen. She mentioned that there had been a brooch. Could it really be as simple as that? A Mackey family heirloom? It was certainly possible that a piece of jewelry owned by Charlotte Mackey could be worth more than he'd earn in a lifetime. Neither did he discount the sentimental value of such an object to the family.

Cobb could understand her connection to the brooch, if indeed it was a brooch he was looking for. Here he cautioned himself to go slowly. It would be a mistake to let supposition run far ahead of the evidence. She hadn't told him if the brooch had been found that tragic night, and he had not asked. It may well have been destroyed in the fire. The fact that it had belonged to Mrs. Mackey made it a lead worth following.

And that led him back to the matter of Miss Morrow's broken heart and the identity of the man she denied even existed. She did not strike him as someone nursing romantic wounds, but then he hadn't been in Bitter Springs to witness her arrival. Mrs. Sterling had. How much trust could he put in someone else's observation?

Gertrude Morrow. Gertrude struck him as a cold, reserved name. It didn't suit her. He'd heard Jenny Phillips call her Tru. Earlier this evening, Mrs. Sterling had referred to her in that same way. It was a better fit.

"Tru." He said it softly, testing the sound, wanting to know the shape of it on his lips. He liked it. He liked her.

That admission was not new to him. The truth was, he had liked her from the moment of their first meeting, not a chance encounter at all, but a maneuver he had planned with some care. She, on the other hand, seemed to be without guile. It was hardly any wonder that Mrs. Sterling felt duty bound to offer her protection. Cobb felt something like that himself. Not that Tru would thank him for it. She practically bristled with righteous indignation if she thought her competency was being challenged. It was another thing he liked about her.

Her prickles didn't bother him. In some odd way they made her more real, more alive, than other women of his acquaintance. He had enough experience with society mavens and their daughters in the course of his work to know he wasn't interested in the thin veneer of civility they often affected. There were exceptions, of course. There always were, and in those cases his encounters were better than merely pleasant, but he never thought of forever with any one of them. Neither did they.

He met women for whom deceit was not merely a tool but a matter of survival. Largely they worked in the cities, sometimes taking positions in the grand mansions as maids. It wasn't unusual for them to be under the thumb of some man who might call himself their protector, but merely took all of the money and none of the risks. They might be prostitutes, but just as often they were swindlers and thieves, and they were always dangerous.

Cobb stopped walking when he came to the large cottonwood at the edge of the graveyard. He leaned into the tree, resting his shoulder against the scaly bark, and stared at the clear night sky. He missed this starry view when he was in the city. There, gaslight and the hulking structures that were deemed progress made the stars something best viewed from a telescope or in a painting.

He smiled to himself, recalling Tru's surprise when she realized he had grown up on a farm. His family said that the city had changed him, although when he pressed them, they could not be specific about their observation. He didn't think it was as much about the city as it was about the job, but his family, with the exception of his father, didn't understand that either. They thought he had the kind of adventures written about in popular dime novels, absorbing and exciting on the page but not real work in real life. Cobb doubted they could imagine that he was standing in the moon shadow of a cottonwood, thinking of them, thinking of home.

Tru was a woman they would like to meet. He barely grasped the implications of that thought as it wandered through his mind, but then it latched on like it had teeth and there was no shaking it off. That was when Cobb Bridger knew he was face to face with the kind of trouble he hadn't met before.

Swearing under his breath, Cobb pushed away from the tree. He ducked his head, presented his pearl gray Stetson to the breeze, and started walking.

Tru could not sleep. She had managed it well enough when she was sitting in the parlor, but once she roused herself to go to bed, she tossed and turned and couldn't find respite.

She did not want to leave the warmth of her quilts and wool blanket, but neither did she relish the idea of just lying there until morning, and she had counted all the sheep she could bear to. Rising quickly, Tru put on her slippers and robe and hurried downstairs. It took some time to fire up the stove and longer to heat water for tea. She warmed her hands mere inches above the stovetop while she waited and wondered how she would ever survive her first Wyoming winter.

People still talked about the blizzard of '86 as if it had happened last week. The stories seemed too fantastic to be true, but as Cobb had pointed out to her, stories and the truth weren't mutually exclusive. The town had been buried in snow. Ted Rush marked the side of his hardware store with a thick blue line to remind everyone how high the drifts had been. On the ranches, cattle died by the hundreds. People slung ropes from their back doors to the outhouses and held on as they struggled to walk between the buildings. Richard Allen, not given to hyperbole, told her once that he couldn't see his hand at arm's length. Dr. Kent had not been able to reach his patients. Terry McCormick's wife lost a baby that winter. Ranch hands died trying to get into town for supplies. Others had toes and fingers amputated because of frostbite. Food stores ran low as no family was prepared for the length of that hard winter. The town's lifeline was cut off when trains were forced to take shelter in snow sheds along the route. For a time they stopped running altogether.

"It's only October," she whispered to herself. Tru didn't

know what she would do when the town realized Mrs. Coltrane had hired a hothouse flower. Bear it, she supposed, because she *would* get her fair share of ribbing. "Bear it," she said aloud, because she was not going away.

The house creaked. Tru didn't jump. She didn't want to move away from the stove. As soon as the tea was brewed, she poured a cup, added a drizzle of honey, and sat at the kitchen table to drink it.

Thump. Tru almost upended her cup. She caught it in time, steadied it, and then pushed away from the table. "Go away," she shouted.

The knock came again, softer now.

"I know you can hear me," she said, rising. "I can hear you. Go away."

"It's cold out here."

"It's cold in here too. I hear the Pennyroyal is warm. Go there." Tru was standing on the other side of the door now and glad he could not see she was smiling. She forced some starch in her voice as she glanced up at the rack above the coat hooks. "I have a shotgun, Mr. Bridger."

"It's Cobb. And I've been meaning to ask you about that. Do you know how to use it?"

"It would be all kinds of foolish to keep it handy if I couldn't."

"That's what I was thinking."

"And yet, it did not deter you."

He leaned against the door. "I was hoping you would only use it on varmints." Her silence spoke for her. "Oh, I see."

"I'm not sure you do. You would need a leg up to rise to the level of a varmint."

He chuckled. "Cruel, Tru. Very cruel."

Tru? Had he just called her Tru? "What are you doing here?"

"I'm talking to you."

She slapped the door with the heel of her hand in the event that he was leaning against it. She was delighted to hear him say, "Ow!" Her laughter was mildly wicked as she imagined him rubbing his ear. "Are you drunk?"

"No. I wish I'd thought of it, though. I'd be warmer. Or

maybe I would just be feeling the cold less. Are you going to let me in?"

She turned the handle and pushed the door open a few inches. "You have to step aside if you want in." He did, and she gave him a wide berth. "You cannot make this a regular occurrence," she said, closing the door behind him. "I have to get up early, even if you don't."

"Then why weren't you in bed?"

"I was, and I couldn't sleep."

"Neither could I."

Tru pointed to the cup on the table. "You might try making yourself a pot of tea instead of roaming the streets."

"Point taken, but Mrs. Sterling doesn't allow guests in her kitchen, and Bitter Springs doesn't have that many streets to roam. I walked out to the cemetery." Without asking if it was all right with her, Cobb took off his coat and hat and hung them up. He followed her to the kitchen table and sat in the same chair as the night before. His lucky chair, he hoped.

"Do you want tea?" She smiled when he pulled a face. "Whiskey, then. Give me a moment." Tru returned with the bottle and a glass and slid both across the table toward Cobb.

"A little in your tea?" he asked, uncorking the bottle.

She covered her cup with her palm and shook her head as she sat. "Did you win tonight?"

"I kept my head above water. Jem Davis was the big winner."

"Oh?"

"He got to walk Miss Harrison home."

Tru chuckled. "I don't suppose his feet touched the ground."

Cobb gave her a considering look as he sipped his whiskey. He felt no need to fill the silence that followed her observation. He thought she seemed comfortable with it as well. Another thing he liked about her. He probably should have been disturbed by the way those qualities were ordering themselves in his mind—but he wasn't.

"You weren't at the Pennyroyal tonight," he said.

"No. Walt brought me chicken broth and biscuits. I sent

Rabbit out after school to tell Mrs. Sterling I wasn't feeling well." Tru felt her cheeks warming under Cobb's scrutiny, but she soldiered on. "A lie, but I'm sure you realize that."

"I had my suspicions. That lie cost you mutton chops. Why didn't you want to be there this evening?"

She stared at him and gave an audible sigh. "I should think it would be obvious after last night. I didn't want to see you."

"Why?"

"You are being obtuse on purpose."

He pretended to give that some serious thought. Finally he said, "No, there's no on purpose about it. My mother says I was born thickheaded."

"Please," she said feelingly. "Do not mention your mother. I am already more embarrassed than I can properly express."

Cobb's slow smile came to the surface. "You will have to trust me on this, but my mother would be more mortified by my behavior than yours. She takes no responsibility for how you were raised, but she knows she taught me better."

Tru's eyebrows lifted a fraction. Her eyes met his. "Are you apologizing, Cobb?"

"No. Did it sound as if I was?"

"Perhaps a little."

"Do you want me to apologize?"

She shook her head the smallest degree. "No. I'm not sure you have anything to apologize for. You told me to warn you off."

"Is that why you're embarrassed? Because you didn't?"

"I don't know. It's complicated. I've never done anything like—" She stopped, shrugged, and smiled at him unevenly. "I wanted to, though. Not before, I mean. But last night, yes. It's absurd when you think about it. You and I were strangers until only a few days ago. I suppose I'm embarrassed because it doesn't feel more wrong. I tell myself it should, but it doesn't, and I don't quite understand that. Last night . . ." Her voice trailed off. She bent her head and stared at the ripples in her teacup. "Last night was outside my experience and contrary to how *I* was raised. I needed time to think about that before I saw you again."

"Have you had enough time?"

She nodded, sparing him a glance. "I have. I wouldn't have let you in otherwise."

"Feeling more resolve, are you?"

"Something like that. And if I waver, there's always the shotgun."

"Good to know." He looked around the kitchen. "As comfortable as it is in here, wouldn't you rather sit in your parlor?"

"Not with you. Besides, you're leaving soon."

"I am?"

"Don't you think that Walt knows you haven't returned from your walk? He makes a point of looking after the guests. He always has, and I don't imagine he'll stop because he thinks you can take care of yourself."

Cobb had never taken into account that his absence might be remarked upon back at the Pennyroyal. He wondered if he could depend on Walter's discretion. "Will you be at the hotel tomorrow?"

"No. I cook for myself on Fridays." She was already shaking her head before he had his expectant expression in place. "Not Friday. Jenny and Jim are coming Saturday for dinner. Jenny's bringing apple tarts. I'm making a roast with potatoes and Harvard beets. Jenny came by the school today and suggested that I invite you. I told her I would think about it."

"And?"

"Dinner's at six."

It was more than he hoped for when he knocked on her door.

"Thank you," he said. He finished the whiskey. "I was thinking I might get a horse from Ransom's tomorrow. Follow the creek and go where it leads me."

"The countryside is harsh looking this time of year, but it's not without beauty. The creek will take you to Hickory Lake if you follow it north. You'll pass Matt Sharp's farm. His son Aaron is one of my now-and-then students.

"His mother schools the younger children, but Aaron's allowed to come into town three days a week to take his lessons here. The family is Mormon. It wasn't always easy for Aaron. There are things about his faith that people don't understand."

"What about you?"

"I know almost nothing about it, but my father was an extraordinarily tolerant man. I'd like to believe I follow his example."

Cobb had no doubt that she did. "What was it like being the rector's daughter?"

"I wasn't teased, if that's what you're thinking. I told you that I was sent away after the fire. My father needed to rebuild the church, minister to the parishioners, and make his own peace with what happened. I believe he thought Mrs. Winston's Academy would be a sanctuary for me. It wasn't, but neither was it unendurable. I made sure that it wasn't. I wasn't a model of rectitude and fine manners."

He regarded her with interest as a picture began to form in his mind. "You were a hellion."

She laughed. "That was one of the kinder things Mrs. Winston had to say about me. I was regularly called forward to confess to some kind of misbehavior. I took responsibility for things I didn't do. You can imagine that made me very well liked by my classmates. They thought I was daring.

"There is not a student in my class as badly behaved as I was, and I thank God for it every day."

"Even Finn?" asked Cobb.

"Especially Finn. That boy is the very definition of mischief. He doesn't have a mean-spirited bone in his body. The same could not have been said of me. I wanted to make everyone around me as miserable and unhappy as I was, but I had a benefactor who saw to it that my behavior never was as important to Mrs. Winston as the money supporting me. Short of burning the school to the ground or skewering Mrs. Winston with a hat pin, I don't think there was anything I could have done that would have gotten me expelled."

Cobb ventured a guess. "Charlotte Mackey?"

"Yes. How did you—" She stopped, recalling what she'd told him about Mrs. Mackey, and reminding herself that Cobb was good at finding the pieces that fit. "Mrs. Mackey wanted to pay my father's debt—and hers."

"I'm thinking her sense of obligation had something to do with the brooch you were looking for the night of the fire."

"That's true, but you would be wrong to suppose it was only that. Mrs. Mackey was a supporter of many social and cultural projects in Chicago. She helped found the Art Institute and remained on the board of trustees for years. Some of the Mackey factories along the river were destroyed in the fire, and she not only oversaw their reconstruction, she also helped families that had no work during that time. As for the church, she was always an influential parishioner, so it was natural that she would use that influence and a good deal of her own money to see that Olde St. John's was rebuilt."

"So she was generous on many fronts."

"Almost to a fault. Her family did not necessarily support her good works, but she never cared for their opinion, whether they agreed with her or not."

"Was she also your champion?"

Tru did not answer immediately. "I've never thought of her in that light," she said slowly, thinking it through. "I'm not aware that she ever defended me to others or that she had any reason to. Mostly she made demands on me that she thought I should make on myself. She was more mentor than champion."

"Did you ever find the brooch?"

"I did. It was wedged in a hymnal. We think it must have fallen off her jacket and landed in the open book. She closed the book without looking, slipped it into the rack behind the pew, and there it remained until I found it."

"You said *we* think it must have fallen off her jacket. Did you mean you and your father, or did you mean you and Mrs. Mackey?"

"I meant all of us." Her features cleared as she began to understand the intent of his question. "Oh, you were wondering if I returned the brooch. You might have just asked."

He shrugged. "Sometimes it's not helpful to ask a thing straight on."

Tru's smile was wry. "Indeed, you have a knack for using the backdoor to get what you want." His grin told her that she was not wrong. "Yes," she said. "I returned the brooch. I held it in my hand so tightly that night that I couldn't open my fingers. My father had to pry it out of my palm. He let me return it to Mrs. Mackey myself. It was days after the fire before we saw her. She smelled of lilac water, and I still smelled of smoke. Father stood by, watching, but I gave it to her. I have a memory of her being quite moved. I thought she would take it out of my hand immediately, but she just stared at it for a long time, and then she took me into her arms and held me for what seemed like forever. She cried, but I didn't. I remember that. Years later, when I was her companion, she told me that she remembered it too."

Tru swiped at her eyes with her index fingers and gave Cobb a watery, regretful smile. "I'm not prone to tears as a rule."

"I'm sorry."

"No. No, it's all right. The memories are bittersweet, not sad. It's good to bring them to mind."

"You cared for her a great deal. I hadn't realized."

"I loved her."

Cobb nodded slowly. "It seems as if she might have felt the same."

"I think she did. I was probably eleven when I learned of her involvement, but by then I was a better student, less bent on making trouble, and coming to appreciate how difficult it had been for my father to send me away. I couldn't hold on to my anger when I already knew that I had found my calling. My experience at Mrs. Winston's started me on my journey to become a teacher."

Cobb decided then and there that if she was lying to him, she had no peer when it came to spinning a story. What she told him had depth and substance, and it seemed unlikely that she could relate it with this fine a degree of emotion and thoughtfulness if it were not fact.

Andrew Mackey III was wrong about Tru Morrow. If something had been stolen, and while Mackey had been emphatic that it had, Cobb thought the man might want to look to his family to find the culprit. Tru did not have it in her to take what she wasn't—

"What is it?" asked Tru.

"Hmm?"

"You're frowning. Your thoughts seemed to have wandered down a very dark path."

Cobb roused himself from his reverie. "What? No. Not a dark path at all. Just thinking."

"About?"

"About the brooch, actually. It seems as if it forged a connection between you and Mrs. Mackey that was very different from the one she had with your father. More affecting, I would say. Their relationship was essentially business, even if the business was the church, but hers with you was not."

Tru was slow to answer. "I suppose that's accurate."

"Did Mrs. Mackey make you a gift of the brooch before she died?"

"No."

Someone less experienced at reading signs might have missed Tru's barely perceptible flinch. Cobb did not.

"Why do you ask?" said Tru.

Cobb noted that she did a credible job of holding his gaze. What she was not able to control was the rising tide of pale pink color that appeared just above the neckline of her nightgown and washed her still features all the way to her scalp. If that were not enough to call her bluff, there was also the lower lip that she pulled in and began to worry between her teeth. The flinch, the color, the worried lip. All subtle indicators that she was prevaricating.

In response to her question, Cobb gave a careless shrug. "It seemed as if it might be something she would do."

"I wouldn't have accepted it."

"Why not?"

"It was passed through three generations to her. It survived the French Revolution. I would have told her that it should remain in her family. Truly, it would have been too extravagant a gift."

Still watching her closely, Cobb said, "So it was not merely a sentimental piece."

"No. Not merely that. But that was its value to her. If it had not been for the meaning she attached to it, she would not have worn it to Sunday services. Unless one looked closely, it seemed more suited to the ballroom than the sanctuary."

"Why do you say that?"

Tru's faint smile appeared. "The brooch's design was the trinity, but it was not immediately obvious. Once you followed the circular pattern of the rubies and the curves of the gold filigree, it became clear. The rubies, she said, represented the blood of Christ. The gold filigree, the crown of thorns."

Cobb whistled softly.

Tru nodded again. "I told you. An extravagant gift."

Cobb sensed she wanted to bring their conversation to a close. He eyed the teapot. "I wouldn't object to a cup of tea."

She blinked at him. "Now?"

"If it's not too much trouble." He suspected that it was the influence of Mrs. Winston's Academy, Tru's tolerant father, and Charlotte Mackey's mannered society that had Tru rising from her chair to get a cup instead of braining him with the bottle of whiskey. "Thank you," he said when she set a cup and saucer in front of him and began to pour. "Honey?"

Tru almost lost her grip on the pot. "Pardon?"

"The honey. May I have some?"

"Oh." Collecting herself, she pushed the honey jar toward him and topped off his cup. She put the pot down and returned to her seat.

Cobb sipped his tea, only narrowly managing to avoid making a face. "So this brooch you recovered remained in the family?"

"I'm not certain I understand your curiosity."

Cobb was aware that Tru's eyes had narrowed and that she was watching him closely. Had he nudged her too hard? Shrugging, he said easily, "Sometimes I don't understand it myself."

She regarded him for a while longer. "Well, I can't help you. I don't know what her intentions were regarding it. It was not something she discussed with me. As important as it was to her, it was hardly her most valuable asset. You must have at least heard of the Mackeys. The family is well known in matters of business."

He smiled wryly. "Not *my* business," he said. "But, yes, now that I am clear that Charlotte Mackey is one of *those* Mackeys, I'm familiar with the name."

"Then you should be able to put the brooch into perspective. It was not what occupied her thoughts toward the end."

And there it was again, Cobb observed, the translucent shadow of pink across her features. Her eyes darted momentarily before coming back to him. "Did you enjoy the role of companion?"

"I did."

He gently moved the conversation to a subject he hoped she would find more palatable. "But it didn't change your mind about teaching."

"No. I was discouraged because my views about the work are not widely embraced, but it never occurred to me to give up." She gave him a slightly crooked smile. "Well, perhaps it crossed my mind, but Mrs. Mackey would not permit it to lodge there. She encouraged me to make application everywhere I could. Sometimes she made an application on my behalf."

"So she *was* your champion."

A smiled edged the corners of Tru's lips. The dimple appeared. "I suppose she was."

Cobb sipped from his cup. "Wasn't Mrs. Mackey worried about losing you?"

"No. Just the opposite. She wanted to know that I was settled and prepared to live my life on my own, and on my own terms." She smiled faintly. "Or perhaps it was her terms. Sometimes I'm not sure. I was as much a nurse to her as a companion. She fought the cancer, and she came very close to seeing out two years. It was when she began suffering that she pressed harder for me to go. She knew that I had nursed my father until he died, and she did not want me to be there at her end. I had to read about her passing in the papers."

"I didn't realize."

"I know I could have stayed. There are still times I wonder if I made the right decision. It was what she wanted, but . . ." Tru's voice drifted away as her thoughts turned inward.

"It was what she wanted," said Cobb. "Period."

Tru's eyes met his. She nodded faintly. "Yes. Yes it was."

"That's better." One corner of his mouth turned up. "You were dangerously close to feeling sorry for yourself."

She blinked, and after a moment to think about it, she chuckled. "You're right. I was. Thank you."

"Thank you? My sisters would have growled at me."

"As well they should."

Cobb did not disagree. He finished his tea and pushed the cup and saucer away. "You were kind to let me in."

"Foolish, perhaps. Not kind. Go back to the hotel."

"Cobb," he said.

"Very well," she said, coming to her feet as he did. "Go back to the hotel, Cobb."

He did. But first there was the matter of a kiss.

Chapter Six

It was indecent, Tru decided, just how often she found herself thinking about that kiss. Sometimes, quite unconsciously, she lifted her fingers to her lips and traced the shape of them, and when she discovered what she was doing she pulled her hand away so sharply that an observer might well have believed she had touched fire. Tru half believed it herself.

She tried not to attach any importance to the kiss. It was one kind of trouble to remember it with so much clarity that she could still feel the pressure of his mouth on hers. It was entirely another kind of trouble to place meaning on it that it did not deserve.

It was a good-night kiss. That was the proper perspective. He simply was saying good night. Of course, he could have actually *said* good night.

It was a thank-you kiss. He was saying thank you for taking him in, for the whiskey, for the tea, for the conversation. She could think about it in that light, except that she had never received a thank-you kiss for playing hostess from anyone but her father.

It was a parting kiss. He had been thinking that it would be Saturday evening before he saw her again. Perhaps that had seemed like a long time. It had to Tru. Not just then, not at the moment he was bending his head toward her, but later, after she closed the door behind him and leaned against it and caught her breath. She had certainly thought Saturday evening was a long way off then.

Now it was upon her, and she was still fussing about that kiss. It was the roast that should have occupied her mind, and if she burned it, she decided that she was not accepting full responsibility, at least not in her own mind. She could not very well present a platter of blackened meat to her guests and explain that Cobb Bridger's kiss was to blame.

The kiss was chaste. Warm. The pressure of his lips on hers was just enough to be felt but could not be mistaken for insistent. The kiss lingered a few beats too long to be called brief, but not so long that it was intrusive. He made no demand, asked for no response. Measure for measure, it was exactly right.

It was a giving kiss.

Tru did not know what she was supposed to think about that.

The sound of water boiling on the stove drew her attention back to dinner preparations. She tossed in the dozen small beets she had washed and gave them a stir before she checked the roast. It was browning nicely, nowhere near to being charred, and the warm aroma was beginning to fill the kitchen in a way that would whet an appetite. She used a long fork to turn the quartered potatoes surrounding the meat so they roasted evenly and then closed the oven door.

Satisfied with the progress of her meal, Tru went upstairs to change her dress. She removed the unflattering brick-colored gown that she had often worn when she worked for Charlotte Mackey. Mrs. Mackey despised it and made a point of telling her every time she saw it, but she also appreciated that it served a purpose even if that was something they rarely talked about. Tru never wore the dress to school or about town. It stayed in the back of her armoire until she was ready to do

Saturday chores. She returned it to where it belonged and turned a critical eye on her wardrobe.

She was fortunate to have choices. It had given Mrs. Mackey considerable pleasure to look through pattern books and fashion magazines while she was bed bound, and she liked to exercise her will over others by insisting her dressmaker attend her regularly. Tru was slow to realize that during the last six months of her service the dresses under construction, whether for day, walking, or dinner were all intended for her use. Upon making the discovery, she protested, but none of her arguments mattered. If Mrs. Mackey had anything to say at all, it was to remind Tru that she wouldn't always want to wear the hideously drab day dress.

And of course, she was right. "Thank you, Aunt Charlotte," Tru whispered. She removed a tailored gown in celadon green with a crossover bodice. It could have been a busy dress with its ribbon striping in different widths, but the effect was a lovely long line that drew the eye instead of distracting it.

She washed, put on a fresh camisole, twisted her hair into a smooth coil and anchored it with two hammered pewter combs. She rolled on pearl gray stockings that complemented the gray cast of the gown's fabric. After stepping into the underskirt and smoothing it over her hips, Tru was ready to slip into the dress.

Tru pulled up the skirt, added the bodice, deftly managed the fastenings, and ran her palm down the ribbon trim to press it flat. It was only after she put on her shoes that she turned to face her reflection in the looking glass.

She was not vain, but she was not unaware that she was a handsome woman. Tru liked that word. "Handsome." And she was not at all bothered to be thought of in such a fashion. She did not possess the dainty sweetness of "pretty" or the delicate features of "beauty." Except for the rather ephemeral nature of the faint indentation in her chin, and the slip of a dimple at one corner of her mouth, her features were bold. She did not believe her face would ever launch a thousand ships, but it could garner a second glance.

Tru pinched her cheeks, examined her reflection again,

and grinned crookedly. "A second glance, indeed. The beets require more attention than your face."

She grabbed her apron and tied it as she fled the bedroom for the kitchen. The beets were tender by the time she arrived at the stove. She removed them from the water, peeled away the skins, and cut them into thin slices. She mixed sugar, cornstarch, added one-half cup of vinegar, and set the mixture to boil for five minutes.

Jennifer Phillips did not stand on ceremony at the front door. She opened it without knocking and announced her presence by calling over her shoulder to her husband to hurry up.

"He's talking to Terry McCormick," Jenny said. "And he's carrying the tarts. Where do you want me to put my coat? Front door or back?"

Tru glanced back at her friend. "Front's fine. I'm waiting for the glaze to thicken for the beets. In another minute it will—" She stopped because Jenny was hurrying toward her, removing her coat as she charged.

"Where *is* he?" she whispered.

"I thought you said Jim was talking to Terry." She looked past Jenny to the front door. "You didn't close the door."

"Damnation." She pivoted, hurried back, closed the door, and hung up her coat. She was slightly out of breath by the time she returned to the kitchen. "I didn't mean Jim," she said as if there had been no interruption. "I was talking about *him*."

"You don't have to whisper. And you do it poorly anyway. Jim and Terry can probably hear you." Tru turned back to her work and lifted the bubbling glaze off the stove. She poured it over the beets and set the bowl at the back of the range to keep the beets warm while they rested. "It's not six o'clock yet," she told Jenny. "I told him dinner would be at six, so the answer to your question is that I don't know where he is. He's not accountable to me for his time the way Jim is to you."

Jenny took no offense. "I have to make him accountable. That man can find six kinds of things to occupy him between home and the drugstore. And that's only one way. He just kind of wanders. I give thanks every Sunday that he doesn't care much for drink because I would surely have lost him to one of the saloons by now."

"You're right," Tru said dryly. "It's a blessing he has never taken to the bottle."

Jenny snorted indelicately. "It's a wonder, is what it is. He tells me regularly that I could drive a lesser man to drink, and he's right. Of course, I tell him that I wouldn't have married a lesser man. That's what passes for sweet talk in our house."

Chuckling, Tru opened the oven door and checked the roast.

"Smells done," said Jenny as the heady aroma wafted through the kitchen. "Is the dining table set?"

Tru grabbed a towel to protect her hands so she could lift the roast pan. "I did that earlier." She set the pan on the kitchen table and spooned some of the hot juices over the meat and potatoes. "It needs a little time to rest, same as the beets, and then it will be ready for Jim to carve."

"Jim? You're not going to ask Cobb to do it?"

"I never thought about it. Why would I do that?"

The expression on Jenny's face indicated that it should be obvious. "Because in these circumstances, he is more than a guest, he is *your* guest, and in my mind, that puts the carving duties in his hands."

Tru rolled her eyes. "In your mind," she repeated. "Honestly, Jenny, I don't always understand your mind. Jim will carve because we know he does it well. I'm not sacrificing my roast to someone who may have no knife skills."

Jenny caved. "My Jim does do justice to a good roast." She glanced back at the front door before she pulled out a chair and sat. "You're sure he's coming?"

"I hope so. You said he has the tarts."

"Stop that. You know I'm talking about Cobb."

"Well, I didn't, but since you are, no, I don't know for sure that he's coming."

Jenny craned her neck to look through the kitchen archway

into the small dining room. She could not see the table in its entirety. "But you set him a place, didn't you?"

"Yes," Tru said patiently. "I set a place for him."

"Did he say he would come?"

"Not really, no."

"What did he say?"

"Should I make gravy?" asked Tru as she studied the roast from another angle.

"That's what he said?"

"Mmm?" Tru's eyes shifted to Jenny. "No, you goose. That's what I'm saying. Should I make gravy? I don't recollect what he said."

"Forget the gravy. How can you not remember what he said?"

"Because it wasn't important. And I didn't really invite him anyway."

Jenny's dark eyebrows shot up. "What does *that* mean?"

"It means I told him that you and Jim were coming to dinner and that you wanted me to invite him. Then I told him dinner was at six."

Shaking her head, Jenny sat back in her chair. Her sigh was more than audible. It carried all the deep notes of exasperation. "You haven't the least notion how to go about these things, do you?"

Tru's head lifted as the front door opened. Jim walked in, Cobb on his heels. She smiled at her friend. "Perhaps not, but let's see how the evening goes before you decide to take me in hand."

Jenny swiveled in her chair to take in Tru's view. She jumped to her feet and whispered to Tru out of the side of her mouth. "Take off your apron. It looks like you slaughtered the cow."

Tru looked down at herself. It wasn't blood that stained her apron, but there were smears and smatterings of beet juice all over it. Sighing much more quietly than Jennifer had done, Tru untied the apron and laid it over the back of a chair. She checked her hands for stains before she smoothed her dress.

One steadying breath later, she left the kitchen to greet her guests.

"Evening, Tru," said Jim, giving her a smile almost as broad as his face. "Good of you to ask us to dinner." He handed her the covered plate of apple tarts and removed his hat. His dark copper hair was flattened just above his temples. He dutifully bowed his head a fraction to allow Jenny to ruffle his hair with her fingertips.

Tru was used to this intimate little ritual between the pair, and she looked at Cobb to gauge his reaction. She couldn't say that he was fascinated, but he didn't look away.

Jim waited for Jenny to step back. He lifted his chin in Cobb's direction. "I met this fellow on the street while I was talking to Terry. I was happy to learn that he was coming here too. Always good to meet new folks, especially when Terry's full of news about them."

Jenny pursed her lips at her husband. "I told you Tru invited him."

Jim hung up his hat. "Did you? I don't recollect."

"Seems there's a lot of folks that are having trouble with their memory," she said, spearing Tru with a glance. To Cobb, she said, "Let me take your hat and coat."

"Thank you, Mrs. Phillips."

"It's Jenny, like I said last time we spoke. Jennifer, if you've a mind to be more formal, but I might not always answer to it." She held out a hand to take his duster and Stetson. "Jim? What did you mean about Terry being full of news about folks? He's usually full of something, but being that we're so close to eating, I'm not saying what that is."

Cobb made a smooth interjection before Jim Phillips could respond. "Good evening, Miss Morrow. Like Jim, I appreciate the invitation."

Tru knew she was holding his look, but it felt as though his eyes were grazing her from head to toe. She was ridiculously glad Jenny had reminded her to remove her apron. "You're welcome, Mr. Bridger. It's the least I could do for the kindness you showed my class."

"And if I make it a point to be kind more often?"

"We'll see," she said politely. "I would not want you to spoil the children."

Jenny's eyes had been darting between Tru and Cobb, but Tru's last comment sent them heavenward. "Goodness," she said. "As if sand tarts are an indulgence. They're the stuff of life."

"So sayeth the woman who owns the bakery," said Tru. "Please, Jim, show Mr. Bridger to the dining room. Jenny will help me with the platters."

They separated with Jenny following Tru into the kitchen. "Didn't you give him leave to call you Tru?" Jenny whispered behind Tru's back.

"No. And if you keep whispering like that, he'll hear you."

"And well he should, *Gertie*."

"Not amusing." Tru set the apple tarts on the table and then took out a platter for the meat and potatoes. She lifted the roast and placed it on the dish before she arranged the potatoes around it and spooned more of the cooking juices over both. Turning back to the stove, she lightly touched the bowl of beets with her fingertips. Warm, not hot. She picked it up and handed it to Jenny along with a serving spoon. "Here. You take this, and I'll bring the platter and the carving knife."

"And the meat fork," said Jenny. "You don't want to bounce up and down from the table getting things."

"Yes, Jenny, I'll bring the fork. And please stop fretting. You're making me nervous. This is hardly the first dinner we've had together."

"It's the first with *him*."

"You're going to drive me to drink."

Jenny nodded. "See? It's a gift."

Cobb and Jim stood as the women entered. Jim took the platter from Tru's hands. She moved his plate to one side so he could set it in front of him. Cobb waited for Jenny to put the beets down and then he held out a chair for her. Once she was happily settled, he did the same for Tru.

Tru waited for him to sit before she asked Jim if he would say grace.

"Guess I should before I commence to carving." Knife and fork at the ready, he bowed his head and gave thanks.

Tru smiled to herself as Jim ended with an emphatic amen. There was never any danger that the meal would grow cold when he was leading the prayer. "Amen," she said more quietly, closely following the echo of Cobb's voice.

Jim sliced and served. Jenny started the beets around. They all had generous portions of everything.

"Perfection," Jim said, tasting the beef. He hummed his pleasure in anticipation of the sweet beets as he speared one. "You make a meal worth looking forward to."

Jenny gave her husband the gimlet eye. "And what do I make?"

"My life worth living, dear. You make my life worth living."

Cobb and Tru smiled appreciatively while Jenny pretended to be only mildly mollified.

Conversation proceeded without awkwardness after that. Jenny and Jim sparred from time to time, but their comfort with each other made them easy company.

Tru had only one newsworthy item to contribute. "I received a letter from Mrs. Coltrane this morning."

Jenny's dark brows puckered. "And you're only telling me now?"

"Well, I'm telling all of you now."

"Yes, but I'm the one that's most interested, *and* I was here first. Jim will only care if she sent you a new book, and Cobb doesn't know her."

Tru looked at Jim. "There was no book this time, but there was a postscript in Mr. Coltrane's handwriting that he would be shipping complimentary copies of *Nat Church and the Runaway Bride* within the month."

"Good to know," said Jim. To Cobb he said, "You are familiar with the Nat Church novels?"

"I am. I believe I've read most of them."

"I have them all. You're welcome to take a look and borrow what you haven't read, but don't tell folks about the shipment coming. People will be waiting at the station every day until it arrives."

"He's right," said Tru. "They're very popular here, and Mr. Coltrane enjoys feeding the town's appetite for them. Mr. Collins was disappointed when I didn't open and read the letter right there in the station. Every bit of anything from the Coltranes is interesting to Bitter Springs."

"That's certainly the impression I have," said Cobb. "Can I anticipate meeting them soon?"

Tru shook her head. "It seems unlikely. Mr. Coltrane indicated they were on their way to Pittsburgh and then New York."

Jenny tapped her fork against her plate, drawing everyone's attention. "That's all very well, but Mr. Coltrane merely added the postscript. What did Mrs. Coltrane write?"

Laughing, Tru shared tidbits from the letter, mostly related to the Coltranes' travels. "Oh, and this was something quite extraordinary. She also wrote that while she and her husband were in Memphis, she had an interview with a gentleman interested in teaching here in Bitter Springs. Apparently this man, and she did not share his name, was late discovering the notice she placed in the Chicago paper. She claims he was a determined gentleman."

"He was if he found her in Memphis," said Jim. "That would impress her."

"Yes," Tru said. "He definitely made an impression. She wrote that he had considerable experience and good character references in addition to his professional ones."

Jenny could not hide her distress. "Why would she write such awful things to you? Does she mean to release you from your contract?"

Tru reached for Jenny's hand and covered it, quieting her drumming fingers. "Calm yourself. Mrs. Coltrane meant nothing unkind by her remarks; in fact, her intent was the opposite of that. She wrote that by all accounts—and I take that to mean my own *and* Mrs. Sterling's—it appears that I am happily settled in Bitter Springs, and she is very glad to know it. As much as she was impressed by this gentleman, she still is confident that she made the correct choice."

Jenny had nothing to say except, "Oh."

Amused, Jim raised an eyebrow at his wife. "That's what is known as a horse of a different color."

Tru saw that Cobb was watching Jenny as if he thought she might stab her husband with her fork. It was not an unreasonable suspicion, but if Jenny considered it, she heroically restrained herself.

At the end of the meal, Tru stood to clear the plates. Jenny started to rise to help her, but Tru waved her back. "It will only take me a moment. I'll start the coffee and warm the apple tarts." Jenny sat back down, but when Tru began to gather plates, it was Cobb who got to his feet and stayed there, collecting the meat platter and the bowl now empty of Harvard beets. He was so quick about it that Tru could not very well tell him to stop what he was doing. She thanked him instead and bit her tongue as he followed her into the kitchen.

"The bowl goes in the sink," she said. "Put the platter on the table. I have to wrap what's left of the meat and potatoes."

She placed her armload of dishes in the sink and turned around. He was standing in front of her, blocking her path to the stove. She saw the platter was already on the table. He still had the empty bowl in one hand. He reached around her and dropped it in the sink.

"I need to brew the coffee," she said.

"I know."

"And warm the apple tarts."

"So you said."

Her eyes darted in the direction of the dining room. Standing where they were, they could not be seen. "What are you—"

Cobb did not let her finish. He bent his head and kissed her. He did not know if it was surprise or wanting that kept her still, but no part of her shied away while his mouth moved over hers. Except for his lips, he made no attempt to touch her. His fingers folded over the rim of the sink on either side of her waist. When he lifted his head, he kept his hands exactly as they were.

"I've been wanting to do that since you met me at the door. What color is that dress?"

She blinked. "My dress? It's celadon."

"I thought it was gray. Sometimes it looks more green than gray. I guess that explains why a color like that has its own name."

"You've been wondering about that?"

"All through dinner. It was either that or keep thinking about your mouth. I could spend a lot of time thinking about your mouth."

Tru pressed her lips together.

He smiled. "You can pretend you disapprove if it comforts you."

"I'm not pretending."

"I'm realizing that I am fairly tolerant myself. I don't even mind if you lie."

Tru brought up her hands between them and gave his chest a good shove.

"Go back in the dining room," she said, waving him that way. Her voice dropped to a whisper as he turned. "And stop thinking about my mouth."

Cobb was still grinning when he sat down at the table.

Jenny's eyes narrowed on him. "You're putting me in mind of a cat that's been licking at the cream."

Cobb shook his head, sobering. "No. I got my knuckles rapped for trying to swipe one of your tarts. I didn't see that wooden spoon coming." He rubbed the back of his hand for effect and then studied it as if checking for a bruise. "She's fast on the draw."

Jim chuckled. "My ma was like that. For a lot of years I thought she kept a spoon up her sleeve." He regarded Cobb thoughtfully. "Do you reckon you're faster with a gun than Tru is with a spoon?"

"Let me put it this way, I wouldn't want to challenge her or bet on the outcome."

"Oh, for pity's sake," Jenny said, throwing up her palms. "Terry appointed him marshal, didn't he?" She turned on

Cobb. "And you accepted, didn't you? Goodness, why so much secrecy?"

"Challenge me about what?" asked Tru. She handed the tray of plated tarts to Jenny to pass out while she poured coffee.

"Guns versus spoons," Jenny said as if Tru should be able to make sense of it. "This has something to do with what Jim and Cobb were discussing with the mayor before they came in." She held her husband's apple tart at his eye level and just out of his reach. "Out with it."

Jim didn't even glance at Cobb before he caved. "Cobb's been appointed our new marshal."

"Is that right?" Tru asked, her eyes swiveling to Cobb. "You accepted?"

"Yes."

Tru set the coffeepot down before it slipped from nerveless fingers. "So this means you'll be staying."

"Yes. For a while. At least until a more suitable candidate steps forward."

Without taking her eyes off of Cobb, Jenny managed to lightly stab her husband's hand with her fork. "How can you eat at a time like this?" Not really expecting an answer, she lifted the fork and smiled at Cobb. "Finding someone else could take a long time. You figure you'll really stick around until then?"

"We'll see. I've only had the position since this morning."

"What about lodging? You're not going to stay in those rooms above the office, are you? I've seen them. They're not fit."

"The mayor tells me there is money in the budget to pay for my room at the Pennyroyal. My board too."

"Then you negotiated a good contract."

"Actually there was no negotiation. Terry offered it straightaway. Come to think of it, no contract either. We shook hands."

Unsure if he was telling the truth, Jenny's look was vaguely suspicious. "I notice you're not wearing a gun."

"I wasn't expecting a shootout at dinner."

"He'll know better next time," Jim said in an aside to Tru.

Tru nodded. "Jenny, Jim's right. Let him be."

Jenny's mouth opened, then closed.

"Eat your dessert, dear," Jim said. "It's delicious."

Tru sat in the parlor, huddled in her robe in her favorite chair while she sipped whiskey and took stock of the evening. She judged that inviting Cobb to dine with them was not a mistake, although Jenny's questioning over dessert had the feel of an interrogation. Fortunately, Cobb had seemed amused, not offended.

After dinner, they had moved to the parlor where they played dominoes as teams, first with the women matched against men, again with Jenny and Cobb against Jim and Tru, and finally with husband and wife facing teacher and marshal. Whatever the configuration, it was invariably Jim's team that won. He was charged with putting the dominoes away for being so very good at it.

Their play had been relaxing, without real competition, and the barbs they exchanged were easily laughed off. Good whiskey had likely contributed to that, and the spirits might even have explained why Jim always won. He didn't imbibe.

"Sly devil," Tru said. She started when an ember popped in the stove and then chuckled quietly as she realized the source of the sound. It was because she was expecting Cobb, she realized. He'd given her no indication when he left that he intended to return. Not a nod, not a look, not a quiet word. He had walked out the door after Jenny and Jim so he had an opportunity to say *something*. She had waited, then . . . nothing.

It was the kiss in the kitchen that confused her. And his talk about her mouth and the color of her dress. Not just what he said, she remembered, but the way he said it. That voice, she heard it now, and it was still as smooth and warm as whiskey. It was hard to tell if it was his voice she felt stirring in the pit of her stomach, or the drink.

Perhaps he wasn't coming because he was now the law in Bitter Springs. He would have the authority to arrest people who caused disturbances by pounding on doors in the middle of the night. He probably had realized that and was acting accordingly. Tru was not entirely certain she appreciated his caution in this instance.

She had wanted to ask him why he changed his mind about the position, but when Jenny began peppering him with questions, she kept hers to herself. There would be time to ask him later; it didn't have to be tonight. She supposed they would share a table again at the Pennyroyal. He would not be breaking any laws.

Tru pressed her hand to her mouth as she yawned. She set her glass aside, but she didn't get up. She was physically tired but still too alert to find sleep. She shifted in her chair to get more of the stove's heat and reached for *Oliver Twist*. It dropped like a stone the moment she heard the back door open.

"Tru?"

Her heart was in her throat as she shot to her feet. "Stay right where you are, Cobb Bridger!" She picked up the lamp and started for the kitchen. "What happened to knocking?"

"I did." He crossed himself. "Swear."

Tru had only one free hand to set on her hip, but she used it effectively. He was already turning to hang up his coat and hat by the time she cornered him. "Not very loudly."

"Loud enough, I thought. When you didn't answer, I tried the door. It wasn't locked. I thought that meant you were expecting me. Was I wrong?"

"It's never locked."

He stepped into the kitchen at the same time he asked, "Do you want me to leave?"

Did she? Hadn't she just been thinking about him? Tru raised the lamp higher. The glow from it highlighted his features and burnished the gold threads in his hair. After he'd taken off his hat, he'd swept a hand through his hair, but it was still tousled. She couldn't decide if she wanted to smooth it or give it a proper yank.

"Let me take that," he said, reaching for the lamp. "It doesn't look steady."

It wasn't. Tru realized her hand was trembling.

Cobb lifted the lamp and slipped past her. "That's better. Now you can rest that hand on your other hip."

That was when Tru understood she was posed like a teapot. She blew out a long breath and lowered her hands to her sides. "Do you want to sit down?"

"Yes. The parlor?"

"You know how I feel about—"

He turned back the wick on the lamp. The flame sputtered, then was extinguished, and the kitchen was blanketed by darkness. "Better?"

"Hardly," she said.

"Give it a moment."

She followed the sound of Cobb placing the lamp on the table. She could make out the darker shadow that was the breadth and length of him. "Close your eyes," he said, and his voice was very close to her ear. Tru didn't move, but she did close her eyes. She felt his lips brush her temple and wondered that he had found that sensitive spot without searching for it. Tru placed a hand on his chest. "I don't think—"

"Don't think," he said. He kissed the hollow below her ear.

Tru tilted her head away but that merely made a present of her neck. Cobb did not require a light, she realized, not when he had the tracking instincts of an Army scout. A shiver sprinted up her spine. He responded to it by slipping an arm around her back and pressing her closer.

"The parlor?" he asked again.

"All right."

Cobb swung her into his arms. Her arms flew to his shoulders for purchase as her feet were lifted out from under her.

He carried her into the parlor and lowered her onto the sofa. He followed her down, sitting near her knees as she angled herself more comfortably but also away from him. Cobb set one hand on the back of the sofa and the other on the arm, creating a loose cage about her shoulders. He leaned forward. "Do you want me to close the curtains?"

Another ember popped in the stove. Firelight slipped between the vertical bars of the grate. The glow threw hulking shadows onto the wall, but inside this room, she and Cobb were largely invisible. "Leave them," she said. What she meant was, *I don't want you to leave me.*

Tru realized she was holding her breath. In her mind it was as if Cobb was suspended above her, hovering, watching her, waiting. She searched his face. His expression remained maddeningly remote, and then she realized he was also holding his breath.

Tru lifted her face. She cupped his roughly stubbled cheek in her palm. Their breaths mingled, and then she touched his lips and his breath was hers. He came with her when she leaned back into the curve of the sofa. His arms folded around her shoulders, slipped under them. He cradled the back of her head in his hand. His fingers stroked soft, golden strands of hair.

That first kiss tempted Tru to want more. The tentative nature of it faded into certainty, and she claimed the corner of his mouth, then his jaw, and finally touched the tip of her tongue to his ear. The sound that he made at the back of his throat was hers, she thought. She was responsible for that.

Slipping one hand between them, Tru tugged on the belt of her robe. Her fingers tangled with Cobb's as he moved to help her. He yanked the belt from around her waist and tossed it over the back of the sofa. He slid his hand under her robe. Her cotton nightgown was an insubstantial barrier to the heat of his palm. His thumb made a pass at the underside of her breast.

Tru felt her nipple stand erect. The fabric of her gown brushed against it as she shifted. Pleasure rippled through her. She could not get close enough to him. She opened her mouth wider and deepened the kiss.

Cobb followed her lead, matching her hunger because it was real for him, too. He hadn't lied when he told her he had been thinking about her mouth. Hell, he was envious of the fork she put between her lips, jealous of the crumb of apple tart that lingered at the corner of her mouth, and damned resentful that it was her tongue that darted out to lick it away and not his own.

Trouble, he reminded himself. Deep trouble. And then he surrendered to it.

Tru felt a change in him. She couldn't have said that he was holding himself back before, but she knew it now. Whatever he had been resisting was gone. She slowly raised one knee. It pulled her nightgown taut until she tugged on the fabric. He ran his hand up and down her leg from ankle to knee, each pass a bit longer, a fraction slower, than the one before. When he finally crested her knee, his palm glided with infinite care down the slope of her inner thigh.

Tru sucked in a breath as he released her mouth. She thought she might have said "please," but the word sounded guttural and unintelligible to her own ears. She might have said anything, meant anything.

Cobb laid his hand over her mons. Her hips jerked once, and then she lay still. He watched her face, her eyes. Her splendid mouth parted. He saw the tip of her tongue peep out. She was concentrating. Good.

Cobb slipped a finger between those other moist lips. She was slick with dew. He opened her wider. She made a little sound, bit her lower lip, but her eyes remained on his, and when his finger went inside her, she shivered in a way that had nothing at all to do with the temperature.

Tru found the buttons on his vest and fumbled with them. She tugged at his shirt, pulling it up. His undershirt and drawers impeded her quest to touch his flesh. He had on more clothes than she.

It was frustrating, but then his fingers began to stir and she could not think of anything beyond what he was doing to her. Of its own accord, her neck arched. She felt her shoulders press against the wide curve of the sofa's arm as the small of her back lifted. She tilted her hips. It was a brazen gesture, and a helpless one, she thought—when she *could* think. Cobb had turned her nerves inside out and was exposing them to sensations both delicate and sharply edged. She no longer knew if she was offering herself or simply, selfishly, acting on the demands of her own body.

Tru stretched, feline-like. She felt her calves tighten and tingle, then just tighten. Without warning, the long, smooth muscles in her left calf knotted into a painful ball.

"Oh! Oh, my! Ahh!" Tru pushed the heel of her hand into Cobb's shoulder and began to wriggle out from under him. He did not make it difficult for her. Although he blinked several times, as a man might if he were disoriented, he slowly sat up and slid away. Tru scrambled awkwardly to her knees, flexing her foot as she pushed at her nightgown. She could hear him breathing; it was neither loud nor labored, but measured, as though he were trying to gain control.

"No," she said. "You don't understand." She scooted toward him on her knees and laid one hand on his shoulder. She used the other to knead the painful cramp in her calf. "This room. The sofa. It's the sofa. It's too short."

Cobb hunched forward, and rested his forearms on his knees. She was right about the sofa. It was neither long enough nor wide enough to accommodate them comfortably or in any other sensible manner, and the floor was an even poorer alternative.

"You might have said something when I set you on it . . . but you sure as hell should have mentioned it before you hiked your shift all the way to . . . to *France*."

Tru was still on her knees, reaching behind her to rub her calf. "All the way to France? Did you really say that?"

Cobb stood and moved to the stove. To keep his back to her, he pretended to warm his hands. "Yes. I really did." He thought she might be smiling, but he didn't turn to find out. It was too much just now to know if she was regarding him with the same quietly amused smile she reserved for errant schoolboys. He already felt as awkward as one.

Tru eased her aching leg over the side of the sofa and kept the other one under her. She pulled her robe closed. She remembered that he had thrown the belt over the back of the sofa, but she made no attempt to get it. "I'm sorry, Cobb. I know how it seems, but you don't know how it *is*."

"I should have remembered you're a minister's daughter."

"It's not for you to remember. I never forget it." Tru flexed her foot again. "I had a cramp in my leg. That's why I pushed you away. That's why I said the sofa was too short. The parlor is not where we should be. My room is, and I am going there. You can come or go as you please but if you ever hope to see France, Mr. Bridger, you'll want to follow me."

Tru stood, tested her leg, and limped lightly toward the staircase. Halfway up the steps, she looked back at him. Firelight limned Cobb's still figure. He had not turned away. She was not confident that he would.

Once she was in her room, Tru lighted the lamp on her night table and set a match to the kindling in the fireplace. When the flames spread, she added wood to take the chill away. She closed the curtains at both windows, lingering in front of each just long enough to see that, except for waning moonlight and the Pennyroyal Saloon and Hotel, Bitter Springs was shuttered for the night.

Tru laid her robe over the back of a chair and turned over the covers on her bed. Sitting on the edge of the mattress, she massaged her calf again as she toed off her slippers.

Creak. Tru cocked her head to gauge the direction of the sound. Not Cobb, she thought, but the house settling. She crawled into bed but did not lie down. Putting a pillow behind her back, she leaned against the walnut headboard and drew her knees close to her chest. She sat huddled in just that posture as she reviewed what had happened below stairs. Most troubling was that she could not decide if she was feeling relieved or sorry for herself. It did not seem possible that she could be harboring both, but the uncomfortable pressure in her chest was an indicator that perhaps she was.

"Am I still welcome?"

Tru's head snapped up. Cobb Bridger was there in her open doorway, leaning against the jamb, looking for all the world as if he had been there far longer than she had been aware.

How was it that she had been alert to the settling sounds of the house and hadn't heard him climbing the stairs?

"Yes," she said. "You're still welcome."

His nod was short, almost imperceptible, but his long exhale was easily heard. He didn't move from the doorway. "I'm sorry."

Tru smiled faintly and remained skeptical. "Do you even know what you're apologizing for?"

"For not trusting you. For not hearing you out."

"I didn't like that."

He did not make excuses for it. "Is it enough?"

"It is."

When she welcomed him with a smile *not* reserved for young rascals, Cobb thought she was being more gracious than he had any right to expect. He stepped into the room, shut the door with the heel of his boot, and began to remove his jacket. "How is your leg?"

"Tender where the knot was but otherwise fine."

"Let me see."

Cobb tossed his jacket on top of her robe and sat down on the bed. Tru lifted the quilts high enough to get her bothersome leg out from under them. Cobb inched closer. He raised her leg the few inches necessary to slide beneath it, and then rested her calf on his lap. His fingers curled under her calf and searched along the length of it. He felt her wince when he found the tender spot.

"You're still tight here," he said.

Tru whistled through her teeth as he kneaded the muscle. Her fingers curled in the bedclothes.

Cobb gentled the massage. "Why didn't you say something?"

"I thought I did."

He remembered it a little differently than that, but he said, "All right. I suppose my first instinct would have been to push you out of the way, too. Do you remember where we left off?"

Tru felt a contraction in every part of her body *except*

where Cobb's fingers were working over her leg. Her throat was so tight that she could barely move words past it. "I remember." She put her fist against her lips and coughed. "I remember," she said in a voice that at least sounded like her own. "But I don't think we should start there."

His chuckle was quiet, faintly wicked. "No. You're right. I was thinking we would start here."

Chapter Seven

"Here?" she said in a voice that was unlike her own.

He nodded. "Here."

Then to Tru's way of thinking, he did an astonishing thing. He cupped her heel in his palm and raised her foot at the same time he bent his head. He kissed her instep.

Her lips parted around a perfect O, but no sound emerged. When he turned his head sideways to gauge her reaction, she felt her mouth pulling to the left in a bemused and lopsided grin.

"How lovely," she whispered. "And how peculiar."

He cocked an eyebrow at her. "You think so?"

She nodded.

Rather than matching her crooked smile, Cobb sobered as he lowered her foot to his lap. "You're certain about this, Tru? I need to know you're certain."

"I am." She hesitated. "I can't . . ."

Cobb waited. He lightly stroked her foot from ankle to toe.

"I can't explain it. Don't ask me to explain it."

"All right." He slid out from under her leg and stood to

unbutton his vest. He angled his head toward the lamp on the bedside table. "Do you want to put out the light?"

Tru glanced at the lamp. A small vertical crease appeared between her eyebrows, and she began to worry her lower lip.

Cobb chuckled. "Do you want me to decide?"

She blew out a small breath and nodded.

"Very well." He took off his vest and folded it before he laid it on top of his jacket. He approached the table and turned back the lamp's wick just enough to mute the glow.

Tru stared at the lamp. "I should have been able to decide." But she knew why she hadn't, why she couldn't. She said nothing about that.

"Decide this," he said. "Right or left?"

She had no idea what he meant, but that made it easier to answer. "Left."

"Then move over."

Tru found she had the wherewithal to smile. She scooted toward the middle of the bed and then a little beyond.

Cobb sat in the space she made for him and removed his shoes. Tru hardly heard them drop to the floor for the hammering of her own heart. After he took off his socks and tucked them into his shoes, he shrugged off his suspenders and unfastened the fly of his trousers. He stood again, this time just long enough to shed his black woolen trousers and suspenders and add them to the carefully folded clothes on the back of the chair.

"You're very particular," she said.

Cobb turned to face the bed as he unbuttoned his shirt. "What?"

"You're particular," she said, pointing to the stack of clothes.

He glanced at the pile. "I suppose I am. In my family, if you didn't take care of it, it couldn't be handed down. We looked out for each other that way."

Thoughtful, Tru inclined her head. "That's nice."

"That's necessity." Cobb tossed his shirt over his shoulder but couldn't resist glancing back to see if it landed on the chair. It did. He was wearing a half-smile and his drawers when he returned to the bed. Tru lifted the covers, and he crawled in. "Warm," he said. "Thank you."

"I know." Tru was lying on her back. She looked at him askance. "I wish I had chosen differently."

Chuckling, Cobb turned on his side to face her and propped himself on an elbow. "You can move this way now." Under the quilts, he ran his free hand over the space that still separated them. "It's warmer right here." When she didn't stir, he said, "Or, I can move."

Tru released a small breath as he edged closer and caught it again when his hand rested in the curve of her waist. She stared at the ceiling, aware that he was studying her from his slightly higher vantage point.

For a long time, he did nothing except listen to her careful, deliberate breathing. He waited her out, and his patience was rewarded when she turned her head just that fraction necessary to look at him.

"Aren't we going to kiss?" she whispered.

"I was wondering that myself."

"Oh. Were you? I suppose I could begin."

"You could."

She nodded. "All right." Tru turned on her side. Her movement did not dislodge his hand. She was glad of that; it grounded her. Leaning into him, she found his mouth. It was so simple after that.

There was no hurry, no reason to. She kissed him at her leisure, softly and carefully, exploring the shape of his lips with her tongue, touching the ridge of his teeth. Her mouth parted to draw in his lower lip. She worried it gently the way she often worried her own. His mouth was damp, warm. He tasted of peppermint and a hint of whiskey. Her lips parted. She changed the slant of her mouth, testing the kiss from one angle and then another. She found she liked them all.

She brushed his jaw with her knuckles and beneath the stubble she felt a muscle jump in his cheek. Her finger moved toward his ear, and she tucked a strand of hair behind it. She laid her palm against his neck. His pulse beat steadily under her hand.

The lamp was behind him when she drew back. A halo of light surrounded his head. His face was shadowed, but his hair gleamed with threads of gold. She touched the crown, flicking at an unruly thatch with her fingertips. It made no difference what she did. There was no taming it.

"I want to touch you," she whispered.

"You are touching me."

She shook her head and laid her palm on his chest. "Here," she said. "I want to touch you here."

He withdrew the hand resting on her waist and touched the uppermost button on his union suit.

Tru put her hand over his. "No. I want to do it." She returned his hand to her waist and unfastened the first button. One after another, she unbuttoned his suit from neckline to navel. When she glanced at him, she saw he was watching her face, not her fingers. She wondered what he was thinking.

Cobb pushed his elbow out, lowering his head a fraction so that lamplight grazed the side of his face and spilled over hers.

Tru glimpsed his satisfied, secretive smile. She poked him in the chest with her fingertip. It wasn't the way she imagined touching him, but moments ago she hadn't thought she possessed the courage to ask him about the thoughts behind his hooded stare.

"What?" she said.

"Your tongue," he said. "I could see it at the corner of your mouth."

She clamped her lips together, tongue safely on the inside.

"Don't do that on my account. I like your tongue."

Tru stopped pressing pointedly against his chest and tapped it lightly instead. "You say extraordinary things, Cobb Bridger."

"Your mouth is . . ." He paused, studying it. "Succulent."

Those succulent lips sipped air in response to the last extraordinary thing he said. She couldn't think of anything to say except, "Goodness." She rested her hand against his chest. Her fingers splayed. She felt his heartbeat under her palm, still strong and steady and, yes, faster.

Tru's hand made a pass upward toward his throat and then down toward his groin. His skin retracted slightly in anticipation of her touch. She felt the murmur trapped at the base of his throat as a vibration against her fingertips, and as she explored the breadth of his chest, she sensed a stirring in him just below the surface of his skin.

Tru traced the line of his collarbone and rested her hand against his shoulder. It required only the slightest pressure to make him bend toward her. She inched closer, found his mouth, and kissed him again, this time long and hard and deeply.

She did not know precisely when or how the tables were turned, but she thought later that it had probably happened sometime during this kiss. She insisted. He persisted.

Tru found herself on her back. It was incidental that her hands were clasped behind Cobb's neck. She wasn't restraining him. He was not going anywhere. When he turned on his side, his hip nudged hers. There was no mistaking the press of his erection for anything but what it was. She felt him shift again, raising a bent knee so that it rested across her thighs.

Tru never had the sense that she was trapped. He did not rest heavily against her, and the knowledge that he would let her go if she asked made it possible for her to remain just as she was.

His fingers plucked at the ribbon closure at her neckline. When he parted the fabric, his thumb rested at the base of her throat while his finger stroked her collarbone. Tru made a small sound of protest when he broke the kiss and lifted his head. His eyes grazed her face. She stared back, waiting, and when he lowered his lips to her neck, she turned her head slightly to offer him what they both wanted.

His mouth was warm against her skin. The prelude to the touch of his lips was a teasing flick with the damp edge of his tongue. He marked her twice, first with that fleeting pass, then with the suck of his mouth. He found a cord in her that made her fingers curl with pleasure. Between her thighs she felt a contraction.

He left her neck eventually. Her lips parted in anticipation of his mouth returning to hers. Instead, he inched lower. His mouth followed the path his hand had taken, and when his palm slid over her breast, Tru knew she could expect that his lips would eventually do the same.

It was a delicious sort of friction that he applied. He did not fully part the neckline of her nightgown. Instead, he laved the tip of her breast through the fabric, creating a damp circle that would have revealed her pink aureole in better light. The cotton puckered along with her nipple and the sweet, rhythmic suck of his lips snapped every one of her nerves to attention.

One of her heels dug into the mattress as her hips lifted involuntarily. She felt a second contraction, this one deep in her womb. He gave her room to move, repositioning his knee, sliding it between her legs. Until then she hadn't known the hem of her nightgown was lying across her thighs, and she did not give a moment's thought as to how that had come to be. His mouth was making a trail to her other breast. She concentrated on that, taking shallow breaths and biting down softly on her lower lip. She was very nearly light-headed by the time his mouth closed over her breast.

It seemed the most natural thing in the world to close her eyes. Tru did . . . and then opened them almost immediately. She needed assurance, and looking down, she found it in the threads of sunlight in his hair. Cobb. That was all right then, but she kept her eyes open just the same.

Her fingers tangled in the curling strands of hair at the back of his neck. She tugged and ruffled and smoothed them. She lightly stroked his nape. The rhythm she found was the same as his.

He spread her neckline wider and slipped part of it past her shoulder. The next time he touched her breast, there was nothing between his mouth and her flesh. The heat of that caress had Tru pressing her nails into Cobb's back and arching her neck.

A whimper lodged in her throat. She sucked in a breath to clear it.

Cobb slowly lifted his head. He said nothing, merely arched an eyebrow.

Tru's hands left his back and came to rest on his shoulders. "I'm not afraid," she said. "You don't make me afraid."

His eyebrow lifted a fraction higher.

Tru did not offer an explanation. Her fingertips found his nape again and applied just that amount of pressure needed to invite him closer. He did not return his attention to her breast. He covered her mouth, and this time his touch ignited a firestorm.

Tru felt heat infuse her blood and course her veins. It seemed as if her heart might explode. The thrumming reached her ears, and she could not hear anything outside of the rush and roar in her own head.

It was beyond what she was able to imagine that she could feel this way.

He moved over her, setting his forearms on either side of her shoulders, taking most of the weight she was so willing to bear. Her arms circled his back. Her hands ran the length of his spine. His muscles bunched and unwound in response to her touch. She raised her knees with no prompting and made a cradle for his hips. It was then that she felt the rigid outline of his erection. Her heels found purchase in the mattress. There was no conscious thought in the effort; it could not even properly be considered an effort. It happened of its own accord. Her pelvis lifted and ground against him.

Tru was staring at him unblinkingly when he tore his mouth away from hers. He searched her face, but she had no idea what he expected to find. The boldness of her unwavering stare vanished when she swallowed hard.

He lowered his hips a fraction; hers jerked against him.

"Do you want a pillow?" he asked.

She didn't know. How was she supposed to know? Was he trying to make her comfortable or smother her? "Yes," she said because it seemed as if it were the better choice no matter what his intentions were. She started to raise her head.

Cobb grabbed one of the pillows that was teetering on the edge of the bed and pulled it under the covers. "Lift," he said.

Now that his purpose was clear to her, Tru wished she had said no. When he came up on his knees to give her space, she raised her hips in spite of her wish to do otherwise, and he pushed the pillow under them. The act of it made her feel as though she were being prepared for sacrifice. It was a disturbing image, and she felt herself go cold inside. Closing her eyes even briefly did not help.

She averted her gaze as Cobb lowered himself once more between her legs. She stared at the ceiling instead, at the play of light and shadow across it compliments of the flickering lamplight. There was a hairline crack in the plasterwork just above her head. She had never noticed it before. She wondered if Walt would be willing to look at it. He repaired almost everything at the Pennyroyal.

"Tru?"

His voice came to her as though from a distance. Her eyes shifted from the ceiling to his face. Between her thighs, she felt him stirring. There were no longer any barriers between them. Her nightgown was caught in the crease of her hips. While she was thinking about plasterwork, he had laid himself bare.

"Where did you go?" he asked.

She laid her palm against his cheek and chose to answer obliquely. "I'm here now." When Cobb's eyes narrowed, Tru tilted her pelvis and pressed against him. It was enough. He expelled a breath of air on the back of a quiet groan and found her wrist. She let him draw her hand to his cock. Her fingers folded around it without instruction or encouragement from him.

She did not have to think about what she was doing then. It was better that way. Sometimes she responded to instinct, sometimes to images she still held behind her closed eyes.

She helped guide his entry. In spite of her willingness to do so, she still winced as he came into her. The care he took only added to her distress.

"Quickly," she whispered. "Do it quickly." And when he balked, Tru bit down on her lip and thrust hard against him.

It was all she needed to do to push him past whatever hesitation or sense of reason he still harbored. He settled himself heavily between her thighs as his mouth came down hard on hers, and when he tore his lips away, she tasted blood. She knew she was both the cause and source of it and wondered if he understood that as well. It seemed as if he might because he rocked her body backward the next time he pushed into her.

Tru did not hold on to him. She sought the sheet under her. Her fingers scrabbled at the fabric until she had enough bunched to make fists around it. The pillow under her bottom kept her hips angled toward him but did nothing to help her accommodate the girth or length of his cock. The pressure never eased. Downstairs, he had made her wet for his fingers. It was not that he had misjudged her readiness here. She had. Or perhaps she had not misjudged at all, she thought, but fooled herself instead into believing she was eager for the act when she was only ever eager to have it done with.

His stroking, long and hard and even at first, shortened. He pumped his hips. She had never tried to match his movements, but if she had, she would have failed now. He swore under his breath. The coarseness of the word, and its relationship to the act they were engaged in, made her blink.

Tru uncurled her fists and released the sheet. She set her hands on his shoulders, tentatively at first, and then felt her way to his back and finally up and down his spine. The caress was not an act of desire but born of the need to comfort, though whether she was comforting him or herself, she wasn't entirely sure.

She felt as if all of him contracted at once. The tension in his long frame was palpable. He seemed to stretch over her, rising, falling, rising again, and then he groaned deeply and shoved away from her. He did not go far. He shuddered as he came against her belly.

Tru did not move. She took careful, measured breaths and

waited for Cobb. In those last moments before he left her, she had felt the pounding of his heart. She remembered that now. She listened to his breathing, harsh at first, then more softly until it was no longer audible. She imagined his heartbeat slowing, quieting.

Cobb turned on his side then his back. He laid his forearm across his eyes. "Was that what you wanted all along?"

Tru didn't hear him. Under the covers, she was touching her belly with her fingertips. It was wet with his seed. So was one of the folds in her nightgown. Her fingers slipped lower. The sticky evidence of what she had let him do to her was there on her mons. She withdrew her hand and pushed her nightgown over her hips.

Cobb lifted his forearm long enough to glance in her direction. Lamplight highlighted her profile but not her expression. Her eyes were open. Had she ever closed them? She was staring at the ceiling again. When he posed his question a second time, it was not merely impatient but accusing as well.

A frown line appeared between Tru's eyebrows. "All along?" she asked. "I don't understand."

Frustrated, confused, Cobb ground his fist hard into the mattress. It was not nearly as satisfying as smashing it against something as solid as a wall. Beside him, he felt Tru tense. "Jesus, Tru. I don't know what happened. I didn't set out to rape you."

"You didn't." She turned her head to look at him. His forearm was resting across his eyes. "You didn't," she said again, this time with more conviction. She sat up, dragging the quilts on her side with her. She shoved the pillow away and drew her knees close to her chest and hugged them. Her voice was tremulous and hardly more than a whisper. "Is that how it seemed to you? As if you were raping me?"

Cobb was silent as he tried to find better words to explain himself, but Tru was too impatient to wait.

"And you are asking if that's what I wanted all along?" She gave him no opportunity to answer. Her voice was brittle. "How dare you. How dare you ask me that." Tru swept away the covers, throwing them over him. She climbed out of bed and stood at the edge. The floor was cold, but it felt warmer than the chill that was settling in her bones. "Get out."

Cobb raised his forearm and used it to push back the blankets. He sat up and swiveled his legs to the side of the bed. He hooked his heels against the frame and tugged on one shoulder of his union suit. Without looking back at Tru, he began to button up. When he was done, he stood and went to the chair where his clothes were carefully folded and stacked. He did not expect her to attempt to stop him, and she didn't.

Neither of them spoke as he dressed. He sat down in the chair long enough to put on his socks and shoes. When he stood, he smoothed the front of his vest and fastened his jacket.

"I'll show myself out," he said, nodding once in her direction.

"I expect you will."

Still he hesitated. He had apologized earlier for not hearing her out; he did not want to make the same mistake again. "Tru."

She said nothing. Her eyes moved pointedly toward the door.

Cobb went. At the threshold he paused a second time and looked back at her. "Just to be clear, Tru, I don't know what happened here." His eyes grazed her still figure. "And now I'm wondering if you do either."

Tru stayed precisely where she was until she heard the back door close. She walked around the bed to the washstand, stripped off her nightgown, and performed her ablutions in a mechanical manner. When she was done, she stepped over the soiled shift and took out a clean one from her armoire.

At her bedside, she extinguished the lamp. In that last flicker of light, she saw her hand was trembling. Tru crawled into the bed, burrowed deeply under the quilts, and stared at the fireplace.

It was then, under the cover of absolute darkness, that she

could finally surrender to the lump in her throat and the ache behind her eyes.

Not for the first time during the Sunday service, Jennifer sneaked a sideways glance at her friend. If Tru noticed, she didn't respond. Jennifer was afraid to whisper, knowing that Tru was right and that she would be heard three pews front and back if she made the attempt. She felt Jim's large hand on her knee. He squeezed it lightly, cautioning her. She supposed that not even her sideways looks were surreptitious. Annoyed with herself as much as her husband for knowing her so well, Jenny deliberately moved his hand to his own knee and gave her attention to Pastor Robbins at the pulpit.

Tru carefully let out the breath she'd been holding. For a moment, it had seemed that Jenny was poised to make a remark. The thought of what her friend might say had the power to make her heart stutter. Tru was so sure she was behaving as she did on any other Sunday, at any other service, but Jenny's fleeting looks in her direction were an indication otherwise.

Earlier she had wondered if she should even go to church. It served no purpose to entertain that argument again, not when the force that propelled her out the door was fear of her own cowardice. Fear, Charlotte Mackey had told her, never presented itself from the outside. It lived inside us, she'd said, and facing it was the act of holding up a mirror to one's soul. Mrs. Mackey had been staring down death when she said it. Tru thought that going to church this morning was the very least she could do to honor the woman who faced her fears so bravely.

Tru rose with the rest of the congregation to say the Lord's Prayer and stayed standing to sing the final hymn. The rich bass timbre of Jim's voice so close to her almost caused her to miss the baritone notes coming from somewhere behind her. Tru's fingers tightened on her prayer book. She did not dare turn around. She knew that whiskey voice, knew with certainty that it had not been present at the start of service.

Sometime during Pastor Robbins's remarks on the Reformation, Cobb Bridger had slipped quietly into church. That he had been able to do it without causing a stir among the congregants made him seem more preternatural than not.

At the end of the service, Tru hung back and spoke to Mrs. Burnside while Jenny shooed her husband away and cooled her heels in the center aisle. When she was confident that she had given Cobb enough time to leave the church, Tru gently disengaged herself from the druggist's wife and sidled up to Jenny.

"What's wrong with you?" asked Jenny.

Tru feigned surprise. "I don't know what you mean."

"Ha!" Jenny pointed an index finger at Tru's nose. "If you can tell me that I don't know how to whisper, I can tell you that you don't know how to pretend even mild astonishment. In point of fact, you're a very poor liar."

Tru merely shrugged.

Jenny went on. "Do you know why? It's because you don't practice it nearly often enough. And don't think I'm suggesting you start lying now, with me." She stopped pointing at Tru and placed the same finger at the side of her own nose. "I have a smell for it. Always have. Tell me what's wrong. Is it about that letter from Mrs. Coltrane? I *knew* that was bothering you."

Tru sucked in her breath. It was exactly the right thing to do before she began lying through her teeth. "How do you always know these things, Jenny? It's frightening sometimes."

"I know, isn't it?" She looped her arm in Tru's. "So what foolish things have you been telling yourself? Are you worried about your position? I swear to you, the town won't have it."

"I don't want to be a bone of contention," said Tru. "I won't allow people to take sides for or against me."

"That might not be your choice."

"Promise me you won't stir the pot. Nothing's happened."

"I'm a baker, not a cook. I let things rest and rise."

"Then do that now." Tru squeezed her arm when she sensed Jenny hesitating. "Please."

"Very well. I promise."

Tru nodded. She looked down the aisle to where the pastor stood at the door. There were only a few people remaining in line. Even Jim had moved outside. "Come on. We'll thank Pastor Robbins for his insights into the scripture, and you and Jim can walk me home."

"There were insights?" asked Jenny. "Are you sure?"

"I'm sure. There always are."

Jim was waiting for them when they stepped out of the church. Cobb was not with him. In spite of herself, Tru looked around for him.

"He went back to the Pennyroyal," said Jim, following Tru's eyes.

Jenny asked, "Who went back to the hotel?"

Jim grinned broadly at his wife, enjoying being a step ahead of her for once. "Our marshal, that's who." He tipped his chin in Tru's direction. "That's who you were looking for, wasn't it?"

Tru did not attempt to lie. She did not want Jenny pointing at her nose again. "I was. I guess I wasn't mistaken that he was at the service."

"He was?" asked Jenny.

Her incredulity made it easy for Tru to laugh. Jim joined her.

"He was," Jim said. "Four rows behind me and out in front of the congregation when it came time to leave. I caught up to him before he left the yard. He's going to come by later and look over my collection of Nat Church novels, maybe take a few to read."

"Did you invite him to dinner, Jim Phillips?"

"No. Was I supposed to?"

Jenny rolled her eyes. "Seeing how's he's coming by, it would have been the polite thing to do." She looked at Tru. "It's too bad that you're having dinner with the pastor and Mrs. Robbins."

"No, it's not," Tru said, and meant it. "I enjoy their company, and they're kind to have me. I hope you don't mean to push me at Cobb Bridger."

"I was hoping I wouldn't have to. I thought the two of you got along very well." She poked her husband in his side with an elbow. "Jim thought the same, didn't you, Jim?"

Jim gingerly removed her elbow. "I recollect saying something like that."

Jenny snorted. "He was more interested in crowing about winning at dominoes."

"It *was* impressive," said Tru. She glanced over her shoulder at Pastor Robbins. "Will you excuse me? I forgot to ask him if there was something I could bring."

"Don't you want us to walk you home?" asked Jenny.

Tru shook her head and waved them off. "No. It's all right. Go on. This is never a short conversation." She waited for them to walk away before she turned and retraced her steps to the church. There, she asked to be excused from joining the pastor and his wife for dinner. She wasn't feeling well, she told him. No, nothing distressing, and nothing that required the attention of Dr. Kent. A headache, she explained, one that was sitting directly behind her eyes. She merely needed to take a powder and rest.

Unlike Jenny Phillips, Pastor Robbins never suspected the lie.

Tru worked all week, but she ate dinner at the hotel only on Monday and Thursday. Cobb was there on Monday, seated at a table with the land agent and his wife. Ted Rush came in later and took up the empty chair. She noticed that the dining room was more crowded than usual at this particular hour and realized people were coming in specifically to meet the man their mayor had appointed marshal. She didn't know why she was surprised that word had spread through Bitter Springs so quickly. She should have been used to it by now.

By Thursday the dining room accommodated only the usual guests and a few new arrivals coming off the four-thirty train from Omaha. Cobb was absent, and Tru did not inquire about it.

Renee offered the information without being asked. "The marshal is taking his meal at the jail tonight."

Tru thought how easily Cobb had slipped into that role in Renee's mind. He was no longer Mr. Bridger. *The marshal.*

"Mrs. Sterling sent Walt down to the office with two trays. One for him and one for that fella that stepped off the train as drunk as two Indians."

"Renee!"

"As drunk as an Irishman then," Renee said. "I didn't mean anything by it. It's just an expression. I guess they say something different where you're from."

"If they do, they don't say it in my hearing."

Renee put her pert nose in the air and affected frosty accents. "Well, pardon me."

Tru sighed. "You're telling me Mr. Bridger has already arrested someone?"

"I was trying to, but you didn't let me get that far, now did you?"

Tru wisely did not interrupt.

"The way I heard it from Walt, who was at the station posting letters when the train came, this fella—I think his name is Westin, Westover, something like that—staggers off the train and falls flat on his face. Broke his nose on the platform. Must have been a sight. Mr. Collins sent Walt for Marshal Bridger. There was a little scuffle when the marshal got there. Apparently Mr. W. was feeling pugnacious." She paused. "That's a word, isn't it?"

Tru nodded. "It's a word. It means combative."

"Right. I got that sense from when Walt said it, and he got it straight from the marshal. Imagine Bitter Springs having a marshal who talks like that. Dan Sugar never did, I can tell you. I can't say about Mrs. Sterling's husband."

Tru had reason to wonder about the wheels she had set in motion. There was no applying the brakes now. Cobb had a small circle of acquaintances as a gambler, but now the entire town was embracing him as their lawman. "So this gentleman and Mr. Bridger fought?"

"That's right, only I don't know that I'd call him a

gentleman." Renee's voice dropped to a confidential whisper. "And here's another thing: seems strange that our marshal hasn't taken to wearing a gun, but Walt said he wasn't strapped. Didn't see the need, is what he told Walt. I suppose he was right because Walt said he dodged those swinging fists just fine and landed a blow that drove that man straight to his knees. Made him puke, too." Renee finally heard herself. "Sorry, Miss Morrow. I probably could have left that last part out."

"It's all right," said Tru.

"Anyway, Walt helped Marshal Bridger toss that fella in the back of the station buckboard and took him straightaway to jail. It's been a long time since we've had someone use the facilities. Mrs. Sterling was glad, I can tell you. Mr.—" Renee paused again, her brow furrowing. She snapped her fingers as it came to her, and her face cleared. "Westerman," she said triumphantly. "That's his name. Westerman. He was supposed to stay at the Pennyroyal so there's no one here who's unhappy about him sleeping off his drunk in jail. Mrs. Sterling's going to charge him for the meal, too. Usually that comes out of the marshal's budget, but she doesn't cotton to the idea of the town paying for it, especially since it saved her from cleaning up after Mr. Westerman." Renee wrinkled her nose in distaste. "What she meant by that was that it saved her from ordering me to do the cleaning up, and that's a fact."

"I'm sure you're right."

Renee nodded and gestured to Tru's plate. "Are you finished? Doesn't look to me like you ate even half. Do you want me to fetch you something else? There's some stew left from last night that'd be fine to heat up."

Tru shook her head. She had spent more time pushing dumplings through the chicken and gravy than she had eating them. "I'm not especially hungry tonight."

"Cil said you weren't here last night or the night before. Are you sickening for something?"

"No, at least I don't think so. I don't seem to have much of an appetite."

Renee picked up the plate and swept away the utensils.

"You know what's good for that? Dessert. Baked apples tonight."

"It's tempting."

"See? I'll bring you a dish when I come back with the teapot. That will set your appetite straight."

Tru hoped she was right.

Cobb looked up from his book as the door to his office opened. He dropped his chair onto all four legs, swung his feet off the desk, and greeted Jefferson Collins.

"Don't trouble yourself to get up on my account," Collins said.

Rabbit and Finn squeezed past their grandfather when he was slow to move out of the doorway. "Hey, Marshal," they said as one.

"Hey, boys."

Collins addressed his grandsons. "You two have a seat over there on that bench. I'd be obliged if you'd leave some space between you. Say, arm's length. Pretend you're bookends."

Cobb suppressed a grin as the boys hung their heads and dragged their feet on their way to sitting down. Wanted posters, most of them several years old, were tacked to the wall above the bench. It was no accident, Cobb thought, that Mr. Collins had pointed Rabbit and Finn in the direction of those posters. There were chairs in the room that they could have had, but the wanted notices would keep the boys occupied at least long enough for Collins to state his business.

"Bookends," Mr. Collins said, critically eyeing the distance between his grandsons. "Or I'll ask the marshal to put you in the same cell and see what comes of that." He turned to face Cobb. "They've been fussing with each other since school let out. I had to get them out of reach of their granny's broom before she took to whacking them or me with it." He scratched his chin as he looked thoughtfully in the direction of the door that led back to the cells. "I don't suppose you'd consider locking *her* up for the night. It would give me considerable peace of mind."

One corner of Cobb's mouth lifted. "And it would give me considerable grief. No, thank you. I'm a great admirer of your wife."

The station agent snorted, but he was grinning.

"Is this just a social call?" asked Cobb. "Or is there something I can do for you?"

"Mostly social. Thought I'd ask after that Westerman fellow, see how he's coming along. You dropped him pretty hard. 'Course he dropped his own self harder before you got there. I don't think I ever saw a man go down like he was felled. He didn't even put out a hand to save himself." He glanced toward the rear door again. "So how's he doing?"

Cobb put a finger to his lips. "Listen."

Collins cupped his ear so it captured noise coming from the back. Mere moments passed before he heard what sounded like the swarming of hundreds of angry bees. The buzzing stopped abruptly. A few heartbeats later, it began again. "Sounds like someone's poking a hive back there."

Cobb laid his hand over his book. "That's what I thought. It's been going on for hours. Mrs. Sterling sent food, but I couldn't rouse him long enough to eat it."

"Won't hurt him to have it cold," said Mr. Collins. "Better that he sleeps it off, I suppose."

"Dr. Kent came by and looked him over, set his nose, and gave me a poultice for his eyes. I can't get him to keep it on. Mr. Westerman is going to have two shiners."

"Serves him right. He didn't do me any favors falling on the platform. I have to file a report with the railroad."

"Someone cares about what happened?" asked Cobb, surprised.

"No one cares. Still, I'm required to file a report. Unusual circumstances. That's what they call it, and the reason they want to know is because he was liquored up. Temperance women make a lot of noise about these things. The story will get out, mark my words, and the railroad likes to have the details before the ladies organize a protest at every station from New York to Sacramento."

Cobb whistled softly.

Collins nodded. "Yep. That about sums it up." He looked over at his grandsons and saw they were still quietly occupied. "I guess you changed your mind about that letter."

"What letter?" asked Cobb.

"The one you wanted to send but didn't want to get there fast. You can tell me it's none of my business because that's true right enough, but curiosity's a powerful thing. I was wondering if you took my suggestion after all and decided to put off writing it."

Cobb set *Nat Church and the Ambush at Broken Bow* on the desk and sat up straighter. "I *did* write the letter. In fact, I went to the station the day after we spoke to post it. You weren't there. I gave it to Mrs. Collins. She assured me she would give it to you."

The station agent's eyebrows came together over his spectacles. Frowning deeply, he rocked back and forth from toe to heel, heel to toe.

"Mr. Collins?"

"You remember me saying I was going to put your letter on a westbound train?"

"I remember."

"Well, I never got the letter and Mrs. Collins wouldn't have known to do that. What about your handwriting? Was it difficult to read?"

"Sure was," Finn said, casting that aside over his shoulder.

Cobb and Collins exchanged glances. Simultaneously, their heads turned toward Finn.

"Finn?" Collins asked. "Turn around and tell me what you know about it."

Finn spun on his knees and then dropped into a sitting position. Almost immediately, his legs began to swing under the bench. "Granny couldn't make heads or tails of what he wrote. She said it was on account of not having her reading glasses, but I think she was just saying that because when I offered to get them, she asked me to read the address to her instead." He shrugged. "So I did."

"*You* could read it?" his grandfather asked.

"Sure. I seen it before."

"Saw. You *saw* it before."

"Uh-huh. Like I said." Finn looked to Cobb to confirm the truth of it. "Ain't that right, Marshal? Even Miss Morrow said you didn't practice making your letters enough."

Sighing, Cobb nodded in the station agent's direction. "He's telling you the truth. I stopped by the school one afternoon. That's where Finn saw my slate work."

"He brought sand tarts," said Finn. "But I don't think Miss Morrow liked the interruption. Leastways, I figure that's why he ain't come around again."

It was second nature for Collins to correct Finn. "Why he *hasn't* come around again."

"Uh-huh."

Collins knuckled his jaw. "So you read the address to your grandmother?"

"Yes, sir. Pretty sure I got it right. Chicago doesn't look like any other word that I know."

"And that's all you did? Read it to her?"

Finn nodded. "She wanted me to cross out what Mr. Bridger wrote and put the address down in proper script, but there wasn't enough room on the envelope for me. I still make my letters kinda big."

Cobb felt a little of the pressure that was building in his chest begin to ease.

"Granny said she couldn't see to do it herself," said Finn. "That's why she asked Rabbit. It was real important to her that Mr. Bridger's letter have a proper send-off, but she said she would have done it for anyone because it was the right thing to do."

Some of that pressure returned and settled uncomfortably close to his heart. He could feel it pounding. "Rabbit helped his grandmother?"

"Sure he did. I heard Pap tell you all about her broom."

"A powerful motivator."

"If you're talkin' about her swing, you got that right."

Jefferson Collins stopped knuckling his chin and made a circling motion with his finger while he looked at Finn. His grandson dutifully rose to his knees, turned around, and made a credible show of studying the posters.

Collins looked at Cobb and rolled his eyes in Finn's direction.

Understanding the offer that was inherent in the gesture, Cobb shook his head. "They can stay. We wouldn't know half of what we do if Finn didn't keep his ear to the ground."

"He gets that from his grandmother."

Cobb pointed to the chair on the other side of his desk. "Why don't you sit down? I'm getting a crick in my neck."

Collins sat and struck at the heart of the matter. "Did you alter the address at all?"

"No. I didn't want that to be a question at the other end." He didn't say that he could explain away his handwriting, but that pretending he forgot the address, or even that he transposed the numbers was not something he was willing to do. It was too careless a mistake, the kind he didn't make. It was his reputation that brought him to Andrew Mackey's attention, and his reputation that Mackey was paying for. In Cobb's experience, people rarely hired the man; they hired what they *thought* of the man.

"How long before the letter reaches its destination?" Cobb asked.

The station agent counted backward, ticking off the days with his fingertips. When he stopped, he shook his head slowly. "I'm sorry, Cobb. I reckon it could be there now. Maybe arrived yesterday. Maybe today. It's almost certain to be there by Saturday."

"I see."

"Is that going to be a big problem for you?"

"I don't know."

Jefferson Collins glanced around the office. Except for adding a couple of posters and a new coffeepot, nothing much had changed since Deputy Sugar sat behind the same desk.

"Doesn't alter what you're doing here, does it? Can't say that you're exactly settled in."

Cobb pointed to the dime novel. "I don't require much to settle. A cup of coffee. A book. Something to look at on the wall. That does me fine."

"Then you're not runnin' off."

"No. I'm not running off." He observed that his answer seemed to satisfy the older man. "It's not your fault about what happened to the letter."

"Did I give you the impression that I thought it was?"

"As a matter of fact, you did."

Collins shrugged. "Well, maybe I do feel I wronged you. Never thought I wouldn't be there when you came by with it. Never thought . . ." He fell silent, shook his head.

"Never thought I'd trust the letter to anyone but you," Cobb finished for him. "That's my fault. I was so sure . . . Well, it's done.

"If there's a reply, I'd like to know as soon as it arrives."

"I'll take care of it myself."

"Thank you."

Collins stood. "Let's go, boys. Hop to. Your granny's waiting, and you have school tomorrow. Don't tell Miss Morrow what you've been reading tonight. She's not likely to think much of you cuttin' your teeth on reward notices."

"You might be surprised," Cobb said softly. "You might just be surprised."

Andrew Mackey tapped the point of his letter opener against his chin. The tip unerringly found the cleft and rested there momentarily, hidden in the nest of his neatly cropped beard. He glanced at the envelope he had pushed to the side and wondered again what he was supposed to make of it. The scrawl was Cobb Bridger's, he was sure of that. The script matched the handwriting on the note inside. Fortunately, Bridger wrote in the same manner he spoke: short and to the point. The man did not use two words when one would do. That made the contents of the letter less laborious to decipher.

The other writing on the envelope puzzled him. It was the cursive style of a careful hand. A child's, he thought. Or child-like. However it had come about, he was glad of it. Cobb's letter might have been a long time coming left to the poor eyesight and hapless sorting of the postal clerks.

"What are you thinking?"

It was his cousin Amelia who spoke. Andrew set the letter opener on top of Cobb's note and regarded her first, then the rest of the family gathered in his study. "I'm thinking that in all of the Wyoming Territory there is probably not a more desolate place than this one. Have any of you ever heard of Bitter Springs?"

To a person, and there were seven of them, they answered in the negative.

"That's what I thought. Frank, will you bring the atlas? It's in the map drawer." He gestured vaguely in the direction of the first column of floor-to-ceiling bookshelves. "We should probably all have a look."

"You've decided then?" asked his uncle Paul. "You're going?"

"There's the labor dispute to deal with first. Not that the Pinkertons can't enforce company policy, but it's my obligation to see it through to the end. Is someone else volunteering to go in my place?" This time he only regarded the men. They numbered four. No one responded, and he did not expect that anyone would. "I've reviewed the case law, read every decision that I thought might turn things our way. You know what I know. Are any of you doubting that Gertrude Morrow is a thief?"

"And a witch," Frank said, dropping the atlas on his cousin's desk. Only Andrew didn't laugh. "How else do you explain that Aunt Charlotte couldn't see that woman's true nature for looking at her? I'm telling you, Charlotte Mackey wasn't bed bound. She was spellbound."

Andrew opened the atlas and leaned forward to address the family. He had a tight-lipped, narrow smile, and deep parenthetical lines on either side of his mouth. His neatly clipped mustache and beard were the ginger color his hair had been in his youth. At thirty, there was no longer any hint of red in his thick thatch of hair. It was as brown as his eyes, an exact match until his eyes darkened with the strength of his conviction. They were very nearly black when he said, "A witch? Frank might be wrong, but I'd be a fool to rule it out. I am not a fool."

Chapter Eight

Cobb was six weeks into his new position as marshal when he decided he needed to make another attempt to close the distance that separated him from Tru. The problem was, all indications thus far pointed to her being satisfied with their current arrangement. No matter how often he thought back to the night she told him to get out, he was no closer to understanding what he had done to make it all go sideways.

There had been opportunities to speak to her, but they occurred in public and conversation was limited to the weather, health, and whatever topic the third or fourth party present introduced. He joined her for dinner on several occasions but never once when she was sitting alone. If Howard and Jack were with her, he invited himself to the table. The same with Ted Rush and Mrs. Garvin. In all that time, she had only asked him to sit with her once, and he remembered thinking the words must have tasted like ground glass. He did not fool himself that he was welcome; rather he sat down with the knowledge that Tru did not want to be John Westerman's sole dinner companion. Mr. Westerman had been out of jail four full days at that point, and cut a somewhat pathetic figure with his black eyes and bandaged nose, but whatever sympathy he mustered for his bruised countenance, he lost when his attempts at exacting speech made it clear that he had no intention of going through life sober.

Cobb put Mr. Westerman on the noon train heading to Salt Lake City the next day. Mrs. Sterling rewarded him with an extra large slice of currant pie that night. The mayor clapped him on the back as he passed the table, and Ted Rush told a story about how he had almost escorted a scoundrel out of town once. Tru did not have a word for him.

Cobb kept an eye on her, not through any sense of civic duty, but because it was harder to ignore her. The truth was, he liked watching her, and admitting it didn't come at any cost. She had a particular way of walking that made him think she must have practiced deportment with a book balanced on her head. Even on a windy day, she seemed to be able to keep her hat in place when every woman around her was tugging on her bonnet ribbons or clamping a hand to the crown of her hat.

Tru's carriage was correct, not stiff, but invariably contained. She was not given to open-armed gestures or covering the ground in long strides. She was free with her smile, though Cobb rarely saw it cast in his direction. Humor made her green eyes brighter, and the appearance of her single dimple meant that she was at least thinking about mischief.

He never observed a sign that she was thinking about him.

Her students adored her. He had seen her in places outside of the schoolroom where children too young to be in her class trailed after their older brothers and sisters just to say hello to her. The littlest ones were often tongue-tied, but he had never known Tru not to be able to coax a string of gibberish from them. She spoke their language fluently, while he generally required a translator.

Children came up to him, too. Boys asked him how many men he had killed. The girls wanted to know why he wasn't married. He had no idea what the youngest among them said if Finn wasn't around to tell him.

As of this afternoon, there still had been no reply from

Chicago. Rabbit and Finn came by his office to let him know nothing was waiting for him and stayed to practice their whittling. Wood shavings littered the floor on either side of his desk. They sat more or less as he did, leaning back in the chair with their heels propped on the desk. Neither of them had mastered finding the proper tilt and balance for keeping the chair on its rear legs. They tried at least once during every visit, usually with one or both of them landing flat on his back. Cobb thought it was a wonder that they hadn't knocked themselves out.

Cobb dropped his chair back on all fours and stood. "I'm getting coffee," he said. "You boys want a ginger beer?"

"Sure," said Rabbit. "But maybe we should split it. Granny says it gives Finn gas."

Finn rolled his eyes. "Gives Granny gas. I'm just a scrapegoat."

"Scapegoat," Cobb said.

"Are you sure?"

"Pretty sure."

"Scapegoat." Finn tested the word several times under his breath before he returned to whittling.

Cobb carried a bottle of ginger beer and two glasses back to the desk. "One pours, the other chooses." He left them to sort it out while he got his coffee.

"Miss Morrow does that," said Rabbit when Cobb was once again comfortably situated behind his desk. He held up his glass of ginger beer so Cobb would know what he was talking about.

"How about that," Cobb said.

Finn held up his glass and examined the contents against the lamplight. He eyed Rabbit's glass to confirm that they were indeed equally full. "Sure keeps kids from scrappin'."

"It works for adults, too."

"How about that," Finn said.

Cobb not only heard his words coming back to him but the exact tone as well. Finn was truly frightening.

Rabbit watched Cobb as he sipped his drink. He swallowed,

licked his lips, and asked, "When are you comin' back to visit us?"

"I was at the station yesterday, remember?"

"I meant dropping by the schoolhouse."

Finn nodded. "Yeah. There's been talk."

"Talk?"

"Sure," said Rabbit. "Kids talk."

"I'm aware," Cobb said, sparing a pointed glance for each of them. He couldn't decide if they were oblivious or only pretending to be. In any event, they were undeterred. Cobb found himself eyeing the broom standing in the corner.

Rabbit said, "Robby Fox thinks you haven't dropped in because you're marshal now and up to your neck in villains. I told him there hasn't been a villain in town since Mr. Coltrane run out the Burdicks, but Robby's got his own ideas about things like that."

Finn nodded. "He thinks Mr. Westerman was a villain only we didn't know it because he was a better drunk than an outlaw."

"Robby might have a point," said Cobb. "The work keeps me pretty busy, boys."

Rabbit eyed the book lying on the desk. "Uh-huh."

Finn followed his brother's glance. The dime novel's lurid cover got his full attention. "Hey! Ain't that *Nat Church and the Frisco Fancy*?" He angled his head almost completely sideways. "Did you know if you look at it just right, you can see up that dancin' girl's petticoats all the way to France?"

Cobb tipped his chair forward, grabbed the book, and flipped it over on its cover. "Enough."

Finn let out a long, disappointed sigh. His lower lip actually vibrated with the strength of it. He pressed his glass of ginger beer against it.

Rabbit simply shook his head. "Finn's a trial, Marshal."

Cobb recognized Heather Collins's voice coming out of Rabbit's mouth. She said the same thing about her older grandson, though not as often as she did about the younger one. She had a martyr's affection for each of them.

To move the conversation away from the Frisco fancy, Cobb asked, "Is Robby Fox the only one with an opinion?"

"No," said Rabbit. "Sam Burnside says that since you gave up gambling, you can't properly afford sand tarts. It's all right, Marshal. Everyone knows lawmen aren't pocket rich the way gamblers are."

"Everyone knows that, huh?"

"Yes, sir," said Finn.

Rabbit nodded. "Priscilla thinks you're too proud to drop by without a treat, but Charity Burnside says it's on account of Miss Morrow that you ain't been around."

"Charity probably got that idea from me," Finn said shamelessly. "I told her how Miss Morrow made you sweep the classroom and especially mind that you get the mud from under Sam's desk. She cuffed Sam real good on the back of his head when she heard that. Charity's kinda sweet on you, Marshal."

Rabbit said, "All the girls are."

Cobb shifted uncomfortably.

"It's all right," said Rabbit. "None of the boys mind 'cause the girls leave us alone."

Finn nodded. "It's a good thing. Girls are bannoying."

"Annoying," said Cobb automatically. "There's no 'b.'"

Finn thought about that. "Must have been that Granny had a cold when she said it. There's probably no 'b' in 'bapoplectic' either."

Cobb was fortunate not to spew coffee. "Finn, it sounds to me as if the only 'b' you're hearing is the one in your Granny's bonnet."

Rabbit laughed, but Finn only frowned.

"Never mind," said Cobb. "I'll tell you what. Suppose you tell Miss Morrow that you invited me to come by, and then you let me know what she says."

"Lie, you mean? And carry tales?"

Rabbit rolled his eyes. "It's not a lie if we actually invite him. And it's more like an assignment than carrying tales."

"Oh. All right. Like we're deputies. Well then, Marshal, it'd be a real pleasure if you'd come to the school tomorrow, especially if you bring something from the bakery." Finn looked at his brother. "How's that?"

"Pretty good. Only it can't be tomorrow. We've got to tell him what Miss Morrow says about it first."

"Okay." Finn lifted his chin in Cobb's direction. "You're invited to come by if Miss Morrow doesn't make a face about it. That's how we'll know whether you're welcome or not." He pointed to his mouth as he pressed his lips together. "Have you noticed that sometimes it's not what folks say that they mean? I'm partial to watchin' how they look when they say it."

Cobb could not decide if Finn was going to grow up to be a gambler, a lawyer, a criminal, or take the worst aspects of all three and become a politician. "Thank you, Finn. Rabbit. I'd be pleased myself."

The following afternoon, Cobb's earnest deputies delivered their report. Miss Morrow had said he was welcome any time. Finn aped the face she made when she'd said it, and there was nothing in it to indicate that she was speaking anything other than the truth. There was, however, the dimple that Finn pressed into his cheek with his index finger, and Cobb understood instantly that while he was welcome, she was up to no good.

The next day Cobb arrived at the schoolhouse an hour before dismissal. He thought she would appreciate his attempt to minimize the disruption to her lessons, but if she did, she didn't tell him.

He came bearing gifts. Charity Burnside and Priscilla Taylor jumped up to take his hat, gloves, and coat. The boys eyed the bakery box he was shifting hand to hand as the girls relieved him of his outerwear. Tru did not interfere. She asked him to distribute Jenny's frosted cupcakes to the class before inviting him to sit down in her chair.

"I thought it would be a treat for the children if you read to them. We've been reading and discussing Aesop's Fables. You're familiar?"

"I am."

"Good." She opened the book in her hand to a place that was marked by a ribbon and laid it in front of him. "This is a favorite."

He glanced down at the title and was immediately wary. "Of whom?"

She ignored his question. Picking up her cupcake, she carried it to the rear of the classroom. Several children made room for her, and she thanked them for it, but explained that she preferred to stand. "Nice and loud, Marshal. So we all can hear."

Cobb smiled weakly as he blew out a long breath and began reading. "A Wolf in Sheep's Clothing." He looked up. "Loud enough?"

Tru smiled sweetly and nodded along with the rest of her class.

"A Wolf found it a great hardship to get at the sheep owing to the watchfulness of the shepherd and his dogs. But one day the Wolf found the skin of a sheep that had been flayed and thrown aside."

Cobb paused to rub the back of his neck and regarded Tru again. "This is a bloody work, don't you think?"

"The children are familiar with flaying. Go on."

He looked around. To a student, they were staring at him raptly. "Very well. The Wolf took the sheepskin and put it on to cover his own pelt. Disguised thusly, he strolled down the hillside and among the sheep. The Lamb that belonged to the sheep whose skin the Wolf was wearing began to follow the Wolf in Sheep's Clothing; so, leading the Lamb a little apart from the flock, he soon made a tasty meal of her."

Cobb glanced up to see if any of the children were grimacing. They weren't. Tru, in fact, was smiling smugly. Finn was right. Girls were bannoying.

He went back to the story. "For some time the Wolf succeeded in deceiving the sheep, and enjoying hearty meals." He closed the book. "The end."

The children applauded. In their excitement, some of them forgot to put down their cupcakes.

Cobb tried to avoid looking at the carnage.

Tru came forward, gave Sam Burnside her handkerchief, told Mary Ransom just to lick her fingers, and simply shook her head at Finn. He had frosting in his hair. When she reached the front of the classroom, she turned to face her students.

"Is it the end?" she asked them, waving Cobb back into her chair.

He sat down slowly, his torture not yet ended.

Aaron Sharp threw up his arm and wiggled his fingers. He hardly settled down when Tru called his name. "There's still the moral. Marshal Bridger didn't read the moral."

"No, he didn't, did he?" said Tru. "That's because it's not written down. Sometimes we have to work that out on our own. What is the moral lesson in this fable? Who thinks they know what Aesop was trying to tell us?"

Finn's hand shot up. He practically bounced off his bench.

"All right, Finn. What do you think?"

"If there's a wolf around, it's better to be a dog or a shepherd. Everyone knows sheep are stupid."

Cobb covered his mouth with his hand and managed to turn his bark of laughter into a credible fit of coughing. Tru sidled up to her chair and slapped him several times between the shoulder blades. He sobered before she left bruises.

"It's all right," he said, pointing to his throat. "Cupcake crumbs."

"Hmm." She withdrew her hand and addressed Finn. "That's certainly one way of looking at it, Finn. Are there other ideas?"

Several children took a stab at it, and one came close, but it was Rabbit who finally hit the nail squarely.

"Sometimes folks aren't exactly like they appear. Pays to be cautious."

"Very good, Rabbit. A clever person can fool us into believing he is something he is not."

The class nodded as a group. Only Finn looked dubious.

"What is it, Finn?" Tru asked. "You don't agree?"

"No, I understand what you're sayin'." He shrugged. "I was just wondering if I could figure it out before the wolf made a meal of me. I'm pretty tasty, Miss Morrow."

Cobb answered before Tru could. "Finn, if anyone can spot a wolf in sheep's clothing, it's you."

Finn sat up straighter on his bench, puffed out his small chest, and smoothed back his cowlick. The frosting in his hair was now explained.

Flattening her mouth, Tru looked askance at Cobb.

Priscilla Taylor put up her hand.

Tru called on her. "You have a question?"

Priscilla nodded. "For Marshal Bridger." Without waiting for permission to go ahead, she asked, "Have you ever met a wolf in sheep's clothing?"

Cobb thought immediately of the preacher and his son who had ministered to a different sort of flock. "I have," he said, and the way he said it, as much as the look on his face, did not invite more questions.

"What about you, Miss Morrow?"

"Oh, yes." She did not look at Cobb. "Sometimes you're the lamb," she said. Her glance encompassed the whole of the class. "And sometimes you're the shepherd."

Tru expected Cobb to leave when the children did. In fact, she had counted on it. Her nerves were stretched taut from managing her every gesture, every facial tic. She did not believe for a moment that Finn and Rabbit had issued a spontaneous invitation, but she was determined not to be outmaneuvered. It was not possible that he had missed the point of her lesson. Whether it was sufficient to keep him out of the schoolhouse in the future remained to be seen, but she judged his continued presence as an unwelcome sign.

Tru was aware that he had ignored the student benches in favor of making one of the tables his seat. He was settling in, not preparing to go. She busied herself with straightening the items on her desk.

"Should I get a broom?" he asked.

She shook her head. "I'll sweep up tomorrow. Friday."

He picked up a slate and blew away a film of chalk dust. "Finn doesn't help you any longer?"

"Not regularly. He was fickle in his attentions."

Cobb's eyebrows lifted. He smiled faintly. Tru saw neither. He set the slate down again and folded his arms across his chest. "We have to talk."

"We don't," she said. "Not really."

"All right. Then *I* have to talk."

"I can't stop you, but I don't have to listen." She turned, picked up an eraser at the blackboard, and began to wipe away all evidence of today's lessons.

Cobb said nothing. He watched the sweep of her arm across the slate. Her motions were not furious. They were deliberate. He recognized anger here, and stubbornness, both of which she was hiding behind as if they were shelter from the storm.

"You are not going to like what I have to say," he told her. "But you *are* going to want to hear it." He thought there might have been a pause before the next pass of her hand, but it was so short, so fine, that it was easy to dismiss as wishful thinking on his part.

"Don't make the mistake I made and not hear me out to the end."

With only half the board cleared, Tru stopped what she was doing. Clutching the eraser, she slowly turned around to face Cobb. Her eyes narrowed on his face; her voice was crisp. "Just say it then. Say it and go."

Cobb shifted his seat on the table, moving forward so that his hip was hitched against the edge. He angled one leg out in front of him for balance. His arms remained crossed, not defensively, but more matter-of-fact. "I've been in your home several times."

"I know. As you will recall, I let you in."

"I've been in your home several times," he said again. "When you haven't let me in."

Tru required a long moment for full comprehension. Except for the slight flaring of her nostrils as she sucked in a breath, she didn't move.

"Three times," said Cobb. "The Tuesday after we were together. Again, on the Tuesday after that. And finally just a week ago."

Her knuckles whitened on the eraser. "I am a minister's daughter. Not a priest. If you need to make a confession, you should apply to the church, not to the schoolhouse."

Cobb tilted his head a fraction as he studied her. "That's a curious response. Why aren't you asking me for an explanation?"

"Because it doesn't matter. You intend to justify yourself. I imagine you believe that as the marshal, you have the right to go wherever you please, whenever you please." Tru drew a steadying breath. She spoke quietly, intently. "The Wolf wears a tin star and walks freely among the Sheep."

"Yes, Little Lamb. That must be it." He easily dodged the eraser she threw at his head. He turned to watch its trajectory. Like a stone skipping on water, the eraser skimmed the surface of two tables before it thudded softly to the floor. "Nicely done," he said.

It was an effort for Tru to regain her poise, but she forced herself to be calm because the alternative was a tantrum too unpleasant to contemplate. She sat down behind her desk where she could hide her clenched hands in her lap.

"Very well," she said after a moment. "I'll ask. Why? Did you leave something behind?"

Besides my self-respect? He could taste the bitterness of that answer on the tip of his tongue. He bit it back. "No," he said. "I was not looking for something I lost."

"But you *were* looking. It was a search."

"That's right."

"Animal? Vegetable? Mineral? Really, Marshal, that's a game I play with the children. I'm not engaging in—"

"I found the brooch."

Tru stared at him. Her lips parted, closed, and parted again. "You broke into my home to steal my jewelry?"

"Hardly. You still don't lock your door."

Her voice, like her jaw, was taut. "Please, do not try me further. I own several brooches. Which one did you take?"

"I said I found it, not that I took it."

Tru's fingers uncurled. She raised one hand and pressed her fingertips to her temple.

Cobb had seen similar gestures many times in the course of his work. He allowed that she might be responding to the first signs of a headache but that did not make him sympathetic. He recognized the gesture for what it was: a means of delaying her response.

"I wish you would be clear," she said.

"And I wish you would not pretend that you don't understand." He watched her lower her hand. Her chin came up. Her mouth was set stubbornly. She was not going to show her cards until he called her bluff.

So he did. "Charlotte Mackey's brooch."

Tru swallowed, but she didn't speak.

"The trinity set in rubies. The golden crown of thorns."

"I told you that."

"So you did, but you didn't mention the diamond chips that fill the spaces where the three ruby circles intersect or that the brooch would not fit easily into the palm of your hand."

"It's not *that* large."

Taking that as an admission of sorts, Cobb gave her an arch look. "I should have found it the first time. I had it in my mind that it would be in your bedroom. I started with the lacquered box on your vanity."

"I'm only surprised you waited until I was gone. How that box must have tempted you from the vantage point of my bed. You showed remarkable and uncharacteristic restraint."

She spoke quietly in acid tones. Accepting it as deserved, Cobb didn't flinch. "I wasn't there long," he said. "The fact that you have so few things in the other rooms made it easy."

She smiled without humor. "Yes, it was my intention to make it as easy for you as possible. You can appreciate how delighted I am to learn that you pawed through my belongings." Tru sat back in her chair. "Why are you telling me this? I hardly know whether I'm to applaud your perseverance or your cleverness."

"I want you to understand that what I did, I did because it was important."

Tru waved her hand carelessly. "Then go on. I admit to not being able to grasp the finer points."

"As I said, I went back a week later. I looked in your kitchen this time. My mother always kept some money in the flour jar. That way she could tell if any of the rest of us had gotten into it."

"I never suspected. You cleaned up after yourself very well. I don't know if your mother would be proud or disappointed."

He went on as if she hadn't spoken. "I was in church a few Sundays later when—"

"The Lord spoke to you?"

"Something like that. Pastor Robbins was leading the congregation in 'A Mighty Fortress.' I didn't realize it had so many verses." He unbuttoned his jacket and opened it, tapping the star on his vest. "My sheep's pelt was stabbing me. I had to fiddle with it. It almost fell into my open hymnal."

"Ah," she said. "A sign."

"There was no burning bush, but it was a revelation. Last week I found Mrs. Mackey's brooch in your father's Bible. According to the inscription at the front, the Bible was also a gift from Charlotte Mackey. It occurred to me that it probably pained you to hide it there, to cut so deeply into the book the way you did, but it also made sense. The Bible and the brooch kept your father and Charlotte together and connected you to both of them."

She neither confirmed nor denied what he supposed to be true. At this moment, what he thought meant next to nothing to her. "All right," she said. "So you've seen the brooch. To what purpose? You said you didn't take it. I fail to understand why you undertook the search."

Without preamble, he asked, "Did you steal it?"

Tru's answer was immediate and firm. "No."

"Then Charlotte Mackey really gave it to you."

"Yes."

"And you lied to me when I asked you that very question at your kitchen table. You said that if she had offered it, you would have told her it was too extravagant a gift, that it belonged to her family."

"Yes, I lied. I'm not about to apologize for it. It's an extraordinarily valuable piece, an heirloom, and we argued many times about who should have it. She had several great-nieces. One of them, Amelia Mackey Brown, particularly admired the brooch. I encouraged Mrs. Mackey to pass it to her."

"And yet . . ." He lifted his hands, shrugged.

"She believed I was confusing Amelia's avarice for admiration. There was no turning her from that opinion, and truthfully, I don't know that she was wrong."

"So you finally accepted the gift?"

"No, not the way you think. I found it when I unpacked my trunks, but that was after I arrived in Bitter Springs. It was tucked away between two petticoats. I have to assume she put it there. I don't think it was something she would have trusted one of the servants to do for her."

"I thought she didn't leave her bed."

"Your mistake—and mine—is underestimating her determination when she wants something. I had moved into an adjoining room by then. She knew when I came and went. I've given this considerable thought since I found it. It would have been difficult for her, not impossible, but in all likelihood she had been planning it for some time. She had a wardrobe made for me and inspected everything before it was packed. I told you that she was determined that I should leave before she died. The clothes were for beginning again. I suppose she meant the brooch to be part of that new start as well. It would have been relatively simple for her to conceal it between those petticoats."

Cobb listened to it all, parsing every sentence for the truth. "And what about your conviction that it should remain with her family? Did you ever entertain the idea of sending it back to Chicago?"

Tru answered as evenly as she could. "I'm quite sure I don't like your tone. Do I stand accused of something?"

"Not yet."

"Aunt Charlotte *gave* me the brooch."

"Aunt?"

"A title of respect and affection. She insisted."

"That must have caused a stir in the family."

"I can't say."

"I have the impression the Mackeys keep their wagons in a tight circle."

"Yes, Marshal, they did. And I was always one of the Indians." Tru suddenly pushed her chair back and stood. She leaned forward at her desk, arms braced, and glared at Cobb. She spoke in staccatos, each word bitten off. "Why is it so important to you?"

Cobb also stood. His voice was no less harsh. "Because I damn well want to believe you!"

Tru stared at him. The high color in her face started to fade. She felt as cold as she had the night she'd sent him away. "I'm telling the truth."

"Did you ever wonder why she gave it to you?"

"She valued it. She wanted it to belong to someone who appreciated it in the same way, not for its dollar worth. The fact that I still have it speaks in my favor. I've never tried to sell it."

"Is that really something you could do in Bitter Springs?"

Tru regarded Cobb wearily. "I'm not sure that it's enough that you want to believe me. Your skepticism is not merely unflattering. It's draining. Are you going to arrest the schoolteacher?"

Cobb stepped back and hitched his hip on the table again. "No. That was never going to be the outcome of this discussion."

"Discussion? Interrogatory is a better description."

He bent his head slightly, allowing that she was right.

"And what if I had stolen it?" she asked. "What then?"

"Then you would return it." He paused a beat. "You may have to anyway."

Tru's brow creased. "Why? And to whom?"

"The answer to the first is that I may be the only person who will believe you. And about the other, that would be the Mackey family."

"I don't understand."

"Andrew Mackey III," Cobb said without inflection. "I was hired by Andrew Mackey to find you."

"Find me?" Tru's absolute astonishment gave way to laughter. She put up a hand to hide her mouth as she shook her head. "He would never do that," she said, quieting. "He won't spend a penny to save a dime. There is probably no one in the Mackey family with less interest in my whereabouts than Andrew."

Cobb wondered what he had misunderstood. Tru's face was flushed, making it more difficult to tell if she was spinning a story.

Tru sobered. "Did you meet him?"

"I did. In Chicago. He told me you stole something from him, from the family. He never told me what it was."

Tru closed her eyes briefly and pinched the bridge of her nose as she thought. When she opened her eyes again, she became aware of the late hour. Outside the schoolhouse, the lowering sun was already casting long shadows. Darkness fell early as winter encroached.

She tilted her head toward the window on Cobb's side of the classroom. "If we stay here, I'll have to light some lamps. I'm concerned that I will not have enough oil for the first morning lesson. It's barely light when the children arrive."

"Your house, then."

"I don't think so. The hotel." She consulted the watch pinned to her pleated white shirt. "In one hour."

Cobb's eyes narrowed fractionally.

"Do you think I won't come?" asked Tru.

"It's crossing my mind."

"The last train went through here almost an hour ago. There's not another one until morning. Where would I go?"

"Jenny and Jim's."

She mocked herself with a wry twist of her lips. "Well, that hadn't occurred to me. I'll be there," she said. "I promise."

Cobb left his room the moment he saw Tru approaching the hotel. He *had* wondered if she would come. Her promise did not mean a great deal to him. She was not an accomplished liar, but she had proven that she was not above making the attempt.

He was coming down the stairs when Walt opened the door for Tru.

"Saw you crossing the street, Miss Morrow," Walt said. "How you keep your hat on when the wind's stirring is a mystery. I've been studying it for a spell, but I ain't figured it out. Can I take your coat?"

"Certainly." She let him help her out of it. "Is the table by the window available?"

"Sure is. I don't expect it will be for long."

"Why is that?"

"Because you'll be sittin' there."

Tru laughed. "You set me up, Walt." She looked past him to where Cobb was loitering beside the newel post. "Marshal Bridger is going to join me this evening."

The dining room was pinched for space, owing to the arrival of some new guests from the last train. As Tru made her way to the empty table, she smiled politely at the diners who greeted her and paused at Howard Wheeler's side while he explained that Jack's absence was on account of being under the weather. By the time she reached the table, Cobb was waiting for her. She accepted the chair he held out.

"Walt must have saved this table for me," she told him. "Did you notice it was the only one vacant?"

Tru saw that Cobb's eyes were making a sweep of the dining room.

He shrugged. "When Walt told me the hotel's full up, I asked him to save this table until you got here. What did Howard tell you?"

"He was explaining why Jack wasn't here tonight." She fiddled with her fork. "Is that really what you want to talk about?"

"No, but I thought we should have what passes for a conversation before we get to the—how did you describe it?—oh, yes, the interrogatory."

"I think I could actually stab you with this fork."

Recalling how Jenny Phillips had gotten her husband's attention at dinner, Cobb removed his hand to his lap.

"In the eye," she said.

His mouth did not so much as twitch. "I believe you."

"Good." She set the fork down and smoothed the edge of the tablecloth with her fingertips. "I've been thinking about some things you said earlier."

"For instance?"

"Well, you said Andrew Mackey hired you to find me. Coming to Bitter Springs wasn't an act of fleeing Chicago, but I can understand how he might have interpreted it in that light. Aunt Charlotte knew where I was going. I can't speak to her reasons for keeping it a secret, though I have to believe she had my interests in mind." Tru smiled a trifle crookedly. "Then again, perhaps no one asked after me. Most of the family would have delighted in my absence."

"Most?" he asked. "Not all?"

Tru meant to toss off a careless shrug, but the tension seeping into her shoulders made it weighty and uncomfortable. "How many Mackeys did you meet?"

"One. Andrew."

"I suppose he spoke with the blessing of the others."

"That was my impression."

Tru ticked off the clan on her fingertips. "Three great-nieces: Amelia Mackey Brown, Lavinia Mackey Wilson, Susannah Mackey. Lavinia and Susannah are sisters. Paul Mackey is their father. Although he is not in the truest sense one of the greats, as she liked to call them, he is the last of the middle generation of Mackeys. Andrew's father, who was Andrew Charles II, was his cousin."

Cobb nodded slowly, working out the relationships in his head. "Go on. That's four. Five, counting Andrew."

"Great-nephews: Jackson Mackey, David Mackey."

Cobb saw a muscle jump in Tru's cheek as she set her jaw. He did not think she was even aware of the tic. "Seven," he said, watching her carefully, alert to the change.

"And the last of the greats: Franklin Mackey."

"Franklin," Cobb repeated, biding time until her flat green eyes regained their usual radiance. "How is he related to the others?"

"Amelia and Jackson's brother. He is very . . . young."

Cobb wondered how he should interpret "young." He decided that question could wait. He did not want to be on the receiving end of her flat, guarded expression again. "Are you prepared to give Andrew the brooch if he asks for it?"

"I've thought about that, too. No, I'm not. Does that surprise you?"

Cil Ross delayed Cobb's answer. She had tea ready for Tru, but she had to ask Cobb what he wanted. She went off immediately to fetch his beer.

"No," he said as if there had been no interruption. "It doesn't surprise. Not after what you told me about the brooch and what it means to you. Does Andrew Mackey impress you as someone who would be moved by that?"

Amused, she laughed, shook her head. "No. I don't think Andrew is moved by sentimentality. That is surely not the reason he hired you to find me." She raised her teacup, sipped. "How *did* you find me?"

Cobb told her about the newspaper she left behind and how once he learned the content of the missing notices he was able to speak to all of the employers who might have hired her.

"So you met Mrs. Coltrane," Tru said.

Cobb could almost see the metaphorical tumblers clicking into place behind her eyes. She had realized that he was the latest teacher applicant mentioned in Mrs. Coltrane's last letter. He smiled faintly, fascinated. "I did."

Cil arrived with Cobb's beer and their plates. Tonight's fare was a thick slice of ham barely visible under a generous helping of buttered cabbage and noodles. Tru's portion was every bit as large as Cobb's. She eyed it warily. "I only receive plates like this when I'm dining with you."

Cobb waited for her to pick up her fork before he tucked in. "Maybe Mrs. Sterling intends you to share."

"Oh, yes," she said dryly. "I'm sure that's it."

After a few minutes of quiet while they did early justice to the meal, Tru broke the silence. "When I received that letter from Mrs. Coltrane, were you at all concerned?"

"Yes."

"You didn't show it."

"Thank you."

"Naturally you would think that was a compliment."

"In my work, it is."

"About that," she said, pausing with her hand halfway to her mouth. "What *is* your work?"

"The precise word is 'detective.'"

"Not 'bounty hunter?'"

"No. I collect at least half my fee when I accept the assignment. Expenses are paid as I go. No payment, I stop. It's a simple arrangement. The half that was not paid at the outset remains with my client if I am unsuccessful." His smile appeared briefly. "And, Tru, I'm always successful."

Chapter Nine

God help her, Tru thought. She believed him. She swallowed, but she had nothing but spit in her mouth, and not much of that. She set her fork down and chose the tea instead.

"Now that you've found me," she said when she could speak again. "What are you supposed to do?"

"Inform Mr. Mackey."

"Inform him. Not escort me back to Chicago?"

"That's right."

"And have you? Told him, that is?"

"Yes."

The surface of her tea rippled as she released a measured breath. "And?"

"And I haven't heard from him. He might not have received my letter yet."

"A letter? I would have thought you'd send a message by wire."

"I wanted time."

"Time?"

"To be with you."

Tru shook her head, disappointed. "To identify and find whatever it is that I am supposed to have taken, you mean."

"That was part of it," he said. "But so was the other. I was told to make certain you didn't run off, but that had nothing to do with wanting to be with you."

"So you say." Tru felt herself grow warm when his eyes did not shift from her face. She was the one who looked away. "Did you write to him about the brooch?"

"No. The brooch never figured into the assignment."

"What if I'd never told you about it? What if you'd never found it?"

He shrugged. "Then I expect we would be having a very different conversation this evening."

"You are an optimist. If it weren't for that brooch, we would not be talking at all."

"Don't make this about that piece of jewelry, Tru. He said you took something, and he wants it back. I determined that it was probably the brooch, but I don't know that."

She leaned forward. Urgent, but quiet, she said, "Except for the clothes Aunt Charlotte gave me, I don't have anything else."

"Then you'll explain that."

"Maybe I won't."

Cobb heard the starch in her voice. She was looking a bit on the stiff-necked side as well. He judged the better course was not to argue. Returning his attention to his plate, he cut and speared a triangle of baked ham. "Suit yourself."

"I don't like being accused of stealing."

"I'm not sure anyone does."

"The allegation doesn't deserve a reply."

Cobb paused, swallowed, and cut another piece of meat. "There would be plenty of people who would agree with you." Most of them were thieves, but he kept that to himself.

"An explanation could make me seem guilty."

"Done poorly, yes."

Tru took a forkful of cabbage and noodles and lifted it to her mouth. "I think I would do it poorly."

"Quite possibly."

"I would probably have to go through several drafts."

Cobb's head came up. "Drafts?"

"Yes."

"Did I give you the impression that this was something you could do in writing?"

"Well . . ." A crease appeared between her eyebrows. "Can't I?"

"Tru," he said patiently. "I told Andrew Mackey that I found you in Bitter Springs. Nothing else. He doesn't know that I've told you anything about hiring me, doesn't know that I'm marshal here, doesn't know that I think his suspicions about you are wrong. Finding the brooch hasn't changed anything. A letter from you is exactly the wrong way to go about explaining yourself."

She considered that, knew he was right. "And the not wrong way?"

"Face to face. Here, I think. In public."

"That would require him coming to Bitter Springs."

"Yes."

Tru's eyes widened. "Andrew Mackey here? He's coming here?"

"It was always his intention to meet with you. He couldn't have suspected I would find you so far from Chicago. I don't know what he will do. There's been no reply."

For a moment she couldn't breathe.

"Tru?"

She expelled the breath, but the word that came out of her still sounded strangled. "Alone?"

"I don't know. You know him better than I do. Who would accompany him?"

She shook her head, didn't answer. Appetite gone, Tru pushed away her plate. The smell of the cabbage vaguely sickened her.

Cobb looked from her to her plate, and back again. "It's not unreasonable to believe he'll come," he said carefully. "This is at least as much about you as it is about whatever he thinks you took. In his place, I would do the same."

"You've already done it," she whispered. "You stood in for

him, asking all the questions he will want to ask. I won't go through that again. It was demeaning. You demeaned me."

He made no attempt to defend himself. His intentions meant nothing in the face of her humiliation.

"I won't answer to him." Tru's teacup rattled in its saucer as she tried to pick it up. "I'm done answering to Aunt Charlotte's family."

Cobb's eyebrows lifted. What she said surprised him more than her vehemence. Before a clear question formed in his mind, she was speaking again.

"Do you know that they wanted me to be their spy? When it was clear they couldn't remove me from her side, they began applying to me for help." Her short laugh held no humor. "Not a coordinated effort, mind you. They came at me one at a time. Each one with an agenda. Each one asking me to keep the conversation just between us. Andrew Mackey was the least of them. There was some sense to what he wanted, which is more than I ever heard from the rest."

Cobb's mind was flooded with questions, any one of which might stop Tru in her tracks. He continued eating, for all intents and purposes giving her nothing more than his polite attention.

"Andrew was charged with oversight of the Mackey holdings, not the mills and Great Lakes shipping specifically, but the investments, trusts. The stock. Unfortunately he was little more than a figurehead, a public face for the business when Charlotte couldn't get out. She did everything from her bed. Lawyers marched in and out of the home almost daily. I sympathized with Andrew. His grandmother was incapable of loosening the reins. He could not make a decision without consulting her, and if everyone didn't know it, he believed they did. He wanted me to turn over her books to him so he could study them. All the accounts, the numbers. He wanted evidence of every donation she made. He wanted to know how she invested profits back into the companies. He told me he needed to understand all of it if he was going to keep the Mackey empire running after she was gone."

Her fingertips whitened as she palmed her teacup in both

hands. "He was desperate for the information." She regarded Cobb for a long moment. "You're not going to ask?"

"I already know," he said. "You sympathized, as you said, but you turned him down. You turned them all down."

"How did you—" Tru stopped, sighed. "Yes. I turned them all down. Even Andrew made it easy for me in the end. He wanted—" She stopped, shook her head, clearing a memory. "It doesn't matter."

"Were you tempted?"

"No. I never doubted that Aunt Charlotte had her reasons. It was not easy for her to trust, especially in her own family. If she had asked me to taste her food before she ate, I would not have been surprised. It never came to that."

"Would you have done it?"

"Yes. But not without some trepidation. Her wariness was contagious."

Cil came, took away their plates, and left four bars of soft sugar gingerbread behind. When she was gone, Cobb said, "She's quiet this evening."

"Mrs. Sterling's marching orders, I expect. There are new arrivals."

Cobb nodded, picked up one of the bars. He was on the point of biting into it when a movement out of the corner of his eye caught his attention. He turned his head slightly. His peripheral vision caught the figure on the dining room's threshold. He could not say why it was immediately familiar to him, only that it was. He accepted that his conversation with Tru was about to come to an abrupt end.

Tru's eyes followed Cobb's glance to the source of his interest. Her heart slammed once in her chest before it dropped to her belly. When Cobb looked at her again it was because he was gauging her reaction, and it angered her that she gave him one.

"You knew," she said under her breath. "You *knew* he was here."

Cobb had a glimpse of her panic before she shuttered it. Having no expectation that she would believe him, he nevertheless shook his head. She looked right through him.

A moment's paralysis kept Tru in her chair, but it passed, and then she was on her feet. Her dress brushed against Cobb's leg as she walked by him. She felt his fingers touch hers, but she couldn't be sure if it was his intention to caution or encourage her. He had the right to do neither. It was his fault that Andrew Mackey had come to Bitter Springs.

Tru was aware of the heads that turned as she approached the entrance. Eyes followed her, but she did not mistake that she was the object of interest. A stranger in town was always a trump card.

If Andrew Mackey realized that he was the target of speculative stares, he gave no hint of it.

An arm's length separated them when Tru stopped. Her smile was restrained. When he lifted his hands toward her, she placed hers in them. She allowed him to squeeze them once before she withdrew them.

"Mr. Mackey," she said quietly. "I was—"

"I think after six days on a train with no other purpose before me than to see you, you could do me the favor of calling me Andrew."

It was not the first time he had proposed that informality, but in Charlotte Mackey's home, Tru had always resisted. She gave in now because it seemed to be the least of the battles that she might have to fight.

"Andrew," she said. "I'm dining with the marshal tonight. We would be pleased if you would join us." Tru watched as Andrew's dark eyes shifted and his gaze traveled past her. She saw his surprise, quickly masked, but whether at Cobb's presence or to the fact that she had revealed that Cobb was the marshal, she did not know.

Andrew said, "You're very kind to invite me. The man at your table . . . you say he's the marshal?"

"Yes. You recognize Cobb Bridger, don't you?"

He had no immediate reaction. His thin smile was slow to surface. "I wondered at your remarkable aplomb. It appears now that you have been expecting me."

Tru did not respond. Turning over her hand and indicating the table, she invited him to follow her.

Cobb stood as Tru and Andrew approached. He drew an empty chair from a nearby table and set it facing the window. It could not hurt if Mackey was distracted by his own reflection.

"Mr. Bridger," Mackey said. He did not offer his hand. Instead, he held out Tru's chair for her and waited for her to sit before he did the same. Cobb did not yet have his chair under him when Mackey said, "I understand that you are the town's marshal."

"He was appointed by the mayor," Tru said. "It was my idea."

"Was it? How . . . *enterprising* of you."

"Mr. Bridger will tell you it was more in the way of interference than enterprise. He did not want the position. He was bullied into accepting it."

Mackey's glance shifted to Cobb, but he spoke to Tru. "I'm trying to imagine."

Cobb merely tilted his head.

Tru was relieved to see Cil emerge from the kitchen. "This is Miss Ross," she told Andrew when Cil arrived at the table.

"Oh, Miss Morrow," Cil said, "there's no need for introductions. I registered Mr. Mackey same as the other guests that came in on the afternoon train. And I was the one who showed him straightaway to his suite. I reckon we're acquainted now."

Deep, parenthetical lines appeared on either side of Mackey's mouth as he lifted his head and smiled at Cil. "I *reckon* we are."

Tru's eyebrows lifted slightly. She thought it was not beyond all possibility that Cil might swoon. At the very least, the young woman was transfixed. Tru reached out and lightly touched Cil's hand. "Perhaps you'd be good enough to bring Mr. Mackey his dinner."

Nodding, Cil hurried off.

"A suite?" Tru asked. "What did she mean when she said she showed you to your suite?"

"I have no idea," he said. "It's not the Drake."

Cobb said, "I think Miss Ross was referring to the residence on the third floor."

Tru pretended she did not see the wry twist of Cobb's mouth or hear his faintly mocking tone. "Oh, of course. Then you have the very best, Andrew. That is where Mrs. Coltrane lived when she managed the hotel and where she and her husband stay when they return to town."

"Someone *lived* there?"

Tru mocked him with her smile. "You have many faults, Andrew, but snobbery has never been one of them."

It was a flirtation, Cobb realized. Andrew Mackey was flirting with Tru Morrow, and she showed no aversion to it. In spite of that earlier moment of panic, she seemed entirely comfortable with Andrew Mackey. *Andrew*, she had called him. Not once, but twice. If it was a performance, it was a masterful one. He knew she was an unskilled liar, but he had never considered that when she immersed herself in a role, she might be an extraordinarily talented actress. What had she told him about her time at Mrs. Henry Winston's Academy for the Advancement of Education and Refinement of Young Ladies? *I wasn't a model of rectitude and fine manners.*

Miss Gertrude Morrow had a certain devious charm. And, yes, he decided, it was another thing he liked about her.

Cobb made a point of staying out of the conversation. It was more entertaining to remain in the box seats than join the players onstage.

"What a surprise to see you, Andrew, and I hope you can appreciate my confusion. Marshal Bridger says he knows you, but I don't understand how that's possible. Even with the railroad, the telegraph, this country cannot already have grown so small that coincidence accounts for it."

Andrew stroked his neatly trimmed beard with the back of his index finger. He regarded Tru and spoke as if Cobb were absent from the table. "He didn't explain?"

"He might have if I hadn't jumped up to greet you."

"You did leap from your chair. You put me in mind of a jack-in-the-box."

"How you flatter me."

He laughed. "I've missed sparring with you, Gertie."

Cobb tapped the side of his fist against his chest as he choked on a mouthful of beer. He managed to swallow, but it required considerable effort. That Tru was watching him, evincing concern, did not help. Mackey reached over and slapped him on the back. Hard.

"I'm all right," Cobb said, putting up a hand to block Andrew's next blow. "Down the wrong pipe." He saw that he could have saved his breath and the explanation. *Gertie* and Andrew Mackey were already turning away from him.

"I hired Mr. Bridger to find you," Andrew told her.

Tru's gaze slid to Cobb. "Is that right?"

Cobb reluctantly joined the players, hoping he had only the one line. "Yes."

Andrew feigned deep disappointment. "I should not be surprised that you're skeptical. Long hours in my grandmother's company have that effect."

Tru sobered. "I read about her passing. I trust you know how sorry I am for your loss. I cared for her deeply."

He said nothing for a long moment, then, "I thought you did."

The edges of Tru's mouth flattened. "Please say what you mean."

"You didn't stay. You abandoned her."

"I was following her wishes."

"You abandoned all of us."

"Hardly."

"You didn't tell anyone that you were leaving or where you were going."

"Your grandmother knew."

"Yes, well, she took that secret to her grave."

Tru closed her eyes briefly; when she opened them again, her expression was earnest. "I didn't ask her to do that."

Andrew leaned back in his chair as Cil arrived with his plate, utensils, and napkin. She hovered expectantly after setting all of it down. Under the table, Tru nudged his foot. "Thank you," he said at Tru's prompting. When Cil was gone, he remarked to Tru, "That will require getting used to."

"Customs are different here. She merely wanted you to notice her. As you pointed out, this is not the Drake."

He looked at her with concern. "I've upset you. You snipe at me when you're upset."

"I snipe at you because you're infuriating."

He laughed. "It's so very good to see you."

She gave him a cool smile and did not return the sentiment. "You haven't yet explained yourself, Andrew. If I may use Mr. Bridger as evidence, it seems that you went to some trouble to find me. What I still don't know is why."

He shook his head as he picked up his fork. "Not a conversation I care to have here."

Cobb finished his beer. "I can leave."

"No need," Mackey said. He tried the cabbage and spoke around a mouthful of food. "This is very good. Bitter Springs has something to recommend it after all." He swallowed, smiled. "Apart from present company that is."

Since Mackey was looking at Tru, Cobb felt safe in assuming he was not included in that company.

"Where would you like to have that conversation?" Tru asked

"We'll go for a walk. You can show me around Bitter Springs."

"Didn't the station agent's grandsons escort you to the Pennyroyal from the station?"

"They escorted my bags. The ladies rode in the buckboard. I walked with their husbands. Did I miss the tour?"

"A better one than I can give you."

"The boys seemed competent enough fellows, but I prefer you."

"Perhaps you won't after you've spent some time with Rabbit and Finn, but very well, it will be a pleasure to walk with you."

Now that he had secured Tru's promise, Cobb waited for Mackey to fix his attention on him. It happened almost immediately.

"We have business to settle," Mackey said.

"Are we going for a walk?"

Mackey smiled thinly. "I think not. Meet me in my room at"—he checked his pocket watch—"nine."

Cobb nodded. He looked from Mackey to Tru and back to Mackey. "If there's nothing else . . ." He started to rise.

"Actually," Andrew said, "there is."

Cobb put himself back in his chair.

"I'm curious about how you came to be marshal."

"Miss Morrow told you. The mayor appointed me. The position had been vacant for a while. Folks were growing uncomfortable with that."

"So they accepted a stranger?"

Tru interrupted. "Is that skepticism, Andrew? I'm not sure that it's warranted. How much did you know about Mr. Bridger when you hired him?"

"A great deal more than either you or your mayor, I should think. He was employed by Pinkerton."

Tru looked at Cobb. "Were you?"

Cobb's mouth tilted wryly. "I was."

"Well," she said to Andrew, "I'm sure the mayor knows all about that. And my point is really that you have no point. You made the same judgment. I would be willing to wager that Mr. Bridger has spent more time with the citizens of Bitter Springs than he did with you. Everyone here is quite happy with the mayor's choice."

"Do you include yourself?"

Tru hesitated. "Frankly, I was more pleased before I discovered that he was in your employ. I'm not certain what I think about him now."

Cobb was not surprised when Mackey seized the opening she gave him and twisted the knife. "I imagine he lied to you."

"I'm sure he did. Lies of omission at the very least."

"Is it usual for you to have dinner with him?"

"No." She held his gaze and her breath until he turned away. "Neither is it unusual."

Mackey nodded. "I thought so." He continued to eat.

When Cil came to take his plate, he made a point of thanking her and complimenting her dress.

"You'll turn her head," Tru told him after she left.

"Like Mr. Bridger turned yours?"

"Andrew."

He said nothing, merely lifted an eyebrow.

"Please," she said. "Do not make me regret giving you my promise. I was hoping that I could enjoy our walk."

For the first time since becoming marshal, Cobb regretted not strapping on his gun. If Jenny Phillips were here, she would have already stabbed Mackey. He picked up another bar of soft sugar gingerbread and stuffed half of it in his mouth. Across the table, he watched Tru lower her eyes when a movement in the reflective glass distracted Mackey. Her lips actually twitched.

Cobb wasn't sure whether Tru's nerves were unraveling, or whether she was trying not to laugh. It made him want to shove the other half of the gingerbread bar in his mouth even if he choked on it. Her mouth—her lovely mouth—looked even more inviting when laughter edged her lips.

Mackey tore his eyes away from the window and settled them on Cobb. "We're done here. You can do whatever it is you do to see that peace is kept in Bitter Springs."

"Generally I lock up vagrants," said Cobb. "I'd advise you to keep moving on that walk. Don't loiter. There's an ordinance I am duty bound to uphold, and I have the impression you would not like the accommodations."

Cobb pushed back his chair. "Miss Morrow. Always a pleasure." He glanced at Andrew Mackey. "Nine o'clock. I haven't forgotten."

Cobb stopped in the saloon to gauge the mood before he made his rounds. He declined Ted Rush's invitation to join him and the Davis brothers in a game of poker but stayed at their table long enough to answer some of the less pointed questions about Andrew Mackey. Ted had been in the dining room when Mackey arrived and very little had escaped his notice. He hadn't been able to hear the conversation, but that didn't stop Ted from creating one. Cobb corrected a few misapprehensions and let others stand. In any event, it was hard to turn Ted away from an idea once it took root, and if the hardware store owner thought Andrew Mackey looked like the miscreant who robbed a bank up Rawlins way, it just made good sense to have an extra pair of eyes watching their new visitor.

Cobb lingered at the long mahogany bar with a beer while Walt shared his first impressions of Andrew Mackey. Walt would spit in his own soup before he said anything unflattering about a guest at the Pennyroyal, but Cobb noticed he chose his words carefully. He confirmed that Mackey had not been satisfied with the first room he was shown. It was because of Cil's quick thinking—and her desire to please a man who so obviously had deep pockets—that he ended up in the Coltranes' apartments. Ida Mae Sterling was still fit to be tied.

The last thing Cobb did before he left the hotel was to find Mrs. Sterling. She was happy to hand over a spare key to the suite so he could have a look around. "Mind that you take particular account of the books and photographs," she told him. "It's not a lending library, and I don't cotton to the idea of him making free with things that don't belong to him."

That was how he came to be comfortably seated in the Coltranes' residence when Andrew Mackey returned to the Pennyroyal.

Mackey stopped short of crossing the threshold when he saw Cobb. "I see that being the law in Bitter Springs gives you certain privileges." Stepping inside, he dropped his key on a nearby table and reached behind him to close the door. He gave Cobb scant attention while he removed his hat and coat. He carried both into the large bedroom at the rear of the suite.

Cobb was not moved to follow him, but he was aware that Mackey was in no hurry to reappear. He heard water running in the bathing room. The Pennyroyal had amenities not generally found in hotels outside of the big cities. He wondered if Andrew Mackey had an appreciation for that or whether it was simply an expectation. It was hard to believe that it wasn't the latter.

Cobb had no problem with Mackey taking his time. It wasn't yet nine o'clock.

Mackey ignored Cobb when he reentered the sitting room

and went directly to the drinks cabinet. He chose whiskey over brandy or wine and poured two fingers into a tumbler. He did not offer Cobb a drink.

Turning away from the cabinet, Mackey unbuttoned his jacket. He looked around, taking in the conversational arrangement of the sofa and chairs, the bookshelves that lined the alcove where a writing desk was positioned, and the scarred table and unmatched chairs that appeared to be used for dining. His gaze finally settled on Cobb. "What would you call this room?"

Cobb made a point of taking in the room's appointments as if he were seeing them for the first time. In reality the inventory was already logged in his head. "Is it important?"

"Not at all," Mackey said easily. "I was merely curious. It appears to have several functions. For instance, you seem to be sitting in the study."

Cobb had chosen the alcove because when he turned the desk chair it put the window at his back and gave him the widest view of the great room. Not only did he face the door, but also wherever Mackey finally decided to sit, Cobb would have him in his sight.

"I'd hoped I had chosen the place where business is conducted," he said. "And where our business will be concluded."

"Since it's not my desk, I don't suppose it matters where we settle."

"You have my money?"

Mackey nodded but made no move to get it. He sipped his drink instead. "I saw you out earlier this evening. When I was with Miss Morrow. It occurred to me that you might be following us."

Cobb's long legs were stretched in front of him, crossed at the ankles. One boot heel rested on a footstool he had removed from the sitting area. His arms were folded across his chest. His posture was not without purpose. He intended that Mackey should see that he was easy in this setting, as easy as he had been in the far grander surroundings of Mackey's own study. The same could not be said for Andrew Mackey III.

Tru had said Mackey was not a snob, but Cobb had his doubts. "I was making my rounds," said Cobb.

"You do that every night?"

"I do. The mayor expects it."

"So when I saw you behind us . . ." He let his voice trail away, took another sip of whiskey.

"You saw me doing my job."

Mackey nodded slowly. He remained at his post beside the drinks cabinet. "About that job. I want you to resign."

Cobb had expected that. "And . . . ?"

"And leave Bitter Springs."

Cobb tilted his head to one side as though in serious contemplation. He eventually blew out a short breath, grunting softly at the back of his throat.

"I'll pay you."

"You would have to. I like Bitter Springs."

"I think you like Miss Morrow."

"You mean *Gertie*?"

Mackey ignored that. "Your continued presence here is a complication that I don't need. Go back to Chicago, Mr. Bridger. I'm sure you will have no difficulty finding work there."

"I have work here." This time he did open his jacket and reveal the star pinned to his vest. "Satisfying work."

Mackey's expression was skeptical. "Really? Keep in mind that I just had the tour. No vagrants. No disturbances of any kind."

"Thank you."

"I wasn't compli—" He stopped when he realized Cobb had deliberately chosen to misunderstand. "How much?"

Cobb named a figure.

"That's what I owe you. What will it take for you to leave town?"

"I only want what's owed me. Even you aren't rich enough for the other." Before Mackey tried to convince him otherwise, Cobb decided it was time to take the offensive. "Did you ask Miss Morrow about your stolen property?"

"You overstep, Mr. Bridger. What has become of your

reputation for not asking questions? My conversation with Miss Morrow is nothing I care to discuss with you."

"That's fair." He pushed the stool aside and set his feet on the floor. Leaning forward, he unfolded his arms. He pressed his hands together and made a steeple with his fingers. "She's not a thief."

"I wasn't looking for your opinion."

"I know. That's why I'm not going to ask you to pay for it. I thought you should consider the possibility that you're mistaken about her."

Mackey carried his drink to the sofa. He did not sit but rather settled his hip on one of the wide arms. "Is that why you're still here, Mr. Bridger? You think you know Miss Morrow well enough to draw conclusions about her guilt or innocence? She lived in my grandmother's home, virtually in the shadow of my grandmother's bed, for two years. I saw her with some regularity; I spoke to her on numerous occasions. I think I know her capabilities far better than you."

Cobb thought about the sketch he kept in the pocket inside his vest. Andrew Mackey had not been able to describe the shape of her eyes. He hadn't mentioned the asymmetrical dimple. It seemed unlikely that he had ever noticed the faint indentation in her chin. For all that Mackey had attended to Tru this evening, Cobb could not dismiss the impression that the man's interest was serious but not sincere.

"Who is Franklin?" Cobb asked. The question, coming as it did without warning, had the desired effect. Although his face gave nothing away, Mackey's hand tightened perceptibly around his glass. Cobb clarified his question so there could be no mistaking his meaning. "Franklin Mackey."

"More questions, Mr. Bridger?"

"Humor me."

Mackey shrugged. "My cousin. I have to believe you already know that. Why ask?"

"Who is he to Miss Morrow?"

"Still my cousin. A great-nephew to my grandmother. I'm unaware that he is anyone to Miss Morrow. Did she say something that would make you believe differently?"

"No. On the way to her telling me how she came to be in Bitter Springs, she shared a little about being Mrs. Mackey's companion. She mentioned you, of course, and other members of the family. The greats, she called you."

"Yes. She would." He did not pretend that it did not annoy him. "It is how my grandmother referred to us." He pinched the bridge of his nose, rubbed it. "What did she say about Frank?"

"Nothing," said Cobb. "No, wait. She said he was young." He did not add Tru's pause or her inflection, the two things that gave some deeper meaning to the description. It was a meaning he still did not understand.

"Yes," said Mackey. "Frank's young. Recently graduated from Princeton."

"Your alma mater."

"Yes. She told you that?"

Cobb shook his head. "I learned something about you before I agreed to work for you."

Mackey nodded. "Of course you did." He pushed away from the arm of the sofa and stood. Returning to the drinks cabinet, he finished his whiskey and set down the empty tumbler. He reached inside his jacket and removed a folded bank draft. He held it out but not far.

"Your money," he said. "I noticed there is a bank here."

"The Cattlemen's Trust."

"Yes. I assume they'll accept this draft drawn on my account in Chicago."

"It shouldn't be a problem."

"Then as soon as you take this, we're settled."

"We're done," said Cobb, coming to his feet. "I don't know if we're settled." He went forward, took the check, and kept going.

Tru was lying in bed on her back, holding a cold compress to her eyes, when she heard the unmistakable sound of the kitchen door rattling. She'd made a point of using her keys to lock both doors. It had to be Cobb, she thought. Andrew would have come to the front entrance.

Putting aside the compress, she got out of bed, grabbed her robe and belted it on the way to the bedroom at the rear of the house. The window looking out on her backyard did not open easily, but anger gave her incentive and strength.

She braced her arms on the sill and poked her head out. The porch's small peaked roof prevented her from being able to see the trespasser. "Go away!"

Cobb backed off the porch and kept backing up until he had a view of the window. He tipped back his hat and squinted. A break in the clouds briefly revealed the moon, and he could see Tru leaning so far out of the window that it was easy to imagine her taking a tumble.

"You're going to break your neck."

"I'm going to break yours."

"Let me in. Your door's locked."

"I know. I locked it. Go away."

The only movement he made was to rise and fall on the balls of his feet. "I think the Stillwells are sleeping."

"That's what people do at night."

"I don't. Apparently neither do you."

"Don't you have vagrants to round up?"

"All accounted for." Cobb pointed to the Stillwell home. "I think someone's stirring. I see lamplight that wasn't there before." He dropped his hand back to his side but kept watching the Stillwell residence. "The light is getting brighter. It could be that we've attracted the attention of your neighbors."

Tru did not believe him. She was on the point of telling him so when she heard Evelyn Stillwell call out from an upstairs window.

"Is that you, Marshal?"

"It is, Mrs. Stillwell."

"Land sake's, son. What you are doing out there?"

"Just finishing my rounds. I thought I saw someone creeping back this way."

"The Collins boys, I bet. They cut between Miss Morrow's

and this place regular like. Probably sneaked out of the house on some kind of dare. They are a trial to Heather and Jefferson that way, but they don't mean any harm. I'd look for them at the cemetery if I were you. They've been known to go there. I bet if you scare them, that would slow them down for a while."

"That's a good thought, Mrs. Stillwell. Thank you."

Holding out her lamp, Evelyn pushed herself forward and turned her head. "Evening, Tru. I guess you heard the boys same as I did."

"I'm not sure it was Rabbit and Finn," she said. "But I did hear something."

Evelyn nodded. "Good to know the town's got someone looking out for us."

Tru sighed, and although Mrs. Stillwell could not see her clearly, she forced a smile just the same. "It certainly is. Goodnight, Evelyn."

"'Night, Tru."

Cobb watched both of them duck back into their homes like turtles retreating into their shells. He retreated himself, taking a meandering route around the nearby homes before he circled back to Tru's. This time the door was open.

The first thing he looked for when he walked in was the shotgun. It was in the rack. He shed his coat and hat and stepped into the kitchen. Tru had left a lamp for him. He picked it up, peeked in the dining room, and then went to the parlor. The stove was still warm but the light came from embers. He saw that she had drawn the curtains. She wasn't sitting in her favorite chair. He picked up the book she had been reading. *Triumphant Democracy* by Andrew Carnegie. No wonder she left it on the table.

Cobb climbed the stairs. Her bedroom door was open, but he stood just outside in the hallway and knocked. Tru was sitting in a chair by the fireplace. She waved him inside. He set the lamp down. That was when he saw the compress lying in her lap.

"Headache?" he asked.

Not looking away from the fire, she nodded.

There was no twin for the chair she was sitting in, but there was a chair at the writing desk and a padded stool at the vanity with a ruffled skirt. He chose the chair, dragged it by its back legs to the fireplace, and spun it around so he could sit with his forearms resting on the curved back. He had a clearer view of her face although she did her best to keep it averted. She had scrubbed it clean, probably for his benefit, but there was still evidence to suggest she had been crying.

Even as he thought it, she flicked a tear away from the corner of her eye. Cobb reached in his pocket and held out a handkerchief. She took it without making him insist on it.

"Thank you. I left mine on the nightstand."

He glanced in that direction. It looked as if she'd left not just one, but several. "*Triumphant Democracy*?" he asked. The question did what he meant it to do. It provoked her to turn her head and fully face him. "Is the title misleading? It doesn't end well?"

She sniffed, gave him a watery smile. "You saw the book. I've barely started it. Jim is insisting I read it. Jenny won't. She says she'd rather impale herself on a knitting needle."

That made him smile as well. "I thought about Jenny at dinner tonight. It occurred to me that she would not have tolerated Andrew Mackey's nonsense."

"You think I did?"

"I think you did better than hold your own. You bested him. It was my tolerance I was referring to. I gave him too much rope."

She shook her head. "No. I don't think you did. You were right not to interfere. He is . . ." She looked back at the fire.

"Jealous?"

She shrugged.

"Possessive?"

"A dog in the manger," she said quietly. "I was thinking more of a dog in the manger."

His faint smile revealed his appreciation for another moral fable. "I followed you this evening."

"I know. Andrew saw you."

"I wanted him to. Did he confront you about the brooch?"

"He never mentioned it."

"Something else then?"

Her nod was barely perceptible. "Something else."

Cobb did not press. "He paid me tonight. He also told me to leave."

"I thought he might. He thinks you overstepped."

"Yes, he made that clear."

"Are you going?"

"No."

"Even if I asked you to?"

"No, not even then." He waited to see if she would argue, but her confrontation at the window earlier seemed to have left her drained. He regretted that. "Why were you crying?"

Tru had no defenses. She turned over her hands in a helpless gesture. "Dinner was exhausting."

"And your walk?"

"Eggshells all the way."

"I see."

She spared him a glance. "I'm not happy with you either."

"That goes without saying."

"You gulled me from the beginning. I've been thinking about our meeting on the street. You planned that."

"I did."

His easy admission took some of the wind out of her sails. "Dinner that first night?"

"I watched for you from the window in my hotel room."

She turned in her chair and drew her feet under her. "Why did you really come to Bitter Springs? And don't tell me it was because Andrew wanted you to make sure I stayed here. That doesn't require your skills. You could have told him to find someone else and saved yourself the trouble of boarding a train."

"I wanted to meet the woman who makes Andrew Mackey afraid."

Tru blinked. "That was Charlotte."

"I'm sure he feared her. But I wasn't speaking in the past tense. He's afraid of you. He's afraid of you *now*, and I still want to know why."

Tru stared at him. "You're wrong."

"I don't think so."

"You are. Do you know what he asked me tonight?"

Tears unexpectedly welled in Tru's eyes. The handkerchief remained balled in her fist.

"Tru?" He watched powerlessly as her tears spilled past the dam of her lashes. It was then that the answer came to him, and he could do nothing to stop her from saying it aloud.

"He asked me to marry him."

Chapter Ten

Tru swiped at her tears, not with the handkerchief but with her fingertips. She sniffed and turned her chin into her shoulder. It hardly mattered that she was avoiding Cobb's concerned study. She felt his pale blue gaze as if it were a physical touch.

She stared at the flames, unaware that her tears captured the firelight as they slipped over her cheeks. "He's been engaged three times," she whispered. "Did you know that?"

"I did."

"That means three women said yes to him before they said no."

Cobb did not care about what three other women said. He cared about *this* woman. He cared about this woman's answer. He waited her out. Her words, like her tears, spilled slowly over the dam.

"His fiancées ended the engagements. Charlotte told me that. She suspected he provoked them to it."

"Provoked them? How?"

Tru closed her eyes and this time pressed the balled-up handkerchief to each one of them in turn. "I don't know," she said, risking a glance in his direction. He wasn't watching her at all now, but staring past her chair to the window, perhaps even looking beyond it as she sometimes did, looking all the way to the Pennyroyal. "She never said more. I didn't ask."

Tru kept her legs curled to one side, but she sat up straighter. There was no hitch in the next breath she took. "I told him I needed to think about it." That brought Cobb's eyes back to hers. She saw no curiosity, no dread. He merely looked upon her without expression, his features shuttered by the remoteness of his regard. For reasons she did not properly understand, her face crumpled and she began to weep.

Standing, Cobb swung his chair out of the way and stepped into the breach. He tossed the compress in Tru's lap aside before he bent and scooped her up. Far from resisting his effort, she helped him by slipping her arms around his shoulders and burying her damp face against his neck. He carried her to the bed, set her down on the edge, and pried the handkerchief out of her bloodless fingers. He soaked it in the basin of water on the washstand, wrung it out, and used it to catch her tears at first and then finally to erase them.

"Like velvet," she murmured.

"Hmm?"

"Something my mother used to say. When I didn't want my face washed, she'd say she would wash it like velvet. I'd forgotten that until now." A breath shuddered through her, but no tears followed in its wake. "Thank you."

Uncomfortable, Cobb nodded shortly.

Tru's fingers brushed the back of his hand. "You're welcome."

He looked down at his hand then at her. A small furrow appeared between his eyebrows.

One corner of Tru's mouth lifted. She mocked him lightly with that smile. "That's what you say when someone thanks you."

"I'll try to remember that." He laid the handkerchief on the nightstand and looked her over. She was fighting sleep or at least fighting being alone. There was only one way to tell the difference. "I should go," he said. He meant to move, but his brain did not relay the message to his feet. He stood exactly where he was.

"You should," she said. She found his hand again and this time her fingers curled around his. "But don't." She raised her face. Her eyelids felt too heavy to raise her lashes higher than half-staff. She regarded him from under them. "Please don't."

He did not argue with her or with himself. "All right." Withdrawing his hand, he hunkered in front of Tru and loosened the belt of her robe. He watched her ease the robe over her shoulders while he removed her slippers. He rose and helped her to her feet, keeping her steady long enough to toss the robe to the foot of the bed and lift the covers. She slipped into bed on her own and turned on her back. When she started to move toward the center, he put a hand on her shoulder to stop her.

"What are you doing?"

Tru glanced at his hand then at him. "I sleep on this side now."

Cobb nodded, removed his hand. "I'll pull a chair over."

Her smile was sleepy, content. She turned on her side, facing him, but she did not close her eyes. "Thank you."

A brief hesitation, then, "You're welcome."

Tru's smile deepened. She burrowed under the covers and pressed her shoulder into the pillow.

Cobb pushed the chair that she had been sitting in closer to the bed, judging the distance to be just right when he could stretch out his legs and rest his heels on the bed frame.

"You won't leave?" asked Tru.

"No."

"There's a book in the nightstand drawer." She pressed her fist against her mouth to cover a yawn.

Cobb realized that she was fighting sleep *and* being alone, not one or the other. He reached for the drawer, opened it, and felt around for the book. He knew by the size, thickness, and feel of the paper cover that it was a dime novel. "Nat Church?" he asked before he pulled it out.

"No. Felicity Ravenwood. She has romantic adventures and wears extraordinary hats."

Cobb examined the cover and saw proof of both those things. Felicity seemed to be in danger of losing her poise and her hat to a dark-haired villain. At least Cobb assumed the man bending Felicity over his arm was the villain, otherwise the dagger she was clutching made no sense.

He read aloud. *"Felicity Ravenwood and the Wolf in Sheep's Clothing."* Cobb cocked an eyebrow at Tru and appreciated that she had the grace to blush. "No, thank you," he said, dropping the novel back into the drawer and closing it. "I've read the original."

She nodded sleepily, eyes drooping, and then she was still.

Tru had no idea of the time when she woke and no proper sense of how long she had been sleeping. Except for the residual glow of spent logs in the fireplace, her bedroom was almost entirely in shadow. The lamp on her nightstand had been extinguished. So had the one that Cobb carried into the room.

Cobb was still sitting at her bedside. He was asleep now, his head lolled slightly forward so that it did not have the support of either of the chair's wings. She could tell that his legs were still elevated because of the way the blanket covering him was draped. She wondered at what point he had stopped feeding the fire and found a blanket instead.

She inched closer to where he was sitting, her attention caught by the object in his lap. It was difficult to make out at first, partially covered as it was by a fold in the blanket, but she recognized it before she teetered on the edge of the mattress. She resisted laughing out loud but did nothing to suppress her amused grin.

Cobb Bridger had succumbed to Felicity Ravenwood's siren call.

She did not try to feign sleep when he stirred. If he woke, she wanted him to know that she was here, waiting for him, and if he slept on, it merely delayed what was inevitable.

It was an odd notion, inevitable. It might involve a flicker lasting no longer than a single beat of a hummingbird's wing, or it might span all the heartbeats in one's lifetime. There was anxiety in anticipation of it and comfort in its certainty.

Without meaning to, she fell asleep again, this time with inevitably on her mind.

Tru was warm, deliciously so. She backed into the heat, drawing her knees up and settling her bottom against the cradle of the stove. It did not occur to her just then that a stove had no cradle.

"Tru." Cobb laid his hand on her shoulder, shook her lightly. He whispered, "Move over." She didn't. In fact, she snuggled deeper, pressing her bottom hard against his groin. He had nowhere to go that would not have him rolling out of bed. "You told me you slept on the other side." Or at least closer to the middle, he thought. He was sure she had been at least as far as the middle when he gave up the chair and joined her.

His compromise to her comfort and his sanity was to stay on top of her quilts and draw his blanket over him. He didn't know how he ended up under the covers, but he suspected it happened the same way she ended up pushed tight against him. *Naturally.*

Except for his boots, he was still fully clothed. There was a mercy. Not that she wouldn't be able to feel the press of his cock on her backside if she woke. It was what had roused him from a deep sleep. He ached to rub it against her. If not that, then to take it in hand.

He did neither. She ground the cleft of her bottom against his groin. Cobb closed his eyes, groaned.

"Tru." This time he forced her name from between clenched teeth. The sound of it was harsh, guttural. When it failed to move her, Cobb slid his hands between their bodies and laid his palms flat on her back. He pushed. She slid in the direction he wanted her to, but he almost landed on the floor. He flailed and found an anchor in the folds of her nightgown. He bunched the fabric in his fist and held on. She fell onto her back, trapping his hand, but her weight was enough to spare him the ignominy of falling out of bed. He rolled toward her, not at all surprised to find her awake and staring at him so widely that he could make out the whites of her eyes.

"So help me God, Tru," he whispered. "You can't—"

She laid two fingers against his lips, quieting him. She waited to see what he would do, and when he did nothing, she removed her hand from his mouth and slid it behind his neck. She pulled him down and welcomed him back.

Inevitable.

Tru feasted on his mouth. The need to have him, to touch and then to delight in the touching, was what urged her on. Her tongue speared his mouth. She ran the tip of it along the ridge of his teeth. She teased the underside of his upper lip and repeated the sweep of her tongue along the bottom one. There was parry and thrust in this kiss. Maneuvering and play and challenge.

She arched her spine. His hand slipped from under her back. He found her wrist and pinned it against the mattress at the level of her shoulder. She gave him the other one when he groped for it. And the kiss went on.

She stretched under him, rubbing, pushing, testing his will. She never believed for one moment that he was restraining her. He was restraining himself. She admired his effort, and then she renewed hers.

Turning her head, she changed the slant of the kiss. She caught the corner of his mouth, found his jaw. Her lips moved to his neck, and she sipped his skin. That kiss would leave a mark. She knew because he had left his mark on her.

Tru raised one knee. She slid the sole of her bare foot against his calf. She wanted to feel his flesh under her toes. Twisting slightly, she pressed her hip against his groin and wrested her hand from his as he groaned. Her fingers scrabbled with the tail of his shirt, pulling it free of his trousers. Still one handed, she tore at his belt while his mouth hovered over her lips. Tru lifted her head. It required nothing more than the whisper of her mouth against his to seal the kiss.

He loosed her other wrist. She opened his shirt and then unfastened his underwear. Her hands slipped inside the flannel drawers. His skin was warm against her fingertips. She pressed them lightly against his abdomen. He sucked in a breath, taking hers.

She found another button and opened it. One hand remained resting against his flat belly. The other circled his penis. Here the heat of him was like a furnace. Engorged with blood, heavy with desire, his cock jumped and twitched in her palm like a living thing. She tightened her grip, not with any need to hold him back but because she wanted to feel his pulse beat hard against the heart of her palm.

"For the love of God," he said, tearing his mouth away from her. His hips jerked. Tru's fingers uncurled in a spasm that matched his. At the end of it she was cupping his balls. Hardly daring to breathe, Cobb held himself very still, afraid that any movement would end this sweet torture. When her fingernails grazed his sac, he felt pleasure so intense that it edged dangerously close to pain.

Under the covers, he shoved the hem of Tru's nightgown to her thighs and moved between her legs. Just as she had before, she helped him. He did not offer to see to her comfort his time. The pillows remained strewn around the bed.

Her breath caught when he pushed into her. It was the same, this feeling of him filling her, pressing against her both hard and intimately, and yet there was a subtle difference that captured her imagination and made her think she had not known all that was possible from this act.

He moved with more care, with measured strokes, and the rhythm that she had not understood before pulsed under her skin so fiercely that ignoring it was not possible. There were inklings of pleasure. Between her thighs, she felt herself contracting around him, using her body like a fist to keep him close. She raised her knees, lifted, and circled his hips. Her heels pressed against his thighs.

She moved in concert with him. Pleasure skimmed her skin. Her breasts swelled, and when her nipples scraped against the fabric of her nightgown, they pebbled. She lifted her hand, grazed her breast with the flat of it. Pleasure made her drive her hips into him.

Cobb pushed back. He knew what she was feeling now, knew that she was close. He knocked aside her hand and found the tip of her tender breast with his mouth. He laved the pink tip with this tongue until he heard her whimper. Her fingers knotted in his hair. The ache that impelled him to go on was matched by hers.

She said something that she only half understood when her body began to shudder. She clutched him as his hips quickened. She felt his breath on her neck, his fingers dancing over her breast. Pleasure no longer skipped across her skin. It dove deep and raised a flush across her chest that crept up her neck to her cheeks. She was warm, replete.

Moments later, so was he.

Cobb was aware of his weight pressing her down, but when he began to move, her hands tightened at his back.

"Not yet," she whispered. "I don't want you to go."

He remembered telling her once that she would not always get her way, but proving it to hcr now was tantamount to cutting off his nose to spite his face. He didn't move.

Tru felt his heartbeat slowing. She realized hers was finally doing the same. "That was very . . . nice."

Cobb wanted to believe she was not damning him with faint praise. He needed to goad her a little to be sure. "Nice?"

Tru pointed to her temple. "Putty. That's your fault. I don't have anothcr word." Shc hesitated. "Do you?"

"Satisfying."

"It was, wasn't it? I understood the mechanics, but there were nuances that I—"

"Mechanics?"

"Yes. The way things work."

"I know what mechanics are. I just never thought about their application here."

"That's because you grew up on a farm. I never had a pet." She touched his shoulder. "I think I'm ready for you to move."

"Thank God. I couldn't breathe." Cobb eased away from her and sat up. He stripped out of his trousers and shirt and laid both at the foot of the bed before he buttoned up his flannel. Behind him, he felt Tru squirming under the covers to right her nightclothes. He did not join her immediately. "Do you want me to lay more wood on the fire?"

"No." She turned on her side and reached for Cobb. Placing her hand against his back, she stroked him. His muscles were still taut, or perhaps it was only her touch that made them that way. "You want to say something," she said. "I can tell. I'm not going to tell you to leave. You can say anything."

Cobb thought she probably believed that. He didn't know if he did. "You understand that what happened tonight was different than the last time we were together."

"Oh, I understand that."

He heard soft laughter edging her answer. Cobb drew up one leg as he turned sideways on the bed. Her hand fell away, and he missed it immediately. His body blocked what remained of the firelight, but he could make out the shape of her even if he couldn't see her clearly. It didn't matter much about the light anyway. He had memorized her face a long time ago.

"I wasn't referring to the . . . *nuances*," he said. "We can discuss them later. At great length, if you like. I need to know that you're clear about the mechanics."

Tru felt her face grow warm. She was glad for the dark. "Didn't I prove that?"

"You did."

"Then?"

"*My* mechanics."

"Oh. You're talking about ejaculating."

Cobb looked at her in surprise even though she couldn't appreciate it. He cleared this throat. "I was talking about mechanics, but if you—"

"I never had a pet," she repeated. "But I am twenty-six years old, and I *do* read. You should also know that Mrs. Winston's Academy was not a nunnery. There were *medical* journals."

He took care not to choke. He coughed instead and swallowed the laugh that lodged in his throat. "I see."

"I'm not sure you do," she said.

Cobb could only imagine the prim set of her mouth. He didn't try to resist it. Leaning over, he kissed her.

Bemused, she asked, "Why did you do that?"

"Not doing it was harder." He found her hand and threaded his fingers between hers. "You understand there might be consequences. A child. I didn't withdraw this time."

Tru understood. What she hadn't done was think about it. There was part of her that wished he hadn't either. She took a deep breath and let it out slowly. "Why didn't you?"

"Nuances," he said.

She smiled faintly, squeezed his fingers. "Yes. That would explain it." After a few moments, she slipped her hand out of his and raised the covers.

Without a word, he slid under as she scooted back to make room for him. He turned on his side and propped his head on an elbow. Tru was plumping a pillow under her head. He waited for her to settle before he found her plait and began to unwind her golden rope of hair.

"What are you doing?" she asked.

"Amusing myself."

Her tone was dry as dust. "Oh, well, that's all right then."

Cobb chuckled. He did not point out that she hadn't tried to stop him. Finger-combing as he went, he separated the heavy braid until most of it lay in waves over her right shoulder. He lightly ran his palm across the ripples. "I like your hair like this. Why don't you wear it down?"

"Besides being immodest, impractical, and out of fashion?"

He grinned. "Yes, besides all that."

"It tries to smother me in my sleep."

"Really?" Cobb slipped his hand under the waves and lifted them. Her hair spilled between his fingers like a cascade of springwater.

"Yes. If it's not trapped uncomfortably under my shoulder, it's creeping across my face and neck like ivy. You'll see. If I don't braid it again, it will come after you."

"I had no idea." Undeterred, he continued to sift through

the silken threads. "Tell me about Mackey's proposal." Cobb felt the tug on Tru's hair as she stiffened. "Did you think I was never going to ask you?"

"I thought it would be later."

"Later than . . . ?"

"Later than now. Later than later."

"So . . . never."

She nodded, whispered, "I suppose so. What do you want to know?"

"Why you didn't say yes."

Tru blinked, surprised that he would begin there. She reminded him, "I didn't say no either."

"You're getting ahead me. That was going to be my next question."

Tru said nothing for a time. She concentrated on the comforting play of his fingers in her hair. He would wait her out; she knew that about him now. Cobb Bridger was a man of almost infinite patience. Her small sigh was a prelude to her confession.

"It's been some time since I imagined myself as anyone's wife," she said. "I'm not sure if you realize that Andrew Mackey and I have an acquaintance of long standing."

Cobb hadn't, not until this moment. "Because of the church," he said.

"That's right. The Mackeys occupied the same four pews every Sunday. Before the fire burned the church, I used to watch Andrew from the choir loft. I was five or six, I suppose. He would have been about ten. He always sat at attention between his parents. His cousins were not so well behaved, but he was a little soldier. His hair was a helmet of copper back then, more like the color that his beard and mustache are now. Sometimes a shaft of sunlight would spear the stained glass and make his hair as bright as a flame. I especially liked it when that happened. I thought he was the most beautiful boy I had ever seen."

Cobb loosely wrapped a lock of Tru's hair in a spiral around his finger. He was tempted to give it a tug. He forced himself to listen to what he had asked to hear.

"I don't recall the precise moment that I decided I would marry him," said Tru, "but I harbored that notion for all the years I was away at the Academy. I saw him occasionally during that time, usually at a holiday. Once he accompanied his grandmother when she came calling. I allowed myself to be so flattered by his visit, I don't think I said a word to him." She smiled crookedly. "Much later I learned that his father sent him with Aunt Charlotte as a punishment, not a privilege. Naturally, none of that had anything to do with me."

Tru turned her head a little in Cobb's direction. She wished she had asked him to open the curtains. The silver-blue cast of moonlight would have been enough to illuminate his features. "Andrew was away at Princeton by the time I returned home for good. I saw him at the funeral services for his father, then his mother, and then not again until he graduated. He announced his engagement to Miss Beatrice Pennington shortly after his grandmother officially appointed him to a position in the family business. I judged that engagement not to be an insurmountable impediment."

Now Cobb did interrupt her. "You tried to end it?"

Taking umbrage, Tru said, "Of course not."

Cobb bent his finger, pulling on the spiral of hair.

"Oh, very well," she said. "I may have prayed about it once. Twice. No more than three times."

"I see." He was careful to keep all trace of amusement out of his voice. "You must have thought those prayers were answered."

"The first time, yes, but then that engagement was followed by one to Edith Cumberland. I decided it was left to me to accept it so I prayed about that."

"And did you accept it?"

"Yes."

"What about when Edith broke it off?"

"I felt sorry for Andrew. That was all. I never saw it as an opportunity. That's how I knew I'd made peace with my childhood infatuation. When Julia Durance's parents announced their daughter's engagement to Andrew Mackey III, I hoped for a better ending for him, nothing more than that. Perhaps

I should have prayed about it, but by then he wasn't often in my thoughts. I had finished my education at the Normal School and was preparing to be a teacher. I was submitting applications all over the city and assisting my father in the parish just as my mother would have done. That was more than enough to occupy me.

"When Andrew's last engagement ended, my father was already ill. I barely noticed that he was free again. I don't know that I gave Andrew Mackey another thought until his grandmother approached me about becoming her companion after my father died. She wasn't bedridden yet—that came later—but she had already received her first doctor's opinion. I hesitated, though not because of Andrew. I simply wasn't sure that it was the right thing to do. It felt something like charity, and I had already accepted so much of that from her."

Cobb unwound one curl to begin another. "If I've learned anything from you about Charlotte Mackey, it's that she rolled right over your hesitation."

"I'm not sure that she even noticed it. It was within a week of her making the offer that I agreed to it. I never thought that her family would greet my presence with so much suspicion. None of them lived with her, but they visited regularly."

"Vultures," said Cobb.

"She thought so. It didn't take me long to understand that one of my purposes there was to scare them away. I told you at dinner that when they couldn't remove me, they applied to me for help. Every one of them wanted something from her."

"You also said Andrew was the least of them."

"He was. What he asked for seemed reasonable. He was thinking about the future of the Mackey holdings. The rest of them wanted me to fill Aunt Charlotte's head with nonsense about one or another of them. She had no patience with their sniping, so they thought it would be better if I carried tales."

"And the point of all that?"

Tru shrugged. "Her will, I imagine. I always supposed they were trying to position themselves for a more favorable mention in her will."

"Even Frank?" Cobb felt rather than heard Tru's sharp intake of air. She recovered quickly just as he expected she would.

"Why are you asking about him?"

"Wasn't he the youngest of the greats? I thought that maybe he hadn't had enough time to make an impression one way or another. That could have worked to his advantage."

"Perhaps it could have, but he was taking no chances."

"What did he want from you, Tru?"

"What I told you. Aunt Charlotte's ear."

Cobb wished he could see the direction she was casting her eyes or whether she had drawn in her lower lip. The lack of inflection in her voice led him to believe she was being cautious with her words. "What did he want you to tell her about the others?"

Tru was a long time in replying. "Hurtful things," she said at last. "Hurtful, vicious things."

He believed her. "So he's really just a cruel little boy poking sticks at things to see what will happen."

"I don't know. I always thought he had a good idea what the outcome would be."

Cobb thought she was probably right. "So what did he do?"

"Do?"

"When you refused to take his tales back to Mrs. Mackey."

"What makes you think he did anything?"

"Because he's a cruel little boy. A leopard doesn't change his spots." He paused. "Is that Aesop?" His question had the desired effect. He heard Tru snicker.

"That's the Bible," she said. "The Old Testament, from the Book of Jeremiah. 'Can the Ethiopian change his skin or the leopard its spots?'"

Cobb finished for her. "'Neither can you do good who are accustomed to doing evil.' I remember now. And that's my point. What evil did he do?"

Tru's sigh was as troubled as it was heartfelt. "He told them all that I seduced him."

"Charlotte, too?"

"No. He was cleverer than that, or he thought he was. An accusation like that required a more formal address. His uncle Paul took up the matter with Charlotte."

"And?"

"And then she sent for me and made him repeat the accusation. She did not ask me if it were true. She told Paul that she would take care of it and ordered him out. When he was gone she wanted to know if Franklin hurt me."

"What did you tell her?"

"I told her no."

"Was that the truth?"

Tru hesitated. "Mostly," she said finally. "She wanted to believe me, although it was soon after that she decided to move my room next to hers. She said it was for her convenience, and this time I wanted to believe her."

"Did Franklin rape you?"

"No. I fought; eventually I was able to cry out. Andrew was in the house that night, in the hallway. He heard and interrupted."

"So he saved you."

She understood why Cobb would think that. "In a manner of speaking," she said. "What he saw when he came in did not convince him I was the injured party. He believed what Franklin told him."

"Ah," Cobb said quietly. "And you didn't try to defend yourself."

"I judged that to be a waste of breath. He had his own reasons for wanting to believe Franklin. He still wanted to remove me from his grandmother's side. He always thought I exerted influence over her."

Cobb's eyes narrowed. "There's something else. What is it?"

"He thought the best way to accomplish that would be to make me his mistress."

"Jesus."

Tru was silent.

"Jesus," he said again. He untangled his fingers from her hair and pushed himself up into a sitting position, tailor fashion. He set his elbows on his knees, his head in his hands, and closed his eyes. He felt Tru's hand at his back and realized that she was comforting *him*.

"What the hell does he want from you, Tru?"

"Marriage, he says."

He turned his head to look at her. "Do you believe him?"

"He seemed sincere."

"Did you remind him about his previous offer?"

"No. He brought it up himself. He said he regretted it, and he apologized. He does that very well. Apologize, I mean."

"Did you accept it?"

"I didn't make any reply at all. I decided to allow him to interpret my silence for himself." She added dryly, "He knows how to do that."

Cobb's own smile was wry. "You do very well on your own."

"It sounds to me as if you had some doubts."

"I had hopes," he said. "But you don't need me."

"Do you want to hear that you're wrong?"

"Only if it's true."

She sat up and inched closer. She slipped two fingers under his chin to keep his head tilted toward her. "*I'm* Tru," she whispered. And then she kissed him.

He supposed that she did need him, if not in one manner, then another. He could accept that for now, even enjoy it. Cobb pressed her back to the mattress and pulled the covers across them. He took over the kiss, made it his, and liked her more for giving him that.

He cradled her head in his hands. His fingers threaded deeply in her hair. He bent and nudged her lips apart, tasting the upper one first and then sipping on the lower one. He found the sensitive cord in her neck, the hollow below her ear, and bedeviled both places with the rough edge of his tongue until she squirmed and laughed and finally moaned.

He used his teeth to tug on the ribbon that closed her nightgown. She called him a fool and tried to bat him away, but then his teeth found her nipple and gave it a tug. She remembered his name was Cobb, and she said it on a breathy exhalation that made him want to bury himself in her.

He moved over her, exploring the outward curve of her shoulder and the inward one at her waist. He laid his hand on her abdomen and made a pass across her navel with his thumb. Her skin twitched and her breathing quickened. His lips eventually replaced his hand and then went lower. He pushed her knees up, tenting the blankets, and set his mouth between her thighs.

She said his name again but not in a way that was meant to discourage him. She was wet and warm and willing, and all of the blood in his head rushed to his cock. He felt her hand fisting in his hair. Her hips lifted. His tongue curled, lapped. One of her heels pressed hard against his back and she arched her spine. She drew her breath in increments, each one pitched slightly higher than the last.

And when the orgasm overwhelmed her, it was not his name that crossed the minister's daughter's lips, but God's.

He rose over her and eased himself inside her. It was better that it was dark. She couldn't see his smug smile. He moved slowly, carefully, aware that she might be tender and certain that she would not admit it. He held back as long as he could, but she did not make it easy for him. She made it extraordinary, but not easy.

When he came, he rocked them both hard enough to bang the headboard against the wall. He and the bed shuddered.

Blanketed by darkness, it was Tru's turn to smile smugly.

Tru was pouring fresh water into the basin on the washstand when Cobb woke. She had laid a small fire and lighted an oil lamp. For once, he did not have to strain his eyes to see her. He punched his pillow a few times to reshape it until his head was resting at a comfortable angle. That was when she glanced his way.

"You're awake."

"Mm. Sun up?"

In answer, Tru sidled over to the window and parted the curtains a few inches. She gave him enough time to observe the pale blue-gray light pressing against the glass before letting them fall into place.

Cobb groaned softly. He did not have much time if he was going to slip away unnoticed. Walt was certain to have observed that he never returned to the Pennyroyal. Cobb did not expect that Walt would remark on it, but that didn't mean Cobb could arrive unprepared to explain.

Aware of Cobb's regard, Tru scrubbed her face and then used the cover of her nightgown to modestly perform the rest of her ablutions. She was wrestling with her damp nightgown when she heard him chuckle. Shooting him a sidelong look, Tru pushed an arm back through its sleeve. She shook out her hand, stretched her fingers.

"Something amusing?"

"Your contortions. Go on."

"I'm done."

"Behind your ears?"

"Done."

"The back of your neck?"

"Uh-huh."

"What about between your . . ."

"Toes?"

"Yes, toes."

"Done." Tru swept her robe over her shoulders as she approached the bed. Bending, she kissed him. He made it tempting to linger. "I'm going to make coffee," she said. "It will be in the kitchen if you want it." She danced away from the bed when Cobb made a grab for her. Waggling her finger at him, she backed out of the room.

Tru thought Cobb looked remarkably well rested when he joined her at the kitchen table. It seemed unfair that he showed no signs that he had passed a night with very little sleep while she would require another compress for her swollen eyelids. Sighing, she pushed a mug of black coffee toward him.

"I have some cinnamon rolls that Jenny made. Would you like one?"

"No. But you go ahead."

She shook her head. "I'll take one with me."

Cobb wrapped his hands around the mug and lifted it. "Are you going to see Mackey today?"

"If he comes around. It's Friday. I don't go to the hotel on Friday."

"There was some speculation in the saloon last night about you and Mackey."

"I would have been surprised if there wasn't. You cleared it up, I hope."

"I didn't make it any muddier." He took a swallow of coffee. It had the exact combination of bitterness and burn that he liked. He raised his eyebrows, saluting her. "Jessop Davis figured you knew Mackey in Chicago. I explained that he was Charlotte's grandson. Ted wasn't impressed. He thinks Mackey looks like someone on one of the wanted notices in my office."

Tru smiled crookedly. "Murderer?"

"Bank robber."

"Ah, well, you never know."

Cobb grunted noncommittally and set his mug down. "Will you be all right seeing him alone? Maybe you should have supper at Jenny's. Spend a few hours with her and Jim after."

"I'll be fine, Cobb. I'm not afraid of Andrew."

"And if he hadn't come alone?" he asked.

"Don't be unpleasant." She regarded him over the rim of her mug for a long moment. Finally she nodded. "Yes, I would be more cautious if Frank were with him. But he's not. Andrew has some sense about him."

"Does he?"

Tru lowered her mug. "He's not a bad man. Don't make him out to be."

Cobb glanced up at the window above the sink. Shades of gray lightened the horizon and made silhouettes of the peaked rooftops across the way. It occurred to him again that he should go. Other than turning his mug in his hands, he did not move.

"He made you cry," he said.

There was no accusation in Tru's voice when she answered him. Her regard was merely candid. "So did you."

Cobb understood she was talking about the first night they spent together. He hadn't been aware that she had wept. "I *know* I'm a villain."

Tru sobered, sipped her coffee. "No. You didn't know about Franklin Mackey. You didn't know that he used a pillow to make me more accessible to him." She watched the color drain from Cobb's face. "I couldn't tell you then. I hardly understood what was happening myself. I'm not sure I do now. I only know that after you placed the pillow under me, it was as if I were no longer there. It felt as if what you were doing—what *I* was doing—was happening to someone else . . . or maybe to my former self."

"And then I asked you if you meant for me to rape you." Cobb's fingertips whitened on his cup. "I will never be able to make that up to you."

She took a deep breath and released it slowly. "You're wrong. You already have." When Cobb looked as if he meant to disagree, she cut him off. It was done, she thought. She was done. "What will you do today?"

He was slow to respond, but finally, "As little as possible."

"I think you take perverse delight in that pretense."

He shrugged. "Tell me about today's moral lesson. Should I come by and read to your students?"

"Don't you dare. Besides, I have nothing like that planned." She gave him a sardonic look. "I think I've surrendered the right to occupy the moral high ground."

"Do you really believe that?"

Tru turned back to the stove and retrieved the coffeepot. "I don't know," she said, not looking at him. "I'm still trying to make sense of what I've done."

"*I* don't believe it," he said. "Whatever you think you surrendered, it wasn't the moral high ground. I've never heard you claim to own it."

"I'm not so sure," she said quietly, adding coffee to her cup. "Perhaps I should have made a little more noise about it. It's easy to believe you know what you will do when temptation is an academic exercise." She raised her eyes and looked at him. "I'm learning that confronting it at my kitchen table is altogether different."

She mocked herself with a narrow smile. "I came away from my experience with Franklin Mackey thinking that I learned two things about myself. The first was that I was not a woman who could be persuaded to stray from her upbringing. The second was that if someone tried to force me to do just that, I would be able to protect myself."

Tru pointed over her shoulder in the general direction of the back door and the shotgun in the rack beside it. "One of the first things I did after I arrived in Bitter Springs was to learn how to shoot."

Cobb's eyes strayed to the shotgun and then came back to her. "Do you regret that you didn't aim it at me?"

"What I'm trying to say is that I never seriously considered taking it down from the rack. Not once. Franklin Mackey was not a temptation. You were. Are. And you have been since the very beginning. So the two things I thought I learned about myself were merely faulty assumptions, not evidence of moral character or strength of purpose."

Tru's mouth twisted to one side. She shrugged awkwardly. "And there you have it."

Cobb slid one hand across the table and turned his palm up. His invitation was clear, and after a brief hesitation, Tru put her hand in his. His fingers closed around hers. For a long time, neither of them moved. Their coffee grew cold and the sun rose in a cloudless sky.

When they stood, it wasn't to stand apart. Keeping her hand in his, Tru led Cobb back to bed.

Cil Ross poked her head out of the kitchen for the third time in as many minutes. She cast a glance around the dining room, frowned when her quarry was still absent, and retreated quickly before one of the diners asked her to fetch coffee or more biscuits.

Mrs. Sterling flipped a pancake in the skillet. "Get away

from that door, Cil. Do you think I have to look at you to know what you're up to? Come over here and help me with these hotcakes."

Cil dragged her feet, but she went. She picked up a warm platter and held it out for the cook to use. "Do you suppose Mr. Mackey thinks we'll take breakfast to him?"

"I don't know how he'd come by that notion unless you put it in his head. Did you?"

"I never. I told him the same as every guest. All meals in the dining room. No exceptions."

"And then you put him in the Coltranes' rooms. He probably thought he was someone special right off."

"He *is*."

"He's someone rich and that just makes him rich, not special. Anyway, I thought you and Renee were still scrappin' over Cobb Bridger. What happened there?"

"The marshal's all right, I guess, but Mr. Mackey is real easy on my eyes."

Snorting, Mrs. Sterling added two more hotcakes to Cil's platter. "Take these out to Harry Sample. Syrup, too."

Cil grabbed the pitcher of syrup on her way out. When she saw Andrew Mackey seated at the table by the window, she forgot all about Harry Sample.

He smiled warmly when she set the pancakes and syrup in front of him. "You are looking very well this morning," he said to her.

Cil blushed.

His voice dropped to an intimate pitch that only carried as far as Cecilia's ears. "I didn't hear you leave. The next time, wake me."

Chapter Eleven

"Morning, Walt," Cobb said. He held the Pennyroyal's front door open for Walter so the other man could get outside with his broom and bucket and rags. "Isn't it a little early for outside cleaning?"

Walter shrugged his broad shoulders. "Early for some things." He gave Cobb a significant, speculative look. "Late for others."

The yawn Cobb forced for show became quite real before it ended. "I slept in the office. Actually, above it."

"Now, why'd you go do a fool thing like that when you can bed down here?"

"There was a little disturbance last night around the Still-well place. By the time I finished up with that, it was late. Stopped in the office and never left."

Walt set his bucket down and leaned on his broom. "What kind of disturbance? We got reason to be worried?"

"No, no reason. I was either chasing shadows or children. Couldn't catch either."

"Probably Rabbit and Finn."

"That's what Evelyn said. I didn't get a good enough look."

"I'll have a talk with the boys," said Walt. "No reason to mention it to their granny or pap."

"I'm not saying it *was* the boys."

Walt nodded. "Just the same, it never hurts to have a talk with them. The Stillwells are right next door to Miss Morrow. Could be they were making mischief for their schoolteacher. Boys will do that."

By the time he left Walter to his chores, Cobb was feeling a little sorry for Rabbit and Finn. He was feeling a little guilty, too. He decided he would find a way to make it up to them. Maybe new whittling knives would salve his conscience.

Cobb intended to go straight to his room to bathe, change his clothes, and beg for his breakfast afterward. He passed the entrance to the dining room without glancing in and had a foot at the bottom of the staircase when he heard his name. He had no difficulty recognizing the voice behind it. Swearing under his breath, Cobb backed up until he could see into the dining room. Andrew Mackey was half out of his chair, waving him over.

Cobb went.

"Join me, Marshal," Mackey said.

Cobb noted that although Mackey was smiling, there was more command than invitation in his tone. Mackey was already pushing out a chair as Cobb approached. Cobb put up a hand to stop him. "I was on my way to my room, Mr. Mackey. I'm going to eat later."

"They won't take breakfast to you. I learned that. Eat now or go hungry." He nudged the chair with his toe. "Have a seat. The pancakes are good."

Out of the corner of his eye, Cobb could see there was some attention being paid to this exchange. He elected to sit. When Cil appeared carrying a pot of coffee, Mackey waved her over before Cobb could stop him.

"Pancakes for the marshal," said Mackey. "Coffee, too."

Feeling contrary, Cobb said, "No cakes. Steak and eggs." He pushed his empty cup toward Cil. "I'll take that coffee though." She tipped the pot over his cup.

"More for you, Mr. Mackey?"

Andrew nodded, thanked her. When she was gone, he said, "That young woman is very accommodating."

"She's kind to everyone."

"Yes, I'm not surprised that's your perspective." He cut another triangle out of his stack of hotcakes and dragged it through the syrup at the edge of his plate. "When I didn't see you earlier, I asked that rather large gentleman who works here where I could find you. He said you hadn't come down yet, but I could tell he didn't know where you were."

"It's not one of Walt's jobs to keep track of the guests."

"But you're not precisely a guest any longer, are you? I thought as marshal that you would be more accountable to the people you serve."

Cobb chose not to engage Mackey in a senseless argument. He decided to force his hand. "Why did you call me over? What do you want?"

"Certainly not the pleasure of your company." He set his fork down, wiped his lips with his napkin, and then picked up his coffee cup. "I wondered if you'd thought anymore about what I said last night. You seem to be relatively reasonable. It occurred to me that you might have reconsidered."

"Reconsidered what exactly?" He watched Mackey's lips thin in annoyance. "You said a number of things."

"Do you really want to try me, Mr. Bridger?"

"I don't work for you any longer. I remember that quite clearly."

"I admit to having no influence here," said Mackey. "But if it's your intention to work in Chicago again, I think you'll want to tread more carefully."

"Already making a note of it."

Mackey frowned slightly. There was more meaning in the silence that followed Cobb's response than in the answer itself. "You *do* intend to take up work in Chicago, don't you?"

"I like it here."

"Then you're not leaving?"

"Not now. I believe I said that last night."

"Even if Miss Morrow leaves?"

"I'm not sure what you mean."

"Exactly what I said."

"Are you under the impression that she has something to do with my decision to stay?"

"Doesn't she?"

"She's the reason I have this job," said Cobb, shrugging. "I owe it to her to stay put for a while."

"And if she goes?"

"I don't see that it matters."

Mackey's study was shrewd. "And I don't believe you."

"All right." Cobb raised his hands to take his warm plate of steak and eggs from Cil. "No more coffee," he told her, setting the plate down. "Smells good. Be sure to tell Mrs. Sterling I said that. I keep getting on the wrong side of that woman's good humor."

"Oh, that's just Ida Mae, Marshal. She likes you fine." She started to leave, stopped, and spun on her heels to face Cobb again. "I forgot. I saw Mrs. Stillwell on my way to the Pennyroyal this morning. She mentioned there was a little excitement at her place last night. Were you chasing someone?"

"I thought I was."

"She wouldn't say who, but I figure she was talking about Rabbit and Finn."

"I can't say. I don't have any proof."

"Just the same, I wanted you to know I agree with Mrs. Stillwell that it's real nice having someone like you looking out for the town. Even if it was just the boys, it's still nice to know."

"Thank you, Cil. Do you suppose she's going to be telling everyone that today?"

"Most likely. Why?"

"Because people will suspect the Collins boys, same as you, and I don't think that's fair to them."

Cil dimpled as she smiled. "If it's proof you want, I guess you're just going to have to run faster next time."

Chuckling, Cobb waved her off.

Andrew Mackey's stare followed her all the way to the kitchen door before coming back to Cobb. "Is she always so friendly with you?"

Cobb did not look up from cutting his steak. "Asked and answered. Miss Ross is always friendly. Period."

"She seemed something more than merely sociable."

"I didn't notice." He put a bite of steak in his mouth. "Is there a particular reason you thought it was important to comment on it twice?"

"I wondered if she was yet another reason why you are set on staying."

Cobb swallowed and stabbed one of the sunny egg yolks on his plate with his fork. Tearing off a corner from a heel of bread, he swabbed the yolk with it. "How long do you expect to be in town, Mr. Mackey?"

"As long as it takes to conclude my business."

"Do you intend to press charges?"

"Pardon?"

Cobb glanced up sharply. He did not doubt that Mackey had heard him, so what was it about the question that had caught him off guard? "Charges," he said again. "For the theft of your property."

"I haven't decided."

"That *is* your business, isn't it? Taking back what Miss Morrow stole from you?"

"It is."

"Well, you might want to reconsider trying to run me off. I'm the only one in Bitter Springs with the authority to arrest her." He returned his attention to his meal. "And I'm going to need something more than your say-so to do that. Not only will you have to produce whatever it is that you say she took, you will have to prove to my satisfaction that it belongs to you."

Andrew Mackey knuckled his neatly trimmed beard. "And if I decide I don't want to have Miss Morrow charged?"

"You still have to claim your property. I suppose you could steal it back and sneak right out of town. That'd create the least amount of fuss. If Miss Morrow wanted it returned, the burden of proving ownership would rest with her." He looked up again, thoughtful. "But then I'm telling this to someone who knows all about the law. I've been studying Wyoming Territory law myself since I took this job, right along with the town ordinances. I would imagine that most of it would be familiar to you. Women have more rights here, of course, but you probably were already aware of that."

Mackey nodded. "Suffrage."

"That's one of them." Cobb finished off the last of his steak. "You could make this easier if you'd tell me what Miss Morrow is supposed to have taken. If you don't tell me, it's more difficult to support your claim."

"I don't care about difficult. I care about confidences."

Pushing away his plate, Cobb asked, "What did Miss Morrow have to say?"

"Say?"

"When you asked her about the—" He stopped. "Oh. I see. You haven't confronted her. That's probably wise."

"I think so, but why do you?"

"You want to lull her. Catch her unaware. Patience always serves a predator."

"I'm not sure I care for the characterization."

"If the sheep's clothing fits."

Mackey frowned deeply. "How is that again?"

Cobb waved the question aside as he stood. "Good day, Mr. Mackey. It's unlikely that we won't see each other around, but unless you have a crime to report, keep in mind that I'm not at your beck and call."

Snow started falling in the afternoon around the time the children were being released from school. Cobb stepped out of his office to see if he could catch Rabbit and Finn before they headed home, but they were either staying after school with Tru or had been among the first to race off. He heard from no fewer than five people after Cil had spoken to him about what was now being referred to as the ruckus at the Stillwell place. Cobb was not confident that the boys weren't running home to trouble.

He was debating whether he wanted to walk over to the school to see if they were still there when he saw Andrew Mackey, head down and shoulders huddled against the cold, hurrying in that direction. He stayed outside long enough to verify that Mackey's destination was the school and not the bank or the hardware store. When Mackey stepped inside the schoolhouse, Cobb returned to his desk, dragged the heavy law book he was reading onto his lap, and tipped his chair back on its rear legs. He was not entirely convinced that doing nothing was the same as doing the right thing, but he did know that Tru would not thank him for interfering at this juncture.

Glancing at his pocket watch, Cobb decided he could wait half an hour before he wandered over to the school on the pretext of looking for Rabbit and Finn.

Tru was sweeping mud from under Sam Burnside's desk when Andrew Mackey arrived. When she looked up, he was already pulling the door closed behind him and kicking at the floor as he brushed snowflakes from his overcoat. She wished he had not come, but more than that, she wished she had asked one of her students to help her with Friday chores.

She paused, straightening, and greeted him politely if not warmly. "Andrew. How surprising."

"A welcome one, I hope."

"If you're here to help, then certainly."

Mackey glanced around. "I came by to walk you home."

"That's kind of you, but I'm not ready to leave." She began to sweep again, this time more slowly.

"That's all right. I don't mind waiting." He saw the hooks by the door and removed his coat and brushed felt bowler. He stuffed his leather gloves into the pockets of his coat. "Shall I get a dustpan?"

"Thank you." Careful not to show her astonishment, Tru pointed behind her. "In the closet."

Mackey went to get it. "Isn't there someone else who could do this?"

"I'm not sure who that would be. The schoolhouse is my responsibility."

He found the dustpan and carried it to Tru. When she didn't take it from him, he hunkered in front of her and held the pan steady while she swept dust and clumps of mud onto it. "Don't you have any troublemakers to punish with these tasks?"

"Not today." She swept the last of the debris onto the dustpan and pointed Mackey to the front door. "Empty it outside. This is the worst of it, but I still have to sweep the rest of the classroom."

Without a word, he did as she asked and then returned to help with the other piles of debris she accumulated from around the room. On his last trip out to empty the dustpan, he asked, "What about those two boys who drove the buckboard yesterday? The station agent's grandsons, I believe."

"Rabbit and Finn? Do you think they should be helping me? They're not troublemakers."

"Really? I heard their names mentioned in connection with some kind of disturbance last night."

"Oh?" Tru set the broom against the wall. She picked up the damp rag lying on her desk and began wiping down the blackboard.

"Miss Ross was asking Cobb Bridger about it. The marshal and I shared a table at breakfast this morning."

Tru was glad that she was no longer facing him. It was easier to keep her movements smooth than to school her features.

Mackey went on.

"It seems that whatever happened, it occurred at the Stillwell place. I thought that perhaps you'd know about it since they're your neighbors."

"I do. I would hardly call it a disturbance."

"But you saw Bridger?"

"Well, yes. Evelyn and I both saw him. Did Cecilia say that Rabbit and Finn were involved?"

"You don't think they were?"

Tru turned away from the board and dipped the rag in the bucket beside the stove. She wrung it out. "I don't know what the marshal thought he saw, but I sincerely doubt it was the boys. It's unfair to them if people are saying so. Bitter Springs has many good things to recommend it, but the inclination of its citizens to gossip is not one of them."

Mackey's eyes followed Tru as she picked up a slate from

the table closest to her desk and began wiping it down. "He seems to be well liked."

Tru frowned. "Who?"

"Bridger."

"I suppose."

"And dedicated to his post. Did you know he didn't return to the hotel last night?"

The look that Tru leveled at him was dead-on. "How would I know that?"

"Aren't you privy to the marshal's comings and goings?"

"I have no idea why you think so."

Andrew chose one of the tables on the aisle to sit on. He rested his feet on the bench in front of it. "A conclusion I drew from observing you and the marshal last night. Are you saying I'm wrong?"

"I'm saying I don't understand. Mr. Bridger and I barely spoke at dinner. You had my full attention from the moment I saw you."

"That's just it. I saw you first. And I saw how you were looking at him."

Tru put down a clean slate and exchanged it for a dusty one. "I don't want to do this again. I said everything I had to say on the subject of Cobb Bridger during our walk. He should have told me that he was working for you. I don't understand why he thought he had to keep that from me. I would have liked to have known. I never suspected that you would want to find me, Andrew."

That gave Mackey pause. His dark eyes grazed Tru's face. "Do you have an answer for me?"

"No. And I asked you not to press me. I'm still not sure what I think about your proposal. It was not merely unexpected. It was a shock."

"Surely not. There were so many times that I thought I was too forward."

Prior to Andrew telling her he wanted her as his mistress, Tru had no recollection of any such occasion. More often than not, he barely seemed to notice her. She chose not to challenge or contradict his version of events and simply let him talk.

"Grandmother suggested that I proceed cautiously. She took peculiar pleasure in reminding me of my multiple engagements. She said that you would certainly know all about those unfortunate misjudgments and that you were too levelheaded to make a blind leap. She led me to believe that you would look long and carefully. I suppose that's what you're doing now, and Grandmother is proved right yet again."

Tru said nothing. Charlotte had never intimated that she had spoken to Andrew about any such thing.

"Was I too cautious?" he asked. "Perhaps I mistook the matter and should have done more to let you know my feelings."

Tru had heard enough. She put down the slate and held up her hand, spreading her fingers wide. "You're talking to me as if that night with Franklin never happened. I can't pretend that it didn't, and it's insulting that you won't mention it. You were *there*, Andrew. I haven't forgotten. That night is the yardstick that I use to measure all your fine words. You would do well to keep that in mind before you prod me to give you an answer. I don't share your sense of urgency."

Andrew stood. His hands fell to his sides. "I love you."

Tru responded by lowering her raised hand.

"I have for a very long time," he said.

"You asked me to be your mistress first," she said. "Not your wife."

"I was wrong. I told you I was wrong."

"So you did. And now it's up to me to decide if I believe you." Tru saw him flinch. She could almost think she had landed a blow. Tossing the damp rag over her shoulder, Tru rubbed the back of her neck where cords of tension pulled the muscles taut. "You better go, Andrew." She closed her eyes briefly. "I want you to go."

Tru was surprised when he did.

A noise outside Cobb's office distracted him from his reading. He looked up to find Rabbit and Finn peering back at him through the window. They had their hands cupped on either side of their eyes to focus their gaze and reduce the glare on the glass. It was clear they saw him because they began jabbering excitedly and dancing in place. He dropped his chair forward, set the law book on his desk, and waved them inside before they wet themselves.

They might have barreled into his office if they hadn't tried to enter at the same time. As a pair, they were just big enough to be a stopper in the doorway. There was some jostling and poking of elbows and shoulders until Rabbit turned sideways, broke the bottleneck, and Finn fell forward on his hands and knees. Rabbit reached Cobb's desk while Finn was picking himself up.

Cobb put up a hand before the boys began speaking. "One at a time."

Rabbit went first. "There's villains come to town, Marshal. Finn and me thought you should know."

"Finn and I," said Cobb.

"You? Finn and you? He told you already?" He elbowed his brother. "How'd you do that?"

"Ow." Finn rubbed his arm. "I never."

Cobb shook his head. "Forget it. Tell me about the villains."

Rabbit said, "Granny didn't give us time to get out of our coats before she started wantin' to know all about where we were last night. She said she heard you were chasin' us through the Stillwells's yard and all the way up to the cemetery and back."

Finn nodded hard. "She was pretty mad about it. And the broom was close. I thought for sure we were gonna get it."

"Would have been better if we had," said Rabbit.

Finn rapped his knuckles on the desk to punctuate his brother's point. "We told Granny we weren't at the Stillwells last night. We didn't leave the house."

"She doesn't believe us," said Rabbit. "Says we're like the boys who cried wolf."

Finn leaned forward. "First of all, Marshal, there was only one boy in that story. And everyone knows it's the wolves that are causin' all the trouble."

Rabbit looked hopeful. "Maybe that's what you were chasin' last night. Wolves."

"Or villains," said Finn. "I'm still thinking it was villains."

Cobb pointed to the chairs. "Have a seat, boys." When they were down, he said, "I want you to know that I never told anyone I was chasing you."

"Oh, we figured that," said Rabbit. "Granny said she had it from Mrs. Burnside who had it from Mrs. Ransom who had it from her husband who got a haircut this morning at Mr. Stillwell's barbershop. We guess we know all right where the story started."

Finn leaned back in his chair and folded his arms across his chest. Even in his bulky coat he was still just a slip of a thing. "Granny says Mrs. Stillwell has a way of spinnin' facts out of thin air. That's what you call speculation. Rabbit and me know a lot about speculators. We're pretty good at it ourselves."

"Of course you are," Cobb said.

"Did you notice if it was muddy between the houses?" asked Finn. "Because I have to tell you that Sam Burnside had clods of mud under his desk today. I didn't think much of it until Granny told us what happened, and now I'm thinking that it might have been Sam."

"Or Robby," said Rabbit. "Or maybe both of them. Robby told me he's going to marry Miss Morrow. He could have been trying to get a peek in her windows."

Finn snorted. "He's not goin' to marry Miss Morrow. You saw that Mackey fella yesterday. The one Granny told Mrs. Garvin was as handsome as sin. That's who's gonna marry her. I gave up the dream myself when I heard that."

"Are you speculating?" asked Cobb.

Finn's head tilted to the side as he considered it. "Maybe a little, but Pap says that Mr. Mackey asked after Miss Morrow's whereabouts right off. Pap doesn't tell folks things like that without good reason, so he asked a couple questions the way he does, and found out that Mr. Mackey knew Miss Morrow back in Chicago. He'd come a long way just to see her.

Pap and me figure there's only one reason a man travels so far to see a woman."

Grinning, Rabbit put a hand over his heart and mimicked a thumping beat. "It must be love, Marshal."

Finn nodded. "Pretty good speculatin', ain't it?"

"Indeed," said Cobb. He looked from one boy to the other. "Now, let's talk about these villains."

It was shortly after nine o'clock when Tru returned home from Jenny and Jim's. She had been invited to dinner and stayed afterward to help Jenny sort through fabric remnants and cut triangles from the chosen material for a church quilting project. As soon as she and Jenny tidied the kitchen and set to work, Jim disappeared into the parlor with the latest Nat Church adventure. Except for an occasional comment when his wife called out a question, he was happy to ignore them.

Tru lighted the lamp at the door before she removed her coat, gloves, and scarf. It was not until she turned away from hanging things up that she realized she was not alone.

Cobb was slouched low in her favorite chair by the stove, his feet resting on a stool. She couldn't be sure, but he seemed to be sleeping. Tru glanced at the parlor windows, saw he had had the presence of mind to draw the curtains, and picked up the lamp. She carried it into the parlor and set it on the table beside him. Other than occupying her chair, there was no evidence that he had made himself at home. No glass, no plate, no book. He had simply waited.

It was oddly touching, and she smiled.

Tru backed away quietly when he didn't stir and went upstairs to change into her nightclothes. Afterward, she sat at the vanity to remove the anchoring combs from her hair. She brushed it out, began to plait it, and then remembered Cobb's fingers sifting through the waves. She decided a fair compromise would be to tame her hair with a loosely tied grosgrain ribbon.

Tru belted her robe as she went down the stairs. Glancing over to the parlor, she saw Cobb was still sleeping. She retrieved *Triumphant Democracy* from the bookshelf and headed to the sofa, prepared to read until he woke or she fell asleep. She was on the point of skirting his chair when his hand shot forward and circled her wrist. Caught unaware, Tru yelped and clobbered him on the side of his head with her book.

"Ow!" He didn't let go, but he did use his free hand to rub his head as he pulled her onto his lap. "Why did you do that?"

"You scared me." She allowed the book to thump to the floor as she lifted her arms to his neck. Brushing aside his hand, she kissed the spot he had been rubbing. "I had no idea that you were so tender-headed."

Cobb grunted.

Tru laughed softly and kissed him again, this time on the lips. When she drew back, she looked him over and decided he was mollified, at least temporarily. "Have you been waiting long?"

"Less than an hour. Where were you?"

She was absurdly pleased that he hadn't known; it meant he had not been dogging her steps, even at a distance. No matter what he said about his job, he had more to do in the course of a day than watch after her. "I had dinner with Jenny and Jim and then Jenny and I started work on the quilt for the church's box social. We're going to auction it off. Did you eat at the hotel?"

He shook his head. "Mrs. Sterling sent Walt down to the jail with food. I suppose you didn't hear yet that I had to roust a couple of wranglers from the saloon and escort them to jail."

"From the Pennyroyal?"

"No. From Whistler's."

"Are they still there? Who's watching them?"

"I let them go after a few hours. They just needed to settle down. As a precaution, I kept their guns. They didn't like it much, but the fight had gone out of them by then. I told them that they could come by and collect their guns tomorrow morning on their way out of town. They both work for the Gibson ranch. I thought I'd give it a couple of days and ride over to the Bar G, have a talk with Marty Gibson about the boys. I'm guessing the pair of them will be fast friends again by then, but you never know."

"Cards or women or both?" asked Tru.

Cobb held up one finger. "Woman. As near as I could tell they both asked her to dance and then argued over who asked her first. Bill Whistler saw where it was heading and sent for me. They were grappling on the floor when I got there."

"Then they didn't draw on each other."

"No. It began with fists and then they were in too close to get at their guns."

Relieved to hear it, Tru exhaled softly. "I'm glad no one was hurt." To be sure he had not sustained any injury, she leaned back and gave him a thorough look. "What is it?" she asked when Cobb's mouth twisted with tender irony.

He pointed to the side of his head where she had walloped him. "I managed to avoid everything thrown in my direction tonight until I came here."

Tru did not apologize for it. She beamed.

Cobb's attention was arrested by her smile. "Jesus," he said quietly. "You're beautiful."

She put a finger to his lips. "You shouldn't say things like that."

"You *are* beautiful."

"I'm not, but I meant the other. You curse too much."

"That wasn't a curse. I said it with enormous respect and reverence." He kissed her finger before she removed it.

Rolling her eyes, Tru cut him off. "Would you like a drink?"

"No. But you go ahead."

Tru slid off his lap and went to the drinks cabinet. She splashed a tumbler with whiskey and carried it back. When he patted his lap, she merely gave him an arch look and curled into the corner of the sofa that was closest to him. "I think it's better if I sit here."

"Better for whom?"

"Both of us, if you like. You can't spend the night."

Cobb agreed, but reluctantly. "You were right about my absence being noticed. Walt commented on it."

"So did Andrew."

That caused Cobb to cock an eyebrow at her. "He said something to you? I saw him go into the schoolhouse after you excused the children."

She nodded. "That's when he mentioned it. It was a test, of course. I've learned that's the way Andrew does these things. I'm unaware that he's ever practiced law in a courtroom, but he approaches people as if they're on trial. He seemed to think I should know where you were last night."

"I know you didn't tell him the truth, so how did you manage the lie?"

"Evasion."

Cobb chuckled. "You do very well there."

Tru nodded and sipped her drink. "He asked for my answer."

That sobered Cobb. He pushed the stool aside and sat up straight.

Tru went on: "He said I should have known that he had feelings for me when I was in his grandmother's employ. I don't recall a single instance when I thought that might be the case."

"Is it possible you were mistaken about the reasons he wanted you gone? It could be that he wanted to remove temptation." He quickly threw up his hands to ward off the sharp, vaguely accusing glance she sent his way. "Playing devil's advocate."

"He also told me he loved me—something he didn't say when he asked me to marry him last night. I had the impression he had thought about it and was rectifying a mistake. It was . . . calculating, I suppose. He intended for me to be moved by his declaration."

"Were you?"

Tru shook her head. "No. Not at all. I really don't understand what he wants."

"Besides you."

"I know I said that, but I'm not certain it's true. I told you yesterday. Dog in the manger. I can't shake the sense that he wants me only so that no one else can have me. It's not flattering; it's disturbing. But before I give him my answer, I want

to understand his urgency first. I want to know his purpose."
She smiled faintly at Cobb's shuttered expression. "You're
not sure what I'm going to say, are you?"

He said nothing.

"My answer does not hinge on you making the same offer.
You should know that in the event you are tempted to make
a proposal."

"And if I did?"

With more regret than joy, Tru's smile deepened. She said
quietly, "I would want to understand the urgency and know
the purpose."

Cobb nodded slowly. "That's fair." He stood. "I think I
will have that drink." He headed for the cabinet. "Finn and
Rabbit dropped by after school. Finn mentioned that Mackey
asked after you as soon as he arrived at the station. That was
enough for Finn and his grandfather to speculate about Mackey's interest in you. It's only a matter of time before people
learn there's been a proposal, and no one's going to be surprised by it."

"How will anyone find out? Only you and I and—" She
stopped. "Oh, Andrew. Of course. Sooner or later he will want
it known. That's why he asked for me when he arrived. I suppose there is more than one way of pressing me."

"That's what I was thinking."

"Enlisting the town," she said, shaking her head. "I hadn't
considered that."

"It's what I would do."

"No, you wouldn't."

Cobb turned back to face Tru as he was pouring his drink.
"Why do you say that?"

"You're a private person."

"I might surprise you."

"I don't think so. You're not secretive exactly, just private.
I imagine it comes from wheedling information from everyone around you. You guard yours closely."

"It comes from being wheedled," he said. "That's what
passes for conversation at the Bridger table. My mother in

particular is relentless. What I know about interrogatory, I learned from her."

"I envy you your family, you know. I shouldn't. It's wrong." She finished her drink and put the tumbler aside. "I'm sure every one of them holds you in great esteem, and if they try to coax something from you, it's because of their affection and concern. I think you know that."

He nodded. "I do, but it doesn't hurt to be reminded."

"Do they know where you are?"

"Yes. I write regularly."

"Do you?" She did not try to conceal her surprise. "What do you say?"

Cobb returned the bottle to the cabinet and carried his drink to the chair. "Different things about the town, the people. The adventures of Rabbit and Finn."

Tru laughed softly. "Did you write that you're marshal?"

"No. That's better left for later."

"For when you're no longer marshal, you mean."

"I mean for when I'm sitting in the farmhouse at the table. They'll need that much assurance that I'm unharmed."

"I would too," she said. "In their place, I would too."

Cobb raised his glass but didn't drink. Footsteps on the front porch pulled his attention to the door. He glanced at Tru. She was already rising to her feet and regarding him with concern. He had no trouble interpreting her look. She wanted him to leave. She was not up to a confrontation. He set his glass on the table, picked up her empty one and shoved it in his jacket pocket. He pointed to himself and then to the kitchen. She nodded and crossed to the entrance while he made his retreat.

Tru pressed the flat of one hand against the door and covered the knob with the other. The knock jarred the door and both of her hands. She waited a few beats and then asked, "Who is it?"

"Andrew. Let me in. I need to speak to you."

"It's late, and I'm in my nightclothes. We already spoke once today. We can talk again tomorrow."

"Please," he said. "I wouldn't be here if I didn't think it was important."

Tru glanced over her shoulder in the direction of the kitchen. She didn't see Cobb. She had to trust that he was gone. "One minute," she told him. "You have one minute and then you have to leave."

"Yes. Whatever you want."

Tru turned the key in the lock and twisted the knob. She had hardly stepped back before Andrew entered, and he was halfway to the sofa before she closed the door.

"Stop right there," she said. "I didn't invite you to make yourself comfortable. What do you need to speak to me about?"

Mackey ignored her. He went to the table between the chair and sofa and picked up the tumbler of whiskey. Once he had it in hand, he turned on her. "You drink liquor?"

"Obviously I did not pour that for you, so yes, I enjoy good whiskey."

Her answer raised his eyebrows. "I had no idea." He lowered the tumbler to the table. "When I saw it, it occurred to me that you might have been entertaining."

Tru did not think that deserved a response. She said, "Please, Andrew, the point of your visit?"

He nodded. "I received a telegram this evening from Uncle Paul. Frank is coming to Bitter Springs."

Tru felt her stomach turn over and imagined that after only a few seconds passed she had no color left in her face.

"I came by earlier," Andrew said. "Twice. You weren't home, or at least you didn't answer the door."

"I wasn't home. I ate with friends tonight."

His dark eyes narrowed on her face. "You should sit down. You don't look well."

"I'm fine." But she wasn't, and she knew she wasn't. If he plucked another nerve, she would begin to vibrate and never stop. "Did you invite him to join you?"

"No."

Tru thought he seemed surprised that she asked. "I

wondered if you intended to present yourself as the lesser of two evils."

He stiffened. "That's unfair. And cruel. You've changed since you left Chicago."

"Perhaps." If it was true, she was making no apology for it. "When can we expect him?"

"He already left. Uncle Paul was informing me after the fact. If Frank's journey is as uneventful as mine was, I believe he'll arrive sometime Thursday. Mr. Collins thought the same."

Tru nodded. "Thank you for telling me. You were right that I would want to know." She indicated the door. "Goodnight, Andrew."

"I wouldn't mind a drink."

"You're staying at the Pennyroyal," she reminded him. "Have whatever you like. There." Tru put her hand on the doorknob and turned it. "I'm tired, Andrew, and I want to go to bed now."

He came toward her and then abruptly turned in the direction of the kitchen. Tru left the door and hurried after him. She put out a hand to touch his shoulder, thought better of it, and let it fall back to her side. He entered the kitchen first. She was right on his heels.

She was glad she had stayed behind him. That left her free to make her own furtive assessment. The room had only the benefit of the lamplight from hallway and parlor, but it was sufficient for her to see that Cobb's hat and coat were not hanging at the back door. The empty glass he had removed from the parlor was not on the table, and as best as she could tell, not in the sink. She wondered if he had walked out with it as a safeguard or because he forgot he had it.

Tru watched Andrew's head turn left and right. She slipped past him and stood beside the table, her hand resting on the back of a chair. When he glanced her way, she had the sense that he was looking through her. "What is it you think you're going to find?"

Ignoring her, he went to the door. Tru held her breath when

his hand closed over the knob. He twisted it. Expecting the door to open, she gave a small start when it didn't.

"This is locked," he said.

"Yes. I told you I was out." She hadn't locked it, though.

"I thought . . ." Shaking his head, he released the knob, turned, and reentered the kitchen. "I thought I heard something."

It was not difficult for Tru to look concerned. She was. It was impossible for Cobb to have locked the door behind him when he left, not with the key still dangling in the lock. "What kind of noise was it? Sometimes the neighbor's cat scratches at my door. I need to stop feeding him. You might have heard Mr. Peeve."

"No. It wasn't that."

"The house is still settling. It creaks and groans like an old man." She pointed to the window as the glass rattled. "And there's a strong wind out this evening. You'll want to turn up the collar of your coat on your way back to the hotel."

Andrew pointed to the archway behind her. "What's in there?"

"A dining room."

"Perhaps I should have a look."

She moved to block his path. "I don't think that's necessary."

He cupped her elbows, lifted her a few inches, and set her down when he had removed her as an obstacle. "It will only take a moment, and I'll sleep better knowing that you're safe. You can't have forgotten there was a problem here last night."

"The problem was out there, not in here. And you don't even have a lamp. I don't know what you think you'll see in there." But when Tru followed him in, she saw the light from the entranceway was brighter in the dining room than it had been in the kitchen. She watched Andrew bend at the waist to get a better view of under the table. "Andrew. This is really rather foolish."

"Humor me."

"I don't know what I'm humoring," she said. "Is this about Frank? Were you lying to me earlier? Is he here already?"

"No. Frank isn't here. He only left Chicago yesterday."

"All right. Then go." She took the short route back to the entrance, avoiding the kitchen, and opened the front door. An eddy of snowflakes swirled across the threshold. Tru shivered. "Go," she said. "I mean it, Andrew."

He turned up the collar of his coat just as she suggested and paused when he stood in the doorway. "I failed to protect you once before," he said. "I'm not going to repeat that mistake. I *will* take care of you. It's not only what Grandmother wanted, it's what I want as well."

Chapter Twelve

Tru went to the parlor window and parted the curtains the few inches necessary to observe Andrew Mackey's departure. When she saw that he had cleared the porch and was walking in the direction of the Pennyroyal, she stepped back from window and let the curtains fall in place.

"So help me, Cobb Bridger," she called out. "I have a good mind to leave the lamp here and bring the shotgun." In spite of her threat, it was the lamp she carried upstairs. "Don't you dare step out of the shadows and scare me." She proceeded cautiously anyway, holding the lamp in both hands as she walked down the hallway to her room. "Cobb? Say something. I know you're here. Andrew's gone. You can come out."

Nothing. Tru glanced around her room. Feeling slightly ridiculous, she stooped to look under the bed and even opened the wardrobe. The thought that Cobb might be crouched inside was an image worth cherishing well into old age. She was a little disappointed when he wasn't there.

Tru retraced her steps in the hall and went to the first bedroom. It required less than a minute to prove that he wasn't there. There were only a few pieces of furniture to hide behind or under or in. There was just one place left, and even though Tru was no longer as confident of his presence as she had been when she climbed the stairs, she kept the lamp steady and walked into the rear bedroom.

She saw immediately that it was also empty. Frowning, she stood in the doorway for a long moment while she reconsidered how Cobb could have exited the house. He had not left by the back door. She wouldn't have known that if Andrew hadn't remarked on it being locked. She also realized that he couldn't have gone out the front while she and Andrew were in the kitchen. They might not have heard him opening and closing the door, but they certainly would have felt the blast of cold air that action would have invited.

Eliminating the possibility that he had used either of the doors to make his exit led Tru to believe that he had moved into the dining room while she and Andrew headed to the kitchen, and while they were in that room, he had slipped around to the front and taken the stairs. She had been so certain that was his route that she covered for him by engaging Andrew in conversation to mask any noise he might make.

Now it seemed that she had been mistaken. She wondered if she went back downstairs if she would find the kitchen door unlocked. It seemed unlikely, if not impossible, that Cobb could have avoided Andrew's search by circling around to the parlor. And that meant he still would have been in the house when she threatened him with the shotgun. That should have gotten his attention.

Tru lowered the lamp. Out of the corner of her eye, she caught the eerie, ghost-like reflection of that movement in the window and immediately retreated a step. She mocked herself with a wry smile as she realized she was jumping at shadows of her own making. Here was the evidence that she was responsible for setting her nerves on edge.

She raised the lamp again, proved to herself that it was its flame that she had seen, and started to exit.

The light could not have dawned any brighter if the sun had suddenly appeared in the night sky. Tru steadied the lamp as she whipped around and made straight for the window. She felt for the latch first, knowing full well that she had closed it after her conversation with Cobb and Evelyn Stillwell.

It was open now. Tru placed the lamp on the floor, threw up the sash, and leaned out the window exactly as she had done the previous night. Snowflakes drifted into her hair and melted on her face. A half-inch of snow already covered the peaked roof of the back porch. She withdrew from the window to retrieve the lamp and then held it out to make a second examination.

Tru had no difficulty finding Cobb's footprints in the snow-cap. Her eyes followed them to the roof's lip. Judging by swirling patterns there, it looked to Tru as if his coat disturbed the snow when he stooped to make his leap. She hoped he hadn't broken his neck. She very much wanted the pleasure of doing that for herself.

"Now how'd you do this again, Marshal?" Walt Mangold poured whiskey over a cotton pad and set it against the cuts on Cobb's side. Not only didn't he remove it when Cobb winced, he actually pressed a little more firmly. "Told you it would sting."

"You did. I didn't think you would relish it quite so much."

"A man has to find his amusements where he can. You sure you don't want to tell folks this happened in a knife fight? It looks a little like a knife caught you here and there. I wouldn't say different."

"I appreciate the offer, Walt, but there were plenty of witnesses at Whistler's place that know there was no knife fight. I picked up a glass from one of the tables thinking I could use it to knock some sense into Tom Bailey's head—he was on top of Al Farrell at the time—but I ended up dragging him away instead. I don't even remember putting the glass in my pocket."

"I'm still thinking we can encourage people to remember a knife fight. That'd be a mite better for your reputation than folks hearing how you tripped comin' up the steps of the Pennyroyal and pierced your side on a couple shards of glass."

Cobb decided that he needed to establish a little dignity in his lie. "I didn't trip. I *slid*. Someone—and I'm not pointing fingers—hadn't swept the steps."

Walt nodded. "I see where you're going here, Marshal. That's why I'm in favor of the knife fight. No sense the town knowing that you went ass over teakettle in the first itty-bitty snow we had in these parts."

So much for dignity, Cobb thought. "How are people going to know if you don't tell them?"

"Well, you're going to be favorin' your left side for a while. Folks will see that and they're bound to ask. Then there's that shirt you were wearing. It will need to be laundered to get the blood out and repaired by a fine hand so the rent ain't noticeable. That's Mrs. Taylor and Mrs. Garvin that you'll be seeing about those matters, unless you mean to toss the shirt away in which case Cil or Renee will probably come across it and have a few things to say. And you'll most likely want to do something about that pocket. The lining's ripped clean through. I figure it'll take about a day and a half before everyone hears about your misfortune."

"You make a compelling argument, Walt, but I can't accuse a couple of rowdy ranch hands of cutting me to salve my pride."

Walt considered that, nodding slowly. "Guess that's what makes you different than the last man we had wearing a badge. Dan Sugar would have kept those boys in jail and made a case for hanging them. To my way of thinking, that's more proof that you're real good for Bitter Springs. And you're not the first person to fall off the porch, although most of the time it's on account of someone being drunk and wandering the wrong way from the saloon. I probably didn't sweep as good as I should have. Mrs. Sterling will scold, but that doesn't bother me much."

"Let's just say I tripped, Walt. There's no point in you taking the fall for me."

Walt's laughter boomed. "Takin' the fall. That's what they call a pun, ain't it? Usually I don't get those, but that's a good one."

Walt's enjoyment made Cobb chuckle. That slight movement caused him to wince again. He looked down at himself to get a glimpse of his wounds. Walt still had the cotton pad over the cuts. "Let me have a look."

Walt lifted the pad a fraction to see if there was still bleeding. "You got one here that's plenty deep." He dabbed at the wound as it began to seep blood. "It could be that Doc Kent would want to stitch it. And I'm not real confident that I got all the glass out. I should fetch him."

"It's late."

"The doc's used it to. He says there's nothin' that happens on a schedule."

Cobb leaned back against the headboard. "All right. Ask the doctor if he'll come." When Walt began to collect the supplies he'd brought, Cobb stopped him. "Leave the whiskey."

Grinning, Walt slapped the bottle into Cobb's palm. "Mind that you go easy." He picked up Cobb's jacket and shirt. "You want me to look after these?"

Cobb nodded. "Thank you. And if you could remove what's left of the glass from the pocket that would be a kindness to Mrs. Garvin."

"I'll take care of it right after I bring the doc back." Then he was gone.

Cobb was still favoring his left side when he walked into church Sunday morning. He was painfully aware of heads turning in his direction as he made his way down the aisle. Even Pastor Robbins looked amused, although to be fair to the man and his position, there was more grace in his smile than sly humor.

It was Cobb's usual practice to sit beside Jim Phillips if there was room in the pew. This morning that pew was filled. Not only were the Burnsides and their children present, but also Andrew Mackey was sitting squarely between Tru and Jenny. Cobb wondered how Mackey had managed that. Jim had warned him against even trying to separate the two women, and Cobb accepted that Jim knew what he was talking about.

Cobb stood at the end of a pew occupied by the Ransoms

and the Stillwells and waited for them to slide down just enough to make room for him. He felt Doc Kent's stitches pulling at his skin as he sat. The service began as soon as he was seated, confirming his suspicion that the congregation had been waiting on him.

It was little wonder that he felt at home in Bitter Springs.

Jim Phillips caught up to Cobb right after the service. He kicked snow out of the way as he followed Cobb's route off the shoveled path. "I guess you came this way to avoid a lot of questions. I could see that more folks were wanting to line up to say something to you than Pastor Robbins."

Cobb tugged on the brim of his hat, lowering it over his forehead. "What do you want to know, Jim?"

"Is it true?"

"Depends. What did you hear?"

"Heard you broke a glass with your backside tripping on the front steps of the Pennyroyal."

"It's my left side not my backside. The rest is true."

Jim pulled a long face and shook his head. "Did you even consider telling a different story? Maybe a knife fight. Something like that."

"Something like folks would read in a Nat Church adventure?"

"Exactly."

Cobb looked sideways at Jim and said dryly, "I'll keep that in mind."

Jim grinned with his usual good nature. "Glad to help." He stayed at Cobb's side as they crossed the street. "What do you know about that Mackey fellow? He seems friendly with Tru, but Jenny disliked him on sight. She was huffing all through the service about him sitting between her and Tru. I thought for sure he'd hear her."

Cobb gave Jim the short version and then asked, "Didn't Tru tell you all of that when she was at your house Friday night?"

"I didn't hear a word about him. Well, she might have said something to Jenny, but Jenny usually tells me things like that."

Cobb wondered what other secrets Tru was keeping from her best friend.

Jim reached the boarded sidewalk in front of the drugstore first. He waited to make sure Cobb didn't need a hand up.

"I'm not an invalid," Cobb said.

"I wasn't thinking about your injury. I wanted to make sure you didn't trip."

"Funny." It wasn't much of a step up, and Cobb would have taken a knife to his own throat rather than show Jim that he felt the tug of the stitches again. Doc Kent also seemed to think he had bruised a couple of ribs, which explained the ache in his chest when he drew a deep breath. The doctor also had done him the favor of believing he had sustained the injuries falling backward off the steps. Kent only puzzled aloud once about Cobb's momentum carrying him in the wrong direction.

"Oh," Jim said suddenly. "I'm supposed to invite you to Sunday dinner at our house. Jenny's got a ham she's fixin' to bake. She told me to mention that there would be greens and scalloped apples on the side. She said you're partial to scalloped apples."

"I am."

Jim nodded. "So you'll come?"

Cobb wondered if Tru would be there. He didn't ask. "Sure. I have a few things to do first. Can I have an hour or will that make me late?"

"That'll be fine. See you soon."

While Jim headed for home, Cobb turned the corner before the Pennyroyal and took the alleyway to the train station. Avoiding the people still milling around the churchyard was his main objective, but he also did not want to chance being observed by Tru or Andrew Mackey on his way to the station. Even though there were any number of explanations he could make for the trip, he simply did not want to offer even one. The most difficult aspect of his job was performing it under the scrutiny of every citizen in Bitter Springs.

No one was in the station house, so Cobb went around to the Collins residence. Heather Collins came to the door and invited him in. She was a slight woman with a straightforward stare, strong jaw, and firm mouth. He thought she was genuinely pleased to see him, but he couldn't be sure. He asked after her husband.

When Jefferson came at her call, Rabbit and Finn were on his heels. Cobb greeted the boys and congratulated himself on his excellent timing. All of his deputies were accounted for.

"There is a young man on his way to Bitter Springs from Chicago. I'd like to know he's here as soon as his feet touch the platform."

"Plenty of young men come this way and call Chicago home," said Mr. Collins. "You have a name?"

Heather wiped her hands on her apron. "He's talking about Mr. Mackey's cousin. The one that you got the telegram about the other night. Surely you remember that."

"I do," Collins said, a bit of starch in his voice. "Sent by one Paul M. The way I heard it, that's Mr. Mackey's uncle." Jefferson pushed his spectacles up the bridge of his nose as he regarded Cobb. "Mr. Mackey already asked to be notified when his cousin arrived. He wants to meet Franklin—that's his name—at the station same as you. Probably wants to escort him to the Pennyroyal himself."

"That's fine," Cobb said. "I only need to be the first to know."

Rabbit sidled up to his grandmother. She brushed absently at his cowlick as he said, "I think it'd help if we knew what he looked like. Don't suppose you know that."

"As a matter fact, I understand he closely resembles Mr. Mackey. His hair will be more red than brown, but he will have a similar weight and build. He's also younger than Mr. Mackey by seven or so years." Cobb could see they were all fixing the image in their minds. Jefferson Collins was particularly thoughtful. Cobb asked, "Is that enough for you to identify him?"

Finn nodded agreeably. "Sure, Marshal. I can picture him just fine."

Mr. Collins put his hand on Finn's shoulder. "The boys will probably be in school when the train comes in. I expect it to arrive in the afternoon if snow doesn't delay it. Should be Thursday. I told Mr. Mackey that, but it could be a day on either side of it this time of year. I'll make certain you know. Heather can stay at the station counter while I go for you."

"Is he a villain?" asked Rabbit. His grandmother cuffed him lightly on the back of his head. "What? He could be a villain."

Finn gauged the distance between his head and his granny's hand before he chimed in. "Mr. Rush says that Mr. Mackey looks like the man wanted for robbin' that bank over Rawlins way. The marshal's got a notice about it hangin' in his office. I got that picture real clear in my mind, too, and I think Mr. Rush is right."

Cobb shook his head. "That's enough, Finn. Mr. Rush's imagination is second only to yours." He returned his attention to Mr. Collins. "I appreciate your help. I wouldn't trouble you if it weren't important."

"I figure that's true, Marshal," Collins said, showing Cobb to the door. "I figure that's true."

Cobb joined Jim and Jenny for Sunday dinner, but Tru was not there. He learned she was having dinner with the pastor and his wife. He expressed no interest in Andrew Mackey's whereabouts.

Sunday rolled quietly into Monday. Tru did not come to the Pennyroyal to eat. Cobb shared a table with Mrs. Garvin and her two daughters and listened to the details about the wedding dress the seamstress was making for whichever daughter it was that was getting married.

When Tru did not arrive at the Pennyroyal on Tuesday and Cobb had to sit with the couple from Topeka, he concluded she was out of sorts with him for the manner in which he exited her house. Did she think he would have jumped if he'd had another choice? She kept things interesting, he would give her that.

Tru's back door was open. Cobb couldn't decide if it was a trap or an invitation. He entered cautiously and called out to her. The lateness of the hour almost guaranteed that she was in bed. The only light he had seen from the outside was the one in her room. He put his things on the usual hooks and made his way with ease through the dark kitchen. He called to her again at the bottom of the stairs and once more when he reached the top. He thought he heard her stirring as he walked down the hall to her room. Standing on the threshold, he said her name.

He saw immediately that he could have saved his breath. Tru was already sitting up in bed waiting for him, the shotgun lying across her lap.

Cobb rubbed the back of his head, his mouth screwed to one side in deep regret. "I forgot to look for that."

"I'm keeping it close these days."

"Because of Frank Mackey?"

"Yes."

He nodded. "Can I come in?"

"You're late with that question, but I suppose I'll allow it."

Cobb moved the wing chair from the fireplace to her bedside and sat down. It was then he realized that the barrel of her gun was now facing him. He made a circling gesture with his index finger. "Would you mind turning that the other way?"

Tru made a show of reluctance but did more than he asked by moving the shotgun off her lap and putting it on the far side of the bed. "How is your backside?"

He laid his palm against his left side. "Here. Not what I'm sitting on."

"I heard it was your backside."

"You're enjoying this, aren't you?"

"I am. Mostly I want to choke you, but having a laugh at your expense is almost as satisfying." She looked him over. "How badly are you hurt?"

He shrugged. "About a dozen stitches and a couple of bruised ribs."

"You could have broken your neck. Did you think of that before you jumped?"

"I didn't see that I had a choice. I couldn't be sure that Mackey wasn't going to come upstairs."

"You had plenty of time to leave the house. Why didn't you?"

He didn't answer.

"Cobb? Why didn't you leave?"

He knew she wasn't going to like his answer. "I was never going to leave you alone with him. Not here. I don't trust him." Cobb saw that she was about to object. He spoke before she could. "I didn't make a sound in the kitchen. He said he heard something, but he didn't. He was suspicious from the moment you let him in, maybe before that. He expected to find someone with you. Probably me, but I can't be sure. He wanted a reason to look around, and when he couldn't find one, he invented it."

Tru regarded him uncertainly.

"Unfortunately he was telling the truth about the telegram and Franklin Mackey coming here. I spoke to Mr. Collins on Sunday and confirmed it. He's going to let me know when Frank arrives."

Tru's short laugh had a bitter note. "For a moment there I was hopeful that Andrew had made it up." Her eyes darted to the shotgun. "I really don't like sleeping with it, but I thought I'd better get used to having it close."

"I could be that close," he said quietly.

"I'm still angry with you."

"How long do you think that will last?"

"It's hard to say right now. I'm a little less inclined to run you out than I was when I heard you stumbling through the house."

"I didn't stumble."

"I prefer to imagine that you did."

A low chuckle rumbled at the back of his throat. "I really have missed you, Tru. Did you know Mrs. Garvin has twenty-two flounces planned for Millicent's wedding gown?"

She smiled because it was harder not to. "I'd heard."

"And that couple from Topeka?"

"I don't think I've met them."

"It's just as well. They're Shakespearean actors. I listened to soliloquies from *Hamlet*, *Macbeth*, and *Julius Caesar*. Twice."

"I suppose I know now who sat with you at dinner."

"Why wasn't it you?"

She merely arched an eyebrow at him.

"All right. You didn't want to be around Andrew *or* me."

"My, but you do very good detecting."

He grinned crookedly. "I do."

"And so modest too."

Cobb leaned back in the chair and set his boot heels on the bed frame. "I know for instance that Andrew Mackey has not returned to the schoolhouse."

"Are you watching him or me?"

"I'm mostly in my office reading these days. Doctor Kent says I should have a care for his needlework. I have deputies for surveillance."

"You are shameless to use Rabbit and Finn that way."

"I am."

"And shameless to admit it so easily."

"You're right. I am without shame."

Tru could only shake her head. "Did you lock the back door behind you?"

"I did. I was surprised that it was open."

"I locked it Saturday, Sunday and Monday just so you would know I was serious. When you didn't come by any of those nights, I thought this would be the one that would test the limits of your patience."

"Huh. You know me that well?"

"I wanted to believe that, but your leap from the roof is forcing me to reconsider."

"You have some questions about my character?"

"I have some questions about your sanity."

"I told you from the beginning that there were dangers in being a lawman."

"That's your defense? One has nothing to do with the other."

"It's the best I can do. It's late. I'm tired. My ribs ache. And I want you to sleep closer to me than that shotgun."

Tru looked him over again. "I didn't know about your ribs."

"I suppose that's because Dr. Kent is the one person in Bitter Springs who can keep a confidence."

Tru chewed on the inside of her cheek. "You do look weary," she said after a moment. "Do you need help undressing?"

"How much pity do you have for me?"

"About enough to get you out of that jacket and vest and maybe your boots."

"I'll take it."

She threw back the covers and slid out of bed. "It's impossible to stay mad at you."

"I've heard that." He pushed himself out of the chair and bent a little at the knees so she could ease him out of his jacket.

"Your mother?"

"And my sisters. No one else is ever mad at me."

"Imagine my surprise." She folded his jacket, placed it over the back of the chair, and then began to unbutton his vest.

"I can do that," he said.

Tru brushed his hands aside. "I know. But I want to." When she was done, she added it to the jacket and directed him to sit on the bed so she could remove his boots. Kneeling in front of him while he carefully braced his arms on the edge of the mattress, she took the heel and sole and began to work the boot back and forth. The first one came off easily, and with that success behind her, she expected the second boot to be equally effortless. Instead, she found she had to grip it more firmly, work it harder, and when she finally pulled it free, the releasing force toppled her off her haunches and onto her backside.

She sat with her legs splayed wide and her back against the seat of the wing chair. She stared at the boot because she didn't dare look at Cobb. "Don't you laugh. I can be mad at you about something else. That's not hard to do."

"Not laughing," he said. "The ribs. It hurts."

Now she did look at him. Apparently grinning did not hurt him in the least. She put the boot aside before she threw it at his head and scrambled to her feet. "The rest is up to you," she said. She went to the basin to wash her hands. When she was done, she walked around the bed and moved the shotgun to the floor before she climbed in. Cobb was out of his trousers and socks by then, but he was taking some care with his shirt.

Tru knelt behind him and slipped it over his shoulders. She didn't bother folding it and simply tossed it toward the chair instead. She heard him make a small sound of protest in response to her carelessness, but she was not moved. "Let me see where you were cut."

"There's really nothing to look at."

She kept her hands on his shoulders and squeezed lightly. "You're not going to win this one."

Cobb unfastened his flannel union suit all the way to his navel and accepted Tru's help managing the covers and his comfort as he lay back. She reached over him to nudge the lamp closer to the edge of the nightstand. "You're going to be underwhelmed," he told her. "It's nothing."

"Let me judge that for myself." She parted the flannel and carefully bared his left side. There were at least half a dozen scratches marking his skin, but Doctor Kent had only stitched three long, jagged gashes. "There are more than a dozen stitches here." She tapped one of the cuts with her fingertip. "I count twelve in this one alone. It must have been terribly painful."

"Not so bad. Getting the glass out hurt worse than the stitches."

"I can imagine, but I meant the injury."

"I didn't feel it. I had other things on my mind. I was halfway to the Pennyroyal by the time I realized I was bleeding. I needed to get back before Mackey so I didn't get a look at what I'd done until I was in my room. Walt helped me and then went for Dr. Kent."

"I thought the doctor would have wrapped your ribs."

"He wanted to. I've had it done before. It doesn't help much, and it's too restrictive."

"What? You're afraid some binding will make it harder for you to draw a weapon you never seem to be wearing anyway?" Shaking her head, Tru leaned over Cobb again and pushed the oil lamp a safe distance from the edge of the stand.

"Have I needed it?" he asked. "I'll wear it when I need it."

"I know there's an ordinance against carrying," she said, "but that doesn't apply to the marshal, and the ranch hands who only get into town when there's a lack of work or a cattle drive, well, they don't think it applies to them."

Cobb turned on his good side and slipped one arm under his pillow. "They do now."

Tru realized this was the one she was not going to win. She surrendered, although not gracefully. She made the mattress bounce as she jostled for position under the covers and lay back hard. When she glanced over at Cobb to see if he grasped her point, she caught him alternately laughing silently and grimacing with the pain of it. She supposed there was more than one way to exact revenge.

"I've missed you too," she whispered. She found his hand and wrapped her fingers around his. Turning on her side, she backed into him and drew his arm across her waist. "I'm not hurting you, am I?"

"No." He amended that after a moment in which she settled her bottom firmly against this groin. "Not my side or my ribs anyway."

Once Tru was quiet, she felt his penis stirring. "Is that a good idea?"

"It doesn't know good from bad. It only has the one idea."

Tru could not quite suppress her laughter. She thought it sounded, if not precisely evil, then definitely a little wicked. Demonstrating significantly more care for his welfare than when she lay down, Tru turned over to face him. "Show me what to do."

In answer, Cobb palmed her thigh and drew her leg across both of his as he lay on his back. Tru edged closer and when he turned his head, she kissed him. It was a gentle kiss, soft, more like a whisper across his mouth.

The care she took with it made him smile.

Tru drew back. "What?"

"I didn't injure my lips."

She tapped his mouth with her fingertips. "Don't tempt me to rectify that." She kissed him again, this time with more passion than prudence. One of her hands rested on his chest.

She could feel his heartbeat under her palm. That hand slid lightly over his bruised ribs and skirted his injury and finally stopped level with his navel. She deepened the kiss while her thumb repeated a pass across his taut abdomen.

Tru heard the hitch in Cobb's next breath, felt his wince, and lifted her head a fraction to look at him. "I don't know," she whispered. "The spirit is willing but the flesh is weak."

"That's a gross misuse of that passage."

"I'm aware of that."

"In that case, pay no attention to the flesh."

She ran her hand over the arrow of hair below his navel and circled his erection with her fingers. One of her feathered eyebrows kicked up.

"All right," he said. "You can pay attention to that flesh."

Tru snorted. "What if I do this?" *This* was sitting up and straddling Cobb's thighs.

"It's a good beginning."

She released his cock and leaned forward, bracing her arms on either side of his shoulders. He untied the ribbon at her neckline and then tugged on the one loosely binding her hair. As a favor to him, and maybe to herself, Tru shook her head. Her hair cascaded forward, long curling strands dripped over and between his fingers. He sifted through her tresses until she sat back and shrugged out of her nightgown. When the fabric pooled around her waist, his fingers drifted to her breasts.

Cobb's hands were familiar with her in a way that his eyes were not. He knew the curve of her breasts, the weight and firmness of them in the cup of his palms, but had never seen the color of her aureoles. In the glow of lamplight, they were coral. In the full light of day, he thought they would be shell pink. He would ask her to ride out of town with him, all the way to Hemlock Lake, and he would find a place to lie down with her in the tall Wyoming grass. It would be spring by then, maybe summer. When he came west from Chicago, he couldn't imagine that he would want to stay in Bitter Springs beyond a week. Now, because of Tru, he couldn't imagine that he would want to leave it that long.

Tru saw the tilt of his mouth, the promise of a smile in the curve of his lips. Her hands closed over his, held them still on her breasts. The warmth of his palms slipped under her skin and cradled her heart.

She bent her head slightly and whispered, "What are you thinking?"

"I'm thinking about your breasts."

"Oh." Tru was more curious than astonished. "What about them?"

"The tips . . . they're coral."

Tru lifted his hands and looked down at herself. "So they are. It must be the lamplight."

"And that flush washing up from your chest to your face? Is that the lamplight, too?"

"No," she said smartly. "That's me. You make me brazen when I'm actually a very modest woman." As evidence of this point, she covered her breasts with his hands. "See? Modest."

Cobb made a pass across her nipples with his thumbs. She arched her spine in response and thrust her breasts into his palms. "And brazen," he said. "I see that now. That's quite a war you're waging with yourself." She whimpered softly as he drew her down and took the tip of one breast into his mouth.

Tru hummed her pleasure as he suckled her. Her fingers curled in the pillow under his head. She lifted her hips, teased him with the damp cleft between her thighs, and then slowly lowered herself onto him. She took careful, measured breaths until she was seated and then for a long moment, she didn't breathe at all.

Cobb abandoned one breast to give attention to the other. He felt Tru contract around his cock. She held him fast, released, and held him again. The rhythm matched the suck of his mouth. He drew on her. She drew on him.

Tru sat up suddenly, shuddering. She rolled her shoulders; her hair spilled down her back. Placing her hands on her thighs, she rose up on her knees and then lowered herself again. After that it was only her hips that lifted.

Cobb palmed her bottom as she rose and fell. He guided her, keeping her steady, urging her to slow down when that was what he needed and letting go when it was better for her.

Her long strokes quickened. Her pelvis rocked. One of his hands slipped between her thighs. He rubbed her clitoris and watched her eyes close. The tip of her tongue appeared at one corner of her mouth. She was perfectly concentrated on her own pleasure when Cobb's hips bucked and thrust and almost unseated her with the strength of his climax. She clutched his shoulders and held on for the ride and then finished it as hard and as wild and as abandoned as he.

Tru eased off of him and allowed herself to simply topple sideways on the bed. She was deliciously boneless and told him so. When he didn't respond, she looked sideways and saw that he had clapped one hand over his bruised ribs and was investigating the condition of his injuries.

Throwing a forearm across her eyes, Tru said, "I told you the flesh was weak. Did the stitches hold?"

"They did. Kent does good work." Cobb ignored the ache in his chest as he sighed feelingly. "So do you."

Because it was his uninjured side that was parallel to her, Tru felt no compunction about jabbing him with her elbow. When he didn't ask why she had done it, she gave him full credit for understanding.

They lay side-by-side in companionable silence while their heartbeats quieted and the soporific effects of the carnal act ebbed and flowed. When Tru thought she could move without her legs folding under her, she sat up and addressed the condition of her nightgown before she climbed out of bed. She washed at the basin with the same consideration of her modesty as she had before.

Cobb watched, still fascinated. "War's over. Is that it? Modesty won?"

Her smile was both prim and sly. "For now." She wrung out the washcloth and laid it over the edge of the basin before she clambered back to bed. Cobb was already sitting up by the time she was snuggled in. "I could have brought the basin to you," she said.

"I know. I didn't want you to."

Tru gave him more privacy at the washstand than he had afforded her, although occasionally she observed him through lowered lashes. Whether it was in consideration of her or because of his own reserved temperament, Tru noticed that he did not make a bold presentation as he washed himself.

She had seen Cobb reveal caution in his vigilance. At other times his caution was an exercise in patience. But here, now, it seemed that he meant to be respectful. She liked that. When he turned toward the bed, she was smiling.

"What are you thinking?" he asked.

She shrugged a little awkwardly. "Just things."

"All right." He crawled into bed when she lifted the covers and lay on his back. She moved close enough to rest her head in the curve of his arm and shoulder. It did not go unnoticed by him that it was the first time she had done that. "I lied to you," he said.

"You've lied about a few things." Her voice held no rancor. "What one are you talking about?"

"The one when you asked what I was thinking earlier and I told you I was thinking about your breasts."

"You weren't?"

"I was. But that was just a starting point. After that my thinking . . . drifted."

"Drifted?"

He nodded faintly. "I thought about riding out to the lake with you and finding a proper place where we could be together. Just us. Alone. There would be sunshine. Lots of sunshine, and you would be golden. It couldn't be now, of course, so I thought it should be in the spring, maybe early in the summer, and that was when I knew I'd still be here, not in Chicago, and that I would be here because it's where you are."

The ache in Tru's throat kept her from saying a word. Tears pressed at the back of her eyes, but she held them at bay.

"You're going to have to marry me, Tru. You told me that if I proposed to you, you'd have to understand the urgency and know my purpose. I haven't forgotten. The urgency is no different for a drowning man than it is for me. I want to breathe the same air you do."

Tru lifted her head to search his face. "And your purpose?"

"Besides the fact that I love you?"

"Besides that," she whispered. She could hardly hear herself over the pounding of her heart. "If there's something else, I'd like to know what it is."

"Well then, my inalienable right to pursue happiness."

Her heart still thumped, but his answer made her smile. "Very well said. Have you been practicing that?"

"Did it sound as if I have?"

"No, actually it sounded as if you've always known it and finally had reason to say it. It's a noble pursuit."

"I think so." He raised his head so he could kiss the crown of hers. "So is loving you."

"Oh, Cobb."

"You don't have to give me your answer now."

"What about the urgency of a drowning man?"

"I'd appreciate it if you'd help me keep my head above water until you're ready."

"How do I do that?" she asked. "You already have bed and breakfast privileges."

"Tru."

"I'm sorry." She returned her head to his shoulder. "I want to say yes. I *do*."

"But?"

"It makes me afraid. You don't. Marriage to you does. I think I would be endangering you."

Cobb thought he finally understood. "This is about Andrew Mackey."

"Yes. Of course it is. There's something wrong there. I know it. So do you. He's had several chances to ask me about his grandmother's brooch, and it's never come up. I don't understand that. I don't understand why he wants to marry me when I have so little in common with the other women he's been engaged to. And now Frank's coming, and Andrew hurries here to tell me but seems more interested in proving that there's someone in my house. Cobb, if I'm right that he's a dog in the manger, then he won't allow you to stand in his way."

"Maybe I want to."

"I *knew* it," she said. "*There's* your urgency. You're looking for a reason to call him out."

He did not deny it. "It doesn't mean that I'm not drowning."

Tru said nothing for a long time. Finally, "I don't want to argue."

"All right."

The ease with which he conceded to her should have been a balm. Instead, it irritated her. "Maybe I want to argue a little."

"All right."

She blew out a breath hard enough to stir the fringe of hair along her forehead. "Do the women in your family ever throw things at your head?"

"It's happened."

"I thought so."

Grinning, Cobb carefully stretched out an arm and reached for the oil lamp. He turned back the wick. "Pleasant dreams."

He thought that she might have growled just then, but he preferred to believe she purred.

It was still dark when Tru woke. She did not have to make a sweep with her hand to know that she was alone in bed, nor wait for her vision to clear to know Cobb was not in the room. She cocked her head to one side to catch the noise coming from downstairs. It sounded like a chair scraping against the floor.

Tru moved quickly. She left her robe at the foot of the bed but put on her slippers. The location of the shotgun made her hesitate until she remembered that she had placed it on the floor on her side of the bed. She found it more under the bed than beside it. Carrying it pointing down and crosswise in front of her, Tru started down the steps and followed the dim glow of a lamp to the kitchen.

Cobb had taken a seat at the table to pull on his boots. He

looked up when she came in and just shook his head when he saw the shotgun.

"You really do mean to keep that at your side. I don't think I realized how serious you were." He bent his head to concentrate on his left boot. "Please tell me you're not taking that to school."

"Of course I'm not."

"Good. I'd have to relieve you of it. I seem to remember you mentioning the ordinance against citizens carrying."

Tru walked to the back door and put up the gun. When she reentered the kitchen, she moved to the stove where there was some residual heat from making a late-night cup of tea. She crossed her arms in front of her to keep warm.

"Why didn't you wake me?"

Cobb pulled on his right boot and stamped the floor hard to make it a snug fit. "I did give you a nudge, and you didn't stir. It seemed the proper thing to do to let you sleep."

"I'd rather that you didn't. In the future."

"So there is a future."

"Of course. Unless . . ."

"Unless?"

"Unless you've changed your mind."

Cobb shook his head. He plowed his hair with his fingers as much in weariness as frustration. "Still drowning. Still in love with you."

"You don't sound very happy about it."

"Still in pursuit of that."

Tru's slim smile carried all the regret she felt. "I'm so sorry I can't do this differently."

Cobb stood. "I know." And he did. She hadn't said the words yet, perhaps she couldn't, but that did not mean that he didn't understand. "Will you come to the Pennyroyal tonight?"

She nodded.

"Good. I'll look for you. Maybe there will be room to sit at a table with Howard and Jack, or even the Shakespearean couple. You won't have to worry that Mackey will join us."

"I'd like that. Thank you for thinking of it."

He shrugged, then remembered. "You're welcome."

Tru did not want him to leave, and she had no right to ask him to stay. Not really. "Walt will be wondering about you."

"Probably not. He's learned I keep unusual hours." Cobb took a step forward, stopped. "Tru."

"What is it?"

"I don't know . . ." He began, paused, and then began again. "I don't know if it's right to tell you this, but because I agree with everything you said about Andrew Mackey, this is one more thing you need to understand. He's been entertaining Cil Ross in his room for several nights now."

"Entertaining? That's delicately put by the man I've been known to entertain."

"Is that really what you want to say about it?"

She looked down, shook her head. "No. I don't know what *to* say except that I'm worried on Cil's behalf and not offended on my own. Cil doesn't think it's a dalliance. I don't know her well, but I'm fairly confident of that. Yes, she flirts and carries on, and yet I'm not aware that she's ever done any more than that. Mrs. Sterling wouldn't put up with it if she knew. Not after the trouble a while back when the Coltranes were still here."

"You're talking about the Ransom girl."

"You know about it?"

He nodded. "The mayor told me when I took the job. The worst thing that ever happened in Bitter Springs, Terry said. She worked at the Pennyroyal."

"Her younger sisters attend the school. They talk about Emily now and again. You can tell how well they loved her. Maybe you should mention what Cil's doing to Mrs. Sterling."

"I've thought about it, for Miss Ross's sake, but I don't know. It doesn't seem right."

"Because of us?"

"Maybe. Maybe I don't like being a hypocrite."

Tru was struggling with the same notion. "I could try talking to Cil. She might listen to me. How do you know that she's been in Andrew's room outside of her regular duties?"

"I saw her going up one night. I was getting in late myself. She didn't see me then or later when I watched for her the next couple of evenings. Mackey's different around her, too. Not smug exactly, more like he has a right to her."

Tru thought Cobb had explained it very well. "I'll think of something to say to her. Go on. Don't give it another thought." She pushed away from the stove and followed him to the back door. She hugged herself against the chill as he removed his hat from the hook, but that chill went bone deep when she saw his gun belt.

Tru was silent as he strapped it on. The belt was brown leather, the holster a little scuffed, a little worn. The revolver was a Colt Peacemaker with an ivory grip. He looked perfectly at his ease wearing it, as comfortable with it at his side as he was in his own skin. She was the one who couldn't draw a breath.

Chapter Thirteen

Cobb was tacking a new notice to his office wall when the door opened behind him. He glanced over his shoulder, hammer in one hand, a second tack between his teeth, and nodded at Tru. He wondered if this was the first time she had seen the inside of the jail.

She gestured to him to finish what he was doing and began a slow circling tour that included stepping into the back room where the cells were. When she reappeared, he was standing a few feet back from the wall, critically eyeing his handiwork. She came up beside him and joined in the assessment.

"So this is the Wanted Wall," Tru said.

"That's what Rabbit calls it."

"I can see why. It's an impressive gallery of villains, miscreants, and desperados."

Cobb nodded. "From five states and two territories."

Tru took a few steps forward and studied the poster at the center of the wall. "William T. Barrington. He does bear a passing resemblance to Andrew Mackey, although maybe even a little more to Franklin. I can see why Ted Rush made a fuss about it. Has Andrew seen this?"

"No. At least I don't think so. He's never stopped in while I've been here." Cobb pointed to the sketch of the man beside Barrington. "I think he looks a little like our mayor. In fact, at a glance, you could make a case for almost all of them looking like someone you know. The posters are helpful. Evidence is better."

Cobb darted a look out the window to see if there were any passersby. There weren't. He took the opportunity to put his arms around Tru from behind and rest his chin against her hair. She gave him a moment's grief before she settled into the cradle he made for her.

He breathed deeply. "Your hair smells like lavender."

"That's your imagination. My hair smells like chalk dust."

He chuckled. "All right." He let her go and stepped back. "Would you like to sit?"

"No. I wanted to tell you that I spoke to Cil after school. I knew there would be no chance for a private conversation while she was working in the dining room."

Cobb pushed the hammer lying on his desk to one side and made space for his hip. He folded his arms across his chest. "And?"

"And she was not receptive. I didn't tell her that I knew she was regularly visiting Andrew's room, but I let her know that I was aware of her regard for him, and I shared that he had three broken engagements to his credit. I hoped it would serve as a caution to her. It didn't. I don't know what would."

"Let it rest, Tru."

She sighed. "Very well. I'm going home now. I have a lesson to plan for tomorrow. I think I can manage to be at the Pennyroyal around six."

Cobb nodded. He tilted his head toward the doorway. "You're making a timely exit. I have company."

Tru's eyes followed the angle of Cobb's head and saw Rabbit and Finn were preparing to storm the Bastille. "Au revoir," she said brightly. Ignoring the odd look Cobb gave her, Tru opened the door and let the rabble in.

At a quarter past eleven, Tru was still waiting in the parlor for Cobb to arrive. Earlier they'd shared a table at the Pennyroyal with Charlie and Sue Patterson. Sue was well into her fifth month of pregnancy, and Charlie seemed to think that deserved a night outside of the house. Tru had the sense that Charlie just wanted to show his wife off, but when she mentioned it to Cobb, he told her he thought it had something to do with Sue's cooking.

Andrew arrived after she and Cobb were already seated. She was aware of his scrutiny when he entered the dining room, but he sat at the window in the chair that she had come to think of as her own and that put him at her back. After she got over the idea that he was boring holes into her, she had enjoyed her present company.

Tru closed the book in her lap. Jim was going to be sorely disappointed when she told him she still had not finished *Triumphant Democracy*. She felt vaguely guilty about reading *Ninety-Three*, but the arrival of Rabbit and Finn at Cobb's office had put her in the frame of mind to appreciate Victor Hugo's revolutionary France.

She placed *Ninety-Three* on top of Jim's recommendation and feeling restless, she got up to poke at the fire in the stove. She made enough noise at first to prevent her from hearing the back door open, but then Cobb stamped his boots and she felt the vibration under her feet.

"Is it snowing again?" she called to him as she turned away from the stove.

"It is. Hard."

Tru only cared because snow meant a possible delay in the arrival of No. 486 from New York by way of Chicago and Omaha. That was surely the train bringing Frank Mackey to Bitter Springs. She set the poker in the stand and stood at the stove warming her hands behind her back.

When Cobb entered the parlor, his gaze shifted from Tru to the shotgun propped against the sofa. Except to shake his head, he did not comment. He stepped over to the stove and stopped when he was standing in front of her.

Tru shivered slightly. She could feel the cold coming off him in waves. Taking his hands in hers, she carried them to the small of her back so he could warm them as she had done, then she stepped into the embrace of her own making and offered him all of the warmth he craved.

Tru laid her cheek against his shoulder as she unbuttoned his jacket. She slipped her arms under the brushed wool and held him close.

"You wore your hair down," he said.

She nodded. "For a while."

He pressed a smile against her head. "You washed it."

"To get the chalk dust out. It really does smell like lavender now." She tilted her face upward. "What kept you? More trouble at Whistler's?"

"No. It was Walt. I was getting ready to leave the hotel when he cornered me. He didn't want to talk where we could be overheard so we walked down to the jail. He wanted to talk about us."

"Us? You and Walt, you mean?"

"No, I don't mean Walt and me." He stepped out of their mutual embrace and took her by the wrist. He swept up the lamp in his free hand. "Come on. You're more tired than you think. Let's go upstairs."

Tru followed but not before she grabbed her shotgun. Once they were in her room, she slid it under the bed and placed her slippers beside it. She laid her robe over the footboard and climbed into bed. She did not lie down, choosing instead to stuff a pillow behind her back and sit at the head. She tucked her knees against her chest and yanked the blankets up around her shoulders.

Cobb added wood to the fireplace and undressed before he joined her. Tru was stingy parting with the covers, and he had to wrestle one of the quilts away from her. When she agreed to marry him, he was going to present her with a trunk full of blankets. He might even add the quilt that was going to be auctioned off at the church's box social.

"Well?" she asked once he was lying down. She had noticed that he was still favoring his left side. "What did Walt have to say?"

"He knows about us—as in you and me. I told you that he looked after me when I injured myself. He pulled out the largest shards and cleaned out my pocket afterward. Walt's been stocking the bar at the Pennyroyal for a long time. He recognized the glass. Pittsburgh glass, he said. The tumbler was heavier than what Bill Whistler keeps in his saloon. Walt was pretty confident that there are only two places in town where that particular style of tumbler and that weight of glass can be found. One is the Pennyroyal. The other is in your cupboards."

Tru blinked widely and when she spoke it was not much above a whisper. "My glassware. It must have come from the Pennyroyal. I don't think I ever realized that." Still disbelieving, she shook her head. "Almost everything in the house came from somewhere else. I arrived with the clothes Aunt Charlotte gave me, a few photographs, my father's Bible, and a chest of books."

"And the brooch."

"Yes," she said on a long exhale. "And the brooch." She placed her hand on Cobb's shoulder. "You know, it's not so bad that Walt is the one who came to you. Next to Dr. Kent, he's the most reliably closed-mouthed person in town, at least in matters like this. I could almost be tickled for him. People tend to underestimate Walt, but I think he's done some good detecting."

"That also occurred to me."

"Did he press you to confirm his suspicions?"

"No. I think he just wanted me to know that I should watch my step. Literally. It seemed more important to him that I do right by you. I didn't tell him that I was waiting on you to do right by me."

"I'm sure that required considerable restraint on your part."

Tru squeezed his shoulder. "So Walt doesn't really know that you hurt yourself here?"

"No. I could tell he was rethinking the story I gave him that night, but he stopped short of calling me a liar. He just knows I've been visiting you, and that this is where I've been most nights when I haven't been in my hotel room."

She nodded. "I appreciate you telling me."

Cobb reached for the bedside lamp and extinguished it. "Why don't you lie down, Tru? Do you think I don't know why you're fighting sleep? Your eyelids are drooping."

"Are they?" She blinked several times, and they felt heavier each time. Stretching her legs, she inched down the mattress until she was lying beside him. "Tomorrow's Thursday."

"I know."

"Maybe the snow will keep him away."

"A day," said Cobb. "A week. Do you really want to live on pins and needles until then?"

"I guess not."

"Go to sleep."

"I can't. Not yet. Tell me about the farm. How many acres did you have? What did you grow? Did everyone help with the harvest? What was your—"

Cobb put a hand over her mouth. "I'm going to oblige you but only because it's going to put one of us to sleep." He felt her nod, lifted his hand, and began. "The farm's one hundred twenty acres. My grandfather cleared the first quarter himself. He married, had children, and they helped clear more. In turn, Granddad helped three of his boys buy up some of the surrounding land so they would have something when my father inherited the farm. My mother says you can't throw a stone without hitting a Bridger. That's even truer now than when she married my father."

Cobb went on, describing turning over the fields for wheat, oats, and barley, the patches as big as Chicago city blocks, where they grew every kind of vegetable for market, and the acres lying fallow to replenish the soil for a new rotation of crops. He warmed to the subject more than he expected and the memories came easy. He told her about hitching horses to the reaper and driving them through the fields at harvest. He didn't forget that he hated milking cows or that some of his most pleasant days were spent hiding in the apple orchard with a pencil and little notebook that he kept tucked in his pocket.

He had always known that he would leave the farm. He told her that, too. He mostly did what was expected of him, but he never pretended that he was going to live out his life in Lima, Ohio. When the time came, no one discouraged him from joining the Pinkertons.

"Why did you leave the Pinks?" asked Tru.

"Good Lord, you're still awake."

"Of course. I told you I was interested."

"Do you know the motto of the Pinkerton National Detective Agency?"

"No, but I believe you're going to tell me."

"It's *We Never Sleep*. I'm thinking you should work for them."

Tru would not be put off. "Why did you leave?"

"It was too comfortable. I wanted to see what I could do on my own."

Tru turned on her side and propped her head on her elbow. She laid her hand on his chest. "What happened in Indiana?"

"Indiana?" Even though he couldn't see her properly, he knew Tru was shaking her head. She wasn't going to accept that he didn't know what she was talking about.

"Something happened there," she said. "Something when you were on your own."

"You're talking about Hempstead," he said.

She heard it again, just as she had the first time he had mentioned the town, that thread of regret edging his words. She imagined that his eyes were already shuttered. "Tell me," she said quietly. "Tell me the thing that's hard to say."

Cobb placed his hand over hers. He stared at the flicker of shadow and light on the ceiling. "I took the job to accomplish one thing for the town: to find a rapist and murderer. I was never Hempstead's marshal. I lied about that. They already had one. Oliver Yates deputized me to give me the authority

I needed, and I investigated, formed a posse of other deputies, and went on the hunt. When I was hired, no one knew the number of women who were so badly used or how wide we would have to cast the net. I interviewed three young women before a fourth admitted there was a second man involved. Until then, no one had been willing to mention the preacher. Only his son. Nathan Boley made sure the girls believed they would be damned if they said his name. He failed to protect his son in the same way."

"Where is it that you think you failed?" Tru asked.

"How do you know that I did?"

"I don't. I only know that *you* think you did. I can hear it."

He was grateful that the dark hid his narrow, bitter smile. She didn't need to see that.

"You told me you arrested them," she said, prompting. "You took them in. I remember that."

"Yes." He closed his eyes a moment, remembering. "The Boleys never confessed. The opposite, in fact. They never stopped proclaiming their innocence."

"Did they convince you?"

"No. But it was no longer my job to be convinced one way or the other. I finally had two women who were willing to testify. I had evidence in the form of mementos that the Boleys kept. And I had pages of meticulous notes of how they had perverted scripture to support their crimes. Some of those verses were exact quotes from Boley as he was arguing his innocence.

"I had all of that to put before a prosecutor, a judge, and a jury. Where I failed, Tru, was in making that delivery. I failed to understand that the nature of the crimes could turn law-abiding citizens of a town like Hempstead into vigilantes. I failed to protect my prisoners, and I failed to serve justice. They were guilty, Tru. I know that. But it doesn't change the fact that they were entitled to a trial before they hanged."

"The men in your posse? Marshal Yates? The responsibility wasn't your burden to carry alone. Didn't they help?"

"Marshal Yates escorted me to jail and assigned one of the deputies to make sure I stayed there."

"But why?"

"He didn't want me to interfere. Again."

"Oh. You tried to stop them."

"And failed," he said.

"Did you hurt anyone?"

"Not badly. Not permanently."

Tru thought about that. "Is it possible the marshal saved your life by locking you up?"

"Not just possible. Very likely. They lynched the Boleys in the courthouse square. I couldn't see what was happening from my cell, but the deputy went in and out and kept me informed. As soon it was over, he unlocked the cell. Yates came by while I was collecting my things, paid me, and offered to accompany me to the state line. I don't know whose safety he was concerned about then. I told him I'd rather go alone, and I did."

Tru was silent for a long time, then, "I imagine there are a lot of people who would say it was justice that was served and the law that went begging that day."

"There are. I even understand their argument. I just don't agree with it. If the law can't serve justice when we're confronted with twin evils like the Boleys, then it doesn't stand for anything. And neither do we."

Tru dropped her elbow and inched closer so she could rest her head against his chest. He automatically made a cradle for her by lifting his arm around her shoulder.

"I think you are a very good man," she said. When he didn't say anything, she suspected it was because she'd made him uncomfortable. "That wasn't a compliment exactly. More like an opinion. I could be wrong." She felt the vibration of quiet laughter rumbling in his chest. She patted his hand. "I probably am."

He turned his head and kissed the top of hers. "I suppose I could try living up to it."

"If you like."

His head fell back. Cobb thought he was a lucky man more than a good one. What he said was, "I almost didn't take the Mackey job."

Tru's slight frown tugged at her eyebrows. "Really? You had reservations?"

"Some. Mostly because he wouldn't tell me what it was you had stolen."

"I suppose you're used to people trusting you."

He nodded. "I am. When someone hires me, it's with the expectation that I can do something for them that they can't do for themselves. Sometimes finding things is only a matter of following the money. I'm good at it."

Tru chuckled. "Why, Cobb Bridger, I believe you were insulted by Andrew's lack of trust."

"I suspect that's true."

"And how decent of you to swallow your pride."

"He offered me a great deal of money to ignore the aftertaste."

"And that still surprises me. About the money he offered, I mean. Maybe the brooch is even more valuable than I think it is. He might not want to ask me about it for fear that I'll disappear with it again. That's what he thinks I did in the first place. Took it and disappeared."

"Maybe."

"You don't sound convinced."

"Because I'm not. If he wanted the brooch back there are easier ways of getting at it than marrying you. I've been reading up on Wyoming law. That brooch isn't necessarily shared property here in the Territory. The way I understand it, if you can prove that it's yours, you'd have the right to keep it as your own even if you marry Andrew."

"Even if I marry you?"

"Especially if you marry me. I know I don't want it."

Tru thought he sounded certain of that. Satisfied, she snuggled against him, and it wasn't long afterward that she finally fell asleep.

Cobb had a full breakfast of steak, eggs, stewed tomatoes, biscuits, and hot, black coffee in front of him when Mrs. Sterling pulled out the empty chair at his side and put herself in it. His fork hovered at the midpoint between his plate and his mouth.

"Go on," she said. "I'm not here to interrupt your meal. You mostly just have to listen, and if you have a mind to say something, I don't care if you talk around your food."

Agreeing to her terms, Cobb took his first bite.

Mrs. Sterling glanced over each shoulder before she pulled her chair closer. As an extra precaution, she leaned forward. "It's about Mr. Mackey."

Cobb nodded once and continued eating.

"I didn't like it much when Cil let him have the rooms on the third floor. That's a private residence. I don't suppose that Mrs. Coltrane would make a fuss about it, but I would have liked her permission. It feels a little like I'm doing something behind her back, and that doesn't set right with me. Now, Mr. Mackey, he's all paid up so that isn't the problem, but he tells me last night—last night, mind you—that he's got a cousin coming in from Chicago, probably today. Probably this afternoon, in fact, and he's saying it to me like he just learned about it, even though I got wind of the very same thing days ago."

Cobb drizzled honey on a biscuit. "Maybe you should have some pity for him, Mrs. Sterling. He obviously doesn't understand how the grapevine works in Bitter Springs."

"Ain't that the truth? And I'll save my pity for someone deserving of it, thank you."

Deciding that he was better off listening than commenting, Cobb bit off a third of his biscuit.

"Now, you might be wondering why he saw fit to tell me anything, but the answer is that he wanted accommodations here at the Pennyroyal for his cousin. I told him we're full up, but I think he knew that already. We had a vacancy for a couple of days, and he didn't mention it then. It was like he was purposely waiting until he thought I wouldn't have a choice except to give him what he wanted. He told me he did not mind sharing his rooms with his cousin. Said it just like he was doing me a favor. Trouble is, he doesn't want to pay extra. Says his cousin won't either. I told him there would be two beds to make, two sets of linens to put out, double the work for my girls and Walter, but he didn't want—"

Cobb put down his knife and fork and turned to Mrs. Sterling. "I'll take care of it."

She opened her mouth.

"I'll take care of it," Cobb said more firmly this time. "How much is it that you want?"

"A dollar a night. Same as if he had a room on the second floor. And I want a week up front. I don't trust him or his cousin to pay at the end." She pulled her spectacles from where they rested above her widow's peak and set them on her nose. Her mouth curled to one side. "Imagine a man like him fussing about a dollar. Plain as plain can be that he's as rich as a Rockefeller. Every one of his suits made in London, England, Mrs. Garvin says, and she would know. There's a suspicion that his shoes come from Italy. I ask you, what possesses a man to want shoes from Italy when we all know the best shoe leather is cobbled from Wyoming cattle?"

"It's a mystery, Mrs. Sterling."

"Isn't it just?" Her chair scraped noisily against the floor as she pushed it back and stood. "Well, you get my money and solve that conundrum, and I'll swear to it in church that you walk on water."

Cobb's narrow smile curved in wry amusement. "Only when it's frozen."

Jefferson Collins was out of breath when he reached the marshal's office. His Adam's apple bobbed above his collar as he sucked in air and swallowed hard.

"You didn't have to run, Mr. Collins," Cobb said, rising from behind his desk. "Here. Let me get you something to drink. There's fresh coffee on the stove."

"No time for that. I just had word that No. 486 cleared the Cheyenne Pass. There's no good reason for a delay now. Snow's not going to be a problem for that engine. You can set your watch by its arrival at thirty-five minutes past the hour."

"Thank you."

Collins nodded and adjusted his scarf so that it covered his neck. "I have to go. I don't like leaving Mrs. Collins alone for long at the desk, but you didn't hear that from me."

Cobb stopped him before he had lifted a foot. "I wonder if you might leave her alone long enough to do me another favor."

"What's that?"

"Find Mr. Mackey and tell him that No. 486 is waiting in a snow shed on the wrong side of the pass. The delay doesn't have to be long. I don't need more than a half hour with his cousin."

"He's going to know that I lied. His cousin's going to tell him different."

"Blame it on the telegraph operator."

"You think quick on your feet, Marshal Bridger. It's a mite disturbing."

"I know. Will you do it?"

"I don't suppose there's any harm in it, save for my immortal soul."

Cobb simply pointed him in the direction of the door and then watched as the station agent turned sharply right toward the Pennyroyal.

Frank Mackey stood between his brassbound trunks with the collar of his coat turned up against the cold. Shifting his weight from side to side, he craned his neck to see past the station platform and in the direction of the town. The station agent had promised him that someone would be along directly to transport him and his things to the hotel. He glanced at the station. Through the window, he could make out the agent behind the counter. The man seemed wholly uninterested that the most recent visitor to Bitter Springs was going to freeze to death on his platform.

Cobb guided the buckboard up to the edge of the platform and stepped off. Tru had not exaggerated Frank Mackey's resemblance to his cousin. From what Cobb could see of the younger man's features from under his stylish black bowler, the likeness was uncanny. The ginger hair was the most notable difference, but with his hat on, there wasn't much of it in evidence. Even the cut and color of Franklin's beard was similar. Cobb had a vision of them both being attended to by the same barber.

He nodded to Frank as he approached. "I heard the train come and go. I thought there might be someone here who could use a hand with their bags." He looked down. "Or their trunks. George and Amelia Sedgwick operate a fine boardinghouse. You want me to take you and your things there?"

"I know someone who is staying at the Pennyroyal Hotel. That is where I want to go."

"Huh. I could have sworn I heard Mrs. Sterling say they didn't have any rooms to let."

"That's not your problem."

"No, it's not." Cobb grabbed the end of one of the trunks. "The Pennyroyal is expensive, twice as much as the boardinghouse. But I don't expect that much bothers a man who travels with brassbound trunks." He started dragging the trunk toward the wagon. "Keep an eye on that one," he said. "I'll be back for it directly."

"How expensive?" Frank asked when Cobb returned.

"Three dollars a night." Cobb hefted the other trunk by taking the straps at both ends. "A week up front, especially since Mrs. Sterling will plainly see you mean to stay a while."

"Twenty-one dollars? Isn't that steep away from the city?"

"I said it was, didn't I? I can take you to the boardinghouse."

"I'll manage." He followed Cobb to the buckboard and climbed on.

As soon as they were away from the station, Cobb changed course and drove the wagon past Ransom's Livery and in the direction of the stockyards.

Frank looked around. "Where are we going?" He pointed over his shoulder. "Isn't town that way?"

"All roads lead to the Pennyroyal." Cobb snapped the reins, but the mare did not appreciably pick up her pace. She was used to meandering under the guidance of Rabbit and Finn, not being driven off her course by unfamiliar hands. He held her up once the wagon was on the far side of the yard. Loosely holding the reins in his left hand, he held out his right one to Franklin.

"Cobb Bridger, Mr. Mackey."

Frank's ginger eyebrows all but disappeared under his hat. He slowly offered his hand. "Mr. Bridger. Andrew's Mr. Bridger?"

"If you're asking if I'm the man your cousin hired in Chicago, then the answer is a qualified yes. Qualified because I no longer work for him. We settled our business after he got here."

"How did you know I was—"

To keep him off balance, Cobb did not allow him to finish. "Paul Mackey sent Andrew a telegram. If that displeases you, you'll have to take it up with your uncle. Andrew thinks your train was delayed by weather otherwise he would have met you."

"Why did he think—"

"Because it's what I wanted him to think. I wanted to welcome you first. It will be better if you and I reach our own understanding before you speak to your cousin."

Frank's spine straightened. His chin jutted forward. "If it's an understanding you want, Mr. Bridger, you've laid a poor foundation for it. This is more of an abduction than a negotiation. Take me to the hotel now, and I won't report you to the police."

"We're not in Chicago. There are no police."

"Whatever passes for the authorities, then. I won't report you to the authorities."

"Is that what you do when you don't get your way? Make reports?" When Mackey did not reply, he climbed a few rungs in Cobb's estimation. It was unfortunate, Cobb thought, that the younger man started so low on the ladder and that the ladder was so long.

"I don't know the exact nature of your business here," said Cobb. "I don't think Andrew does either. You can explain it to him. I don't care. I just want to be clear that you are to keep your distance from Miss Morrow. If she's coming toward you on the street, you cross to the other side. If you see her dining in the hotel, you wait until she's gone before you take a seat. Don't walk in a store if you know she's in there, and if you don't know, walk out the moment you see her. Give yourself thirty yards distance from the schoolhouse and twice that around her home. The town has one church. If you're inclined to attend, go to Rawlins."

Franklin Mackey did not look away. He returned Cobb's level stare. "That's the understanding?"

"It is. If something else occurs to me, I'll let you know."

Frank's narrow-lipped smile was both amused and derisive. "She's a witch, isn't she?"

"What?"

"Trudy Morrow. She's a witch. Not the Salem, Massachusetts, burn-at-the-stake variety. I'm speaking of the witchery that called to Ulysses from the rocks, although I don't suppose you'd know Homer's epic."

"Sirens. You'd suppose wrong." Cobb watched as Frank made a second assessment. He held still for it because it amused him.

Frank said, "I know when she's put a spell on a man. I've seen it before, and I'd say she's done some of her finest work on you. That's the only thing that explains this . . . this *understanding*."

"Do we have one, Mr. Mackey? I don't care what you think about it. I only care that you abide by it."

Frank shrugged. "It doesn't sound very hard. Now, if you'd asked me to give up drinking, that would have been a hardship. I'm here to see Andrew, and if Trudy Morrow had two words to say about it, they were both a lie."

"Do we have an understanding?"

"I thought that's what I just said."

"Be clearer."

"Then, yes, Mr. Bridger, we have an understanding."

Cobb nodded, gave the mare her lead, and returned to the main thoroughfare. Without another word passing between them, he escorted Frank to the Pennyroyal, helped Walt with the trunks, and lingered at the front desk long enough to make sure that Mrs. Sterling got twenty-one dollars. He noticed she didn't hesitate to take it up, but when Frank was turned away, her unflappable expression vanished, and Cobb felt her regarding him with something more than mere astonishment. He thought she might be starting to believe he *did* walk on water.

Winking at her, he turned to go. "I look forward to hearing what you have to say in church, Ida Mae."

Tru saw Cobb talking to Mrs. Burnside and Mrs. Taylor across the street as she was leaving the schoolhouse. They appeared deeply engaged in conversation. She raised her hand in greeting in the event they noticed her, but none of them returned it. Tru looped her scarf around her neck a second time and began walking. Her skirt glided over the crusty edge of frozen snow until she stepped up onto the sidewalk in front of Johnson's mercantile.

She stood in front of one of the mercantile's large windows for a time and debated the merits of going inside. Jenny was expecting her, but Mr. Johnson had already seen her and was hurrying forward to open the door. It was not the kind of invitation she could ignore.

Tru was admiring a bolt of sage green damask when the door opened again. She didn't look up until she heard the familiar rhythm of stamping feet that she associated with Cobb.

"Hello, Marshal," she said politely as he closed the door behind him.

"Miss Morrow." He touched the brim of his hat. "George."

"Cobb." George Johnson pointed to the array of large glass jars filled with every sort of candy on the counter. "Fresh licorice. And some of that saltwater taffy you're partial to."

"Nothing for me today." He reached in his pocket and set a half-dollar on the counter. "Fill up a bag and send it over to the schoolhouse at the end of the day tomorrow."

"Sure thing." George swept the coin off the counter and

added it to his register. It was only as an afterthought that he addressed Tru. "Is that all right with you, Miss Morrow?"

"It's fine." She had returned to studying the damask. She ran her fingertips along the length of the bolt. "The end of the day, though. That's important." She glanced at Cobb. "That was a generous gesture, Marshal. The children will appreciate your kindness."

"What about their teacher?"

Behind the counter, George Johnson stopped squaring off a stack of catalogs. His head came up, and his deep-set eyes darted from Cobb to Tru and back again.

Setting her jaw, Tru gave Cobb a pointed look. Somewhat stiffly, she said, "As a rule, their teacher appreciates kindness."

"Enough to permit me to walk her home?"

Tru wondered if her father would still think her eyes were a merry shade of green when they were frozen over. She failed to keep her tone as neutral as she would have liked. It was an understatement to say that butter would not have melted in her mouth. "Thank you, but I am not going home."

Cobb's shrug was careless and easy. "That's all right. It would be my pleasure to walk with you wherever you're going."

Tru was aware of the mercantile owner's curiosity in their conversation. He did not even make an attempt to pretend interest in something else. Instead, he was leaning in, his forearms resting on the countertop, his head cocked slightly to one side.

Tru strove to remain polite if not warm. "I'm sure you have more important matters to attend."

"More important than providing an escort for everyone's favorite teacher? I don't have anything like that waiting for me."

George Johnson chuckled. "There is nobody going to fault you if you did."

"Mr. Johnson," Tru said. "Please." She set down the bolt of damask. "I'm only going to Jenny's."

Cobb did not mistake that for an invitation, but when Tru

turned to go, he and Mr. Johnson exchanged a grin before he followed her out.

"What was that about?" Tru asked when Cobb caught up to her. She did not look at him and pulled her elbow away when he tried to take it.

Cobb let his hand fall back to his side. "What? Asking if I could walk you home?"

"Yes. Not only asking, but the *way* you asked it. And in front of Mr. Johnson."

"Would you have preferred that I loiter outside the store until you came out? The town council discourages loitering."

"They do not." She pointed down the street where three of the town's leaders were huddled in deep discussion in front of the land office.

"Oh. Well, I'll take that up with them later."

His thickheaded pretense annoyed her to the point she wanted to stop and stamp her feet, and if she crushed his toes, so much the better. Her irritation was barely in check when she said, "You gave Mr. Johnson the impression that you were courting me."

"You think so?"

"You know you did."

"I admit it was my intention. Good to know that I was successful."

His confession stopped Tru in her tracks. She flung out an arm to stop him as well. "We agreed that it's better if Andrew doesn't know about us."

"Better?"

"Safer, then."

Cobb turned to face her. "It's your safety I care about. I never agreed to ignore that. Andrew Mackey suspects our mutual interest. He has from the first. I don't see the purpose of hiding it any longer. And now that Frank's here, it's not only prudent for people to know my intentions, it's necessary."

The only color in Tru's face was the one pressed into her cheeks by the cold. "Frank's here?"

Cobb nodded. "An hour or so ago."

"You should have told me right away."

"In front of Mr. Johnson so he could see you look like death? I think my way was better." He took Tru's gloved hands in his. She did not try to shake him off this time. "Listen to me. Only you and I know that I've asked you to marry me. What I agreed to was to wait for your answer, your real answer, until you're satisfied that you know what Andrew wants. There's no reason to let him continue suspecting. He needs to know that he has a rival."

Tru searched his face and could not keep the distress out of hers. "You're provoking him. It's that very thing I wanted to avoid."

"I know. But you can't have your way this time, not with Frank here. I want the Mackeys to know that you're not alone."

"What have you done, Cobb?"

He didn't protest his innocence or pretend he didn't understand. He released her hands and placed one of his behind her back. With the slightest pressure, he encouraged her to begin walking again. "I met Frank's train at the station. We had a cordial discussion, and he agreed to my terms. We reached an understanding before we passed the stockyard. He also paid Mrs. Sterling three times what she wanted to charge him for sharing the third floor rooms with Andrew."

Tru did not allow herself to be sidetracked by Cobb's final tidbit. She kept on walking. They were almost to the bakery. "What terms?"

"Simple ones. I told him to stay away from you and explained exactly how he was supposed to go about it."

"And he agreed to that?"

"He said it would have been harder if I'd told him to give up drinking."

"That's something at least. Perhaps that means I am no longer the apple of his eye."

"Even if you are, he'd be better off not acting on it."

Tru let Cobb help her down from the sidewalk so they could cross the street to Jenny's. "I wish you'd told me what you had planned."

"And you know why I didn't."

"I have a right to disagree with you, Cobb."

"I know. You exercise that right frequently." He held her back so she didn't walk directly into a wagon being driven by Matthew Sharp. He waved Matt on to indicate there was no harm done while he helped Tru recover her balance. "Careful. It's damned inconvenient if you throw yourself under a wagon wheel."

Tru added her weaker wave to Cobb's as Matt continued to look back. She could hardly believe she had been oblivious to the wagon bearing down on them, but there it was going up the street and Cobb still had her firmly by the waist. "Are Mrs. Burnside and Mrs. Taylor still talking?" she asked.

Cobb looked to where he had left the ladies. "They are."

"And the councilmen? Still huddled in front of the land office?"

He nodded. "Only their jaws are moving."

"Jenny?"

Cobb's eyes shifted to the bakery where Jenny was standing in the window in anticipation of Tru's arrival.

"And Mr. Sharp?"

"He's looking where he's going now. Not at us."

"That's too bad," she said quietly.

"Too bad?"

She smiled, lifted her face, and rose up on her toes. She put her arms around his neck. "He's going to miss this."

This was a very thorough, very public kiss, and the news of it occupied the good citizens of Bitter Springs for the better part of the evening.

Chapter Fourteen

Andrew Mackey made no effort to hide his displeasure. It irritated him further that Frank either did not notice or did not care. He turned away from the drinks cabinet with a whiskey in hand and merely indicated that if Frank was parched, he could fend for himself.

"I certainly will," said Frank. He heaved himself out of the overstuffed chair and took Andrew's place at the cabinet. "It is my sincere hope that the liquor here does not cause blindness."

Andrew took up the chair that Franklin had vacated. "I don't know anything about the Coltranes except that this is their residence when they visit and that they stock excellent whiskey."

"Good." Frank glanced over as he poured his drink and saw that Andrew was sitting where he had been. "Petty."

Andrew shrugged. "I've come to think of it as my chair."

"You could have said so." Frank tasted the whiskey, made approving noises, and moved to the couch. He sat in one corner with his arm across the back, his legs crossed. "I feel much better now. I appreciate you restraining yourself long enough to permit me to scrub off the stink of travel and change my clothes. I'm in anticipation of a lecture, so please, by all means, begin and have done."

"Go home, Frank."

Franklin knuckled his chin, a slight smile lifting the narrow line of his lips. He waited. Finally one of his ginger eyebrows arched, and he asked, "That's what you have to say? Go home?"

"I find a concise message is apt to be less confusing."

"Ah. I see that drink still sharpens your wit, not dulls it. How many times did you go to the bottle while I was in the bathing room?"

Andrew did not deign to answer. "If I had met you at the station, you would be back on that train."

Frank just shook his head, and the look he gave Andrew was pitying. "Then it is unfortunate that Mr. Bridger was there to greet me instead of you." He shrugged. "But I don't believe you anyway. The proprietress of this establishment was expecting me. She said as much when I registered."

"A precaution in the event you proved resistant to taking my advice."

"Resistant? That train was going west to Salt Lake and Sacramento. Short of stuffing me in one of my own trunks, you could not have persuaded me to step foot on it again, at least not before I bathed and imbibed."

"And now that you've done both? Stuffing you is tempting."

"We'll see," said Frank. "I'm not going anywhere tomorrow. I've only just unpacked."

"Good. That means there will be room in a trunk."

"Did you or did you not ask if there were volunteers to go to Bitter Springs in your place?" When Andrew said nothing, Frank went on. "So you do remember. It is good of you not to pretend otherwise."

"I also recall that no one responded."

"I can't speak for the rest of the family, but I required some time to consider it."

"There's a damn lie. You don't consider. You have never done anything but act on the impulse of the moment."

Frank's slight smile appeared above the rim of his glass

before he sipped. "How like Aunt Charlotte you sound. I wondered which one of us would embrace the moral sniping she was so fond of. A family like ours needs such a person, don't you think? I had thought it would be Lavinia. Uncle Paul has never had the stomach for it, and Jackson is not such a hypocrite. I do believe, however, that you are more suited to the role than dear Lavinia."

"Shut up, Frank."

"My God, but you're peckish." He looked around. "Is there some method of ringing the help? I would be glad for a sandwich."

Andrew explained the limits of the Pennyroyal's hospitality. "You will have to wait until they begin serving dinner. It's likely that you'll see Miss Morrow there. It's her habit to eat in the dining room on Thursdays."

Frank's cheeks puffed a bit as he exhaled. "That presents something of a problem, at least for me. Mr. Bridger has strongly suggested that I make a sincere effort to avoid Trudy."

Andrew set his glass down. "Say that again."

Frank did, and this time added the details of the mostly one-sided conversation. "Oh, and I nearly forgot. He said he is no longer working for you. I took that to mean that he is no longer working for the family since that was at the core of the agreement we had with you. Based on what he had to say after that, I assumed he was telling the truth. I don't know how he thinks he will be able to enforce what amounted to an edict, but I am too fatigued to challenge him this evening. Trudy's influence was more conspicuous the longer he spoke, but we've always known how capable she is in that regard."

"Indeed." Andrew looked down and casually brushed at a nearly invisible piece of lint on his jacket lapel. "Did Mr. Bridger mention who employs him now?"

"No." Frank actually smiled as it came to him. "It's Trudy, isn't it? Just when I think we comprehend the lengths she will go to, I discover we have underestimated her cunning. It's brilliant, actually. I only wish I had anticipated it. How is it that you didn't, Andrew? You tend to be more clear-eyed than the rest of us where Miss Morrow is concerned."

Andrew finally looked up from examining his lapel. His voice was flat. "You're wrong. Bridger doesn't work for her. Not directly. He works for the town. Our private detective is currently the marshal of Bitter Springs. I think that suggests how he will be able to enforce his edict."

Frank's mobile eyebrows arched dramatically. "Marshal. How did he manage that?"

"With Miss Morrow's help. I have it from her and several others as well that she put in a word for him with the mayor. Apparently the position was vacant for some time."

"Brilliant," Frank said softly.

"I don't mind giving Miss Morrow her due, Frank, but this was more serendipitous than brilliant. She didn't know about Bridger's connection to the family when she made the recommendation."

"Did she tell you that?" He put up a hand. "No, don't bother. I can tell that she did. And you believed her. That is what surprises, Andrew. You're making my case for me. I *need* to be here. If she pulls any more wool over your eyes you'll be mistaken for a sheep. It's a sad fact that it will take both of us to manage this. That is what was wrong with your plan from the beginning. This was never something you could do alone."

"Make no mistake, Franklin. Even if I believed that, I wouldn't have chosen you."

"That's ridiculous. We're closer than brothers. I know that because I have one. One pod. Two peas. Even Aunt Charlotte said so, and she was never wrong."

"She never *thought* she was wrong. There's a difference."

Frank shrugged. "It doesn't matter now. You would have gone through the list of candidates—a short list, I must add—and chosen me in the end. And you know why?"

"Enlighten me."

"Because I will do whatever it takes. I won't argue or hesitate. I will act if you don't. That's why I'm here." He finished his whiskey and rolled the tumbler between his palms. "Since we're not going to be able to go to dinner soon, suppose you tell me how far you've come. Can I assume that Bridger is at the very least a fly in the ointment?"

"He is."

"He's clearly protective of her. That seems to come out of genuine feeling for Miss Morrow. Is it your impression that she returns his feelings?"

"It is. I make no judgment about her sincerity."

"So what you've observed may be a pretense."

"Of course."

"But you have spoken to her, haven't you? You've certainly had enough time for that."

"The first evening."

"The first evening?" Frank's tone was rife with disbelief and scorn. "That was precipitous. Remember that when you are on the verge of calling me impulsive. Good Lord, Andrew, you have the experience of three engagements to draw on. Did you even try to woo her?"

"That would only have raised her suspicions. I chose a different tack. I told her that I thought I had made my interest and intentions clear when we were in Chicago."

"You said that? Christ, your interest was getting her into bed and your intentions were to make her your mistress. I bet she pitched that back in your face."

Heat colored Andrew's fair complexion. "I apologized for that."

"I doubt that she believed you even if she said she did. You play apology like a trump card when you can't follow suit. Sometimes you need to throw off, Andrew. Sacrifice the trick to see the other person's cards. Lose a hand, win the game."

"As opposed to you, Frank, who showed your hand when you tried to rape her."

"It wasn't rape."

"Because I was there. Don't forget that. She hasn't."

"She brought it up?"

"Yes. I'm inclined to agree with Bridger. You would do well to keep your distance."

"We'll see. In regard to the alleged attempted rape, your memory is conveniently incomplete." He shook his head. "No, don't make excuses for yourself now. You may need them for Trudy, and they will sound more sincere if they're not practiced." He rose to get himself another drink. "I'd offer to pour another for you, Andrew, but I believe you're at least one ahead of me." When he returned to the sofa, he asked, "Did she give you an answer?"

"She hasn't refused me."

"Then she hasn't given you an answer. Be precise. You taught me that, you know." He raised his glass, smiled at his cousin. "I'm sorry. I'm testing your patience. We are on the same side. The Mackey side. I haven't forgotten that. Did she indicate when she would have an answer?"

"No. But she was clear that if I pressed my suit, she would not respond in my favor."

Frank sighed. "That *is* a problem. Time is not our friend."

"I know that."

"I don't hold out hope that she won't be found eventually. Naturally, without the same assistance you lent Mr. Bridger that has proven to be more difficult."

"Yes."

"Again, it's foolish to be too hopeful. You know, Andrew, contrary to what you think, I've been reconsidering your plan. I may be one of Princeton's recent graduates, but I was also one of its best. By any definition, the scheme you hope to implement comes perilously close to fraud with you as its perpetrator. I am concerned that you, and by extension we, are in at least as much trouble if she says yes as if she says no. Marrying her without fully disclosing what Aunt Charlotte did might only be the beginning of new problems, not the ending of old ones."

When Andrew made no reply, Frank continued. "Have you been inside her home?"

"Yes."

"That's something. Did you find anything to support our contention?"

"That she's a thief?"

"That she's a witch." He chuckled when Andrew's mouth flattened in disapproval. "Of course that she's a thief."

"No. That would require being in her home when she's not there. That opportunity hasn't presented itself."

"You can't wait for it. You have to make it."

"I understand that, but Miss Morrow has watchful neighbors."

"Nosy."

"If you like."

"Well, that limits our options. I could take a look myself and risk being found out, or we can do what I think is our prudent choice at this juncture."

"What is that?"

"Kill her, of course. We are all agreed that she ceases to be a problem if she is dead."

Ted Rush paused at Cobb and Tru's table on his way to join his friends. "I was fixin' to stake all my money on the fact that it was Mr. Mackey who had Miss Morrow's attention, what with the suspicion folks have that he must have come here to make a declaration. I guess it's a good thing I never got around to pullin' that money out of my mattress. I heard it was a hell of a kiss." He gulped guiltily at Tru. "Sorry, Miss Morrow. Didn't mean to cuss. Just come over me."

"It's all right, Mr. Rush." She crooked a finger at him. When he bent closer, she whispered in his ear, "It *was* a hell of a kiss."

Ted's grin split his face as he straightened. "You're blushing, Miss Morrow. I always did figure you for a modest woman." He felt Cobb nudge him. "I'm goin'. No point in hangin' back with a pair of lovebirds. There's no conversation for an outsider there."

When he was gone, Cobb gave Tru a level look. "This is your fault. I don't think anyone but Jenny saw that you initiated that kiss. Ted would have to revise his opinion of you as a modest woman otherwise. Same as I've had to do. What did you whisper to him anyway?"

She smiled primly. "I'm not saying."

"I don't think there is anyone here who hasn't heard about that kiss."

Tru looked around and returned several knowing glances with a brief smile. "Andrew isn't here. I suppose he wanted to dine with Frank. When do you think he'll hear about it?"

"As soon as Miss Ross finds an excuse to leave the dining room to tell him."

Tru sighed. "You're probably right. Perhaps I shouldn't have spoken to her about Andrew. I'm afraid I left her with the impression that I was her competition."

"She would have thought that regardless. She heard the rumors."

Tru nodded and resumed eating. The chicken cutlet was so tender that it all but melted on her tongue. "What do you think Andrew will do?"

"I only know what I would do. Try to talk to you. Preferably without a dozen pairs of eyes gauging the success or failure of my conversation."

"You think he'll come by my house then."

"I would."

"You *do*."

"See?"

Tru didn't smile. "I should see him alone."

"Uh-huh."

She did not mistake his reply for agreement. "There's still the matter of what motivated him to propose. I want to know."

Cobb cut into his chicken carefully and lifted his fork to his mouth. "It's not just Andrew any longer. There is Frank to consider."

"He's certainly not going to propose."

"God, I hope not."

"Hear me out."

Cobb did not see that he had a choice, and the sideways glance he shot her told her so.

"It's better if I invite him to come to me. I can name the

time, the place. Otherwise, I'll have no warning. He'll just show up. It will be awkward and uncomfortable."

"Dangerous," said Cobb. "You left that out."

"Not Andrew. You're wrong about him."

Cobb traded his fork and knife for his beer. "I've hesitated to say this, but you're naïve about Andrew Mackey." He looked around to see if they were being watched as closely as when they came in. The diners nearest to their table seemed to have finally found something else to occupy them. Still, he kept his voice low and pretended more interest in his beer than in Tru. "I'll tell you why Andrew was in the hall when Franklin cornered you in your room. It was a plan hatched between them to get you away from Charlotte Mackey. It's hard to say how far Frank would have gone left to his own devices, but he wasn't acting on his own. He went as far as Andrew allowed him. Don't be confused about who was pulling the strings that night. Andrew was clever enough not to take the tale back to his grandmother. You told me Paul Mackey did that, but I think it was Andrew, not Frank, who saw the wisdom in involving his uncle. Young Frank does not lack for hubris. That was certainly apparent during our brief meeting. It's worth considering that he doesn't comprehend the extent to which Andrew manipulated him. And if he does know, then he will never admit it. Andrew thought you would be so grateful for his rescue that you would agree to become his mistress. I wonder if he shared that with Frank when he set his scheme in motion."

The bite of biscuit in Tru's mouth was paste by the time she was able to swallow it. "You don't know any of that to be true," she said. "It's all speculation." She tapped the side of her head with her forefinger. "It's all up here."

Cobb recalled something Rabbit and Finn had said to him. "I'm a pretty good speculator."

"I thought you depended on evidence."

"I'm not arresting them, Tru. I'm warning you."

"Because I'm naïve."

"Maybe that was the wrong word, but if you're honest,

you'll realize that you still remember some part of Andrew Mackey with the affection you had for him when you were a girl and a younger woman. That colors your perspective. I know. Sometime I'll tell you about Rebecca Frost."

Tru ignored that. "I could ask Walt to deliver a note to Andrew for me. He wouldn't have to come to my home. I could invite him to meet me at the school. He helped me with chores last Friday. If you're so concerned, you can hide in the closet."

Cobb sputtered on a mouthful of beer. Tru clapped him on the back.

"There's really nowhere else for you to go."

Cobb ducked out of the way of her next blow and put down his glass. For the benefit of the attentive gazes that his coughing and her slapping had attracted, Cobb smiled at Tru and talked through his teeth. "I am *not* hiding in a broom closet."

"I'll take the broom out. I can't very well have Andrew going to look for it when you're in there. That's not practical."

"Tru."

She recognized the warning in his tone, and she smiled sweetly if not sincerely. "It's your responsibility to arrive at a better solution. I've offered mine." She pushed her plate away. "Now, if you'll excuse me. I'm going to go home to write out that invitation."

He automatically started to rise when she did. She waved him back in his seat. "You should stay here, Cobb. I believe things will become more interesting once I'm gone."

"They're pretty interesting now." Still, he sat. He thought Tru might kiss him, but if she felt the impulse, she stuffed it in a closet.

Cil Ross did not go to Andrew Mackey's room with her news. She passed it along in the form of a hastily scribbled note that she gave to him when she served his chicken cutlets.

Frank watched the exchange. When Cil sashayed back to the kitchen, he turned to Andrew. "You've had a poke at her."

"Keep your voice down."

"No one heard. There's hardly anyone in here."

"That's because we're eating on Chicago time. In an hour or so everyone who isn't in one of the saloons will be in bed." As if to underscore the truth of his statement, the three councilmen occupying a corner table got up and filed out. Andrew opened Cil's note in his lap.

"What did she write?" Frank asked. His eyes darted to Cobb's table. The marshal did not look up from his cobbler.

Andrew crumpled the paper in his hand and shoved it into his pocket. "It seems Mr. Bridger and Miss Morrow were nearly run over by a wagon this afternoon."

"She thought that was important for you to know?"

"She thought I should know they were kissing at the time."

"Ah. Then you *are* poking her."

Tru lighted one of the candles on the altar and carried it back to the pew where she sat on Sundays. She set the candlestick beside her. The church was quiet, but the silence was peaceful, not eerie. Tru opened her reticule. There was only one thing in it. She took out Charlotte Mackey's brooch and held it in her palm for a long time, admiring it in the candlelight before she opened her coat and fastened it to her blouse just below her throat. It was heavy, and it tugged at the cotton fabric and pulled at the fragile clasp. She placed her hand over it to give it support. The stones were cool against her palm.

Tru folded the hand in her lap and bowed her head. Softly, she began to pray.

"What are you doing off in this corner by yourself, Marshal?" Jem Davis flicked the cards in his hand with his thumbnail. "You're about as solitary as a man can be in a saloon. If you want to be alone, you should head on over to the church."

Cobb used the toe of one boot to push out a chair. "Make yourself comfortable, Jem."

He dropped into the chair and waved his brothers over. "You expecting trouble?"

"No. Praying for it."

"Ah. I know the urge that comes over a man to hit somethin' sometimes. You want, my brothers and I will oblige you by stirring up a fuss. Or you can go on down to Whistler's. Doesn't take much to start something there. Though I got to say, if there's a ruckus, don't put a glass in your pocket."

Cobb's smile was cool but not completely lacking in humor. "Have a care, Jem. That thing I want to hit? It could be you."

Jake and Jessop chuckled as they took seats on either side of their brother. Jake took the cards out of Jem's hand and began shuffling. "You want me to deal you in, Cobb?"

"No, my pockets aren't as deep these days as they once were."

"Deep enough to hold a glass." This time all three brothers said it.

Cobb cocked an eyebrow at them. "I won't hesitate to take out the Greek chorus." He watched the Davis boys exchange confused glances, three square jaws shifting mightily to one side as they puzzled it out. "Forget it," said Cobb. "Play cards."

Cobb tipped his chair so the back rested against the wall and the two rear legs supported him. Lowering his hat a notch, he watched the card game under the shadow of his brim the same as he watched men coming and going from the Pennyroyal. He saw Frank Mackey enter the saloon from the hotel side a full minute before Jessop Davis spied him.

"Who's that?" Jessop thrust his chin at the newcomer on his way to the bar. The question was not directed at anyone in particular, but when his brothers turned to look and shrugged in ignorance, Jessop settled his gaze on Cobb.

"His name's Franklin Mackey. He's from Chicago."

"Brother to that other Mackey? There's a resemblance, that's for sure."

"Cousin. Second. Third. Kissing. I don't know. They're related." He saw the brothers trade grins this time and immediately wished he had not elaborated on the connection between Frank and Andrew—or at least that he had chosen his words more wisely.

"About kissing," Jake said. "We heard Matt Sharp almost ran you and Miss Morrow down in the street."

"Matt was innocent," said Cobb, thinking he could correct some part of the story. "It was Miss Morrow who nearly stepped under the wagon wheel."

Jem waved aside the particulars as unimportant and went to the heart of the matter. "Heard you were so tickled she wasn't hurt that you kissed her within an inch of her life anyway."

Cobb just stared at him.

Jem's jaw slackened a fraction. He shrugged. "Leastways that's what we heard."

Jake poked his brother in the side. "Leave it." He glanced back at the bar. "Hey. Why don't we invite that Frank fella over to take up a hand?"

Jem and Jessop were on the point of agreeing when Cobb said, "No."

They regarded Cobb with identically raised eyebrows. "Something wrong with him, Marshal?" asked Jessop.

"I like him better at a distance." His eyes followed Frank from the bar to a table. "It looks as if Ted, Terry, and Harry Sample invited him to play. Who are the other two at their table? I don't recognize them."

Jake craned his neck to get a look. "The one beside Ted goes by the name of Billy Barry. He just signed on with our outfit over at the Pepperdine ranch. Helped us cut out some of the herd this morning and bring the cattle in this afternoon. Bit of a greenhorn but a hard worker. That fellow on the other side of Mackey is Beck. Don't believe he told us any other name."

"I asked him," Jessop said. "He says Beck is all he answers to."

"They're not bad sorts," Jem said conversationally. "They left their gun belts with Ed Ransom at the stockyard same as we did after Jake explained about the town's ordinance. They didn't seem to mind not carrying. Leastways they didn't make a fuss."

"Good to know," Cobb said absently. He watched Frank take a chair at the table. There appeared to be brief but friendly introductions before Ted named the game and money was tossed into the pot. Ted started to shuffle. He wasn't smooth. The cards were old, well used, and they jammed and stuck several times. Ted kept on talking, unaware or uncaring of his clumsy efforts or that the other players—at least the ones whose faces Cobb could see—were becoming impatient with his lack of attention. Cobb abruptly brought his chair down on all four legs as Frank reached inside his vest. Cobb's hand hovered just above his holster. Frank pulled out a new deck of cards, held them up, and with the approval of everyone at the table, including Ted, passed them to Billy Barry who kept them instead of passing them along.

It was not until Cobb reset his chair in a comfortable tilt that he became aware that the Davis brothers were watching him with more wariness than interest. He heard Jake's chuckle and recognized it as an uneasy one.

"For a moment there, it looked like you might have found something to hit," said Jem.

Jessop nodded. "Yeah. With your gun."

Rather than deny it, Cobb said, "The night's still young."

Frank swept his winnings to the growing pile in front of him. "Perhaps I should sit out a few hands," he said. "And give someone else an opportunity to win. I seem to be extraordinarily lucky this evening." His dark eyes swept the faces at the table. "Unless this is an example of Bitter Springs hospitality and all of you are welcoming the newcomer."

Billy Barry clapped his hand firmly over Frank's before he began stacking coins and bills. "I'm a newcomer myself. So is Beck. If there's hospitality here, seems to me it needs to be spread around a bit more." He released Frank's hand. "The way it generally works in these parts is that the big winner stays at the table and gives the rest of us a chance to win some of our own back. There's no shame in one of us gettin' up if we're done in, but there'd be considerable shame—to say nothin' of trouble—if you was to do the same." He made eye contact with every player. "Is that about right?"

"Well," said Ted. "I don't know if we take our game as seriously as—" He stopped because Billy Barry's lips had thinned. "Well, yeah," said Ted. "That sounds right."

Billy nodded. "Beck, I seem to recall it's your turn to deal." He knuckled the ginger stubble along his sharp jaw as the other ranch hand gathered the cards. "Does this town have a barber? I don't recollect seeing one. I'm not too happy with the shave Beck here gave me." He showed off his chin side to side.

"Mr. Stillwell does the barbering," said Terry. "Just down the street. He opens around eight. Ask for him. Dave Rogers might nick you. He doesn't have the knack for it if you're particular."

"Guess I am. Beck, you goin' to deal or play with yourself?"

Frank smiled narrowly. No one except Beck laughed. The cowhand dealt the cards.

Frank did not win that hand or the next one. That settled Billy Barry down even though Beck took one game and Harry Sample the other. Frank won the next hand with two pair, lost another, and then won again when he drew to an inside straight.

This time it was Beck's large hand that clamped Frank's right one to the table before he could collect his winnings. Billy tipped his hat back to reveal a deeply furrowed brow and a fringe of ginger hair. He rubbed the bridge of his narrow nose thoughtfully while his friend held Frank Mackey down. He reached across the table to Terry McCormick and turned up his palm. He crooked his fingers to indicate he wanted the cards. Frowning himself now, Terry gave them up.

"I would like to have my hand back, Mr. Beck," said Frank.

"Just Beck. And Billy says when."

Except to shake out his free arm, Frank did not struggle. He looked at the other players. "Is there an accusation?"

Billy fanned out the cards face down in front of him. He studied the intricate design and flourish of black ink stamped on them. After a moment he picked one, turned it over, and regarded the seven of clubs with more thoughtfulness than it generally deserved. He put it off to the side, drew another—this time the jack of diamonds—and nodded to himself. He also passed it along to Ted.

"A trick, gentlemen," said Billy. "One I was pretty sure I'd seen before but didn't understand how it was done. Watch." He waved his hand slowly above the overturned cards. He stopped, turned his index finger sharply downward, and pressed it against one. "Six pips," he said. "Diamonds. The same card Mr. Mackey drew to complete his straight."

He turned it over. It was indeed the six of diamonds. Billy Barry was reaching for his gun before he remembered it wasn't there. It hardly mattered. Beck remembered, and he clipped Frank Mackey on the sharp edge of his chin as soon as he started to twitch. His right hand still crushed under Beck's, Frank began to topple sideways. Billy slid his chair out of the way.

"Gun!" Beck said.

No one at the table saw it, or knew who had it or where it was aimed, but they followed Billy's example and shoved their chairs backward. Ted stumbled to his feet. Terry gripped the table and started to heave it on its side to use as a shield.

Frank Mackey's derringer was solidly in the palm of his left hand before his knees hit the floor. He fired at Billy Barry as the man's silver-tipped boot flashed once and then connected with the underside of his neatly trimmed beard. Frank's jaw snapped shut with enough force to crack a molar.

Frank never saw his bullet lodge harmlessly in the upturned table.

Cobb put out an arm and applied enough pressure to get Billy Barry to step back. Jem and Jessop stood ready to restrain Billy if that's what it took to keep him from kicking Frank again. Jake hunkered beside Frank, who was still on his knees. His eyes were closed and not fluttering. Beck looked down at Frank, shrugged, and released the hand he had been grinding in his fist. Beck's hold had been Frank's anchor, and as soon as he removed it, Jake duck-walked backward to get out of the way. They all watched with differing degrees of fascination as Frank weaved slowly for several long moments before he toppled sideways onto the floor and was still.

Cobb bent and took the derringer from Frank's hand. He dangled the pistol by its pearl grip between his thumb and forefinger so everyone could see it. "And this is why the town council saw fit to ban carrying in Bitter Springs after the Burdicks were gone." He pocketed the empty weapon. "Now who wants to tell me what happened?"

Before anyone could answer, Jake said, "Maybe someone should fetch Dr. Kent. Mackey here is bleeding like he's been gutted, except for it's his chin. I think he might have bit his tongue, too."

No one wanted to leave so Cobb directed George Johnson who was closest to the door and on the outer ring of bystanders to make the sacrifice and head over to Dr. Kent's. "Send him to the jail, not here. That's where he'll be stitching Mr. Mackey's pretty face." This was greeted by murmurs of approval and low rumbles of laughter.

Ted stepped forward to begin the explanation, but Cobb stopped him. "Sorry, Ted. I'm afraid he'll bleed to death before you wind down. I need the uncomplicated, short version." He looked to the mayor.

Terry scratched behind an ear as his mouth screwed up to the side. "It's like this. Mr. Mackey was cheating. Mr. Barry proved it and called him on it. Mr. Mackey took exception, and Mr. Beck intervened to—"

"Just Beck," said Beck. "The uncomplicated, short version."

Terry nodded. "And Beck saw the pistol and shouted a warning. I guess you saw some of that yourself, Marshal. I think you were already here by then."

Cobb had been, but he did not confirm it. He had started to get out of his chair when he observed Beck screwing Frank's hand to the table. "Does that sound right you, Mr. Barry?" He glanced down at Barry's silver-tipped boots and then at the man himself. He expressed only mild interest in Barry's answer.

"Sounds right. I can show you what the fella did. The cards

were marked. Looked like a new deck, too. That's what fooled me at first."

Cobb looked around. The cards were scattered everywhere thanks to Terry tipping the table. A good number of onlookers were already bending to pick up a card or two and fixing to study them. "Give me a few of those, Jem." When Jem handed them over, Cobb pocketed them with the derringer. "And you, Beck? Terry's story stands for you too?"

"That's right."

"Good. Then you and Mr. Barry won't mind helping me transport Mr. Mackey to the jail."

"Ah, can't these Davis fellas help you with that?"

"I don't know." He looked at the brothers; they nodded agreeably. "Good. You and Mr. Barry still need to tag along. I want you to swear out a complaint."

Billy Barry rubbed the narrow bridge of his nose with a knuckle. "Don't see the purpose there, Marshal. It's settled as far as I'm concerned. Besides, there're the winnings to divvy up."

Although bystanders had stooped to pick up cards, none of them had taken any of the money lying on the floor. "Everyone," said Cobb. "I need you to pick up the money and hand it over to Jem. It's evidence first. Harry. Ted. Mayor. You come along with the rest of us to get your fair share back."

Jem took off his pearl gray Boss of the Plains Stetson and passed it around to collect the bills, coins, and because Ted was cautious about carrying too much cash, his markers. "Got it," Jem said when the hat came back to him.

"Then the excitement's over," Cobb said. He waved to Walt at the bar. Drinks all around on my tab." That had the desired effect of moving the crowd to the bar and leaving him with only the people he needed. "All right. Jake. Jessop. You take Frank. Everyone else, go on ahead. I'll follow."

When they reached the office, Cobb took down the keys for the cells. "Mr. Barry. Beck. Suppose you take over for the two Jays and carry Mr. Mackey into the back. They've been doing the heavy lifting long enough."

Beck hesitated, but Barry said, "Never hurts to do our share." He took Frank by the ankles and left Beck to exchange places with Jessop at Frank Mackey's shoulders. Frank groaned softly as they slung him between them.

"I think he's coming around," Beck said.

Ted Rush peered out the window. "Just in time. I make out that's Doc and George crossing the street and heading this way."

"Go on," said Cobb, nodding in the direction of the doorway to the back. "Cells are open. You can put him in the first one." He followed, watched them drop Frank none too gently on the hard bunk, and then motioned them to step out.

In concert with them clearing the cell, Cobb drew his Colt and blocked their path to the outer office. "The next one," Cobb said, indicating the second cell with his chin. "Don't test me. I know you men weren't asking for trouble tonight. That probably didn't fit with your plans to rob the bank later."

Neither one moved. Their hands hung loosely at their sides, fingers twitching slightly for weapons that weren't there.

Cobb waited. There was no challenge in his expression, only infinite patience.

Barry and Beck took a step backward. First one. Then another. They both looked toward the exit when the conversation in the office grew louder and more excited with the entrance of the doctor, but they did not make a break for it.

Cobb's eyes never shifted. He held his Peacemaker steady, and he continued to wait.

They stepped into the empty cell with less fuss than Rabbit and Finn had ever demonstrated passing through a doorway.

"Thank you." Cobb couldn't think of a reason not to be polite. He closed the cell door and waved them back toward the far wall before he locked them in. He had just holstered his weapon when Dr. Kent came through, followed closely by Ted Rush and Jem Davis. They all stared at the men in the second cell before they fastened their gazes on Cobb.

Cobb pointed to Frank. "There's your patient, Doctor. I can't figure why a man who paid twenty-one dollars to spend a week at the Pennyroyal decided he wanted to spend his first night here. You don't mind if I lock you in while you stitch him up, do you?"

"Nope. He doesn't look dangerous."

"And don't trouble yourself to make his stitches as pretty as you made mine," said Cobb. "Jem? You'll stay here with the doctor?"

"Sure thing."

"You heard me say you're my deputy, didn't you?"

"I caught some of that when you were jumping up from the table back at the saloon. Jake and Jessop heard it, too."

"Good." He ushered Kent into the cell, locked it, and passed the keys to Jem. "Stay close and yell if you need me. Don't talk to your friends over there. In fact, it's better if they don't talk to each other. It might disturb Dr. Kent."

"All right, but they're not exactly friends. This is the first day I worked with them."

Cobb spared a glance at the pair. They were still standing against the wall. "Seems as if a lot of visitors prefer these accommodations. Mrs. Sterling is going to be insulted." He motioned to Ted to back up into the office.

Ted had hardly turned and cleared the threshold before he was launching into a story about what he had just seen. The fact that he didn't understand what he had observed didn't stop him from trying to explain it.

Cobb was aware that everyone except Ted was looking to him for clarification. He took a step toward the Wanted Wall but halted when the street door opened and Tru walked in. Her eyes went from man to man until they came to rest on Cobb.

"I hope I am not interrupting a meeting," she said. She swept back the woolen scarf from her head to reveal a bounty of loosely anchored golden hair. "Am I?"

"Um, no. Not a meeting," said Cobb.

"Oh." She looked around again. "But I *am* interrupting. I saw the lamps burning from across the street and was curious. I apologize."

Ted Rush tipped his hat. "You're always welcome, Miss Morrow."

Cobb's tone was the opposite of welcoming. "You were out?"

Tru blinked. "Well, yes. That's how I could see the light."

"Alone?"

"I was at the church."

"You were at the church? Tonight? By yourself?" Cobb was peripherally aware that the other men in the room were either shifting their weight side to side or taking considerable interest in their shoes. "Not with Jenny or Pastor Robbins or the ladies circle?"

"I was praying." Her eyes dared him to have something to say about that. She looked beyond his shoulder to where Ted Rush was standing. He was usually easy pickings, but tonight he wasn't quite meeting her eye. She took a second look at Jake Davis, then his brother. Harry Sample and the mayor also avoided her, but she finally intercepted George Johnson's nervous glance. "All right, gentlemen. I'm not leaving until someone tells me what's going on. You know I'll hear about it sooner or later. For once I'd like to be among the first to know." She made sure she was blocking the door in the event that one of them tried to leave. "Well?"

It was then that Jem Davis called out from the back room. "Dr. Kent says to tell you that Mackey's coming around. Guess he doesn't care much for Doc's needlework."

Cobb watched Tru's eyes grow so wide they practically filled her face. He was prepared when her head snapped around. He pointed to the back room. "Go ahead. It's Frank not Andrew. You can look in. Don't take a step past the doorway, or I'll put you out in the street."

The men parted to let Tru pass. She stopped exactly where Cobb directed her and put her hands on the doorjambs to make sure she stayed there. She nodded at Jem and then at Dr. Kent when he glanced up. She wasn't really able to see Frank for the doctor sitting in the way, but the length and breadth of him seemed about right.

"What happened to him?" she asked Jem. "Was he shot?"

"No. He tried to shoot somebody, though. Got a boot to the chin for his trouble." Jem tilted his head to the men in the other cell. "He's going to be all right. I guess you probably know him since he's Mr. Mackey's cousin."

Tru nodded faintly. She was no longer trying to get a glimpse of Frank's face. Her attention was focused on the pair in the other cell. She removed one of her hands from the doorway and pointed to the men. "Marshal Bridger locked them up?"

"He sure did." Jem shook the keys. "Still don't know why. I saw what happened. Far as I can tell, they're the wronged party. Mackey was cheating."

"Oh. Yes, well, maybe he did it to keep them safe."

"Safe from what?" Jem asked, but his question went unanswered. Tru had already ducked out of the doorway and back into the office.

Cobb asked, "Did he have something to say?"

Tru shook her head. "I don't think he could see me. I couldn't see him. Dr. Kent is still working on him."

"It *is* Frank."

"Yes. I believe you." Her eyes swept over him in a single glance, then again, more slowly the second time as she took inventory. "I'm glad you're all right."

"Of course I am. Why wouldn't I be?"

Her eyes darted to the Wanted Wall.

Cobb's smile was modest and a little amused. "They don't know," he said.

"They don't?"

He shook his head. "Frank had everyone's attention. Do you want to tell them or should I?"

Ted frowned and asked the room at large, "What's he talking about?"

Jake shrugged. So did Harry and Jessop. Neither Terry nor George bothered to offer even that much of a response.

"I'd like to," said Tru. She walked over to the Wanted Wall, and with a gesture that she had perfected in her classroom while discussing place names on the map, she extended her arm and pointed to the notice at the center. "Gentlemen, that is Mr. William T. Barrington our marshal arrested this evening. Ted, you're going to spend the rest of your days telling everyone about the time you *almost* captured a miscreant."

Ted took off his hat, scratched the back of his head, and squinted hard at the poster. "Why, the fella back there doesn't look anything like that sketch. Barrington here has got a beard."

Everyone except Cobb and Tru regarded him with a jaundiced eye and an arched eyebrow. Terry said, "It's him, Ted. You can't tell from the poster that he's a redhead. Remember how you said that picture put you in mind of Mr. Andrew Mackey? You were in the right church, wrong pew. Frank looks like his cousin and Billy Barry looks like Frank. Funny how none us of saw it when they were sitting side by side at the card table."

Harry nodded. "Barry asked about a barber. Do you recall that?" When Ted nodded, Harry went on. "That's why we didn't see him for looking at him. Hiding in plain sight, he was. He told us straight out that he didn't like the way Beck shaved his beard."

Tru went to Ted's side and took his arm. "I'm sorry, Ted. I should not have teased."

Ted harrumphed under his breath, but everyone could see that he was pleased to have the apology and the attention. "Don't recollect seeing that other fellow up there. What about the one that calls himself Beck?"

Cobb said, "That's for me to figure out, Ted. The best way to do that is to encourage one of them to turn on the other." He addressed Tru. "So you know, everyone here tonight helped out in some way. They just didn't realize how much until a moment ago."

Jake chuckled. "I don't think Jem knows yet who he is guarding."

"I'll tell him in a while. Mr. Johnson, I'd be grateful if you'd escort Miss Morrow home. Ted, Harry, and the mayor have to stay to figure out the money."

George was happier to oblige Cobb than Tru. She separated herself from Ted's arm because no excuse to remain behind came to her.

"Goodnight, Marshal," she said as Mr. Johnson opened the door for her. "Goodnight, gentlemen." The best she could hope for was that Cobb understood that she did not include him among the gentlemen at the moment.

Chapter Fifteen

Tru asked George to walk her to Jenny's instead of escorting her home. He hesitated because of Cobb, but she promised him that Jim would go with her when she was ready to leave. George agreed and eased his conscience by speaking to Jim before he passed her off.

Jim stepped aside to allow Tru into the house. "What was that about?"

"It's Cobb," she said. "He's feeling inordinately protective toward me."

"Kissing a man in front of God and everyone will do that."

Tru felt the weight of her beaded reticule dangling from her wrist. "I suppose."

"Let me take your coat, Tru. Jenny is in the parlor. She'll have something to say."

"Actually, Jim, I came because I do."

Rabbit and Finn huddled in the deepest shadows of the school-house watching the activity in the jailhouse across the way. Their cowlicks and all the rest of their pale yellow hair were hidden under black woolen caps. The collars were turned up on their coats, and their long knitted scarves were wrapped several times around the lower half of their faces. Rabbit's scarf had wide black-and-gray stripes. Finn's was crimson. He hadn't liked it when he saw it in the lamplight, but in the dead of night, it did not look like any color other than black.

They kept their gloved hands thrust into their pockets and stamped the ground softly to keep warm.

Finn lowered his scarf to uncover his mouth. "Too bad about the snow."

Rabbit nodded. They were nearly invisible staying close to the houses, but when they stepped away, it hardly mattered that there was only a fingernail moon out tonight. The crusty blanket of snow that lay everywhere except on the well-traveled main street made their presence as obvious as chalk on a slate—but only the opposite, Rabbit had hastened to add.

"I don't know," said Rabbit. "Maybe it'll make you more careful. You can't just go running off every which way."

Finn shrugged and jerked his chin in the direction of the jail. "What d'you suppose they're doin' over there?"

"Hard to say. Is that money that they're takin' out of that hat?"

Finn squinted. "Suppose it could be." He sighed because Ted Rush sidled up to the desk and stood directly in their line of sight. "Well, that's that. Hey, do you reckon Miss Morrow's in some kind of trouble?"

"No," Rabbit said scornfully. "She's our teacher. It'd be unnatural."

"Maybe they're hiding something from her. That'd be natural, her bein' a woman and all. They didn't let her stay very long."

"Could be. Mr. Johnson looked like he was in a hurry. You wanna take a peek up at the Phillips's place? There's nothing we can see in the marshal's office anyway."

Finn tugged on his brother's coat sleeve as he shook his head. "I want to show you what I found behind the Taylors' house. We're supposed be looking for villains, remember? That's what you said, and I think I know what Sam Burnside's been up to. C'mon."

Moving as stealthily as the crunch of snow under their shoes would permit, Finn led Rabbit behind the schoolhouse, into the alley, and past several cross streets until they reached the gate that opened on the fenced-in backyard of Taylor's Bathhouse and Laundry.

When Finn reached for the handle on the gate, Rabbit stopped him. "The Taylors have a dog."

"Yeah, I know. Clover. Prissy says she's real friendly, and she doesn't bark at strangers on account of she's used to them because people are always comin' and goin' from the laundry or the bathhouse." Finn opened the gate only wide enough to slip inside. He motioned to Rabbit to follow but threw out an arm to keep him from advancing too far into the yard.

"Notice anything?" Finn whispered. "About the snow, I mean. Like where it is and where it ain't?"

Rabbit did. A dark path leading from the back porch opened to a large, equally dark circle that was almost dead center in the yard. "Where's the dog?"

"See? That's the thing. Prissy says they take her in at night, and Mr. Taylor puts her out in the morning. Ties her up because otherwise she'll dig in Mrs. Taylor's garden." He looked around. "You can't see it now, but there's a patch under the snow somewhere. There's a stake in the middle of that circle, and the path comes from Mr. Taylor walkin' back and forth to the house."

"You're saying Sam Burnside comes here?"

"Uh-huh. Most every morning before school to play with the dog. That's what I'm suspicioning. His folks won't let him have a dog, or even a cat, on account of his sister gets all wheezy and watery around them."

"So that's why she's never with him."

"Maybe. I don't think she knows or cares where he goes. Besides that, Charity gets a little wheezy and watery around him. Good for her to keep Sam at a distance."

Rabbit thought about that. "Only problem, Finn, is that the ground is frozen. Not muddy."

"That was a puzzler, but then I tagged along with Prissy when school let out on Monday and—"

"You told Gran you stayed after to help Miss Morrow."

"Sure, and she thinks we're still tucked in just like she left us."

Rabbit nodded, impressed. "Right. Go on."

"Well, I saw Mrs. Taylor toss a couple of buckets of water out here. Some of it froze, but what with Clover and Mr. Taylor going back and forth, the ground ain't froze solid yet. If you want to test it, just walk in there, but I'm tellin' you, you'll leave tracks."

Instead of going anywhere, Rabbit flung his arm around Finn's shoulders. "This is good work."

Finn beamed. "So maybe it's Sam that's the villain cuttin' between Miss Morrow's and the Stillwells."

"Could be. The Stillwells have a cat. Peeve. We both know Mrs. Stillwell lets him out to prowl at night."

Finn absently rubbed his right arm. "I never saw any scratches on Sam that looked like the ones Peeve laid on me."

"Maybe Sam never knelt on the cat's tail when he tried to pet him." He pulled Finn through the gate and closed it. "Let's go on over to Mrs. Stillwell's, but first we'll check to make sure Miss Morrow is with Mr. and Mrs. Phillips. It'd be better if we don't have to watch out for both of them."

Ted, Harry, and the mayor were still haggling over the money and markers when Cobb was thanking Dr. Kent for his services and seeing him off. As soon as the doctor was gone, Cobb strode over to his desk and threatened to scatter the spoils over the Laramie Range if the three of them didn't conclude their business in five minutes.

"At this rate, you'll be wrangling over the reward money into the next century," he told them.

That brought Ted's head up. "Reward money?"

Cobb pointed to the poster. "Two hundred dollars offered by the Jones-Prescott Bank of Rawlins. And that's only for Mr. Barrington. Beck might be worth a little more or a little less depending on his role in the robbery."

Ted whistled softly. "I wasn't thinking about the reward when I invited them to join us for cards."

Cobb did not reveal his amusement. "That was clever of you, Ted. You dangled just the right bait on your hook."

"That's what I'm realizing. Always was good at getting the fish to bite. Of course, Harry and our mayor had a say in it, too. Leastways they were sitting with me. Share and share alike, I say."

Jake and Jessop Davis were slouched on the bench under the Wanted Wall with their arms folded identically in front of them and their legs slightly splayed and extended. In response to Ted's comment, they exchanged sardonic glances.

"That's real big of you, Ted, to remember us," said Terry. He pushed Ted's portion of the winnings toward him. "All of your markers and your share."

Ted looked at it, frowned. "Seems like there should be more."

"Ted," Cobb said, and looked pointedly at his pocket watch.

"All right. All right. I'm taking it." He scooped up what Terry had passed to him and stuffed it in his pockets. "You fellas want to have a drink at the Pennyroyal?"

"You buying?" Harry asked.

"No."

"I think I'll go home then and let the marshal get on with his business."

Terry held up a hand. "Same for me, Ted. My wife will be waiting."

Cobb said, "If you're going back to the Pennyroyal, I would take it as a favor if you'd let Mr. Andrew Mackey know that his cousin is here. I'm a little surprised he hasn't shown up already."

"Maybe he already knows and doesn't care," Ted said, shrugging. "I wouldn't if my cousin was a card cheat. That Frank fella back there came to the saloon alone, so maybe Mr. Andrew Mackey doesn't want to associate himself with trouble."

"I realize that. Will you tell him anyway?"

"Sure." He gave Cobb a little salute and caught up with his friends as they were leaving. He was still trying to convince them to accompany him to the Pennyroyal as the door closed behind him.

"Maybe I should go tell Mr. Mackey," Jessop said. "I don't know if you can count on Ted."

"No. I want you here. And it doesn't matter if Ted remembers to tell Andrew."

"Then why'd you ask him to do it?"

"I thought since the other two were going home, Ted could use a reason to head up to the saloon. Sometimes a man needs to feel important."

Jake nodded. "That was real good of you, Marshal."

"Don't repeat it. I'll deny it, and it will embarrass Ted."

Jake put a finger to his lips, nudged his brother, and Jessop did the same.

"Anyway," Cobb said, dropping into the chair behind his desk. "I think Ted's right. Andrew Mackey doesn't care much for his cousin."

"Huh," Jessop grunted.

Jake asked, "You goin' to keep him overnight?"

"I haven't decided. Doctor Kent says he has no problem with it if I do."

"Well, I guess one of us should relieve Jem in the back. He's probably bored keeping an eye on Barry, um, *Barrington* and Beck."

"Yeah," said Jessop, getting to his feet. "And he gets a little punchy when he's bored."

"Actually, Jessop, we're going to separate Barrington and Beck. One out here in shackles. The other stays in the cell."

"You're going to talk to them?"

"If I do it right, I won't have to talk much at all."

It was after midnight when Jim Phillips escorted Tru up the front steps of her home. "Do you want me to go inside with you? Have a look around?"

Tru shook her head. "That's not necessary. You saw that everyone's over at the jail. The office is practically ablaze."

"Not everyone. I saw the Davis boys, Cobb, and someone sitting behind Cobb's desk that you say is Barrington. We don't know if Frank Mackey or the other fellow are still in their cells. I couldn't see through walls and neither could you. Cobb might have let them both go already."

"I don't think so."

"Humor me, Tru. After what you told Jenny and me tonight about the Mackeys, I think I need to be humored."

"Very well." She stood on tiptoes and bussed Jim's cheek. "I appreciate you offering."

"My mistake was posing it as a question. Go on." Jim shook his head when Tru opened the door without searching her reticule for a key. "Given the situation as you described it this evening, locking your doors when you go out would not be amiss."

"You're right. I suppose I don't like being the only person in Bitter Springs who locks her doors."

"After word gets around about the bank robbers, I have a feeling you won't be alone."

Tru set her reticule down and lighted the table lamp. She allowed Jim to help her out of her coat. "There are more lamps in the parlor. Light them all if you wish."

"One will be sufficient." He found matchsticks in a drawer and struck one. "Let me walk around once."

"Certainly." She smiled a little to herself as she removed her gloves and scarf. Jenny would be so pleased by Jim's thoughtfulness. She called after him as he went into the kitchen. "I'm going to take *Triumphant Democracy* off the shelf again. I swear I will finish it by Monday."

Jim checked the back door. It was also unlocked. He opened it, stepped on the back porch, and nearly came out of his shoes as a large ball of gray-and-white fur howled and spit and finally leaped over the stairs and into the yard.

"That's Mrs. Stillwell's pet Peeve," Tru called from the parlor. "Did he scratch you?"

"No. But it wasn't for lack of trying." Jim stepped back

inside, closed and locked the door. He looked around the kitchen, the dining room, and then came around to take the stairs.

Tru tucked her book under her arm and let him go. He wasn't gone long, and she was waiting by the front door when he reappeared. "Just so you can be assured that I lock it behind you," she told him.

He nodded, handed her the lamp, and stepped out when she opened the door for him.

"Locking it," Tru said when he was on the other side. "Rattling the key." She heard him chuckling. "Goodnight, Jim."

"'Night, Tru."

Rabbit yanked on the tail of Finn's coat. "Get down," he whispered.

Finn stumbled more than stooped. He followed Rabbit when his brother crawled under Miss Morrow's back porch. "What are we doing under here?" he asked when his heart stopped pounding.

"Hiding."

"Well, yeah, but—"

"Be quiet."

Finn clamped his mouth closed. He thought the cat might have scurried under the porch before they did, but when it didn't claw or squeeze past them, he figured he was wrong.

"That was Mr. Phillips," said Rabbit after a while.

"I heard him same as you. Lucky for us that we were still on the side of the house."

"Lucky for us that he scared the cat. We might have showed ourselves."

"I don't reckon he can run fast. Jeez, Rabbit. Can we go? It's cold lying here."

"No. Not yet. Wait."

Finn had no idea what Rabbit wanted to wait for, but he decided he could give it another minute. In a lot less time than that, Rabbit's judgment was proved sound.

"Peeve! Mr. Peeve!"

Finn's eyes widened as Mrs. Stillwell called for her cat. He craned his neck to get a glimpse of her on her back porch. She was holding out a lamp, and when she turned toward Miss Morrow's house, Finn buried his face in the dirt before she saw him.

"Peeve! I know you're out there. What did you hear? Rascals? Did you hear rascals? I sure heard you. Come on. Come back inside." Evelyn Stillwell waited a long minute before she gave up.

Rabbit exhaled loudly when Mrs. Stillwell and her lamp disappeared inside. "I never heard anyone carry on the way she does. The way she expected Peeve to come, she must think her cat's a dog."

"That's the truth." Finn wiped dirt off his nose with his coat sleeve. "Can we crawl out now? I guess we been just about everywhere tonight. Someone catches us now, they're bound to think that Mrs. Stillwell's right and that we're the rascals."

Rabbit was philosophical. "Sometimes we are."

"Oh, yeah. I'm kinda tired though. We've been to the cemetery and back, seen every dog and cat that belongs to someone and some that don't belong to no one, and I guess we'll have a thing or two to say to Sam tomorrow."

"Go on. You go out first. And start thinkin' about what we're gonna tell Granny when she wants to know how we got so gosh darn filthy."

Finn pulled himself forward on his elbows. "You reckon we're *that* dirty?"

"Uh-huh."

Finn waited until Rabbit joined him out in the open before he said, "You wanna take a peek in Miss Morrow's windows?"

"Now why would you wanna to do that?"

"Two reasons. If we're goin' to be in trouble with Granny anyway, then we might as well be hanged for sheep as lamps, and Miss Morrow might—"

"It's lambs," Rabbit said. "Might as well be hanged for sheep as *lambs*."

"Oh. Huh. That makes more sense."

"What's the second reason?"

"Miss Morrow might have her hair down. I sure would like to see that."

Tru tossed *Triumphant Democracy* onto the sofa after Jim was gone and went to the kitchen to make a cup of tea. She couldn't imagine that she would sleep easily until Cobb came by so it seemed pointless to try. She pumped water into the sink, filled the kettle, then set it on the stove while she laid the fire. Afterward, she sat at the kitchen table and waited for the kettle to boil.

A rustling noise outside her kitchen window caught her ear. She was halfway out of her seat to investigate when another sound, this one a substantial creak from the other direction, made her turn her attention to the entranceway. She finished rising, skirted the table, and quickly headed to the front door. Still an arm's length away from reaching it, she heard the creaking noise again, this time behind her.

Tru grabbed her reticule from the entry table and prepared to swing it as she spun around. "Andrew!" Heart hammering, she aborted the swing of her arm and drew it close, clutching the reticule to her chest.

Andrew Charles Mackey III descended the last three steps almost soundlessly. He did not advance on Tru. Instead, he stood at the foot of the stairs and casually rested his arm on the newel post. "You have a warped tread. Five or six steps up, I should think. It practically groans in protest of being used."

Tru saw his lips move, knew he was speaking, but it may well have been in a foreign language for all that she understood him. What in the *world* was he going on about?

Andrew straightened and removed his overcoat. He draped it over the newel post and then laid his bowler on top. Taking advantage of Tru's silence, he reached inside his jacket and brought out a small envelope. "I received your note. I thought you'd like to know that Walter made the delivery on your behalf. I've noticed that he is conscientious in the performance of his duties, large and small."

Tru's hand dropped to her side. The beaded reticule hung loosely from her wrist. She finally found her voice. "Where did you come from?"

His narrow smile seemed to indicate amusement. He pointed up the stairs.

"I don't understand. Jim went up there."

"Jim. Yes, I heard him. Who is he?"

Distracted by her own racing thoughts, Tru answered almost absently, "A friend."

"You have so many friends here, I've noticed. All of them doing your bidding. Walter. Cobb Bridger. The station agent. And now this Jim."

"What are you doing here, Andrew?"

He shook the envelope to capture her notice with it. His gesture had the desired effect as Tru's eyes moved from his face to what he was holding in his hand.

"I know what I wrote," she said slowly. "The invitation is for tomorrow at the schoolhouse after the children are dismissed."

He tucked the envelope away and made a show of examining his pocket watch. "It's tomorrow." He smiled and angled his head toward the parlor. "Why don't we retire there? I know you like your spirits, and you look as if a drink would not be unwelcome."

Tru glanced at the drinks cabinet. There was a bottle of whiskey sitting out that she could not recall leaving there. "I put the kettle on for tea. I should see to that."

"All right. Take the lamp." He ushered her forward. "I'll bring the whiskey anyway." He managed to retrieve the bottle and still only be a few steps behind her when she entered the kitchen. "You sit by the stove," he said, holding out a chair for her. He took the lamp and set it on the china cupboard. "You'll be warmer. Your cups?"

Tru pointed to the cabinet beside him.

Nodding, Andrew retrieved one along with a saucer and the teapot. He also placed the tea canister on the table. "There. Everything you need, I believe. Are you comfortable?"

A slight frown pulled at Tru's eyebrows. She answered carefully. "I am not uncomfortable."

Andrew pulled out the chair opposite her and sat. "You need time to collect yourself. I understand." He uncorked the whiskey and poured a moderate amount in her cup. He pushed it toward her. "Here. You don't want to wait for the water to boil and the tea to steep."

"Aren't you going to join me?"

"No. I had a drink earlier."

Tru tried to remember if she had seen a glass on the cabinet. "While you were waiting?"

He shook his head. "No. At the Pennyroyal."

"But you were waiting, weren't you? For me. In the dark."

"For a while. Not so long. I heard you and—Jim, was it?—talking on the front porch. I realized he was going to have a look around. Rather like I did not so long ago."

"And your response to that was to hide?"

"I came because I want to hear your answer, not answer for myself. Hiding, as lowering as it was, struck me as the better choice." He regarded her frown. "Ah. You want to know where I was. It is fascinating that you can't move past such an unimportant detail. Will you be amused to know that I was under your bed?"

"Nothing about you being here amuses me."

"Have a drink. It will change your perspective."

Tru did not touch her cup.

"No," Andrew said, pushing the cup and saucer closer to her. "I wasn't making a request. Have a drink."

Tru lifted the teacup by its dainty china ear. In the brief second before she struck, her eyes telegraphed her intent.

Andrew ducked sideways and the cup and its contents sailed over his head. Some of the whiskey splashed his shoulder, but when he sat up, he showed her that he was largely unscathed. Even the cup survived. Andrew bent again to pick it up and poured twice as much whiskey into it as he had before. He calmly set the cup back in the saucer. "Drink. It will steady your nerves . . . and your aim."

Tru raised the cup in both hands this time. The reticule dangled awkwardly from her wrist. She had forgotten about it. She drank. Before she could draw it away from her lips, Andrew reached across the table and pushed on the bottom of the cup so she was forced to take another swallow.

After a moment, he withdrew his hand. "Better?"

Tru nodded faintly.

"Good. You required some Dutch courage, I believe." He sat back and folded his hands on the table in front him. "I'd like to hear your answer."

Tru stared at him. She could hear the water in the teakettle behind her begin to boil.

"Leave it," he said as she started to rise. "You can see to it in a moment."

Tru slipped her reticule's black cord off her wrist. "May I show you something?"

Andrew shrugged. "If you would like."

Tru loosened the drawstring around the neck of the reticule. She opened it and withdrew Charlotte Mackey's brooch. She did not hand it to him. Instead, she turned her bag inside out and laid the brooch against the black silk lining to display the stones to their best advantage.

He glanced at the brooch and then at her. "Yes?"

"Don't you recognize it? It's your grandmother's brooch."

"I could hardly mistake it for anything else."

Andrew's response to the brooch puzzled Tru. The flash of interest she saw in his dark eyes was absent in his voice. "I thought you might be curious as to how I came to have it."

"Since Grandmother rarely failed to remind us that you were responsible for finding it after the fire, I imagine she wanted you to have it."

"She did."

"Well? So she gave it to you. Did you think I would begrudge you that piece? I don't." He reached across the table for it, but she pulled on the drawstring and the bag and brooch slid toward her. Andrew's fingers curled around nothing and he withdrew his hand. "You see, it supports my long-held contention that you exercised extraordinary influence over Grandmother during the last years of her life."

Tru frowned. "But you just said that you imagined she wanted me to have the brooch."

"I did say that. To you. I am not going to repeat it to anyone else, and I will certainly deny having said it at all."

"I don't understand, Andrew." She watched him shake his head slowly as though he were disappointed in her.

"No, you don't, do you? But let's have your answer first. There's that business to settle before we will discuss the other."

Her eyes widened slightly. She palmed the brooch. "My answer is no, and I will never believe that you are surprised to hear it." She waited for him to say something, but he remained quiet for a long moment, his eyes dark with thought, even a trifle sad.

"Surprised?" he said finally. "No. I don't suppose that I am. But I was hopeful. For a while I was hopeful. I don't know what I think about it now. There are so many considerations. May I see the brooch?"

Tru raised her hand as he reached out with his. Her thumb flicked the fragile clasp. She felt it fall open as Andrew's hand slipped under hers. With no hint or hesitation, Tru slammed the brooch down so the clasp's sharp pin pierced the flesh of Andrew's palm.

He howled in pain. Tru vaulted out of her chair. She grabbed the kettle, careless of the steam and the hot handle, and threw it blindly in his direction as she charged for the door. He saw it coming and threw up an arm. The kettle tipped, splashed some of its scalding water on his hands and neck, but most of its contents stayed inside until it bounced on the floor and lost its lid. Swearing, he pulled the brooch's stickpin out of his palm and launched himself at Tru. His arms swept the air but got nothing of her.

Tru knew she couldn't hope to get the locked door open before he reached her. She didn't try. Her goal was the shotgun rack. Her hands closed over where the shotgun should have been before her eyes registered the fact that it wasn't there.

"I took it," Andrew said evenly. He stood on the edge of the kitchen and the rear entryway absently rubbing his injured palm with the thumb of his other hand. "As a precaution. It seems I was right to do so. Hard liquor. Guns. You *have* changed, Gertrude, and not in ways that I could have embraced if you were going to be my wife. Come. Back to the table. I'll pour you another drink."

Tru hesitated, but when he stepped back to let her pass, she went. Her only thought in doing so was that if she were injured struggling with him now, she would be less able to defend herself later. She returned to the table, righted her chair, and sat. Aware of a slight trembling in her hands, she set them firmly in her lap. Her chin came up. Regarding him with what she hoped was more defiance than fear, she asked, "Now what?"

"Did you hear that?" Finn whispered. He grabbed Rabbit by the back of his collar to bring him up short.

Rabbit swatted at Finn's hand and turned sharply to face him. "Stop doing that!" He grabbed Finn by the collar and dragged him into the deeper shadow of the Stillwell's front porch. "How do *you* like it?"

Finn wrested himself free. "Didn't you *hear* that?"

"I got things on my mind, Finn. Like not getting caught crossin' the street. Did you think of that?"

"Well, I got somethin' on my mind, too. Wolves. I think I just heard one."

"You're crazy."

"Am not. I heard it. Swear." He crossed his heart. "Hope to die. It *howled.*"

"Then we should go. It ain't safe here if it's a wolf."

Finn shook his head. "No. I think it came from inside Miss Morrow's house."

"That's stupid. We both had a peep in the kitchen window.

You saw same as I did that she's got company. C'mon. We need to go."

Finn dug in his heels when Rabbit tried to pull him along. "I'm going back. Maybe it was Mr. Mackey I heard."

"You said it was a wolf."

"I said I *thought* it was a wolf. I figure a man might howl like that if he's hurt. I do."

"That's because you're not a man. You're a baby."

"I'm going back." He eluded Rabbit's attempt to grab him and started off.

Rabbit called after him as loudly as he dared. "How are you gonna see in the kitchen window if you don't have my shoulders to stand on?"

Undeterred by this very good question, Finn trudged on.

"Granny's right," Rabbit muttered to himself. "You are a trial." Sighing deeply, he began to follow his brother. When he caught up, he said, "There's other reasons a man howls, Finn, but I reckon we can talk about that later."

"Sure," said Finn. "We're gonna have a lot of time in the woodshed."

Andrew tipped the whiskey bottle away from Tru's cup. "Go on. Drink."

She stared at the teacup. Andrew had filled it nearly to the rim. "I can't. I've had too much already. It will make me sick." She pressed one hand to her stomach. "I don't feel well, Andrew."

"I'm sorry for that. I am. But I have to insist. You'll thank me for it. When you hear what I have to say, when you understand what I have to do, you'll thank me."

Tru wrapped her hands around the cup and carefully lifted it to her lips. It seemed heavy, its weight out of all proportion to its delicacy. She sipped once. Twice. At Andrew's urging, she took a deep swallow. The whiskey burned her throat and settled uncomfortably in her belly. She set the cup down but did not release it. "I can't do more. Not now."

"In a little while, then."

Tru was aware that she was feeling the effects of the first

round Andrew had poured, but she was still clearheaded enough to understand that he did not mean for there to be a long reprieve. "Tell me," she said. "While I still have the hope of comprehension."

Andrew moved the bottle to the side. "Yes. I should. I do want you to understand. Did you know that in making a will the mind of a testator must be free and not moved by fear, fraud, or flattery? Many states have something similar in their codes, but I am quoting Illinois law. That's what is pertinent here. The testator—in this case, my grandmother—lived in Chicago all of her life, so there is no question that the statutes of Illinois apply."

He pointed to Tru's teacup and waited for her to drink again before he went on. Taking the brooch out of his pocket, he laid it on the table in front of him. "My grandmother's mind was not free, not around you. I will testify, and the family will support me, that she would never have given this to anyone other than a Mackey if she had been free of fear and flattery." His thin smile mocked her. "Even I can acquit you of fraud."

"What makes you think your grandmother ever asked me for advice? She didn't. Moreover, I certainly did not threaten her." Tru pressed the fingers of one hand against her temple to quiet the throbbing. The gesture had no impact. She closed her eyes briefly, tried to gather the thread of her thought, and continued when she grasped it. The words came to her tongue more slowly than they came to her mind and the delay made her stumble. "She was . . . she was dying, Andrew. She had nothing to fear from me. And . . . flattery? Have you ever known Charlotte Mackey to have her head turned by smooth . . . smooth talk? She was unimpressed by . . . by sycophants, and she numbered quite a . . . quite a few of her family among the worst of them."

Andrew tapped the brooch. "You persuaded her we were undeserving. Before your arrival, my grandmother dealt with us fairly. Her expectations were high, but not unreasonable. She held firm opinions, but she was not intractable. You changed that. How could she hear any one of us with you constantly whispering in her ear? It was what I feared from the beginning. I never made any secret of the fact that I did not want you there. You poisoned her against us."

Tru's head drooped slightly. She felt the heaviness and forced herself to sit up straight. "Didn't," she said softly. "I didn't. The lawyers. There were always the lawyers."

"Yes. The lawyers." Andrew gestured to her to pick up her cup again. When she had it in her hand, he helped her tilt it to her lips. "A little more," he said. "It will help your headache. You have one now, don't you?"

Tru nodded slowly. She set the cup down and covered her mouth with her hand.

"Don't be sick. You'll only have to drink it again."

She let her hand drop. On the way to her lap, her fingers struck the edge of the table hard. She regarded her hand as though it had betrayed her. She nursed it gingerly.

"The lawyers," Andrew said again, drawing her eyes to him. "She paid them to listen to her. And they did. From your mouth to Grandmother's ear. The lawyers might as well have been talking to you. I never said you weren't clever."

"Not . . . clever. Tired. But you're sind to kay so." Tru frowned. "Kind to say so." Her head drifted forward again. She didn't lift it until her chin touched her chest. It was difficult to focus her gaze on Andrew. She stared at the brooch instead. "Your grandmother loved that piece."

"She did. So much so that I intended that she should have it pinned to her funeral gown. I was prepared to bury her with it. I looked for it with that in mind. Of course, I didn't find it. I have to say that it never occurred to me that you would have it. I actually thought she might have lost it again." He turned over his hand and studied the spot where she had driven the pin into his palm. He chuckled softly as he looked at Tru. "That damn clasp."

"You wouldn't have . . . buried it. Not that. Mackeys don't put a fortune into the ground. They take it out."

"Ah, yes. That. A fortune. You're right that I wouldn't bury a fortune. But this? I could have buried this. It's worth its weight in sentiment."

Tru frowned deeply.

"Paste, Gertie. It's paste." He shrugged. "It seems she didn't tell you everything after all. I suppose she kept it from you because she put so much stock in you finding and returning it to her. That meant a great deal. You know that." He pointed to her teacup. "Finish it. We're almost done here."

She was aware of him watching her closely. The thought of drinking more made her want to retch. She knew what good whiskey should taste like, and what he was insisting that she drink was not something she would have kept in her cabinet. The bottle was hers. She was sure of it. The bitter aftertaste in every sip was not something she could explain.

She wanted to sleep. She wanted to put her head down on the table and go to sleep. And because it seemed to be what Andrew wanted too, she drank. When she was finished, he smiled at her like a proud parent. It did not occur to her not to return the smile.

"I only learned the truth myself a few years back," said Andrew. "I made the mistake of telling her that if she wanted to keep supporting that museum, perhaps she should stop pouring money into the project and donate something that she valued personally. I suggested the brooch. That's when she told me that she couldn't because it would involve an appraisal, and she already knew the brooch was essentially worthless. She had been prepared to have the clasp repaired after you returned it to her all those years ago, but when the jeweler examined it and informed her that it was so much colored glass, she decided to keep it exactly as it was."

He idly turned the brooch with his fingertip. "Glass and gold-plate. That's all this is. And now you know it too. The jeweler is dead. I asked. The truth is it doesn't matter any longer that it's worth so little. Its real value to me is what you *thought* it was worth and the importance my grandmother gave it as a Mackey family treasure. When I take it back, it will be appraised as part of her estate, and I will be as shocked as the rest of my family upon learning that it's paste."

Tru gave a start when Andrew hit the tabletop with the flat of his hand.

"That's better," he said when she blinked at him. "Do you understand what I'm telling you? This piece of glass is perhaps the best evidence I possess to have my grandmother's will declared invalid. Her mind was *not* free. Had her judgment remained sound, she never would have given you the brooch. That's what people who knew her will say. And by extension, it will be clearly understood that she would not have named you as heir to one third of her personal fortune."

Andrew's short laugh was devoid of humor as the impact of what he'd said made Tru push herself fully upright and press her spine against the back of her chair. Her hands were braced on the edge of the table to support her rigid posture. "Yes," he said. "I see that *now* I have your full attention. Not quite sober, I think, but no longer listless. That will have to change, of course." He pulled her cup toward him, filled it halfway, and then pushed it back.

The room tilted as Tru shook her head. She heard someone moan and realized only after the fact that she was responsible for it. She set her jaw mutinously. She hated that he merely looked amused.

"In a moment," he said. "I know you're curious, and I always intended that you should know how well you manipulated a woman I thought could not be bent. As I said, she left you one third. Most of the remainder of her fortune will be divided equally between Olde St. John's Church and the arts museum. I say most because you were clever enough to make sure she did not write us out of her will altogether. We could have contested that and perhaps won. But no, the greats are all named. She left us one hundred thousand dollars to share equally. That's twelve thousand five hundred for each of us. A not insubstantial sum until one considers the depth and breadth of Grandmother's wealth. If I cannot challenge her will, we stand collectively to inherit less than three percent of her fortune."

Tru was vaguely aware that there was something here that she needed to grasp. He was explaining something to her that she should understand. She was frustrated that he insisted that she drink and then expected her to comprehend the forest when she could only see trees. She shivered.

"Are you cold?" he asked. "I can fix that. I *will* fix that. A fire, I think, is what will help. You'd like a fire, wouldn't you?"

His stare, as much as his words, drove ice into her marrow. She remembered the fire. The Great Fire. Andrew Mackey could set her ablaze right now and she would still die cold.

"Why isn't Frank with you?" Tru asked suddenly.

Andrew did not try to hide his surprise, but he answered the question in spite of it. "He's in jail."

"Oh. Yes. I remember now. Cheating. He was cheating."

"That's what Miss Ross told me."

Tru pointed a finger at him. "You should leave Miss Rosh . . . Miss *Ross* alone."

"Eventually. I left her sleeping soundly."

"In your room," Tru said.

"In my bed."

"In your bed," she repeated. "You should leave her alone."

"Yes, you said that. I was with her when she fell asleep, you know. And I'll be with her when she wakes up. She'll swear I was with her because she doesn't know differently."

"She cares for you."

"I know. I wonder how things might have turned out if you had cared for me."

"I did once." Her mouth formed a perfect O; her eyes opened almost as widely. She quickly covered her lips with her fingertips. From behind them, she whispered, "I wasn't going to tell you." She giggled. "When I was a little girl I wanted to marry you."

It was then that Tru was finally able to step back far enough to see the forest. She tried to make herself sober in his eyes, but the best she could do was to flatten her rather ridiculous smile as she leaned forward and set her folded hands on the table. Her earnestness was undermined by a gaze that had dimmed and remained slightly unfocused. When she spoke, she heard the halting cadence and heavy accents of a drunk.

"Thass why you want to . . . marry me. You don't *love* me. I'm an heiress now. 'Magine that. You'd be rich." She blinked.

"*Richer.* All my money for yourself. I don't think you would share a nickel of it with your family. Is that why Frank's not here? You don't want to share?"

"Frank's in jail," he reminded her.

"Riiight. In jail. And Cil's in your bed. Thass very bad of you. Cobb says you're a bad man. I told him he was wrong. Frank's bad. You're . . . *weak.*" Tru could not get out of the way as Andrew struck. The flat of his hand connected hard with her cheek, knocking her head sideways. She put up an arm to defend herself, but he was already withdrawing by then. Tru laid her palm against her hot, stinging cheek and stared at him, her expression more pitying than accusing.

Andrew's hands curled into fists, but he moved them to his lap. In a flat voice that did not encourage argument, he said, "Finish your drink."

The thought of another sip made her stomach roil. In spite of that, she picked up her teacup. Would it be such a bad thing if she were sick? Perhaps not. Andrew would be furious. He might even hit her again, but that was surely better than whatever was coming.

Tru knocked back her drink. She set the cup down hard, rattling the saucer, and gave Andrew a defiantly drunken smile. That smile was still in place when her eyes glazed over and she toppled face forward. Her head banged the tabletop. The teacup upended and the saucer slid sideways. The whiskey bottle jumped. Only Andrew was still, and that changed a moment later when everything else quieted and he was the only one moving.

For once Rabbit and Finn did not charge through a doorway simultaneously. Rabbit was indeed as quick as his namesake and arrived a full four seconds before Finn.

Jessop and Jem Davis leapt up from the bench the moment the door crashed open. Jessop grabbed Rabbit by the coat collar and yanked him back before he reached Cobb's desk. Jem scooped Finn under one arm and held him fast in spite of his squirming.

Cobb stood at the side of his desk, not behind it. William T. Barrington was sitting in the chair, his legs shackled together. Barrington looked at the newcomers. Cobb continued to watch his prisoner.

Rabbit pointed to the bank robber. "That's him! From the wall!"

Finn stopped squirming and looked to where his brother was pointing. "You got a villain, Marshal!"

Without looking away, Cobb said, "Put him down, Jem. Jess, let Rabbit go. Stay where you are, boys. Do your grandparents know you're here? Are they all right?"

"No," said Finn.

"Yes," said Rabbit.

Cobb didn't try to sort that out. "Tell me why you're here."

"On account of Miss Morrow," said Rabbit.

Simultaneously Finn said, "On account of a wolf."

Cobb heard neither of them clearly from behind their scarves. "One at a time." He gestured for them to pull their scarves down. "Someone begin."

For once Finn deferred to his older brother. Rabbit said, "We just come from Miss Morrow's house. We were looking for rascals ourselves. You know, because we got blamed for stirring up a fuss over that way, remember?"

"I remember."

"Well, we were looking around here and there. Evidence, you know. And we took a couple of peeks in Miss Morrow's kitchen window to see if . . . just to see."

"Uh-huh."

"Finn stood on my shoulders and then I stood on his. First time we were there we—"

"You were at her house twice tonight?"

Rabbit nodded. "Goin' out and comin' back. Ow!" He glared at Jessop for cuffing him lightly on the back of the head. "What was that for?" He stepped away when Jessop merely raised an eyebrow at him. "You didn't let me finish. First time she wasn't even home so we just looked around, not in. Later, on our way to headin' home, she was just getting back with Mr. Phillips."

"Mr. Phillips? Don't you mean Mr. Johnson?"

"No. After she left here, we saw Mr. Johnson walk with her up to the Phillips's place."

"Imagine that," Cobb said under his breath. "Go on."

Rabbit told Cobb about Mrs. Stillwell's cat and hiding under the porch and how they would have left if Finn hadn't come up with the idea of seeing Miss Morrow with her hair down. This time it was Finn who got cuffed and Jem who delivered the soft blow.

"That's when we saw Mr. Mackey," said Rabbit. "Don't exactly know—"

"Mackey?"

"Yeah. Mr. Andrew Mackey. Not the other one."

Cobb stepped away from his prisoner. "Jem, take Mr. Barrington back to his cell. You and Jake stay here. There's a shotgun in the closet in the back. It's loaded. Jessop, you come with me." Cobb grabbed his hat and duster. "Rabbit. Finn. You go on home now."

Finn got out of the way as Jem moved to take care of Barrington, but he dogged Cobb's footsteps to the door. "Don't you want to know what else, Marshal?"

Cobb stopped and looked back and down at Finn. He could barely keep his patience in check. "What else?"

"He *howled*. That's why we went back, and that's how I know he's a wolf."

Rabbit came up behind his brother. "It's on account of the whiskey."

"He's drinking?" asked Cobb.

"No," Rabbit and Finn said together. "She is."

Chapter Sixteen

They saw the fire's eerie glow against the night sky just as they turned the corner to Tru's street. Starting to run, Cobb ordered Jessop to roust the Stillwells and the other neighbors and shouted back to Rabbit and Finn, who were still following with what they imagined were stealth-like movements, to ring the church bell to roust everyone else.

It was the back of the house where the fire was fully engaged. Cobb knew that the boys had last seen Tru at the kitchen table. In order to keep moving, to keep his mind clear, he could not allow himself to believe she was still there.

The front door of the house did not submit to his shoulder or his boot. He drew his gun and slammed the pearl grip against the parlor window. Glass shattered, and he heard the consuming rush of flames. It was impossible not to imagine the fire leaping forward in search of fresh air. He roughly cleared out enough glass to allow him to crawl through the opening. Smoke billowed toward him as he holstered his gun. His eyes stung. He bent, pulled a handkerchief from his pocket, and tied it around the lower half of his face.

Above the pop and crackle of the flames, Cobb heard the

church bell. At this time of night, no one could mistake its violent, incessant peal for anything but a call for help.

Cobb stayed down and quickly searched the parlor and then the dining room, aided by the fire's terrible glow. Heat kept him from reaching the kitchen. He tried to see in, tried to get closer, and was always held at bay. He could make out the stove, the china cupboard. The table was engulfed. Flames attached themselves to the walls like red-hot ivy and defied gravity by turning at right angles to advance across the ceiling. The floor was a carpet of fire.

The kitchen window exploded. The fire roared again, and this time Cobb was beaten back. Turning, he headed for the stairs. What he had not seen in the kitchen was a body.

Taking the steps two at a time, Cobb passed the back bedrooms, where the fire would soon break through, and went straight to Tru's room. He found her lying facedown on the floor beside her bed, one arm stretched out under it. The shotgun? Had she been trying to reach her shotgun?

Cobb couldn't give more than a cursory thought to the explanation. Beyond her windows, he could hear shouting. Once he thought he heard his name. It would be all right. He told himself that as he turned Tru over and lifted her under her arms into a sitting position. Except for her head lolling forward, she didn't stir.

He straightened and pulled her to some semblance of standing as he rose. He knew she was deadweight in his arms and completely unable to help him, but with his heart hammering in double time, he was able to hoist her over his shoulders without effort or awkwardness. When she was secure, he started for the staircase.

And discovered the fire had beaten him to it.

It was only a high, thin wall of flames that was climbing the steps, but Cobb couldn't trust that the underside of the stairs wasn't already under attack. If they collapsed while he was on them, he would lose Tru. He retreated to the relative safety of her room and unceremoniously dumped her on the bed. He opened the window that looked out onto the street and down on the narrow and uncovered front porch. The pumper had not arrived from the livery where it was kept, but people who had gathered had already formed a bucket brigade that started somewhere behind Taylor's Bathhouse and Laundry.

Jessop Davis saw Cobb first and shouted for someone to get a ladder before Cobb called out the same request. Immediately, Mr. Taylor and Ted Rush stepped out of the brigade and began running toward Ted's hardware store.

Cobb ducked back inside and left Tru's room to see how far the flames had climbed the stairs. It was concerning to see they were already halfway up the steps and that the tallest among them was spiraling toward the hall railing. He went to Tru's bedside, hunkered down, and laid his palm flat on the floor. The wood was warm, even hot in places. Smoke was rolling in, and it was harder to breathe now. Cobb decided that he could not wait for the ladder, not for Tru. Perhaps not for himself.

Hoisting her as he had done before, Cobb carried her to the open window. From across the street, Evelyn Stillwell pointed to him and heads all around her lifted in his direction. He shouted his intentions and half a dozen men, including Jessop, Mr. Stillwell, and Walt Mangold, broke the line to rush forward and position themselves under the window.

It was impossible to get Tru through the window without banging her against the sash and sill. For the first time since he found her, he was glad she was insensible. Behind him, he heard the fire moving closer, the flames fanned by the new rush of night air. He held Tru tightly by her wrists as he lowered her as far as he could without falling through the window himself. She was still dangling six feet or more above the men prepared to catch her when Cobb let go.

There had been no time to get a blanket, let alone stretch it under the window. Tru's rescuers stood in a circle and made a spider's web of their arms. They moved a little to the right and then a little closer to the house as they watched Tru fall. Her drop brought two of them to their knees, but the web held. It was Walt who was left to cradle her when all the other hands released and untangled.

Cobb watched them safely clear the porch as flames shot

through the window directly below him. People were moving out of the way to make room for the team of horses and pumper truck coming down the street. Walt gave Tru over to Jenny Phillips. Several women came forward and quickly circled Tru as she was lowered to the ground. They covered her with their own coats.

Jessop stood in the middle of the street and waved his arms wide at Cobb. When Cobb waved back, Jessop cupped his hands around his mouth and yelled, "The ladder's not here yet. Jump!" Without waiting for Cobb's reply, Jessop called the other men forward again and headed back to the front of the house. This time the flames kept them from getting close.

Mr. Stillwell directed the men with the pumper to aim their hose at the part of the fire that was preventing him and the others from approaching the house. Cobb leaned out the window. He felt the spray of water and the flash of heat on his face. Under his feet, there was only the spread of heat.

There was no retreating now. There was no chance to save anything for Tru if he was going to save himself. Cobb laid his hand against his chest for a moment, not precisely over his heart, but over the pocket in his vest where he kept the sketch he'd made of Tru. For luck, he thought, or at least as much luck as he'd had the last time he jumped from the second floor of her house.

Cobb sat on the windowsill, brought his knees up, and pivoted. He dropped his legs over the side. Fire licked at his boot heels. Water sprayed down the front of the house. He was aware that people were yelling, waving, encouraging him to jump quickly, but he only had eyes for the circle of women protecting Tru. It seemed the most natural thing in the world that they should part suddenly and that she would be there, standing more or less on her own with Jenny close at her side. He yanked down on his kerchief and grinned at her.

He jumped then, and he thought he saw Tru crumble before he had cleared the window. The wooden porch absorbed his impact better than the ground, but Cobb had to drop and roll to displace the rest of the energy. He was quickly surrounded and hustled away from the house so the hose could be properly aimed again. Without looking back, he told the volunteers to save the Stillwells' property.

Cobb dropped to his knees beside Tru. She was sitting up, supported by Jenny's hand at her back. Away from the reek of smoke, he could tell that she smelled of whiskey and sickness. He didn't care. Pulling her into his arms, he held on. She shuddered in his embrace. Profound relief was in her weak laughter and in her tears. She squeezed her arms out from under his and looped them around his shoulders. When he stood, she rose with him.

"It was Andrew," she whispered.

"I know."

"You were right about him."

He did not respond to that.

"I'm so tired," she said. "So very tired."

Cobb nodded and gently removed her hands from his neck. "Go with Jenny. I'll come for you there after I'm done."

Weary with drink and despair, Tru still understood what that meant. She wavered on her feet but didn't move away. "You're going after Andrew." It wasn't a question.

"I am."

"Alone?"

He nodded. "I have to. You know why."

She did. "He told me he was going back to the Pennyroyal." Tru jumped as another window in her house shattered. "Cecila's there. He drugged her, I think. The same as he did to me. It was never the brooch, Cobb. He says it's paste. It's because of Aunt Charlotte's will that he—"

Cobb put a finger to her lips. "Later. You can tell me later. Go with Jenny." He kissed her on the brow and turned her into the curved arm that Jenny held out for her. "I won't be long."

Tru caught his sleeve and held on.

Cobb stopped. "What is it?"

She beckoned him closer, and when he came, she tilted her head forward so that she would have his ear. "I love you, and my answer is *yes*."

The promise that was inherent in Cobb's usual smile was

fully realized as he searched Tru's upturned face. "You saved a drowning man."

She released his sleeve and gave him a gentle push. "Go now, and come back to me."

Jessop Davis stepped up to accompany Cobb, but Cobb shook his head. "Stay here. You, too, Jim." He nodded to several others who wanted to fall in with him. "You're all needed here. The fire isn't finished with us yet."

No one argued the point. They had the water and the will to stop the fire, but Cobb had the gun. Thanks to Rabbit and Finn, Andrew Mackey's name was a curse on the lips of every man slinging a bucket or pumping furiously at the truck.

Cobb ignored the ache in his ribs as he sprinted toward the Pennyroyal. Andrew Mackey's life would end on a rope before he saw the inside of the jail if the town burned. Cobb knew it could come to that anyway.

No one was left in the saloon as Cobb strode past, and Mackey was not standing on the hotel's porch with the other guests who had been roused from their beds. They tried to stop him to ask whose house was burning on the other side of town, but he ignored them all. He was halfway up the stairs before someone thought to close the door behind him.

Andrew Mackey's hubris was no less than his younger cousin's. It was the only thing that Cobb could think of to explain why Mackey hadn't bothered to lock his door. In his own way, the lawyer was as insensible to the danger around him as Tru had been.

Cobb drew his gun but held it at his side as he entered the suite. There was a lamp burning on a table inside the door. It was immediately evident that Mackey was not in the large, open sitting and dining area, but the room to his left and the other two to his right were dark and silent. "It's Cobb Bridger, Mr. Mackey. There's a fire. Everyone has to leave the hotel."

Cobb knew Mackey could not be asleep and that any delay in his response was merely a pretense. He counted out fifteen seconds under his breath before he called again. Sure enough, he heard movement coming from the bedroom on his left. He walked toward it.

"Marshal here, Mr. Mackey. You have to leave." He stood in the doorway and could make out Mackey sitting up on the edge of the bed. "Is there someone with you?"

"Miss Ross."

"Why isn't she getting up?"

"She drank rather freely last night, I'm afraid." He stood and grabbed his trousers. "Did I hear you right? There's a fire? Here in the hotel?"

"No. Miss Morrow's house."

Mackey paused. "My God. Is she all right? What happened?" Holding his trousers, he moved to the window and peered out. The distant fire briefly lighted his face as he swore softly. "Is she in there?"

Cobb's voice was flat. "We have to assume she didn't make it out. No one's seen her. The fire isn't contained, and no one could get in. Get dressed." He holstered his gun and approached the bed. Putting a hand on Cil's shoulder, he shook her. When he let go, she simply rolled back into her sleeping position. "You can carry her," Cobb said. "Everyone has to leave. Wrap her in a blanket and bring her clothes."

Mackey finished tucking in his shirt. "Is that necessary, Bridger? She has to live in this town. Why don't we go down, and if the fire moves this way I'll go back up then and get her. No one else needs to know."

Cobb pretended to think about it. "All right."

"I want to help," Mackey said.

"Good. We need as many hands as we can get. You didn't hear the church bell?"

"I heard it," he said, pulling on his jacket. "I didn't know what it meant. Let's go, Bridger."

Cobb followed him out of the bedroom and waited while Mackey got his coat, hat, and gloves, then he waved him on and stayed a few steps behind as they headed down the stairs.

Mackey looked back once. "Why did you have your gun drawn when you came in my room?"

"Habit. I wasn't sure you were awake enough to be thinking clearly. Your cousin wasn't."

Andrew nodded. "So I heard."

"In fact," said Cobb as they stepped out onto the porch. "I could use your help clearing the jail. I can't leave my prisoners there. If the wind changes, the fire will move straight toward them. I can take care of Barrington and Beck if you'll look out for Frank."

Mackey looked off in the direction of the fire then at the guests still milling about on the porch. "Why are you standing here? People need help. Go, for God's sake." Shaking his head, he stayed at Cobb's side down the steps to the street. "I don't suppose any of them were in Chicago during the fire in '71." He looked back to see that two of the men looked as if they had the intention to follow. "If you think it's better for me to go with you, I will."

"Good. That will make things considerably easier."

And it did. It was always better, Cobb thought, when the prisoner didn't know he was one until the cell door closed behind him.

Epilogue

"I think I'll be nostalgic for these rooms when we're gone," said Tru. She was curled in one corner of the sofa, her bare feet tucked under the hem of her nightgown. She held a mug of coffee in her hands and continued to look around as she drank.

Cobb was still eating breakfast at the table, but he leaned back in his chair holding a strip of bacon between his fingers and joined Tru in her thoughtful inspection of her surroundings. "Huh. I don't think there's a place here where we haven't made love."

"Cobb Bridger!"

Grinning, he glanced over at Tru. "You're blushing like a maiden schoolmarm, and I know darn well you were thinking the same thing."

"I was not."

"Liar."

She wrinkled her nose at him. "Nobody likes a know-it-all."

Cobb was still grinning as he bit off the end of the bacon strip. "How did you convince Mrs. Sterling to let Walt bring our breakfast up here?"

"I thought you did it."

"I wish I had, but I didn't. I suppose that means Walt's going to be in trouble with her."

"It might have been her idea, you know. A gracious send-off because she's happy that we're finally leaving the Pennyroyal."

He chuckled. "That sounds as if it could be right." He took another bite of bacon. "That's all you're going to have? Coffee?"

"For now. I'll do justice to Mrs. Sterling's breakfast in a little bit, so don't think you can have more than what's fair."

In answer, he lifted the domed lid off the stack of silver-dollar hotcakes and speared four of them with his fork. "That's three left for you."

"You can have one more."

He didn't hesitate to stab another and heard her chuckle softly. He could not imagine that he would ever tire of hearing her laughter. Pushing the cakes off his fork and onto his plate, he said, "You're pleased about leaving, aren't you?"

Tru regarded him with surprise. "Of course. I never meant for you to think otherwise. I appreciate Mr. and Mrs. Coltrane's generosity in allowing us to stay here while our home was being built, but three months of living in a place that's not ours, well, it's been a little like wearing someone else's shoes. I am grateful to have had them, but I'm happier to be wearing the ones that were made for me." She paused, looking at him over the rim of her mug. "For us."

Cobb smiled at that. It was apt. He picked up his cup and raised it in the gesture of a toast. "To us."

Tru lifted her mug as well. "Yes," she said. "To us." She rose then and moved to the table, taking a seat across from him after she had kissed him on the cheek and run her fingers through his hair.

Cobb helped her fill her plate until she batted his hand away and told him to look after his own meal. He did, but mostly he took his pleasure from watching her.

She was right that three months was a long time to live in someone else's place, but now that they were on the cusp of leaving the hotel, it was hard not to look back and think that much of that time had passed too quickly.

The remains of Tru's house were still smoldering when they exchanged vows in Grace Church. It seemed to Cobb that the entire town showed up for the wedding, but that was probably because they all talked about it as if they were there. Some things about Bitter Springs would never change, and Cobb thought they were all probably the better for it.

Frank Mackey only spent one night in jail with his cousin. Cobb released him the following morning and moved him and his trunks to Sedgwick's boardinghouse. He kept the Davis brothers on as deputies so they could take turns keeping an eye on Frank until he was called to testify at Andrew's trial. As soon as Frank answered all the questions put to him in the land office, which on this occasion doubled as a courtroom, Cobb put him on the next eastbound train. He had Mr. Collins send a telegram to Paul Mackey, informing him that Frank was finally on his way home and that Andrew, pending the most likely outcome of his trial, was on his way to the Territory prison.

Frank argued all the way to the station that he was due at least some part of the reward for capturing Barrington and Beck, both of whom had been transported to Rawlins for trial. Cobb told him he could take it up with the three men who were going to claim it, as long as he made his case from Chicago. No one in Bitter Springs wanted to see him again. Frank had nothing at all to say about Andrew, probably because he said everything he cared to say under oath, including what he swore was the truth about the card game that landed him in jail.

The cards weren't his, he told the judge and jury. He didn't know they were marked because Andrew gave them to him and never saw fit to mention it. Winning that night had nothing at all to do with cheating, even drawing to the inside straight was luck. Frank advanced the prosecution's theory that Andrew had wanted him out of the suite that night, wanted a better, more credible alibi than his own cousin. Miss Cecilia Ross was meant to provide that alibi.

Cobb did not know if he believed Frank's testimony, but because it saved Cil from having to admit that she had gone willingly to Andrew Mackey's room, he never told anyone except Tru about his doubts. To the court and all the followers of the four-day trial, it appeared as if Andrew had used drink and drugs to make Cil receptive to accompanying him. All these months later, there was still no evidence to suggest that something more than sleeping in his bed had ever occurred. Cil continued to work at the Pennyroyal, although her flirtations were considerably less animated and she regularly allowed Tom Bailey to escort her around when he was in town on Bar G business. It was good for Tom, too. He hadn't asked a saloon girl to dance in a long time.

Judge Abel Darlington came in from Rawlins to preside at the trial. Andrew wanted to represent himself, but he had no standing in the Territory to do so, and reluctantly accepted the defense attorney recommended by the judge. Cobb doubted that Andrew could have done any better for himself, although he seemed to have had his say, constantly whispering advice in his lawyer's ear.

Frank's testimony that first day was damning in its own right, and followed by what Cil had to say, Cobb could tell the jury was prepared to find Andrew guilty right then and be done with it. Judge Darlington would have none of that. He wanted to hear everything and that meant the jury would also.

On the second day, the prosecution called Cabot Theodore Collins and Carpenter Addison Collins to take the stand. The boys were so unused to hearing their names that they continued to sit at the back of the courtroom until their granny tapped them on the back of the head. Finn had to wait outside while Rabbit answered questions first, but then he was invited to take a seat beside the judge and promised he would tell nothing but the truth, even the parts that sounded like stories.

Jim and Jenny Phillips testified later that day to what Tru had told them when she stopped by the same night as the fire. They laid the framework for the relationship between Tru and her former employer and for the antagonism that existed between Tru and the Mackey family. They also introduced the brooch into the record.

It was Cobb who discussed evidence on the third day. He had turned over everything to the prosecutor: the bottle of whiskey he found in the burnt remains of Tru's kitchen and the one he took from the bedside table in Andrew's suite; the brooch he removed from the pocket of Andrew's coat after his arrest along with Tru's note that asked Andrew to meet her at an entirely different place and time; and finally, a copy of Charlotte Mackey's last will and testament sent from Chicago by express mail from the law firm of Paxton, Oliver, and Kingery. The attorneys who thought they had had Charlotte Mackey's complete confidence for more than a quarter of a century were very glad to learn the whereabouts of Gertrude Morrow. Cobb produced correspondence from the firm in which Mr. Kingery ruefully admitted that Mrs. Mackey had not seen fit to trust them with this last vital detail in spite of repeated requests that she do so. She put them off, afraid they could be turned by her family, but she always made it known that she intended to tell them before she died. In the end, she left it to too late. Mr. Kingery further regretted that the firm's efforts to find Miss Morrow had not been met with the same success as the Mackey family's, but he wanted it to be known that they had not given up. They meant for Charlotte's final wishes to be realized.

Dr. Kent came to the stand afterward to support Cobb's claims that something—in this case, a concentrate of laudanum—had been added to the whiskey. A residue of the extract still clung to the bottle that had been in the fire, but there was more than enough left in the bottle that Cobb had found in Andrew's bedroom to clearly identify the contents.

Mr. Abraham Stern, a respected watchmaker and jeweler in Cheyenne, was invited to come to Bitter Springs to appraise the brooch and testify regarding its worth. Cobb thought he would never forget the look on Andrew Mackey's face when he realized that his grandmother had lied to him. Mr. Stern told the jury that the conservative value of the brooch was forty-five thousand dollars. The judge immediately ordered the brooch to be removed from the courtroom and delivered by Cobb and one of his deputies to the safe at the Cattlemen's Trust until they sorted out proper ownership.

The sorting out occurred the following morning when Tru delivered her testimony. She kept her explanations brief, and they were all the more powerful for it. She held the courtroom as rapt as she held her students, and when she finished describing how Andrew Mackey had carried her from her kitchen to her bedroom with the intent of further harming her before he set fire to the house, some women wept and all the men scowled.

Tru had saved herself. She was not as helpless as she had made herself seem, and she managed to roll out of the bed before he trapped her. The fall was the catalyst she needed to finally purge the whiskey and opium that was still in her stomach, and being sick was the thing that drove him away. He left her lying on the floor beside the bed reaching for the shotgun he had hidden there earlier. She could recall hearing him hurrying down the stairs and remembered that she tried, and failed, to get up. Her next memory was watching her house burn from across the street and seeing Cobb sitting on the sill of her bedroom window. She had been told that he jumped, and she believed the accounts, but she could not recollect it for herself.

Against the advice of his attorney, Andrew testified. None of the greats traveled from Chicago to offer a defense on his behalf. It turned out they had the family business to manage. While Charlotte Mackey had left them no part of her personal fortune, the operation of all the Mackey enterprises was still in family hands. If Andrew was convicted, he would be removed permanently from the circle, and that apparently influenced their decision to stay home to calculate the best way to administer their spoils.

It was this, the fact that Charlotte Mackey had left her grandson with the means to make his own fortune, which persuaded the jury that they could not trust his testimony. In spite of his impassioned protests that Miss Morrow was the cause of these circumstances, not the victim of them, they saw him as so profoundly greedy that they wanted to hang him on principle.

The law only allowed them to put Andrew Charles Mackey III in prison for fraud, arson, and attempted murder for the rest of his life.

Cobb was more satisfied with that outcome than the jury. Tru understood, and her understanding was all that mattered to him.

His brilliant blue eyes darkened at the center as he watched her drag a bite of hotcake through the molasses syrup on her plate. A droplet of syrup remained on her bottom lip as she chewed. He anticipated the moment the tip of her tongue would appear and take the droplet back. It was always worth waiting for, and when it happened, he just smiled.

"What are you going on about?" she asked.

"I haven't said anything."

"Do you think that matters?"

He laughed. "I guess it doesn't. All right, I was thinking that later today I will have the opportunity to carry you across the threshold of our new home."

"Uh-huh. And?"

"And I'm wondering if I can do it." He placed a hand on the left side of his rib cage and regarded her doubtfully.

"It's been three months since you threw yourself out a window. I think you're healed."

"We should test that theory."

"Ah. Now I understand." She set down her fork. "And that was *not* what you were thinking."

"It started with your tongue, but it ended there."

Sighing deeply, as though her surrender were a reluctant one, she raised her arms above her head. "If you can get me out of this chair, Marshal Bridger, you can have me."

Cobb accepted the challenge, which was her purpose in issuing it. He groaned for effect as he lifted her, but she wasn't fooled and told him so. Rather than deny it, he pretended that he was going to drop her. That made her hold on tighter, which also was the purpose in doing it.

He announced they were crossing the threshold as he entered the bedroom, and she congratulated him on having made it so far. He did toss her on the bed then, but he also followed her down. They made love in happy haste, teasing, laughing, finding pleasure in the ridiculous and the sublime, and having no thought of a moment more distant than the one they were in now.

And afterward, when Cobb was holding his left side, this time because his heroic effort to keep Tru from tumbling out of bed had given him a stitch, she leaned over and kissed him very sweetly, first on his mouth, and then between the fingers splayed over his ribcage.

"You are not a well man," she said.

"I was. I should have let you fall on your head. It couldn't hurt. How did you get all turned around?"

"You should know. You were doing the turning." She flopped on her back, tugged down on her nightgown, and then moved close enough to rest her head against his shoulder. "And the tickling. You were doing a lot of that."

"You should have told me to stop."

"I did."

"Huh. I had no idea you were saying anything like that."

Tru nudged him with her elbow. He merely smiled, and they lay like that for several long minutes. It was Tru who finally broke the silence.

"I've been thinking about what you said about the money, Cobb."

"You have?"

"And I think you're right. I'm going to put most of it in trusts. The town will manage one for the school and another for the library that we're going to build. I think it would be lovely to have a park here, a place for adventuring children who do not want to sneak away to the cemetery." She smiled a little at that. "Although I suppose there will always be rascals among us."

"I hope so. I hope they're ours."

"Yes," she said softly. "I hope so, too."

Cobb let her hold that thought for a while before he asked, "What else, Tru? There's something else."

She nodded. "It's so much money. Unfathomable, really. You're right that if it doesn't change us, it has the power to change the way people think about us. I don't want either one of those things to happen, not because of this fortune, not because we can *bathe* in money if we like."

"There's a picture."

"I'm serious."

He put his hand over hers. "I know. I'm sorry. It doesn't have to drive us out of Bitter Springs, Tru. Charlotte Mackey trusted you above anyone to know what to do with the fortune she left you. The art museum and Olde St. John's will make the most of her investment in them, and a lot of people will benefit, but what you do with it will spread her money farther and wider."

"Maybe. But right now I can't see much beyond Bitter Springs."

"You will. It will come to you."

And it would, he thought. He had married a farmer, not a teacher. She planted seeds every time she spoke to a child. She would always think of the children, and the money would follow. The school. A library. A park. Their own children someday. There would be scholarships and grants and hundreds of occasions for children as rascally as Finn and Rabbit to succeed. It was only a matter of time, a matter of turning a corner in her mind where she could embrace Charlotte Mackey's gift as an opportunity and not be overwhelmed by it.

Until then, and then for the rest of their lives, he would stand by her, lie with her, and love her as deeply as a heart could bear, because each time he realized he was a better man for it, he knew it was Tru.